Song of the Silent Harp

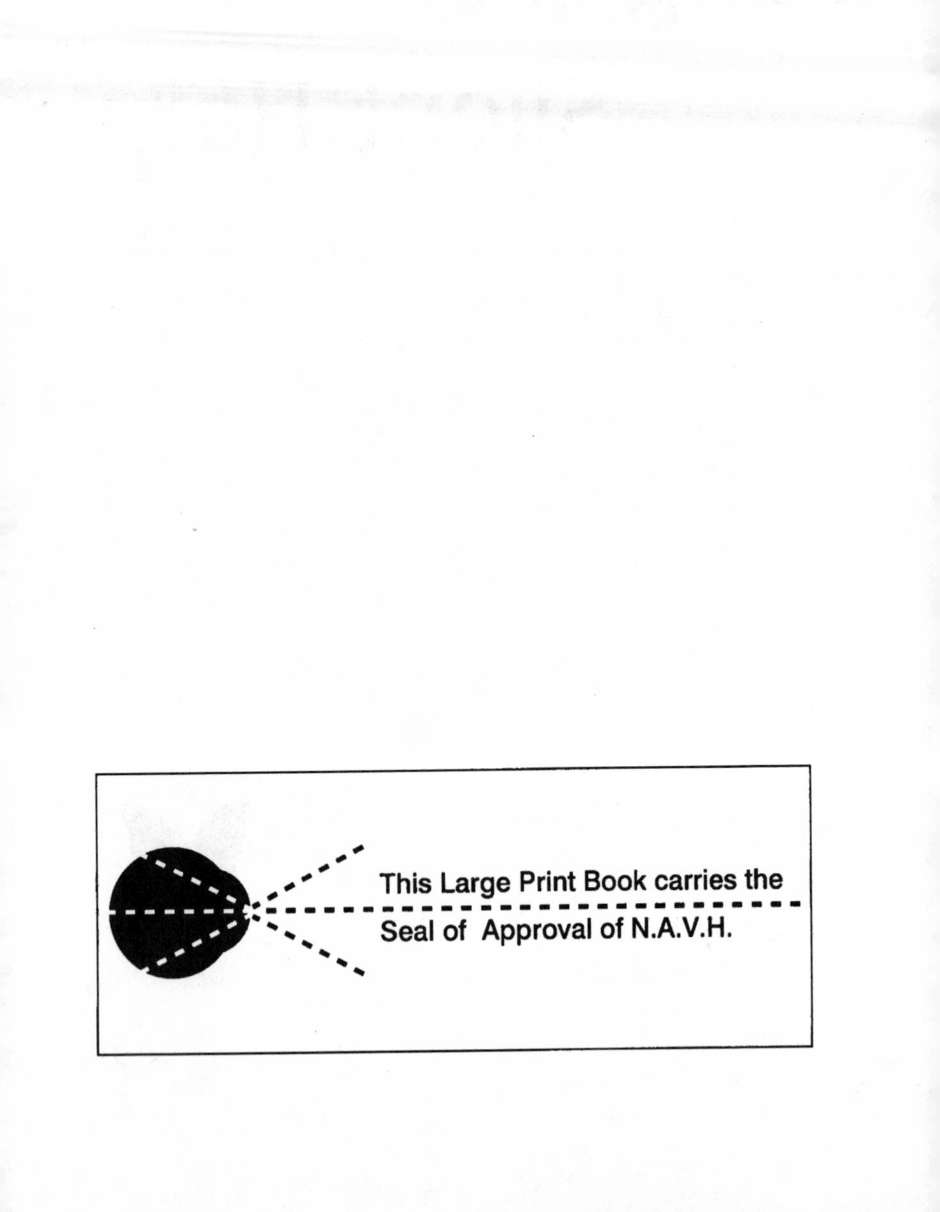
This Large Print Book carries the
Seal of Approval of N.A.V.H.

B. J. Hoff

Song of the Silent Harp

Walker Large Print • Waterville, Maine

Published in 2002 by arrangement with Bethany House Publishers.

The text of this Large Print edition is unabridged.
Other aspects of the book may vary from the original edition.

Set in 16 pt. Plantin by Minnie B. Raven.

Printed in the United States on permanent paper.

ISBN 1-4104-0030-1 (lg. print : sc : alk. paper)

For Jim —
My Hero . . .
My Husband . . .
My Best Friend . . .

Acknowledgments

I'm very grateful to Dr. Eoin McKiernan of Minneapolis for the information and assistance he has so kindly and patiently provided.

Many thanks also to the following individuals for their gracious assistance:

Ivor Hamrock, Senior Library Assistant, Mayo County Council, Castlebar, County Mayo, Ireland

John R. Podracky, Curator, New York City Police Museum

Thomas Gallagher, New York City

A special note of appreciation to the reference librarians at the Fairfield County District Library, Lancaster, Ohio, for their continuing and always cheerful efforts on my behalf.

And thanks to Carol Johnson, Sharon Madison, and Penny Stokes of Bethany House Publishers for your encouragement, your help, and your faith in the story.

Contents

PART TWO
SONG OF SILENCE • THE WAITING

PART THREE
SONG OF FAREWELL • THE PASSAGE

Pronunciation Guide for Proper Names

Aidan	Ā´den
Aine	Än´ya (Anne)
Caomhanach	Kavanagh
Conal	Kôn´al
Connacht	Kôn´ot
Drogheda	Draw´hē guh
Eoin	Ōwen (older form of John)
Killala	Kil lä´lä
Padraic	Paw´rig (Patrick)
Sean	Shôn (form of John)
Tahg	Tīge
Tierney	Teer´ney

On the willow trees
in the midst of Babylon
we hung our harps.
For there they who led us captive
required of us a song. . . .
Our tormentors and they who
wasted us
required of us mirth.

PSALM 137:2, 3 (AMP)

prologue

Eoin

These are the clouds about the fallen sun,
The majesty that shuts his burning eye:
The weak lay hand on what the strong has done,
Till that be tumbled that was lifted high.

W. B. YEATS (1865–1939)

Drogheda, Ireland
1649

"Eoin Caomhanach, your harp will sing no more until the evil of Black Cromwell has been forgotten in the land and the survivors of his butchery return from exile."

Eoin's harp rode his shoulder in silent obedience as his grandfather's command echoed throughout the dim upstairs room. For a moment the old man looked as if he would say more; instead, he turned and went to stand at the narrow window, where a pale blade of late evening light struggled to pierce the gloom. Like a shadowed statue, Conal stood gazing down upon the ruins below.

Drogheda had finally fallen. After a seemingly endless siege and a three-day orgy of savagery and slaughter, the town's destruction was complete. The massacre of its defenders had been swift and thorough, the slaying of its innocent people brutal and merciless. The streets, now virtually deserted, were haunted by the eerie hush that follows disaster. The only sounds to break the silence were the cries of the wounded, an occasional angry shout between soldiers, and the screaming of the gulls over the River Boyne.

Yesterday, Eoin had crouched on one of the breastworks with his bow, watching as the wall around the town was breached by the hordes of Cromwell's New Model Army. He had stared in stunned disbelief as the first wave of shouting, blood-crazed troopers came pouring through the break. Today his heart raced and pounded in his ears as he remembered the surging tide of round black helmets and rust-red doublets exploding on the town in demented fury, chanting psalms and screaming curses in the same breath. On foot and on horseback, with muskets cracking and swords clanging, they hacked and shot and stabbed until the breach was soaked with blood and littered with fallen soldiers.

Losing his bow, Eoin was quickly swept up in the wave of retreating men, then stalled in the chaos and press of the massacre. From there he gazed in sick horror as Sir Arthur Aston, the defending commander of the city, was upended by a mob of jeering troopers, then bludgeoned to death on the bridge with his own wooden leg. As if in a daze, the lad watched the brightly colored feather from Aston's hat wave bravely in the warm harvest breeze before sailing to the ground in final defeat.

Eoin could no longer remember his route of escape. He vaguely recalled hearing the voices of the people at St. Peter's singing the *Gloria* just before the wooden steeple roared to a blaze; within seconds the church's shelter became a funeral pyre. He dimly remembered trying to avoid stepping on the dead bodies as he raced toward home. His ears still rang with the ominous drum of marching boots on cobblestones, and his nostrils still burned with the stench of smoke and gunpowder and death.

Somehow he made his way through the alleys and back streets to his house, only to find his mild-natured father slain just outside the open door, his young mother and two sisters savaged and mutilated within.

Blood . . . his home had been a river of blood.

Half-crazed with shock and grief, he had stumbled blindly down St. John's Street, deep into the Irish quarter to the home of his grandfather. Now the two of them waited, as did the other survivors of Drogheda, to learn their fate. Already lands had been seized, the garrison destroyed, their clergy and scholars humiliated, then slain alongside the town's defenders.

They would be driven from their home, his grandfather said, then either killed or taken prisoner. Rumors ran wild, but most believed that survivors would be sent to Barbados as slaves or relocated to barren Connacht in western Ireland. Eoin thought he would prefer death to being a slave or a prisoner — not that he would have a choice.

"Did you hear me, lad?"

Eoin blinked, forced back to his surroundings by his grandfather's voice. Conal had left the window and stood watching him.

"I did, Grandfather. But —"

"I am charging you with the custody of the Harp of Caomhanach. You have been taught the covenant."

"Aye, sir," Eoin said softly. The harp was the symbol of a generations-old covenant between the Caomhanach family and their God. A clan chief in the time of the kings had decreed that the harp was to remain silent in time of exile, that it should sing only for a free people.

"So it has ever been with our ancestors," Conal now intoned, "and so it is to be with you, Eoin, the eldest and only surviving son of Dermot."

A fierce conflict of emotions flooded Eoin.

He was still raw with pain at the loss of his parents and sisters, still bewildered by the enormity of what had happened to him and his neighbors, and while he loved Conal deeply, he resented the old man's stern directive, especially at this moment.

Lifting his eyes to the ruins of his grandfather's craggy face, Eoin realized that the old man would be woefully unprepared for the rebellion of his only surviving grandson. No less than the fullest measure of respect would be anticipated, for no less had ever been given.

In his prime, the old warrior, like past generations of male Caomhanachs, had been a giant of a man. Year after year of battle and bloodshed, however, had finally defeated him, leaving him shrunken and wasted, a scarecrow whose flesh draped his once-mighty frame like the useless folds of a tattered cloak. Now his hair and beard were purest white, his eyes faded, his hand unsteady. His tunic and breeches hung loosely on his bones.

Eoin answered Conal carefully, denying the pity that rose deep within him. Such an emotion in the face of a chieftain would be an unforgivable insult. "I'm sorry, Grandfather, but I cannot abide by the old ways. The Harp of Caomhanach will no longer be a silent harp of exile. I intend to let her have her voice."

"No!" Conal pounded a fist on the wooden table in front of him, causing Eoin to jump back into a large Venetian vase. It tipped, crashing to the floor. Mindless of the broken vase, the old man went on shouting. "It is forbidden! The harp is to sing only in its own land, to its own people! You would not *dare* break the covenant."

Anticipating his grandfather's opposition to what he was about to say, Eoin nevertheless longed for the old man's understanding. "Grandfather, please, hear me. I can no longer be faithful to the old order, don't you see? To remain silent is to ignore all that has gone before. If we allow our past to be forgotten, we lose not only our land, but our hope as well. Surely you would not have it so. *God* would not have it so."

Ashen-faced, Conal stared at Eoin in breathless silence. "And so, do you now speak for God, Eoin?" he questioned softly. "Would you truly break a vow with our Lord?"

"But don't you see, Grandfather, I wouldn't be breaking the covenant! The vow between our family and God was that the harp would sing for our people as long as the Lord is among us and freedom is ours. If—"

Shaking his head like an angry lion and pointing a thin, accusing finger, Conal leaned toward Eoin. "You forget the rest of the vow! We are about to be an exiled people — perhaps even a people *enslaved!* Whether we flee to the west or go to the islands in chains, we will be slaves. The devil Cromwell and his demons will have our freedom and our faith at their feet."

"No, Grandfather, they will not," Eoin said quietly. "Wherever they send us, we will take our memories. And our faith. And as long as we have our past and our faith, do we not also possess at least a remnant of dignity and freedom — and a future? The Lord promised us 'a future and a hope,' did He not?"

Conal's disdainful glare made Eoin rush to defend his own words. "We will not be leaving God behind, after all, will we? Nor will God desert us. Has He not promised that He would never forsake us?" Forcing a strength into his voice he did not feel, Eoin pressed on. "As long as our God is with us, Grandfather, I say we are free. Free, and at liberty to allow the harp to declare our freedom, to call to mind our heritage and our hope of what God in His mercy will do for us in a new day."

"You rave like a roaming minstrel! An unseasoned child of fourteen years, and you dare to break the pledge of centuries between a people and their God?"

With a stab first of uneasiness, then anger at his grandfather's words, Eoin hesitated, struggling to control his feelings. "I am no child," he answered harshly. "I have seen my family butchered, my townsmen massacred, my land stolen. I have seen evil of a kind that men three times my years have not witnessed."

He moved a step closer to Conal, intent now on making his grandfather understand. "I saw him. Cromwell. I saw that pious hypocrite on his knees. He was praying, Grandfather. Only moments before he himself stood in the blood-soaked breach of the wall and urged his soldiers to break through and slaughter our people — *he . . . was . . . praying*. I saw his rage — he was wild with it, in a white-hot passion for our blood! 'No quarter,' he said. 'Kill them all!' Our soldiers said he intends to bring all Ireland to its knees. They said he believes himself to be the divine instrument of God's judgment upon the Irish!"

Even now the memory of the Puritan general's gaunt, sour face, the sound of his vile name, made Eoin's head roar. "Would you have the ugly truth about that monster go untold? Would you have his name remain free of the guilt it ought to bear?"

At last Eoin stopped. His heartbeat slowed, and the ringing in his ears subsided. He was drained, his anger cooled, his passion depleted.

After a long, tense silence, Conal nodded sadly. "What you say is true. The Puritan and his army purport to carry out the will of our merciful Lord, while in truth they have no mercy at all — none at all. But, then, Drogheda is not the first, nor will it likely be the last field of battle where the Hatchet of Hell proclaims itself the Sword of Heaven."

Their eyes met, and Eoin drew a deep breath. "Grandfather, two nights past, before the massacre, I had a dream. In the dream, God" — he faltered — "God spoke to me."

Conal's chin lifted, his eyes flashing first with incredulity, then something akin to dread as he listened.

"Our Lord has given me a clear vision of — of His will for my life." Eoin spoke haltingly, yet he felt his conviction grow as he went on. "That's how I know I am to take the harp into exile, wherever we go. And not as a silent harp, but as a voice. A voice for our people. The Harp of Caomhanach will be our emblem of freedom, an unchanging reminder of God's presence with us and His promise for us: a promise that one day we will be truly free. A free *Ireland*, Grandfather."

Silence hung between them. When Conal finally spoke, his voice trembled as violently as his hands, causing Eoin's heart to wrench at the pain he knew he had inflicted. Gone was the challenge in the old man's eyes; instead, there was only sorrow.

"Do what you must do, then, Eoin. I will only caution you this one last time, for soon I will no longer be with you to dampen that fiery spirit you possess."

Eoin stared at him. "What do you mean, Grandfather? Of course, you will be with me."

Conal shook his head. "No, lad. I'm old, and I'm ill, and I'll lay my head down for the last time on my own sod. As Drogheda has been my home, so will it be my tomb."

Stunned, Eoin moved toward him, but Conal stopped him with an upraised hand. "I do not fear those stone-faced zealots, lad. With what can they threaten me? Death?" He made a small sound of laughter. "They cannot threaten a sick old man with heaven, now can they? No," he said, again shaking his head slowly, "I do not fear death, so long as I can die in Drogheda."

When Eoin opened his mouth to protest, Conal ignored him. "But as for you, if indeed God has spoken to you, then of course you must obey."

Tears scalded Eoin's eyes, and he quickly lowered his head to hide them.

"Come here, lad," Conal beckoned him kindly. "Come here to me now."

Eoin went to him. Standing with one hand behind his back, the other steadying the harp on his shoulder, he suddenly felt very much the child Conal had accused him of being.

"If indeed you are leaving, Eoin, you must leave now. Go by the river. Use the opening in the cellar, behind the stone. Go up the river, not down, where the ships are. Swim until you find a boat. Go tonight," he said, his voice urgent, "before the moon rises."

"But I can't —"

"You must!" The old man clutched at Eoin's arm. "There's a sack of coins beneath the cellar floor — take it with you. Hide it somehow; you may need the gold later, to buy your safety."

Conal paused, then tugged at Eoin's arm to draw him still closer. "If you believe with all your heart the words you have spoken to me, Eoin, that the harp is free to sing, then let it sing for me this one last time. Sing a lament for Conal Caomhanach, whose spirit has already departed the land and waits for his flesh to follow."

Eoin stared at his grandfather for a moment. At last he eased away from Conal and turned, knowing the old man would not wish to see the tears that now spilled from his eyes. Steadying the harp, which some long-dead ancestor had hollowed from a single block of willow, he slowly began to pluck the strings.

He sang in a voice still boyishly high. He sang for his grandfather, and he sang for himself.

> "My harp will sing across the land
> across the past and years to be. . . ."

Eoin's voice caught, and he had to stop and swallow hard before going on.

"No loss or grief nor death itself
will still its faithful melody . . .
To sing the presence of a God
who conquers even exile's pain —
Who heals the wandering pilgrim's
wound
and leads him home in joy again . . ."

ONE

SONG OF SORROW

The Hunger

They who are slain with the sword
are more fortunate
than they who are the victims of hunger.

LAMENTATIONS 4:9 (AMP)

1

Daniel

Write his merits on your mind;
Morals pure and manners kind;
In his head, as on a hill,
Virtue placed her citadel.

WILLIAM DRENNAN (1754–1820)

Killala, County Mayo (Western Ireland)
January, 1847

Ellie Kavanagh died at the lonesome hour of two o'clock in the morning — a time, according to the Old Ones, when many souls left their bodies with the turning of the tide. A small, gaunt specter with sunken eyes and a vacant stare, she died a silent death. The Hunger had claimed even her voice at the end. She was six years old, and the third child in the village of Killala to die that Friday.

Daniel kept the death watch with his mother throughout the evening. Tahg, his older brother, was too ill to sit upright, and with their da gone — killed in a faction fight late last October — it was for Daniel to watch over his little sister's corpse and see to his mother.

The small body in the corner of the cold, dimly lit kitchen seemed less than human to Daniel; certainly it bore little resemblance to wee Ellie. Candles flickering about its head mottled the ghastly pallor of the skull-like face, and the small, parchment-thin hands clasping the Testament on top of the white sheet made Daniel think uneasily of claws. Even the colored ribbons adorning the sheet mocked his sister's gray and lifeless body.

The room was thick with shadows and filled with weeping women. Ordinarily it would have been heavy with smoke as well, but the men in the village could no longer afford tobacco. The only food smells were faint: a bit of sour cheese, some onion, stale bread, a precious small basket of shellfish. There was none of the illegal poteen — even if potatoes had been available from which to distill the stuff, Grandfar Dan allowed no spirits inside the cottage; he and Daniel's da had both taken the pledge some years before.

All the villagers who came and went said Ellie was laid out nicely. Daniel knew their words were meant to be a comfort, but he found them an offense. Catherine Fitzgerald had done her best in tidying the body — Catherine had no equal in the village when it came to attending at births or deaths — but still Daniel could see nothing at all *nice* about Ellie's appearance.

He hated having to sit and stare at her throughout the evening, struggling to keep the sight of her small, wasted corpse from permanently imbedding itself in his mind. He was determined to remember his black-haired little sister as she had been before the Hunger, traipsing along behind him and chattering at his back to the point of exasperation.

Old Mary Larkin had come to keen, and her terrible shrieking wail now pierced the cottage. Squatting on the floor beside the low fire, Mary was by far the loudest of the women clustered around her. Her tattered skirt was drawn up almost over her head, revealing a torn and grimy red petticoat that swayed as her body twisted and writhed in the ancient death mime.

The woman's screeching made Daniel's skin crawl. He felt a sudden fierce desire to gag her and send her home. He didn't think his feelings were disrespectful of his sister — Ellie had liked things quiet; besides, she had been half-afraid of Old Mary's odd ways.

Ordinarily when Mary Larkin keened the dead, the entire cottage would end up in a frenzy. Everyone knew she was the greatest keener from Killala to Castlebar. At this moment, however, as Daniel watched the hysterical, withered crone clutch the linen sheet and howl with a force that would turn the thunder away, he realized how weak were the combined cries of the mourners. The gathering was pitifully small for a wake — six months ago it would have been twice the size, but death had become too commonplace to attract much attention. And it was evident from the subdued behavior in the room that the Hunger had sapped the strength of even the stoutest of them.

Daniel's head snapped up with surprise when he saw Grandfar Dan haul himself off the stool and go trudging over to the howling women grouped around Ellie's body. He stood there a few moments until at last Mary Larkin glanced up and saw him glaring at her. Behind the stringy wisps of white hair falling over her face, her black eyes looked wild and fierce with challenge. Daniel held his breath, half-expecting her to lash out physically at his grandfather when he put a hand to her shoulder and began speaking to her in the Irish. But after a moment she struggled up from the floor and, with a display of dignity that Daniel would have found laughable under different circumstances, smoothed her skirts and made a gesture to her followers. The lot of them got up and huddled quietly around the dying fire, leaving the cottage quiet again, except for the soft refrain of muffled weeping.

Daniel's mother had sat silent and unmoving throughout the entire scene; now she stirred. "Old Dan should not have done that," Nora said softly. "He should not have stopped them from the keening."

Daniel turned to look at her, biting his lip at her appearance. His mother was held in high esteem for her good looks. "Nora Kavanagh's a grand-looking woman," he'd heard people in the village say, and she was that. Daniel thought his small, raven-haired mother was, in fact, the prettiest woman in Killala. But in the days after his da was killed and the fever had come on Ellie, his mother had seemed to fade, not only in her appearance but in her spirit as well. She seemed to have retreated to a place somewhere deep inside herself, a distant place where Daniel could not follow. Her hair had lost its luster and her large gray eyes their quiet smile; she spoke only when necessary, and then with apparent effort. Hollow-eyed and deathly quiet, she continued to maintain her waxen, lifeless composure even in the face of her grief, but Daniel sometimes caught a glimpse of something shattering within her.

At times he found himself almost wishing his mother would give way to a fit of weeping or womanly hysteria. Then at least he could put an arm about her narrow shoulders and try to console her. This silent stranger beside him seemed beyond comfort; in truth, he suspected she was often entirely unaware of his presence.

In the face of his mother's wooden stillness, Daniel himself turned inward, to the worrisome question that these days seldom gave him any peace.

What was to become of them?

The potato crop had failed for two years straight, and they were now more than half the year's rent in arrears. Grandfar was beginning to fail. And Tahg — his heart squeezed with fear at the thought of his older brother — Tahg was no longer able to leave his bed. His mother continued to insist that Tahg would recover, that the lung ailment which had plagued him since childhood was responsible for his present weakness. Perhaps she was right, but Daniel was unable to convince himself. Tahg had a different kind of misery on him now — something dark and ugly and evil.

A tight, hard lump rose to his throat. It was going to be the same as with Ellie. First she'd grown weak from the hunger; later the fever had come on her until she grew increasingly ill. And then she died.

As for his mother, Daniel thought she still seemed healthy enough, but too much hard work and too little food were fast wearing her down. She was always tired lately, tired and distracted and somber. Even so, she continued to mend and sew for two of the local magistrates. Her earnings were less than enough to keep them, now that they lacked his da's wages from Reilly the weaver, yet she had tried in vain to find more work.

The entire village was in drastic straits. The Hunger was on them all; fever was spreading with a vengeance. Almost every household was without work, and the extreme winter showed no sign of abating. Most were hungry; many were starving; all lived in fear of eviction.

Still, poor as they were as tenant farmers, Daniel knew they were better off than many of their friends and neighbors. Thomas Fitzgerald, for example, had lost his tenancy a few years back when he got behind in his rent. Unable thereafter to get hold of a patch of land to lease, he barely managed to eke out an existence for his family by means of conacre, wherein he rented a small piece of land season by season, with no legal rights to it whatever. The land they occupied was a mere scrap. Their cabin, far too small for such a large family, was scarcely more than a buffer against the winter winds, which this year had been fierce indeed.

Daniel worried as much about the Fitzgeralds as he did about his own family. His best friend, Katie, was cramped into that crude, drafty hut with several others. She was slight, Katie was, so thin and frail that Daniel's blood chilled at the thought of what the fever might do to her. His sister had been far sturdier than Katie, and it had destroyed

Ellie in such a short time.

Katie was more than his friend — she was his sweetheart as well. She was only eleven, and he thirteen, but they would one day marry — of that he was certain. Together they had already charted their future. When he was old enough, Daniel would make his way to Dublin for his physician's training, then come back to set up his own practice in Castlebar. Eventually he'd be able to build a fine house for himself and Katie — and for his entire family.

There was the difference of their religions to be considered, of course. Katie was a Roman and he a Protestant. But they would face that hurdle later, when they were older. In the meantime, Katie was his lass, and that was that. At times he grew almost desperate for the years to pass so they could get on with their plans.

A stirring in the room yanked Daniel out of his thoughts. He glanced up and caught a sharp breath. Without thinking, he popped off his stool, about to cry out a welcome until he remembered his surroundings.

The man ducking his head to pass through the cottage door was a great tower of a fellow, with shoulders so broad he had to ease himself sideways through the opening. Yet he was as lean and as wiry as a whip. He had a mane of curly copper hair and a lustrous, thick beard the color of a fox's pelt. He carried himself with the grace of a cat-a-mountain, yet he seemed to fill the room with the restrained power of a lion.

As Daniel stood watching impatiently, the big man straightened, allowing his restless green eyes to sweep the room. His gaze gentled for an instant when it came to rest on Ellie's corpse, softening even more at the sight of Daniel's mother, to whom he offered a short, awkward nod of greeting. Only when he locked eyes with Daniel did his sun-weathered face at last break into a wide, pleased smile.

He started toward them, and it seemed to Daniel that even clad humbly as he was in dark frieze and worn boots, Morgan Fitzgerald might just as well have been decked with the steel and colors of a warrior chief, so imposing and awe-inspiring was his presence. He stopped directly in front of them, and both he and Daniel stood unmoving for a moment, studying each other's faces. Then, putting hands the size of dinner plates to Daniel's shoulders, Morgan pulled him into a hard, manly embrace. Daniel breathed a quiet sigh of satisfaction as he buried his cheek against Morgan's granite chest, knowing the bond between him and the bronze giant to be renewed.

After another moment, Morgan tousled Daniel's hair affectionately, released him, and turned to Nora. The deep, rumbling voice that could shake the walls of a cabin was infinitely soft when he spoke. "I heard about Owen and the lass, Nora. 'Tis a powerful loss."

As Daniel watched, his mother lifted her shadowed eyes to Morgan. She seemed to grow paler still, and her small hands began to wring her handkerchief into a twisted rope. Her voice sounded odd when she acknowledged his greeting, as if she might choke on her words. " 'Tis good of you to come, Morgan."

"Nora, how are you keeping?" he asked, leaning toward her still more as he scrutinized her face.

Her only reply was a small, stiff nod of her head before she looked away.

Daniel wondered at the wounded look in Morgan's eyes, even more at his mother's strained expression. The room was still, and he noticed that the lank-haired Judy Hennessey was perched forward on her chair as far as she could get in an obvious attempt to hear their conversation. He shot a fierce glare in her direction, but she ignored him, craning her neck even farther.

Just then Grandfar Dan moved from his place by the fire and began to lumber toward them, his craggy, gray-bearded face set in a sullen scowl. Daniel braced himself. For as long as he could remember, there had been bad blood between his grandfather and

Morgan Fitzgerald. Grandfar had carried some sort of a grudge against Morgan for years, most often referring to him as "that worthless rebel poet."

"Sure, and that long-legged rover thinks himself a treasure," Grandfar would say. "Well, a *scoundrel* is what he is! A fresh-mouthed scoundrel with a sweet-as-honey tongue and a string of wanton ways as long as the road from here to Sligo, that's your Fitzgerald! What he's learned from all his books and his roaming is that it's far easier to sing for your supper than to work for it."

Now, watching the two of them square off, Daniel held his breath in anticipation of a fracas. A warning glint flared in Morgan's eye, and the old man's face was red. They stared at each other for a tense moment. Then, to Daniel's great surprise, Morgan greeted Grandfar with a bow of respect and, instead of goading him as he might have done in the past, he said quietly, " 'Tis a bitter thing, Dan. I'm sorry for your troubles."

Even shrunken as he was by old age and hard labor, Grandfar was a taller man than most. Still, he had to look up at Morgan. His mouth thinned as they eyed each other, but the expected sour retort did not come. Instead, the old man inclined his head in a curt motion of acknowledgment, then walked away without a word, his vest flapping loosely against his wasted frame.

Morgan stared after him, his heavy brows drawn together in a frown. " 'Tis the first time I have known Dan Kavanagh to show his years," he murmured, as if to himself. "It took the Hunger to age him, it would seem."

He turned back to Daniel's mother. "So, then, where is Tahg? I was hoping to see him."

Nora glanced across the kitchen. Tahg lay abed in a small, dark alcove at the back of the room, where a tattered blanket had been hung for his privacy. "He's sleeping. Tahg is poorly again."

Morgan looked from her to Daniel. "How bad? Not the fever?"

"No, it is *not* the fever!" she snapped, her eyes as hard as her voice. " 'Tis his lungs."

Daniel stared down at the floor, unable to meet Morgan's eyes for fear his denial would be apparent.

"Nora —"

Daniel raised his head to see Morgan searching his mother's face, a soft expression of compassion in his eyes.

"Nora, is there anything I can do?"

Daniel could not account for his mother's sudden frown. Couldn't she tell that Morgan only wanted to help?

"Thank you, but there's no need."

Morgan looked doubtful. "Are you sure, Nora? There must be something —"

She interrupted him, her tone making it

clear that he wasn't to press. "It's kind of you to offer, Morgan, but as I said, there is no need."

Morgan continued to look at her for another moment. Finally he gave a reluctant nod. "I should be on my way, then. The burial — will it be tomorrow?"

Her mouth went slack. "The burial . . . aye, the burial will be tomorrow."

Hearing her voice falter, Daniel started to take her hand, but stopped at the sight of the emptiness in her eyes. She was staring past Morgan to Ellie's corpse, seemingly unaware of anyone else in the room.

Morgan shot Daniel a meaningful glance. "I'll just be on my way, then. Will you walk outside with me, lad?" Without waiting for Daniel's reply, he lifted a hand as if to place it on Nora's shoulder but drew it away before he touched her. Then, turning sharply, he started for the door.

Eager to leave the gloom of the cottage, and even more eager to be with Morgan after months of separation, Daniel nevertheless waited for his mother's approval. When he realized she hadn't even heard Morgan's question, he went to lift his coat from the wall peg by the door. With a nagging sense of guilt for the relief he felt upon leaving, he hurried to follow Morgan outside.

2

Morgan

Oh, blame not the bard if he flies to the bowers
Where pleasure lies carelessly smiling at fame;
He was born for much more, and in happier hours
His soul might have burned with a holier flame.

THOMAS MOORE (1779–1852)

Despite the frigid evening air, they walked all the way to the edge of town, heading toward the pier. The lines of Killala's low, grim buildings were smudged by the gathering darkness, their stains from the wet Atlantic winds scarcely visible. It was a heavy, menacing dusk, thick with the inhospitable silence of a village in mourning.

Although he held a near-sentimental fondness for the village, Morgan had long ago observed that Killala was much like Ireland throughout: at a distance it presented an alluring appearance, with its gently sloping grounds, its fertile meadows and groves, and its picturesque setting by the bay; seen closer up, however, the beauty was spoiled by disorder and squalor, by a dismal aimlessness among its winding streets and its poverty-stricken inhabitants.

Despite its location in Mayo, the wildest and poorest county in all Ireland, Killala had once been a cheerful, bustling town, the center of episcopal authority. Years ago, however, most of the trade had moved south to Ballina, destroying Killala's economy. Eventually the church consolidated its jurisdiction in Tuam, adding to the village's declining prosperity.

The cathedral still stood at the center of the town, as did an ancient round tower, from which Killala's three main streets diverged — one turning west toward the miserable hamlet of Palmerstown, one going south toward a site known as the "Acres," and the other leading east. The tower was the only building of any real interest; even the cathedral was spare and plain. In addition, Killala boasted the handsome residence of the Protestant clergyman — still referred to as "the palace" — a small Wesleyan meeting-house, a Roman chapel, and a schoolhouse that was often without a master.

As they walked through the town, Morgan's distress for its ruinous conditions grew. Still, he should not have been surprised; the same oppressive death pall that now hung over Killala had draped all the other villages he had passed through during the last few months. Like the dreaded potato blight that had settled over the country's fields for two consecutive growing seasons, an uneasy hush seemed to permeate the whole of Ireland. It was, Morgan knew, the silence of a people whose hope was dying, a people who had lost sight of tomorrow. The sound of the fiddle and pipes had been exchanged for the mourners' keen; the rhythm of dancing feet had slowed to the dirge of the death cart, the cadence of the burial march, and the desperate, shuffling steps of a homeless people in search of refuge.

They must have passed twenty or more poor, uprooted wretches before they came to the outskirts of the village. Most of them stood huddled and shivering around their tumbled cottages, waiting for night to fall so they could creep back beneath the remains of their roof and walls to shelter themselves until daybreak.

Morgan knew their ways, for he had encountered hundreds like them. For days they would hover close to what was left of their houses — houses often destroyed for payment by some of their own neighbors. Unwilling to break the final tie to the land on which their homes and those of their ancestors had long stood, they would spend the night in the tumbled shelter, then crawl outside before dawn to avoid discovery by one of the agent's henchmen. Making themselves scarce until evening, they would then repeat the ritual all over again. Eventually they would have to leave and take to the road.

Evictions were routine now, the sufferings of the homeless a pandemic tragedy in Ireland. The nation was fast becoming an open graveyard, burying its memories, its traditions, its spirit — and its people.

People were dying by the thousands: dying from hunger, from the vicious fevers that never failed to accompany a famine, and from the total despair of utter hopelessness. From their ancient beginnings the Irish had been a valiant, generous people of open doors and open hearts, who in the very worst of times were never without their poems and songs, so gregarious by nature they made a festival out of a wake. Now they lurked behind locked doors, quaking in fear and dread and defeat.

And it was killing them. Morgan had seen the dying wherever he went — not all of it physical, not by far. The people were losing their sense of themselves — their homes, their dreams, their pride, their very *identity* — to a faceless, seemingly invincible enemy.

And who would bear the guilt for the changes that ravaged Ireland? People blamed the British, who continued to claim Ireland as her own personal breadbasket, ruling her with an incredible lack of Christian conscience. They accused the greedy absentee landlords, who owned enormous chunks of the small island, yet cared nothing about their properties except for the collection of exorbitant rents. They condemned the land agents, who managed estates for the absentee landlords, often with a total disregard for the lives and health of their tenants. And they vilified the disease itself, which was, with a vengeance, claiming the children of Eire by the thousands.

But despite so many areas to which communal guilt could be apportioned, Morgan reflected, Ireland's great destroyer was the *ukrosh*. The Hunger. The life-destroying, heart-freezing, soul-stealing Hunger —

"Morgan? Morgan, *look!*"

The lad's voice at his side brought him up short from his brooding. He looked at Daniel John, then followed the boy's gaze to see what had caught his attention.

Across from them, in a ditch off the right side of the road, huddled a woman and two wee girls, all clothed in rags. Both the mother and the children were without coats or shawls, and their dresses were so tattered they might as well have been wearing paper ribbons. Even in his cloak, Morgan was chilled; he could not imagine how these poor souls could bear the cold with no protective outer clothing. They were clearly half-frozen and in the throes of starvation. The woman appeared to be watching their approach through glazed, dull eyes; but as they drew nearer, Morgan saw that her gaze was the empty, fixed stare of one whose strength is so depleted she could see nothing beyond the mists of gathering death.

He glanced down the road and saw others on their way out of the village: an old man and woman, both coatless, plus a number of other walking skeletons covered only by rags or torn sacks. Some hovered lifelessly in the ditches on both sides, while others marched in the wooden, moribund gait of impending death. Some were grown; some were children; many were carrying infants.

Where had they all come from? Not from the village, Morgan suspected; Killala was a wee place, fourteen or fifteen hundred at most. Besides, from the looks of these stricken souls, many had been traveling for days. Most likely they were refugees from other towns in search of work or relief or shelter — none of which they were likely to find.

As they came abreast of the woman and her little girls, Morgan put a hand to Daniel's shoulder, indicating the lad should wait for him. He turned toward the ditch where the small family huddled. The woman watched his approach with no real show of interest or emotion. One of the girls, the smaller of the two, fastened dazed, unseeing eyes upon

Morgan; he sensed she was but hours away from death. The older lass seemed to be holding the smaller one up, as if to keep her from falling into the ditch. Both were gaunt like their mother, with skin hanging in folds and cavernous eyes that burned a tunnel to Morgan's heart.

"Sure, and you'd not be on the road, you and your lasses?" he ventured by way of greeting.

The woman stared at him. When she opened her mouth to speak, it seemed to require great effort. "We are that."

"Where is your man, then?"

Again the woman gave him a blank look, as if she didn't understand. She was shaking so hard and her voice was so weak and phlegmy that Morgan could scarcely make out her words. "Dead two weeks now, from the fever."

"Here, in Killala?"

She shook her head. "We come from Rathroeen. The agent turned us out yesterday."

What kind of man, Morgan wondered, *could throw a starving woman and two wee girls into the snow?* But he already knew — a man such as their own local agent, George Cotter. More beast than some, less man than others. And the island had more than her share of them.

"Do you have someone here in the village?" he asked. "Family, perhaps?"

Shivering, the woman drew her children close against her, as if to gather some warmth from them. Neither showed any sign of awareness, but simply continued to stare at Morgan with hollow eyes. "Not here," she answered dully, her voice shaking as hard as her body. "We are going to Kilcummin; my man's family is there."

"Kilcummin?" Morgan stared at them with dismay. "Your little girls are not up to the road. Haven't you anyone nearby?"

The woman turned her head without replying, as if she had not heard. Morgan looked from her to the tiny girls, clutching their mother's ragged dress. With a mutter of frustration, he pried open the pouch tied about his waist. "Here," he said, fishing out a coin and handing it to her. "There's a woman on the Rathlackan road who lets rooms. It's not a tavern, mind, but a decent place. Give her this and tell her Morgan Fitzgerald says she should give you a room and some food until you're able to go on to Kilcummin."

The woman stared at Morgan's outstretched hand as if it held a rainbow. Her eyes went from his hand to his face, then back to the money he was thrusting on her. At last her stiff fingers reached for the money with a jerk. "God bless you, man," she mumbled, stuffing the coin down the front of her dress. "May God in His mercy bless you. You have saved us."

Morgan started back to the road, but before he could reach Daniel John, he was stopped. As if a call had been sounded to a host of phantoms, raggedy marchers swept in upon him like a flock of buzzards, grasping, crying, whimpering — all reaching for him at once. They clawed at his clothes, wailing and pleading that he must help them, too.

"I can't — I'm sorry, but I can't —" In vain he tried to make himself heard, but his protests were lost amid the clamor.

Throwing up his arms as a shield, he tried to draw back without striking out. He stood more than a head above them all, yet so desperate and determined was the press of their bodies that he knew a moment of alarm for fear they'd bring him down and trample him.

He was shouting now, but in vain. Afraid they might turn and swarm the woman and her little girls, Morgan twisted around and shot her a warning look, jerking his head toward the road. It took her a moment to react, but at last she moved, dragging the children with her. Stumbling and weaving, they finally managed to leave the ditch for the road.

Over the heads of the crowd, Morgan saw Daniel John; the lad had left the road and was running toward him. *"No!"* Morgan shouted above the din. "Stay there!"

Still unwilling to turn the power of his own large, healthy body against the starving, pathetic scarecrows encircling him, Morgan flung his arms up, snapping himself sideways like a whip through the first opening he spotted. The force of his movement caused a tear in the frenzied crowd, and they began to fall back.

Finally free of them, Morgan felt himself seared by their accusing eyes as they followed his retreat. A hot, irrational flash of guilt struck him in rebuke of his own well-being.

Daniel John had managed to skirt the mob and rushed to his side, his face milk-white. "Are you all right, Morgan? Did they hurt you?"

"No, no, lad, I'm fine," Morgan assured him, straightening his clothing. "How could the poor creatures hurt me, and them so near death?"

Not wanting the boy to know just how badly the incident had shaken him, Morgan forced a note of gruffness into his voice. "We must be getting back. Your mother will be furious with the both of us — especially with me, keeping you out in this cold so long."

"Let's just go the rest of the way to the pier first, Morgan. Please, can't we? Like we used to?"

Morgan hesitated, then slung his arm around the lad's shoulders, catching his breath at the sharpness of bone he could feel beneath the thin coat. "All right, laddie, but only for a moment, and then we must be off."

They reached the edge of the rude pier and

stood in silence, staring across the dark, sullen waters of the bay, now thick with ice. Wind laced with mist stung their faces, and Morgan pulled the scarf from his neck and wrapped it about the boy's throat. "So, now, is it true what I've heard — there have been numerous deaths in the village from the Hunger?"

Daniel John nodded, touching the scarf at his throat with a grateful smile. "Aye. From the Hunger or the fever — or both."

Morgan stooped to clasp the boy's shoulders. "I want the truth now, Daniel John. Have you food, you and your family?"

The lad hesitated, and Morgan could almost see Nora's pride at work in her son. He knew a sudden stab of anger with her for shifting her own stubborn self-sufficiency onto those young shoulders, and yet he understood. In her fierce need to better herself, Nora had learned to suppress any hint of weakness. He supposed he might have expected Daniel to be struck with the same branch.

"You're to tell me the truth, lad," he insisted softly.

The boy looked away. "Mother is proud, you know."

Morgan nodded. *Proud and stone-stubborn,* he thought. "Aye, she is that, and pride has its place. But it's not among friends such as us." He paused for a moment before asking,

"Owen had nothing put by, then?"

Again Daniel John avoided meeting his eyes. "He did, but it's long gone."

Morgan tightened his hold on the boy's shoulders. "Well, see here, now, you're not to worry. I'll work something out for you and your family."

"But *how?*" the boy blurted out. "Grandfar says your pockets are as empty as your promises." Too late, he threw a hand over his mouth, his eyes wide with dismay at his words.

Morgan grinned, dropped his hands away from the boy's shoulders, and straightened. "True enough. But I believe I can still help a friend when the need is there."

Stretching up on the balls of his feet, he looked up for a moment at the night sky, so heavy with clouds they looked to be dropping into the bay. "What about evictions, lad? Have there been many so far?"

"Aye, and more every week. The Conlons were turned out just last Saturday, in the worst of the ice storm. They're living in one of the squatters' abandoned huts near the shore."

Morgan looked at him. "Brian Conlon, is it?"

Daniel John nodded. "Cotter had their place tumbled practically around their heads."

Morgan frowned angrily and spit out the agent's name like an oath. *"Cotter!"* The memory of the swine-featured agent was still all too clear in his mind. He was the devil's own spawn, that one.

A question nagged at the fringe of his thoughts, but he wasn't sure he should ask it. Still the boy seemed to feel easy about confiding in him. "And what about *your* rent, Daniel John? Do you know if you're behind at all?"

"We owe for the last half year," the boy said quietly, without hesitation. He bit his lower lip for a moment, and added, "Grandfar says it will be the road for us before spring if we can't pay what we owe to date and the next half as well."

The old anger and resentment flared up in Morgan as he searched the lad's worried eyes. Impulsively, he pulled him into the circle of his arms and held him. "Didn't I say I would help, and that you're not to worry?"

"Aye, Morgan."

He heard the uncertainty in the boy's muffled reply. Taking him by the shoulders, he set him away from him just enough that he could see his face. "Let's have a smile now," he said, forcing one of his own. "You must not forget that your granddaddy is a great one for making big out of little." He tousled Daniel John's unruly black curls. "Well, am I wrong?"

Shaking his head, the boy managed a small smile. Morgan opened his cloak, pulling

Daniel John into its shelter, close beside him. "Come along, now," he ordered, putting his arm around the boy's shoulders and turning him back toward town. "Suppose while we walk you advise me of your progress with the harp. Yours and Tahg's."

Daniel John grinned up at him. "Do you know, you always say that, in the exact same way, each time you come back home?"

"And haven't I the right, being the one who taught you all your music?"

"Tahg says I'm sounding more and more like you all the time when I play."

Morgan grinned down at him as they walked. "Oh, does he, now? Well, we shall have to be seeing about that, I expect." He felt a tug at his heart at the boy's pleasure, and he found himself wishing, not for the first time, that this tenderhearted lad with the wise blue eyes were his own.

As well he might have been, man, had you not been so intent on playing the fool. The thought stabbed Morgan before he could shield his heart against it. *But best not to turn down that road.* "And Tahg, then? How does he fare with the harp?"

The boy's face clouded. "Tahg isn't strong enough to play these days. He can scarcely sit up in bed now."

The image of Nora's oldest son fastened itself upon Morgan's mind — all pale skin and slashes of bone; good, guileless eyes, and a heart equally pure. Tahg was the sober one, the down-to-earth, sensible planner and doer. A lovely lad, destined to be a fine, strong man. But now?

They walked the rest of the way in silence, both ducking their heads against the sting of the snow and the wind whipping at their skin. Neither spoke again until they reached the walk to Daniel John's cottage.

"I'll leave you here," Morgan said. "Your mother will be anxious and want you with her."

The boy clung to his hand, and Morgan could see Daniel John's reluctance to go inside. "Morgan . . ."

"Aye, lad?" The boy's eyes were fastened on Morgan in a look of mingled trust and confusion.

"Do you believe —" He stopped, then went on. "You know how we're always saying 'God is good'?"

Morgan frowned down at him and nodded.

The boy hesitated. "Well . . . do you believe it?"

Morgan stared at him. "Why would you ask such a question, lad?"

Daniel John didn't answer, but simply stood staring up at him, waiting.

Morgan sucked in a deep breath, glancing over his shoulder toward the road for a moment as he attempted to form his reply. When he turned back, the lad was still watching him expectantly. "Aye, Daniel John, of course I believe that God is good. But that doesn't mean," he went on, running a hand through his hair as he measured his words, "that all His *creatures* are good. Though He made us in His image, there are those who have badly distorted His original notion, it seems to me."

He paused, sensing that the struggle going on inside the boy was the same kind of conflict between faith and doubt that took place all too often in his own spirit.

"You see, lad, what seems to happen is that God's goodness is often overshadowed by His creation's meanness. Do you understand what I'm saying?"

After a moment the boy nodded. "I think so. But ever since Da was killed and Ellie died and Tahg was taken so ill —" He stopped, as if unable to capture the words he needed to explain himself.

Morgan waited, comprehending the boy's struggle all too well. "It's a hard thing, I know. If God is truly good, you're wondering why He gives evil so much quarter, isn't that it?"

Daniel John nodded, his gaze clearing somewhat. "Some of the villagers are even saying that God has abandoned Ireland altogether."

"Well, lad, I confess to having had that thought myself upon occasion," Morgan admitted. At the boy's expression of surprise, he tried to explain. "Being a man doesn't necessarily mean you cease to doubt and to question, Daniel John. But I have come to believe that God's ways were never meant to be entirely understood. Perhaps the fact that I cannot perceive the reasons for His doing what He does or does not do only serves to point out that I am human, and He divine."

The boy seemed to consider Morgan's words for a moment, but his eyes were still troubled. "It seems so unfair, the bad things that are happening. Like Ellie's dying. She suffered so before she went, and Ellie never hurt a living soul."

"Ah, lad, don't make the mistake of expecting life to have the qualities of God. Learn now, while you're young, not to compare the two, or it may well drive you mad one day. Life is life, and God is God, and it's nothing but folly to confuse the two. Life will never be fair, Daniel John, but we must *believe* that God is never *less* than fair. That is the truth, even though it's often a hard truth to cling to, especially in times like these."

Morgan was grateful to see a faint light of understanding dawn in the boy's eyes. "I will have to think on that, Morgan."

"Aye, lad," he said, putting a hand to the boy's shoulder. "I am sure you will. But it's inside with you for now."

"Morgan?" The boy still made no move toward the door. "Will you be staying for a while this time?"

Seeing Daniel John's hopeful gaze, Morgan felt a pang of sorrow for all the losses the lad's young heart had suffered, the loneliness he now must be bearing. His delay in answering caused the boy to press. "Will you, Morgan?"

"I have something I must do first," he began. Seeing Daniel John's eyes cloud with disappointment, Morgan hurried to reassure him. "It will not take but two or three days, I'm sure. Then I'll come back, and when I do — yes, lad, I plan to stay for a time. These long legs of mine are growing stiff and sore from roaming about in the cold. Perhaps a nice long rest would be just the thing for me."

The boy beamed. "I should think so, Morgan. A *very* long rest at home, that's what you need."

Home. The word struck a note of regret in Morgan. For more years than he could remember, home had been the road — or, at best, a bed in a friend's house or a pallet of straw in a kind farmer's barn. Home had never been much more than a word, never meant more than a dream or two of what might have been if he had been a different man, a good enough man, for Nora.

Ah, well. Home tonight was a corner near the fire in his brother's kitchen. After seeing the lad safe inside, Morgan turned and, pushing his hands into his pockets to keep them warm, went on down the road.

3

Nora

But I, being poor, have only my dreams;
I have spread my dreams under your feet;
Tread softly because you tread on my dreams.

W. B. YEATS (1865–1939)

Squeezing her eyes shut against the pain grinding at her temples, Nora stopped her spinning wheel and waited for the dizziness to pass. There was still enough late afternoon light in the kitchen that she could work, but she was so weary she thought she could not possibly go on.

She was weak to the point of collapse. There seemed to be no end to the days, and the nights dragged on forever. The daylight hours brought enough work for two women, but it was the darkness she minded most. No matter how exhausted she might be when she threw herself onto her bed, sleep refused to come. Night after night, her mind continued its torture, forcing her to relive Owen's death, then Ellie's, before assaulting her with a fresh seizure of fear for Tahg and the threat of imminent disaster for them all.

Only a week had passed since Ellie's burial, but things had gone from bad to worse throughout the village. The Hunger was upon them with a fury now, and its companion, disease, continued to seek out more and more victims, afflicting entire families at once. Mary Conlon had died just last night, and before dawn death claimed her youngest son. Last week alone, half a dozen families or more had been evicted and turned out on the road; before week's end the bitter January gales had felled three of the homeless children.

Though the Kavanaghs fared better than some, in their own cottage Old Dan was visibly failing. Night before last, while trying to plug a hole in the thatch on the roof, he had grown faint and come close to falling. He would not admit his weakness, of course, but it had been painfully obvious that he was spent. Nora had found Daniel in tears beside the fire shortly afterward; he was a brave lad, never crying for the pain in his own empty belly, yet unable to disguise his worry for those he loved.

Nora's hope was stretched thin, hard put to find even a slender thread to cling to. She had heard talk of soup kitchens and new relief centers to be added. Some said help would come any day now; others believed it would be spring before aid would arrive here, in one of the most remote sections of Mayo.

Spring would be too late. Their pig was gone, and the hens; the cow alone was left, and she was starving. Only her milk and a few old turnips stood between the family and starvation. There was grain in the barn, but it was marked with the landlord's cross for rent and could not be touched. Old Dan said they must begin to sneak a bit of it for food, but if they were caught it could bring eviction.

Nora shuddered at the thought of being homeless. With the old man so weak, and Tahg growing worse every day, they would die in the ditch in no time.

Tahg. He was suffering his life away. Every night he coughed and groaned until Nora thought she would surely go mad from the sounds of his misery. Old Dan suspected that Tahg had the fever, but she would not even consider the possibility. The boy's lungs had been poorly ever since he'd had pneumonia as a wee wane; he'd always been frail, Tahg had. This fierce winter had simply weakened him even more, but when spring came, he would be stronger. *Please, God.*

Dropping her hands to her lap, she began to rub them together. The cottage was cold; she kept the fire low, for the turf was nearly gone. Soon the only thing left to burn would be the few sticks of furniture they hadn't already sold, not nearly enough to see them through the rest of the winter.

A wave of despair rolled over her. It was impossible not to speculate on what might lie ahead. She had tried, at least until recently, to fix her mind on God's promises of provision for the future; but lately she lived with such fear, such dread, that it was becoming nearly impossible not to surrender to utter despair. The very act of living, of *surviving*, required such a fierce effort that there was little strength left over for its added burdens.

Who would ever have dreamed that the appearance just two summers past of some small brown spots on the potato plants would herald the nationwide disaster they now faced? Even when the dreaded blight had come again in '46, stealing its way across the land in a great white, silent cloud, those who had felt the eerie, unnatural quiet could not have envisioned the doom about to fall on Ireland's fields. The vile, sulphurous stench on the wind might well have been that of hell itself, so disastrous was its onslaught.

Some said the blight was God's judgment on the land, that Ireland's own sin had condemned her. Old Dan had remarked testily that only the British would believe that kind of foolishness, but Nora no longer knew *what* to believe. It was difficult to fathom how a merciful God could allow infants and children to starve to death or die in the agony of the fever, yet the horrors now sweeping Ireland seemed to defy any hint of mercy. The all-powerful God who could have stayed the destruction at any moment had not moved to do so; indeed, the storm of pestilence and devastation raged more fiercely than ever.

More and more often, questions came to nag Nora's conscience and attack her faith. If, as some insisted, the Hunger *was* an act of God's judgment, then how high a payment would He exact from her — from them all — before His divine justice was satisfied?

In the curtained alcove behind her, Tahg coughed and gasped, and Nora got up to go to him. When she stepped inside the small, windowless room, she saw that he was still sleeping. As she stood, unmoving, watching him, an ugly phantom of fear rounded the corner of her mind to assail her. *First Owen, then Ellie. Would Tahg be next?*

Owen had once accused her of being partial to their eldest, though of course she had vigorously denied it. Now she seemed to hear a guilty whisper in her mind, repeating her husband's accusation.

It's true . . . you know it's true; you've always favored Tahg . . .

It was *not* true, she silently insisted — at least not entirely. It was more that she had always been able to *know* Tahg, to understand him. He was so much like her, so close in spirit that she seemed to know his heart as well as her own. The two of them seemed to share a special communion, an unspoken sameness.

Daniel John, on the other hand, had been a mystery to her almost since his first word. At thirteen the boy already had the look of a long-armed, long-legged plowboy, but his head held the mind of a dreamer, a scholar, a poet. The lad was as starved for books and knowledge as most boys his age were for food and fun. Forever running to the schoolhouse when there was a master, he would soak up what he could of history and the old language and the heroes' tales, then run home to share all he had learned. His deepest pleasure was found in reading from a tattered book of poems or strumming achingly lovely tunes on the ancient Kavanagh Harp, tunes that somehow made Nora want to weep.

She had long ago accepted the fact that her youngest son would forever be a question, perhaps an exasperation, to her own cautious, practical nature. No matter how deeply she cared for Daniel John, she knew she would never really understand him.

Indeed, she wondered if *anyone* would, except perhaps for Morgan Fitzgerald, who had once called Daniel John a "boy-bard with a soul of old sorrows and a heart born to break." But, then, Morgan Fitzgerald was cut from the same cloth, she thought with a bitterness she refused to examine too closely. Hadn't the man been a dreamer his lifelong, with his precious books and his songs and his poems — his *words?*

Words. Morgan was never without them. They were living things to him, riches such as jewels would be to a king. Well, much good had they done him. He lived the life of a penniless vagabond, traipsing about the country, teaching in one schoolhouse after another, then wandering off to barter an occasional poem for food and lodging. He seemed to care not at all for hearth fire and comfort, but was more at home with the wind at his back and an untraveled road just ahead.

Ah, but once, Nora . . . once you would have died for the lad . . .

With a start, Nora gave the curtain a yank and returned to the kitchen, where Old Dan had come in from outside and was punching at the fire. "Work as if there is a fire under your skin," he muttered, straightening, "and there will ever be a fire in your hearth. Ha! No truth at all in that old saying, not in these times."

Nora smiled at him. "You've got it burning well enough, though. It will ease the chill, at least."

The old man's concern with the fire was a recent concession to Nora's worsening fatigue. As the woman of the house, maintaining the hearth fire was entirely her responsibility. In the old days no housewife would have thought of letting the fire go out, day or night; it was the heart of the home, the perpetual symbol of family unity. That an old one like her father-in-law would deign to share this traditional woman's chore was a distinct act of love, an act that endeared him to her that much more.

"Where's the lad?" he asked now, clasping his hands behind his back to warm them.

Nora sighed, knowing the truth would bring a sour retort. "I believe he went to the Fitzgeralds."

As she'd anticipated, the old man uttered a grunt of disgust. "With his harp, I suppose."

Nora felt a quick stirring of defense for her son and an even sharper stab of anger at Morgan Fitzgerald. No sooner had he left Ellie's burial site than he'd taken to the road again, leaving behind a disappointed, but still loyal, Daniel John. Every day since, the lad had watched the road or gone to the Fitzgerald cabin to inquire, never saying a word about Morgan's defection.

"Well?" the old man pressed.

"His harp? No, he left his harp at home today."

"Ach, so he's given up on the rogue for now, eh?"

Not answering, Nora went back to the spinning wheel and, after smoothing the lumps from a roll of thin wool, set the wheel singing with a hard spin. Old Dan crossed to the small, narrow window at the front of the kitchen and peered out.

"It's going to snow again," he said with a

heavy sigh. "What a winter this has been. 'Tis the worst I remember since Peg died."

Nora watched him as she worked, frowning with concern at his wasted appearance. Old Dan was seventy-three, but he still had a full head of curly gray hair, and his beard was as thick as cotton batting. He was toothless, but this was seldom noticed since he was a solemn man, not given to many smiles. Until a few months ago, he had been a strong man, healthy and vigorous for his age. Now he appeared to be little more than bone, with his tall, stooped frame and his long, rope-thin arms. Lately, Nora thought, his skin had turned as gray as his beard.

"I'm thinking of sending Daniel John for the doctor tomorrow," she said. "Tahg is getting no rest at night."

The old man turned around from the window. His face was glum. "And how is it we will be paying him?"

"He's been kind enough to take fresh milk before. I'm sure he'll do so again." Nora paused, then ventured her next words with care. "I thought we might have him take a look at you as well."

"Well, keep your thoughts to yourself, woman. There's not a thing wrong with me that a good meal wouldn't cure! And as for the fresh milk — the cow is going dry, and well you know it! She can't live on roots and rocks any more than the lot of us."

Groping for patience with the irritable old man, Nora stopped the wheel and gave him a level look. "Sure, and weren't you the one recently reminding me that this winter will not last forever? 'Spring will come,' I heard you say only days ago."

He uttered something unintelligible and crossed the room with a stiff, unsteady gait. "I'll sit with our boyo a bit," he said, disappearing behind the curtain.

Once he was out of sight, Nora wiped a hand over her eyes to blot the tears of weakness and frustration she'd fought to hide. The raking dryness of her palm caused her to frown at her hand with distaste. She had always been vain about her hands, had done her best to keep them smooth and soft while Owen lived, for he had liked to hold them between his when they sat by the fire in the evening. Now her skin was as rough as tree bark, her nails peeled and broken.

Again she lifted a hand, this time to her hair. Another vanity, God forgive her. It was still long and thick, but had grown dull and felt nearly as dry as her skin. *What more?* she wondered wearily. *What more?*

Merciful God, don't let me lose my teeth, too!

She shuddered against the sudden thought, then just as quickly breathed a prayer to ask forgiveness for her wicked vanity. Of course, she would eventually be toothless. These days more women were than not, at least those she had seen in the village. The Hunger spared no one from its ravages, not even foolish women with forbidden pride.

"*Nora!* You'd best come!"

Her father-in-law's cry from Tahg's room shocked her out of her thoughts, and she knocked the stool over in her haste to get up. Old Dan was holding the boy awkwardly by the shoulders as Tahg writhed and choked in the throes of a coughing spasm.

Nora went to him, forcing a note of calm into her voice as she took Old Dan's place by the bed. "Here, now, *asthore,*" she crooned, bending over to take him in her arms. Holding him gently, she grieved at his appearance. At fifteen Tahg looked more like a man in his middle years, so great had been the toll of his illness. The angry flush on his hollow cheeks, the wildness in his fevered blue eyes, the limp strands of dark hair falling raggedly over his forehead gave him a peculiar, deranged look. Gripped as he was with a furious fit of coughing, he seemed even weaker than usual. The look of him tore Nora's heart and stabbed her with fear, but she forced a smile and continued to make small sounds of comfort until the spasm passed.

Finally he drew an easier breath, then another. A thin ribbon of blood trickled from the side of his mouth, and he lifted a frail hand to wipe it away. When he finally looked up at her, his eyes were still glazed with pain, and for an instant Nora thought he didn't recognize her. But after a moment his lips moved with the effort to smile, and he whispered, "I'm fine now, Mum."

At her side, she was aware of the old man shaking his head and mumbling a prayer.

"God have mercy on him," Old Dan murmured. "Ah, dear God, have mercy on him . . ."

And on us all, Nora added silently. *And on us all.*

4

Michael

I am come of the seed of the people,
The people that sorrow,
That have no treasure but hope,
No riches laid up but a memory
Of an ancient glory.

P. H. PEARSE (1879–1916)

New York City

Michael Burke loved New York — except, that is, in the winter. In the spring the city was a capricious, blood-stirring flirt of a lass, but in the winter she turned to a bad-tempered woman, spitting her nastiness and flaunting her ill breeding as if to put a man off. Her sky became a grim, pewter shield, her avenues teemed with dirty snow and frozen refuse, and her sullen harbor waters churned with ice and floating debris.

January in New York meant driving snow and bitter wind, and today had brought a relentless attack of both. It was still snowing hard as Michael turned down Pearl Street and headed toward home. He pulled the collar of his greatcoat higher about his throat, feeling uncommonly relieved that his watch was over.

He was tired, bone-tired. Fridays were always the worst of his week, but this one had been even more trying than most, with two murders, a series of knifings, and a vicious attack on Sal Folio, the grocer — all within the last three hours. One of the murder victims had been a newsboy, a small, scrawny lad who routinely turned over his wages to one of the countless gangs that ran the streets day and night. More than likely a member of that same gang had done the killing, but since the incident had gone unobserved, the chances of ever catching the murderer were slim indeed.

It was becoming increasingly difficult these days for the police force to make any real mark on the wave of violent crime sweeping the city. The force had grown appreciably, but was still far too small for a city of New York's size. Until '44, there hadn't even been a professional police force — merely two constables, a small group of appointed marshals, and a "watch" made up of men who patrolled the streets at night. Even with the significantly larger new force of day and night policemen, the city's lawlessness remained out of control. Jails were badly overcrowded, laws remained inadequate, and widespread corruption existed throughout the entire legal system.

More and more these days, Michael found himself angry and frustrated with his job, discouraged one minute and furious the next at the way the entire force seemed to be losing ground to the criminals. Even worse, a rising number of Irish immigrants were to be found among the thugs roving the streets. Hundreds of his own were fast becoming the very kind of predators from which they'd thought themselves to be escaping when they'd fled the auld sod. Once they found the golden streets of their dreams to be paved with garbage instead of gold, and once they learned that the good jobs were seldom if ever available to anyone whose name began with *Mac* or *O* in front, they often turned on the city with a vengeance and seized whatever they could from her.

A bitter root was taking hold in the leprous tenements these days, a root Michael knew would yield even more hatred and a vast new crop of crime and corruption. It had been bad before, but never more so than in the months since Ireland and other parts of Europe had been devastated by famine. They were coming by the thousands now, arriving hungry and ill and desperate, and neither New York nor any other American city was prepared to handle the problems the people brought with them. The streets were filled with a variety of races and nationalities, and there seemed to be no end to the continuing flood of immigrants deluging the shores of the East.

Michael's eyes took in his surroundings. A crush of people crowded along the gaslight-lined streets. Nobody seemed aware of the lateness of the evening or even the bitter wind and stinging snow. There was such a busy, noisy stream of bodies, he felt certain every nation in Europe must be represented somewhere amid the throng. Over there was the fez of a Mohammedan; just ahead the brimless hat of a Persian; farther up a cluster of Italian women with brightly colored shawls and heavy skirts. Mixed in among them were Irish newsboys, Negro laborers, Germans and Spaniards and Orientals — they were all here in the streets, making their fortunes, chasing their dreams, loving and marrying, robbing their countrymen, even killing their neighbors. What was to become of them all, he couldn't imagine.

He was nearing Krueger's bakery now, and he managed a pallid smile for Margaret O'Handley, who worked for the German. As was often the case lately, the woman appeared to be waiting for him, giving him one of her long-toothed grins and a coquettish wave as she watched his approach. Michael instinctively quickened his step as he passed by the storefront, anxious to avoid an encounter.

He was hungry and could smell the bakery's delights, but his step didn't falter as he hurried on. The widow O'Handley had taken to pushing small packages on him once a week or more, insisting they were the leavings from the day and that he "might just as well take them home to the boyo." The leftover pastries were always grand, but Michael was determined to avoid any further kindnesses from the woman.

Some had hinted that he could do worse than consider Margaret O'Handley as a wife. But it was impossible for him to think of the stout, eager-eyed woman as a replacement for his Eileen. Not only did he suspect the widow O'Handley to be considerably older than himself, but he saw a certain meanness in her nature that made him wary of her outward geniality. In short, he simply did not trust the woman.

Aside from his mother, Michael had loved only two women in his thirty-six years, and he wasn't at all convinced he had it in him to attempt a relationship with another. Perhaps his Eileen had been no beauty, but she'd been fair enough in her way, small and sweet-natured, with a quiet voice that gentled his world and an adoring smile that never failed to make his heart leap. He had loved his wife, truly loved her. Her death from the stillbirth of their second child would have crushed him had it not been for the need to go on and look after their son, Tierney. Gone ten years this winter, Eileen still warmed his memories like the tender touch of sunlight on a bitter day.

Before Eileen there had been only Nora Doyle — Nora *Kavanagh* — but they had been little more than children when he'd fancied her. Besides, she had never been able to see him; Morgan Fitzgerald stood ever in the way. Except for those times when a brief letter from Morgan would send his thoughts straying back to Killala, he had given Nora little thought over the years.

From time to time he considered marrying, but mostly out of concern for Tierney. His son wasn't a bad boy, just motherless since he was four. Growing up as he had, in a city that viewed all things Irish with contempt and in a neighborhood that keened with the endless sorrows of its people, it was small wonder that the lad inclined toward rebellion. A woman's touch might just be the thing to bring some gentling to Tierney's fiery spirit and volatile temper, but only the *right* woman could ever hope to —

A cry from the midst of the dense crowd just ahead brought Michael to a dead stop. It took him only an instant to spot the trouble and take off running, shouting as he went.

A sandwich-board man — one of the numerous fellows who walked about with two advertising signs slung over his shoulders — was down in the street, shrieking at the top of his lungs. A row of young toughs had formed a menacing circle around the poor man, who lay on his back, a virtual prisoner of his signboards. The thugs — four of them, Michael noted as he ran — were kicking the man and brandishing knives as they taunted him and jeered at his terror.

"Here, you!" Michael shouted. Twirling his stick from under his arm, he blew his whistle and took off running, pushing pedestrians out of his way as he went. Some scowled or cursed at him, and one dark-skinned Arab spit in his direction.

A crowd had gathered to watch the assault on the sandwich-board man, and the press of their bodies kept the thugs from seeing Michael until he was nearly on top of them.

"Leave off, scum!" he roared at the largest of the four. This one was whipping a knife dangerously close to the sandwich-board man's horror-stricken face.

"Copper!" The warning shout was from one of the punks, a small, ferret-faced boy with freckles.

Michael lunged for the big brute first, clubbing him with a fist as he waved off the other thugs with his stick. Out of the corner of his eye he saw the other three take off and go darting down the street. There was nothing to do but to let them go and concentrate on this one.

The crowd was cheering vigorously, and Michael wasn't surprised to realize that the cheers weren't for him: they were rooting for the tough with the knife. A piercing flash of hot rage surged on him as he hurled himself at the wild-eyed thug and knocked the knife from his hand.

Pressing his stick across the throat of the pimply-faced youth, glaring into his defiant eyes, Michael was tempted to inflict a well-deserved blow. Instead, he fought for control. "It will require no effort at all on my part to snap your scrawny neck if you've a mind to resist arrest," he grated out in a tightly controlled voice. "It's your decision entirely, punk."

At that moment Denny Price, another policeman, parted the crowd, approaching Michael and his captive. "Thought you might need some help, Sergeant, but I can see you don't. I'll tend to the sandwich-board man."

The sandwich-board man seemed shaken, but otherwise unharmed. Price helped the man to his feet, straightened his signs, and turned back to Michael.

"Sure, and your watch is over, Sergeant. Why don't you go along home and let me take this worthless pup in for you? I can manage him without a bit of help at all."

Too tired to argue, Michael gladly took Price's suggestion. As he resumed his trek homeward, he wondered, not for the first time, whatever had possessed him to take on this thankless job.

The answer, of course, was the same as always: It was one of the few decent jobs available to an Irishman in New York City.

5

Do You See Your Children Weeping, Lord?

Pale mothers, wherefore weeping?
Would to God that we were dead –
Our children swoon before us,
And we cannot give them bread!

LADY WILDE [SPERANZA] (1820–1896)

Killala

The road to the Fitzgerald cabin was a highway of the dead and dying. Frozen corpses lay heaped in ditches on either side. Some, Daniel knew, had died of starvation and the cold; others of fever. Meanwhile, the living continued their death march, limping silently down the snow-pitted road. Few expected to escape their inevitable doom, but simply wandered in a bewildered haze of aimlessness and dejection.

They fell when least expected, one by one or at times as an entire family. Many died on their way into the village in search of food or shelter; others died as they left Killala to seek survival elsewhere.

Encountering former friends and neighbors dead along the road was almost past the bearing, and yet there was no escaping the evidence of the famine's unyielding hand. Daniel's heart was laden with feelings so heavy he thought the weight of them would stop him in his tracks; he always seemed to carry with him a bitter mixture of fear, confusion, and anger.

He *did* stop now, standing off to the side of the road, his gaze falling for a moment on the round tower on Steeple Hill. Its dark silhouette thrust into the late afternoon sky filled him as always with a mixture of wonder and yearning. Again he found himself questioning how long it had stood there, this monument to a past no man could date. What battles had it seen throughout the centuries? How many generations had it watched from birthing to burial?

The past beckoned and tugged at Daniel's imagination. He longed to look across the years and see what had gone before, study it, and perhaps preserve its memory as a part of his own.

In truth, he believed there was no real separation between past and present and future. He felt that somehow, in a way known only to God, the three were one and the same. Mere humans were incapable of seeing things from beginning to end, and so they had to isolate the times, one from the other. But God, he was certain, had no need for such distinctions; He could undoubtedly view at once everything that had ever been and everything that would ever be.

He had once attempted to explain his thoughts to Morgan, who'd had a word for his theory. Morgan had a word for everything, of course, but this was a particularly grand one, which Daniel had never forgotten: *panorama*. "God's panorama," Morgan called it, saying, "I believe, lad, you may have excavated a great truth for yourself, one well worth a measure of careful study."

Now, as Daniel stood staring at the tower, he was convinced that if God were sharing this moment with him, He would more than likely be seeing not only a black-haired boy gazing at a round tower but the mysterious builders of that curious structure as well. Morgan said the towers scattered throughout Ireland had long been a source of controversy among the scholars and the poets. For his part, Morgan held that the ancient buildings had been watchtowers from which the approach of the enemy could be seen in advance. Probably, he said, they had once served as places of refuge, into which the monks could retreat when the barbarous Norsemen invaded the island.

But, wise as he was about most things, even

Morgan could not be certain of the towers' origins. God *did* know, however, and Daniel thought that was a wondrous thing indeed. God could see the giants and the heroes who had walked the land before the coming of St. Patrick, the ancient warriors and mythical creatures from which the great legends and epic poems had arisen. God could see the inhabitants of the *raths* — the stone ring-forts, where hundreds of jagged stone stakes enclosed the dwellings of pre-Christian inhabitants. God knew all about the clan chiefs and the druids, the high kings and the bards, and He could see the French fleet landing in the bay during the ill-fated rising of 1798.

Knowing that, believing it, Daniel also had to assume that God saw the corpses of the children and the elderly lying along the road, the starving infants in the dim, unheated cabins, and all the dreadful atrocities taking place beneath the watchful eye of the old round tower. What puzzled him was how God could see it all and do nothing about it. The very One who could end the suffering and the dying in a whisper of an instant made no move to do so.

Knotting his hands into tight fists, Daniel thrust them deep inside his pockets. *Life is life and God is God, and it's nothing but folly to confuse the two.*

The words Morgan had spoken the night of Ellie's wake returned again, as they often had in the days since. They didn't actually help to ease the worrying, and certainly they answered none of his questions. Yet Daniel found an inexplicable measure of comfort when he considered them. Somehow the words relieved his need to *blame* God, thereby allowing him to maintain faith in the Lord's compassion. He sensed there was much, much more to Morgan's words than he'd so far been able to glean, some important truth that continued to elude him.

Perhaps, he thought with a sigh, he simply needed to pray harder about it. Grandfar said too much thinking was a waste, that time and effort were far better spent on one's knees. But Daniel found it virtually impossible to separate the two. It seemed his thoughts were forever interfering with his prayers.

A frigid blast of wind-driven snow shook him out of his reverie for the time being, and he hurried on. He passed half a dozen *scalpeens* on the way to Thomas Fitzgerald's cabin. Their numbers were increasing every day. The hastily built lean-tos were thrown together from whatever thatch and beams and rafters could be salvaged, then anchored against a roadside bank or stone ledge to secure them. Inadequate as they were for one alone, most were crowded with whole families and sometimes even a "lodger" or two. In these hard times, the people inside the rude shelters counted themselves fortunate to have even this much respite from the weather.

Hunched stiffly against the shrieking wind and snow, Daniel was eager for some shelter of his own. His boots, entirely too small for his feet, were worn so thin they provided little protection. His cramped toes felt like chunks of ice, and his stomach was empty, making him lightheaded and a bit queasy. He felt a growing need to see Morgan, and he prayed his friend might have returned by now.

Veering across the road, he started through the field leading to the Fitzgerald cabin. In truth, the "cabin" was little more than a hut in the hollow of a hill. Its walls were shaped by the hillside itself, its front made of mud, its roof sparsely thatched with fern and straw.

Deep ice-glazed ruts in the field sucked at Daniel's feet, slowing him down and freezing his toes. He lifted his face to catch some snow in his mouth, hoping to appease the gnawing in his belly; instead, he caught a sharp breath at the sight of the doctor's trap in front of the Fitzgerald place.

His heart pounding, he began to run. Catherine Fitzgerald had been poorly most of the winter; Daniel had heard his mother voice her concern more than once about her friend's failing health. If the doctor were there, it could only mean Catherine had taken a turn for the worse.

He gave a perfunctory knock, then opened

the door and stepped inside; the Kavanaghs and Fitzgeralds went in and out of each other's dwellings freely, like family. His automatic greeting of "God bless all here" met no response, for the only Fitzgerald in sight was ten-year-old Johanna, who was both deaf and mute. She stood staring at Daniel, a fist stuffed against her mouth. Thinner yet than her older sister, Katie, the girl looked pale and not entirely well. Her torn frieze dress, mended more times than the cloth could bear, hung on her like a sack, and her dark red hair was tangled and wild. Her face was so pinched and pale that the freckles banding the bridge of her nose appeared almost black.

Daniel gave her a smile, but she didn't respond. He was struck by a keen sense of something wrong. The cabin was silent. Silent and cold. No family was gathered about the table, and the peat fire had gone out. There was no sign of life, except for Johanna, who stood still as a stone, watching Daniel with frightened eyes.

The Fitzgeralds were a family given to noisy laughter and much teasing — all except for Thomas, who tended to be solemn. Their cabin was normally a loud and lively place, even in these bitter times. The present hush was entirely unnatural, and Daniel's apprehension sharpened still more.

At that moment the curtain at the back of the room parted, and Katie Fitzgerald appeared. As soon as Daniel saw her red-rimmed eyes, he knew she had been crying.

As if anticipating the reason for Daniel's visit, she shook her head. "Morgan isn't back yet, Daniel John."

"But the doctor is here, I see."

Katie nodded. "Mum is awful sick again, she is."

She came the rest of the way into the room then, and Daniel frowned at her appearance. A terrible pallor had settled over her skin, fading it to an almost unhealthy gray. Her face and neck were thin, almost transparent; she looked sad and troubled and somewhat ill.

"Where is your da?" Daniel asked, looking around the room.

Johanna came to stand beside her older sister, and Katie clasped her hand. "He took Little Tom to stay with the grandmother, so he wouldn't be pestering Mum." She paused and her voice faltered. "And . . . and then he was to go for Father Joseph."

Daniel looked at her with dismay.

"Dr. Browne said he should." Katie's voice had dropped to little more than a whisper.

Daniel stood staring at the two sisters, not knowing what to say. Katie's reddish-blond hair was damp around her thin face, her eyes desperate. At her side, Johanna continued to stare down at the floor, clinging to Katie's hand.

If the Hunger could fell the once strong and steady Catherine Fitzgerald, how much more easily could it devastate his small, frail mother?

Unbidden, the question struck Daniel with a force that made him sway. For one dreadful moment he wanted to run, to flee the Fitzgeralds and their tragedy. But the look of utter helplessness and pleading in Katie's face held him captive.

Johanna was tugging demandingly at her sister, whining in an odd, voiceless manner, but Katie seemed scarcely aware of her presence. "Daniel John . . . do you think you could go for your mother? Perhaps it would help Mum if Aunt Nora were here . . . They're such friends . . ."

"Aye, I'll go straightaway. Katie, I —" At a loss, Daniel fumbled for some word of comfort. Finding none, he simply repeated, "I'll go now."

Ashamed of his eagerness to get away, he turned and started for the door, willing himself not to run.

As soon as he closed the door behind him, however, he *did* run. Paying no heed to his half-frozen feet or the sharp wind knifing his face, he ran as fast as he could over the field to the road. He ran until he thought his chest would explode, furious with himself for his lack of courage.

I don't understand you, God. Why are you letting this happen to Catherine . . . to Katie and —

and to all of us? You're allowing the good to die with the bad, and even if you're not the one doing the killing, you're letting it happen, and that's the same now, isn't it? It's not fair! You know it isn't the least bit fair to take mothers from their children and let little babes die. What have we done to make you turn on us so, to make you so angry with all Ireland? Don't you see what is happening to us? Don't you care?

It was almost dusk as Morgan tramped the last half mile toward his brother's cabin. He was relieved to be back in the village, though disgruntled that his expedition had not been as successful as he'd hoped. His men had given generously of their meager supply, but they, too, had families to feed — some, entire villages.

There were few ships to plunder on these stormy winter waters, and those that *did* brave the sea usually did so with naval escorts. Ever since the looting in Blacksod Bay a few months past, the government had been more cautious with their sea trafficking. Still, the lads had provided him with a measure of barley, flour, and dried beef. Morgan had carefully limited his portion, taking only what he could carry on his back; he dared not chance discovery of his mount, leaving it, as always, with his men in the hills.

He neither knew nor cared which particular land agent might be short a few head of cattle or a barrel of flour. He had closed the door on any personal guilt when he'd come to grips with the truth about England's handling of the famine: While Ireland starved, British ships sailed out of her harbors with enough Irish-grown oats and wheat and cattle in a year's time to feed twice the population of the entire island.

Other countries — France, Germany, Holland — had also suffered from the potato blight during the last year, but these, not being ruled by the British, stopped all exports of other food at once in order that their own people would not go hungry. Not so in Ireland. Under the pitiless hand of British rule, tons of home-grown food left the country's harbors every day on British ships, leaving the already starving Irish to survive on nothing but their failed potato crop. Even the grain stored in the farmers' barns was not available to the people; it was marked for rent, to be collected by the agents, while the very ones who had grown it died lingering deaths from the Hunger.

No, Morgan no longer allowed his conscience to keep him awake nights with recriminations. He had no illusions about the road he had taken: He was a wordsmith turned outlaw, a patriot turned rebel, and if he were caught he would die at the end of a rope.

If he were caught . . .

Should that be the case, he suspected that even the Young Ireland movement — which presently viewed him as an influential, if not entirely irreproachable, member — might be less than eager to claim him as well. All the essays and verses he had written for their journal, *The Nation* — not to mention the funds he and his lads had poured into their coffers — would not inspire them to come to the rescue of a common brigand. While he had done his part to convince Ireland's masses that "peaceful negotiation" with Britain would never bring about a free Ireland, his writings stopped a bit short of the militant, inflammatory tirades some members of the movement would have preferred. He was no favorite of Mitchel or Thomas Meagher, and the fanatical Lalor despised him.

In truth, the entire movement had progressed to an extremism Morgan found both ineffective and foolhardy, and *The Nation* was fueling its fire. He had held both its chief contributor, the now deceased Thomas Davis, and its founder, Charles Gavan Duffy, in high regard. But besides himself, only a few supporters, like Smith O'Brien, still shared the original concepts on which the Young Ireland movement had been founded — that of an Ireland with its own identity, a right to its independence, and a nationalism of the spirit that would embrace both

Protestant and Catholic, peasantry and gentry.

No, there would be little help for him from the movement. No matter; he wrote what he wrote, not for the movement, but for himself and the few in the country who still wanted to hear the truth. As for the rest of his "labors," he liked to think they were for those who were too weak or oppressed to save themselves. And, of course, for those few he loved: Thomas and Catherine, their little ones . . . and Nora and her lads.

He had reached the top of the hill behind his brother's cabin now and, stopping, he shifted the bag of provisions from one shoulder to the other. He frowned when he saw no sign of life below — no smoke from the fire, nobody moving about. But in the remaining gray mist of evening he could just make out blurred hoofprints and tracks from a carriage.

His uneasiness grew as he stared down at the desolate-looking cabin. Finally he moved, taking the hill at a leap, sliding most of the way down in his urgency to reach the bottom.

He knew it was bad as soon as he was through the door. Thomas sat at the table with Johanna in his arms, both of them weeping. His brother's face was stricken, his eyes stunned and vacant.

Then he saw Nora Kavanagh, and knew it

all. Joseph Mahon was leading her and Katie from the curtained room at the back. Nora's thin shoulders were stooped beneath the priest's supportive arm, and she was sobbing quietly. The silver-haired Mahon met Morgan's gaze with a sorrowful shake of his head.

Swallowing down his own sense of loss — for he had set a great store by Catherine, fine Christian woman that she was — Morgan dropped his bag onto a chair by the door, then crossed the room to Thomas. His brother wiped his eyes and grabbed for Morgan's hand; Morgan could feel the wet from Thomas's tears on his own skin. "She just . . . slipped away, Morgan. So quietly . . . so quickly . . ."

Katie now came to stand beside Johanna, and Morgan released his brother to gather both little girls into his arms, giving them a hug and some feeble words of comfort before handing them back to their da. He turned and walked uncertainly toward Nora. When she lifted her face to look up at him, her grief was a raw, painful thing.

Gently he eased her away from the priest, and she came to him with a choked sound of despair. As he held her, Morgan felt her trembling, sensed her frailty. The knife of sorrow dug even deeper into his heart, sharpened by a sudden thrust of fear for the small woman in his arms. Instinctively he tightened his embrace.

"She is gone, Morgan. Catherine is gone." Muffled against his chest, Nora's voice was little more than a whisper.

"Shhh, *Nora.*" He rested his chin gently on top of her head. "Catherine rests now. Her struggle is done."

While the priest prayed with Thomas and the girls, Nora went on crying softly in Morgan's arms. He longed to console her, but at this moment he, who had spent most of his life fashioning just the right words for his feelings, could summon none at all to assuage her grief. He could only hold her steady and let her weep.

After a time, her trembling subsided and she backed away, avoiding his eyes. "The old man is ailing now," she said abruptly. "He took to his bed late this afternoon and has not got up since."

"Old Dan?" Morgan frowned. He shouldn't be surprised; the elderly and small children were among those hardest hit by the Hunger and its companion diseases. But Big Dan Kavanagh had always seemed as invincible as the mountains of Mayo themselves, as enduring as the round tower on Steeple Hill.

"I must get home," Nora said, taking another step backward to free herself from his arms. "There's no more I can do here for now, and I left Daniel John to see to Tahg and the grandfather."

Morgan nodded, noting the sooty smudges of exhaustion beneath her eyes, the ashen pallor of her thin, drawn face. "I'll see you home, then."

"That's not necessary," she said stiffly.

"It will soon be dark. Besides, you may need me to go for the doctor for Old Dan."

She shook her head. "I wanted to go myself this afternoon, but he wouldn't hear of it."

"Even so, I'll see you home."

She looked at him, saying nothing, then turned and went to have a word with Thomas.

Outside, the last light of day had almost faded. The gloom-draped dusk was heavy with snow, and the sorrow from the cabin seemed to be carried on the wind.

They walked along without speaking until Morgan broke the silence between them. "So then, how is Tahg? Any change at all?"

Nora stumbled on a jutting ridge of ice, and he took her arm to steady her, tucking it firmly inside his own. "He's so terribly weak," she answered worriedly. "It's as though he's coughed away all his strength and has no more left inside himself. He coughs all the time now, night and day. The medicine Dr. Browne left with us doesn't seem to help at all."

Morgan pressed her hand. "This cold weather is hard on a cough. Sure, and he'll do better once spring comes."

When she said nothing, he added, "You

must get some rest yourself, Nora. You'll be no help to your family if you're ill."

She gave a small, apathetic shrug but didn't answer. Morgan felt her shiver and attempted to pull her closer to his side, but she firmly resisted.

"It was all so much easier when we were young," he said with a sigh, primarily to himself. He was remembering other walks they had taken through the snow, in happier days. "Life was kinder then."

"For you, perhaps," she said tersely. "I hated being a child."

He looked at her. "Because of your mother." It was no question, merely a statement of what they both knew.

"There was that," she said quietly. He winced at the hurt in her voice, remembering all too clearly Nora's shame.

"Nobody thought the less of you for her, Nora," he said awkwardly, meaning it.

"Nor the better of me either, I'm sure." A harsh, choked sound of derision escaped her.

"Many thought you were a grand girl," Morgan said evenly after a moment. "I, for one. And Michael, another."

He could scarcely hear her reply, so soft were her words. "Aye, I remember."

He looked down at her, but her eyes were fixed straight ahead.

"Have you heard from him of late?" she asked.

"Michael? Not since last fall."

A ghost of a smile touched the corners of her mouth as if she, too, were remembering. "You were the lads, the two of you. You, always in trouble, with Michael guarding your back."

"And both of us playing the fools over you." He said it quietly, not thinking. She didn't seem to hear. If Nora was remembering, she was keeping her thoughts to herself.

Where had it gone, that time in the sun? The years of being young and brimming with life, when every wish was a promise and every dream still within reach . . . when Nora had been but a slip of a lass, with him and Michael standing as tall as heroes in her eyes?

Ah, where had it gone . . . and so quickly?

Where have the years gone? Nora wondered, a terrible sense of loss pervading her spirit. Had it really been so long ago that the three of them roamed the village as childhood friends and adventurers?

They had been great companions, those three, young and more than a little foolish at times, but faithful one to the other for all their youthful follies . . . so different in so many ways, and yet somehow so close in spirit that each could finish the other's thoughts.

Nora had been in Killala first, before either

Michael or Morgan. Born in the village, the only other town she had ever stepped foot in was Ballina. She was a child of shame, the oldest of four children, all born on the wrong side of the blanket to a woman who was the scandal of the village. Their father had been a womanizing British sailor who promised Nora's mother the stars and delivered only stones. It was thought he had left a wife in England, for when Nora was eight years old he went back to the sea and never returned.

After that, her mother had taken in one man after another until she became such a slattern she could find no companion but the bottle. Nora and the younger children were left to fend for themselves as best they knew how, and over the years Nora provided what she could in the way of motherly care to the little ones.

She grew up in abject shame: the shame of her mother, their mean, dilapidated hut, her own raggedy clothing and the cast-off garments she and her siblings were forced to wear — but, most of all, the shame of rejection: that of her mother for her own offspring and that of the village for the lot of them. So heavy had been the burden of that shame throughout the years that when her mother died only weeks before Nora gave birth to Tahg, her first thought — may God forgive her — was one of relief: relief that her own children would never need to know their maternal grandmother.

Michael came to the village the year Nora turned nine, the same year a diphtheria epidemic took the lives of her two younger sisters, leaving only her and her wee brother, Rory, to defend themselves against their abusive mother. Three years her senior and already possessing the instincts of a born leader, Michael Burke had immediately taken Nora under his protection. He took his self-appointed guardianship seriously; no longer did the children of the village dare to wag about Nora and her brother, much less taunt them face-to-face. Michael was brawny and rock-solid even then, and he had a look about him that clearly said he was not to be trifled with.

To the lonely, timid Nora, the Burkes were a great wonder of a family, and she often made believe they were her own. Michael's Roman Catholic mother had been an actress in Dublin; his Protestant father the son of a clergyman. Both had defied their families and their churches to wed, eventually settling with their two sons in Killala on a small square of land that had once belonged to Michael's grandparents.

Unloved and neglected, Nora was charmed and entirely in awe of the gregarious, unconventional Burkes. Their generosity of affection, their intelligence and wit, their flair for the dramatic, and, more than anything else, their enthusiastic love for one another attracted her to them like the warm sun draws a dying blossom from the snow. The statuesque, vibrant Madeline Burke appeared to Nora as grand as the legendary warrior-queen Maeve of Connacht. She was beautiful, clever, and endowed with a heart as big as the Irish Sea. The men in Madeline's family adored her, as did the Doyle waifs, who over the years put their feet under the Burkes' kitchen table far more than under their own.

Then came Morgan. In Nora's twelfth year, a long, lean man named Aidan Fitzgerald appeared out of nowhere one autumn day with his two sons in tow and a poke on his back that appeared to hold the sum of their worldly possessions.

Aidan Fitzgerald claimed to be from the southern County Kerry — a long way, indeed, from Killala. He said he was on the road in search of a schoolmaster's position, and when he learned there was an empty schoolhouse in the village he simply moved himself and his lads into an abandoned hillside cabin and stayed. Over the years he kept a school of surprising excellence, managing at the same time to keep the nearby taverns busy accommodating his thirst, which was considerable.

A great deal of mystery surrounded the new schoolmaster and his sons. Aidan was obviously a highly educated, even cultured man, despite the fact that he routinely drank himself witless. He never seemed to be without funds, yet they lived a crude, Spartan life in their womanless cabin. Not a mean-spirited man, he nevertheless appeared to be indifferent to his sons. Indeed, the only time he appeared to show them any interest at all was when he was instructing them in some long-dead poet like Virgil or, more appropriately to Nora's thinking, in the legends and history of ancient Ireland. Of course, Aidan might just as well have been whistling jigs to a milestone with poor Thomas, who cared for nothing but the land; but Morgan soaked it up like the bog in a downpour, always eager for more.

Never a word was spoken of Morgan's mother, and for a reason Nora did not entirely understand, she knew she was not to ask. Once, when they were older, Michael did make a cautious attempt to inquire, but Morgan's curt "I never knew her" was the only reply.

Rumors circulated the village, as was always the case where a mystery was involved. One particularly popular story had it that Aidan was a fugitive from the law, on the run from some terrible deed in his past. Nora found it difficult to imagine Morgan's distant, hollow-eyed father possessing either the passion or the energy to commit a dastardly crime. Other tales hinted of scandal or tragedy somewhere in the Fitzgeralds' background, and Nora found these far more likely. Another account, one that was never entirely put down, had to do with Aidan's family being gentry of means, who, for reasons never quite fully defined, had disowned him and set him and his boys on the road.

Whatever his past, Morgan was nearly as much on his own as was Nora. They were the same age, though to Nora it seemed that Morgan was years older than she — older, even, than Michael. Considering the friendship that quickly developed among the three of them, it seemed entirely natural that Morgan and his brother Thomas would soon pull up their chairs at the Burkes' supper table and be assimilated into the family. Thus Nora found herself with *two* protectors rather than one.

She soon recognized, however, that while Morgan might enjoy the companionship of Michael and his family, his solitary, restless nature had no real need of a permanent family unit. In contrast to the serious-minded, land-loving Thomas, Morgan had a yen for the road and could often be seen wandering in or out of town, his harp riding his shoulder, his poke slung over his back.

Differences among the three of them might have been expected. In matters of faith, for example, Nora and Michael were closest, both being a part of the small remnant of Protestants in the village. Nora had sought out the small Wesleyan meetinghouse on her own when still a wee girl; her mother was held in such disgrace by most of the Catholics in Killala that Nora could not bear to attend the Roman chapel. As for Michael, although his younger brother Tim had opted for the Catholic faith, Michael himself was impatient with what he termed the "fuss and bother" of it all — he liked the orderly but simple style of worship he found at the meetinghouse.

Morgan was of a different cut entirely. His da never went to church at all, although Aidan was widely known as a "lapsed Catholic." But while Thomas faithfully attended mass whenever it was offered, Morgan went only occasionally. Nora knew that Morgan was a believer, but he claimed no particular denomination or doctrine. Sometimes he showed up at the meetinghouse; sometimes he attended mass with his brother. His odd churchgoing habits made him suspect in the village, of course. Even Nora was bothered by his lack of interest in any formal religious practice. Still, she had to admit that the freedom of Morgan's faith somehow seemed to suit him.

She had a fierce love for both her defenders, though a far different kind for each. She adored Michael Burke as a grand older brother, but Morgan she loved with all her heart. Morgan loved her, too, at least he claimed to as they grew older, and for a time she clung to her hopes that they would one day wed. However, near the time when she reached an age to marry, Morgan left Killala. Apparently there were enough nuggets left in Aidan's mysterious pot of gold to pay for the furthering of his son's education, so Morgan set off for France.

To Nora's dismay, the Burkes took it upon themselves shortly thereafter to announce their intention to leave Ireland as well. They were of a mind to travel to Van Diemen's Land — Australia. Michael, however, having no interest in his parents' plans, declared that *he* would be sailing for America and stunned Nora by asking her to accompany him as his wife.

Once she recovered from her shock, Nora was sorely tempted to accept Michael's proposal. The prospect of losing both Morgan and the entire Burke family terrified her; she could scarcely bear to face life in the village without them. But in spite of her despair, she knew she could not marry Michael Burke. She simply did not love him in the way a woman *should* love the man she weds. Nor could she find it in her heart to leave Ireland and start her life anew in a foreign land among strangers.

So she reluctantly let Michael go, and

when Owen Kavanagh began paying her great attention at the meetinghouse and eventually came calling, she put aside her memories of both Michael Burke and Morgan Fitzgerald. Older than Nora by several years, Owen was still a handsome man. More importantly to Nora, he was a *good* man: sober, industrious, and sensible, with goals she could share and the respect of the entire village. Owen's dreams were simple but worthy ones, and closely related to Nora's own; he had it in mind to make a proper marriage, farm a piece of land, supplement his income by working for Reilly the weaver, and raise a family.

Nora was happy as Owen's wife. If she sometimes allowed a longing thought of Morgan Fitzgerald to cross her mind, she immediately dismissed it and asked forgiveness. Although he drifted in and out of her life now and then, making an appearance in the village whenever he'd a mind to, their paths crossed only casually. She could not help the way he looked at her with those searching, sorrowful eyes of his; but she was a woman grown, a wife and mother, and so she quickly turned away and pretended not to see.

Seventeen years had passed since Nora had kissed Michael Burke goodbye and wished him the blessing of God as he left for America. Now she was a widow who had buried her little girl as well as her husband, lost her dearest friend to death, and given up her only brother to a life on the sea as a sailor. She had gray in her hair and winter in her bones and a brimming cup of sorrow in her heart. It was nearly impossible to believe there had once been a time when she had run through a mountain field of wild flowers on the arm of a tall copper-haired lad who played her love songs on his harp and wrote verses about her smoke-gray eyes.

Nora Kavanagh looked up at the bronze-bearded man leading her over the snow, and unwillingly found her heart aching, not only for Owen and wee Ellie and Catherine, but for the young Nora Doyle and Morgan Fitzgerald, for their now silent laughter and long-forgotten dreams.

The time for dreams, Nora knew, had come and gone.

6

And the Fool Has Condemned the Wise

From Boyne to the Linn
Has the mandate been given,
That the children of Finn
From their country be driven.

FEARFLATHA O'GNIVE
(SIXTEENTH CENTURY)

Killala
Early February

George Cotter, land agent for Sir Roger Gilpin's holdings in County Mayo, considered himself a victim. He was given to brooding about the various acts of unfairness he had been forced to suffer since childhood. This continual litany of woes had long since become much more than a means of reconciling himself to his miserable existence; indeed, it had become the very *essence* of that existence.

Among his afflictions he numbered poor health, a short, round physique with a flat-featured face, and a history of unfortunate financial circumstances. The bane of his entire life, however, was his father. George could not remember a time when he had not hated his father, hated him with an almost debilitating passion.

Richard Cotter had been a Dublin barrister with a terrible thirst for the spirits and an even greater lust for gambling. He would bet on anything, no matter how foolish the risk, and he proved to be incredibly unlucky in all his endeavors. While still a young man, he had gambled away not only his own small inheritance from his physician father, but most of his British-born wife's humble dowry as well. It was widely held in the village and surrounding countryside that Richard Cotter was a weak, dissipated, totally immoral man whose lifelong conduct would have shamed a field of tinkers.

Fortunately for the family, George's maternal grandparents owned a modest estate and two small but successful farms in Connacht, which, taken together, provided the Cotters with a home and an adequate livelihood. Even so, George grew up a bitter, rebellious young man: bitter because of what he considered their humble station in life, and rebellious in response to his father's frequently expressed contempt for his only son.

George's mother died before he reached his eighteenth year, and his father's excesses finally took their toll a few months later. Richard Cotter's only legacy to his son was more than a decade of verbal and sometimes physical abuse, and George felt nothing but relief and even a sense of satisfaction when he buried the man.

Cotter was left with virtually nothing; his grandparents' lands had so many liens on them by then that they immediately fell to Hamilton Gilpin, an "absentee landlord" who owned vast tracts of property throughout County Mayo — but who was never seen to step foot on any one of them. When Gilpin's agent, a kind enough man, offered the penniless young George Cotter a job on the Gilpin estates, he saw nothing else to do but take him up on it, albeit grudgingly.

Cotter had worked for the Gilpin family ever since, rising to his present position as land agent not through any real ambition or even competence, but because he was one of the few men in the area who could read, write, and do sums. The "big lord" was now Sir Roger Gilpin, who like his father before him, avoided any involvement with his Irish holdings, except what was required to collect the rents.

It was a Friday night, and Cotter sat morosely in his shabby fireside chair, his gouty leg propped up on a stool, his belt unbuckled to free his protruding stomach. He scowled at the letter in his hand. His mood was as ugly as the wild, shrieking snowstorm he'd only recently escaped. Chilled and in agony with the gout that plagued him more and more bitterly these days, he lifted his tumbler of whiskey and drained it dry.

It was easy enough for these absentee landlords like Gilpin to wave their pens over their fancy stationery and sign eviction orders, he thought. It would not be *their* hides if a mob of village riffraff took it upon themselves to have their revenge on those responsible for turning them out. Agents like himself suffered the consequences of the landlords' greed. And all because they had no choice but to do as they were told.

Retaliation by some of the locals was a distinct possibility. Cotter had heard enough, all right, to know it was happening all across Ireland, even right here in backward Mayo. Displaced tenants were striking out, venting their rage like a bunch of mindless savages on the land agents. Just last month an agent near Ballina had been knifed and clubbed to death by a group of peasants he'd evicted.

Mass eviction. That was the cause of it. Not just tumbling a few squatters' cabins or the huts of those worthless whiners who were continually in arrears, but the large-scale eviction of dozens of families who had lived in Killala and similar communities all their lives.

His throat tightened. It would be easy to

imagine men like O'Malley, a known faction fighter, and Rafferty, the worst kind of drunken troublemaker, rising up and taking arms against their betters.

Head pounding, Cotter tipped the tumbler to his lips. Finding it empty, he hauled his ponderous, aching frame from the chair, grunting with the effort. He went to the window and looked out, down the hill toward the village; but there was nothing to be seen except sheets of wind-driven snow piercing the night. His anger swelled along with the pain in his head, and he limped across the room to pour another whiskey.

The thing to do, he thought as he swilled his drink, *the expedient thing, would be to torch the entire dismal village.* Not only would it remove an unsightly blot from the landscape, but it would settle those miserable wretches in their hovels once and for all, before they took it upon themselves to make trouble up here on the hill.

With a stab of apprehension, Cotter recalled the rumors blowing about the county: tales of a band of rebels and malcontents, sweeping down from the mountains just long enough to fire the houses and barns of agents throughout the county, stealing their livestock and pantry contents, then depositing their spoils in the yards of the starving peasants.

One band in particular raised the hair on

his neck — the rabble who followed the brigand called the *Red Wolf*. Outlaws, every last one of them, and not beyond stirring up an enraged peasantry to rebellion. Thugs was what they were: low-browed, hulking primitives, for certain, and their leader — the one they fancifully called the *Red Wolf* — was undoubtedly the worst of them all. Tales mounted weekly about *that* one, most of them undoubtedly blown all out of proportion. They tended to make him a creature far bigger than life and more a menace than the predator from which he took his name. George had his suspicions about their *Red Wolf*'s identity, and while the great brute might be entirely human, he was still a formidable enough enemy.

A hot pain stabbed upward from his foot to his knee, and he cried out, fumbling for the desk to steady himself. At last he staggered across the room, sinking weakly down into his chair and leaning back with a moan. As the pain subsided, he tried to think what to do. One thing was certain: he would need every man of the constabulary he could get. First thing in the morning he'd call in the bailiff and have him alert the police. It was best to begin at once, before some of the riffraff in the village got wind of what was coming, as they seemed to have a way of doing.

Cotter started to crumple his employer's letter, then stopped, realizing it might not be smart to destroy Gilpin's written orders. It also occurred to him that he might be wise to arrange for protection for himself when he talked with the bailiff. No point in taking chances. Considering the fate to which he would be subjecting these poor devils, it wouldn't do to relax his guard.

There was an unmistakable smell of trouble in the air, and he didn't intend to be caught unawares. Those starving barbarians in the village were capable of anything, of that he had no doubt. Once the evictions began, who could tell what mischief they might wreak?

Two weeks after Catherine's burial, Morgan was still trying to soften Nora's reserve toward him, with no success. He thought he understood the way she had retreated into herself after Catherine died. On the heels of the death of both her little girl and husband, losing her dearest friend had to be near devastating to Nora, both physically and emotionally.

But he wanted to see her, to help if he could, to comfort if she'd let him. He wasn't dim-witted enough to try to start things up with her again. Not only was she in mourning, but the two of them had long ago faced the truth that no matter how deep their feelings for each other, they simply had no future together. He was one way, and she another; involving himself in her life in any manner other than as a friend could only lead to problems, even pain, for them both.

That being resolved, why, then, did she still flicker like a flame in the shadows of his mind? Why did his heart ache so when she deliberately ignored his overtures to see her? If he called at the cottage, she merely exchanged a few words with him at the door, never once inviting him inside. If he passed by her place — which he made it a point to do at least once a day — and happened to spot her in the yard tending to the cow, she offered a distant greeting, then hurried inside before he could stop her. She was deliberately avoiding him, he had no doubt; as to why, he wasn't sure.

Although getting past that iron-hard stubbornness of hers had been a bit like boring through a mountain, he had finally convinced her to accept the provisions he'd brought back with him from the hills. At first she had argued, her mulish pride resisting the suggestion that she needed his help. God forbid that she should accept charity from one such as Morgan Fitzgerald! Finally, though, she had acquiesced and accepted his offering. It had been the last real conversation they had shared.

Thus, he reluctantly decided to attend tonight's farewell to-do for Tim O'Malley. Ordinarily he would have avoided the event. He had never been the man for these provincial traditions, nor did he particularly enjoy being a part of a group. Added to his solitary nature, however, was his physical discomfort this night; he had a monster of a toothache that had been paining him since sunup, and the O'Malley's cabin was cold as a grave, which only served to aggravate the pain.

He was here for one reason only — to see Nora, who so far had been maddeningly successful at ignoring him entirely. He had expected that, of course, but it scalded him nevertheless, the way she would look in a different direction each time he managed to catch her eye.

The "American wake," as it was called throughout most counties — or more commonly here in Mayo, the "feast of departure" — had been observed only on rare occasions before the famine. Lately, however, it had become commonplace, although the nature of the event had changed drastically, given the destitute conditions across the country. For many of them, indeed, the act of leaving Ireland seemed the closest thing to death itself. Dying was epitomized by the departure from home; the ship came to represent a coffin, separating the voyager from his loved ones and setting him on his way to "Paradise" — America.

During the best of times the custom made for a bittersweet occasion. The evening ordinarily began with dancing and singing, drinking and eating, then declined to a maudlin wallow in nostalgia and painful farewells. Until recently it was not uncommon for a family to go the entire affair on tick — on credit — depending on the one going across to repay the debt once he attained his fortune. With the extreme poverty in the village these days, however, tonight's gathering for Sean O'Malley's Tim held little hint of merriment and even less of a feast. Without the luxuries of tobacco or the illegally distilled poteen, the occasion was a solemn, almost dismal affair.

By late in the evening the talk had drifted round to the heart of the wake: America, and her limitless opportunities for success, wealth, and happiness. The men, most of them gaunt and somewhat desperate-looking, stood with their arms folded across their sunken chests, listening with avid expressions to young Tim and another hopeful emigrant repeat their collected tales about the promised land. Most of the stories were based upon letters received by other village residents who had family already settled in America, family "growing richer by the day."

The women, hunched for the most part in a dimly lighted corner across the room, were noisily reviewing the contents of the letters to which they had been privy. This group, while loud enough in its own right, was far more somber and inclined to expound in great detail about the horrors inflicted upon unsuspecting voyagers who, alas, had not lived long enough to see the sweet shores of America.

Morgan noted that Nora didn't seem to be a part of either group, nor of the smaller cluster of young girls who sat off to themselves, giggling and casting an occasional flirtatious glance toward the lads across the room. Instead, she stood off to herself, her eyes dull and fixed.

An unexpected rush of desire to comfort her seized him, only to ebb as he accepted the fact there was nothing he could do. The kind of loss Nora had suffered over the past months was a grief only God himself could relieve. Still, he could not quite dismiss the frustration of wanting to encourage her, all the while knowing that Nora would no more turn to him for consolation than she might to an Englishman for mercy.

When Daniel John walked up at that moment, Morgan spoke before he could conceal his annoyance with the situation.

"Ah, I was beginning to think I was invisible to the Kavanaghs this evening."

The boy gave him a blank look.

"Your mother has as yet been unable to see me."

Daniel John was quick to reassure him, but Morgan didn't miss the lad's troubled expression. "Mother is sad, is all, Morgan.

She . . . she has very little to say these days, even at home."

Disgusted with his own churlishness, Morgan forced a smile. "I know, lad. I suppose I've always been a bit touchy where your mother is concerned."

"But why, Morgan?"

The question on the boy's face was entirely innocent, and Morgan hesitated, uncertain as to how to reply. "Well, now, I expect it's because I've always valued her good opinion, you see. Your mother is a grand woman, and why wouldn't I want her to think well of me?"

"Oh, but she *does*, Morgan! I know she does! You were great friends once, after all. It's just that . . ."

The boy faltered, and Morgan hastily changed the subject. "Pay me no mind, Daniel John. I've a toothache that's been driving a dagger up my skull for most of the day; it's made me as cross as a bag of cats. Come along now," he said cheerfully, slinging an arm about the boy's thin shoulders, "let us go and say hello to your mother."

At their approach, Nora's eyes took on the startled expression of a skittish foal. Morgan sensed with impatience that she was vastly uncomfortable in his presence. He supposed he deserved that from her, but it grieved him to see her look at him so.

More than her awkwardness around him, though, he was concerned about her appearance. Her always willow-slim frame was thin to the point of gauntness; she looked wan and frail and not entirely well. He wondered if she were eating, wondered as quickly if she and the family still had food left from what he'd given her. He would make it a point to get Daniel John alone before the evening ended and see what he could learn about their situation.

She finally managed a smile — for her son's sake, Morgan suspected — and a murmured hello. They exchanged stiff, uncomfortable bits of conversation for a time, with the boy doing his best to alleviate the tension. Morgan did manage to learn that Tahg was no better — he was, in fact, worse — and that Old Dan's condition had also deteriorated.

When Daniel John eventually drifted off to talk with another lad from the village, Morgan stepped closer to Nora to prevent her from escaping him. "And you, then, Nora, how is it with you?"

She tensed, avoiding his gaze as he stared down at her. "We're getting on. As well as the next, I'm sure."

"That's not entirely reassuring, given conditions in the village."

She shrugged, still not meeting his eyes. "They say we're to have more relief soon. New soup kitchens and distribution centers." Clearly she was unconvinced. "Have you heard so?"

She looked at him, her eyes so large and anxious that he hadn't the heart to tell her what he knew. Even if more relief *were* to come to their all-but-forgotten village, it would likely be too late for most of Killala, just as it had been too late for so many other towns throughout the country. True, numerous centers had been established all across Ireland, but they were far too few, and the soup served by most of them was little more than worthless greasy water, a pitiful excuse for even the most meager nourishment.

"Aye, I have heard," he mumbled. Now he was the one to look away.

"What requirements will there be, do you know?"

He looked back at her. "Requirements?"

She nodded. "Sean O'Malley is saying you must meet certain requirements to be eligible for the relief. He says the rules are strict."

"I would expect so." *Strict and entirely unrealistic,* he thought bitterly.

When he said no more, Nora went on. "I must be certain we will qualify. For Tahg and the Old Man, especially."

For a moment, Morgan felt a hot stab of resentment and anger at the helpless fear in her eyes: resentment that one so innocent and good should be degraded to such dependency, and anger at himself for being virtually powerless to help her.

"As I understand it," he said, carefully

choking back the bitterness he felt, "recipients must be certified to have no means of support. They must have no animals, and their potato patch must be a total waste." Pausing, he then added, "And you must give up all land more than a quarter acre."

Her eyes widened with alarm. "But the land is all we have!"

Wanting more and more to avoid this conversation, he gave a small nod of agreement. "They know that only too well, I should imagine."

A reluctant understanding dawned in her eyes. "You're saying they don't *want* us to survive, aren't you? That even when the famine ends, they mean for us to die."

"That possibility has occurred to some," he answered sourly. "The land, you see, will be far more profitable to the landlords as grazing land, rather than parceled out as it presently is, in tenant farms. Some believe that Mother England intends to clear the land of people so she can populate it with cattle. Perhaps," he finished, "the lads like young Tim there are doing the Queen a great turn by sailing for America."

Nora searched his eyes for a moment. "And is that what *you* believe?"

He answered her question with a shrug, feeling a tinge of relief when Sean O'Malley walked up just then, sparing him the need to say more.

"Did I see you bringing your harp inside this evening, Morgan?"

"You did, Sean."

The older man's expression was sober and somewhat strained. "Would you give us a tune, then? A song for Tim and his mother, perhaps?"

Morgan put a hand to O'Malley's once burly shoulder, keenly aware of the sharp protrusion of bone beneath his fingers. "I will do that, Sean, and gladly. Have you a special one you fancy?"

"One of your own, I should think, Morgan, if it's no trouble. Something just for the lad, if you would."

Ashamed of his eagerness to escape the pain in the grieving father's eyes, Morgan gave a short nod and started for the corner by the fireplace to retrieve his harp. Even as he crossed the room, a song began to form on his tongue. Words and melodies had ever been within easy reach for him. From the time he was a lad it seemed that the Lord had placed a storage box of songs within his heart, from which he never had to do more than simply lift the lid and reach inside to select the one he wanted. He knew that he was known more for his words — his verses, and lately his essays in *The Nation* — but in truth he found his greatest pleasure in choosing words to fit melodies equally his own.

And so he sang his song for Tim O'Malley,

and although it was a sad song that poured forth from him, he was able to give it a touch of hope as well. For while the lad undoubtedly had a terrible, bitter time ahead of him, he was at least doing something to save himself and perhaps eventually some of his family, too.

Morgan cradled the harp against his shoulder and plucked the brass strings with his fingers. The sound vibrated into his chest as he caressed the ancient instrument with the familiar touch of a lover returning to his beloved. For a moment — for just a moment — his heart vibrated too, with the hope of something better to come. But the fleeting echo died as quickly as it had begun, and when the last strains of Morgan Fitzgerald's song for Tim O'Malley had ceased, darkness closed in around the poet's soul once more.

By the time he had finished, the "wake" had reached the hardest moment of all, the time of the final parting. The guests would commiserate with the family, then make their tearful goodbyes before departing to allow the O'Malleys a private farewell. Afterward, young Timothy would exchange embraces with his family, then turn and leave, for the last time, the cabin in which he had grown to manhood. Off he would go with his paltry worldly goods and a brave wave of his hand as he put behind him forever his loved ones, his past, and his heritage.

The closing of the coffin, as it were. How many from the village, Morgan wondered, would repeat this same scene in the weeks and months to come? Indeed, how many would *survive* long enough to repeat it?

His eyes went to Nora. Her face was stricken, drawn with grief for her friends and, he sensed, dread for her own family. At her side, Daniel John's face was ashen and taut with his own bewilderment and unanswered questions.

At that instant Morgan felt a suffocating hand of apprehension slip down and close around his throat. He was struck so hard he almost reeled at the power of his unspoken but ever-present love for these two. The small woman in the coarse black dress was as lovely and as noble to his eyes as if she were a princess in satin, and the long-legged boy at her side might have been his own son, so dear to his heart had he long been.

Sudden fear for them both loomed up as strong as a physical presence, and he knew at last why he had returned to Killala long before he had planned. His intention had been to stay with the lads in the hills, dropping down at night only when he had a need to. There he could think and write and even find a bit of temporary peace. But something had called him back, some urge he could neither name nor resist.

He recognized it now and was infinitely

thankful to have heeded its call. Without knowing how he would accomplish it, he knew he was here to save Nora and her sons from the darkness gathering on Killala's horizon. How much he could do and how soon he should act depended in part on Michael's response to the letter he had written him — the letter he should have received by now.

If Michael were willing to help, and if Nora were willing to go, there was still hope for her and the boys. But one thing was certain: Every day that went by eroded their hope and compounded the danger. To wait too long might well mean disaster.

And yet wait he must. In the meantime, he would do what he could to help them survive.

If Nora would let him, that is.

Nora asked young Moira Sullivan from up the road to pay a call at the cottage while she and Daniel John attended the O'Malley farewell supper. Old Dan had grown far too weak to be of any real help to Tahg; more and more Nora feared the old man might fall, with nobody nearby to help *him*.

Moira had already gone when they returned home, so Nora went immediately to check on the old man, then Tagh. Both were asleep, though Tagh was tossing and moaning. Ashamed that she had left him for so long, Nora hurried from the room to get a cloth and some cool water.

She stopped just inside the kitchen at the sight of Daniel John, framed in the open doorway, standing as still as a statue.

"Ach, Daniel John, close the door! 'Tis cold enough in here as it is, without —" His white, stricken face stopped her in mid-sentence. "What is it? What's wrong?"

"The cow is gone!" he blurted out, his eyes wide and frightened. "Someone has taken Sadie!"

Fear clutched at Nora's heart as she stood staring at him. Then she bolted across the kitchen and out the door. Coatless, she scarcely noticed the damp, stinging cold of the night as she ran around the side of the cottage with Daniel John right behind her.

As he said, the cow was gone, rope and all. Panic rose like a flood tide as the dreadful reality of their situation washed over her. Their one remaining source of food was gone.

"Perhaps she wasn't taken, though . . . perhaps she simply broke her rope and is roaming about . . . somewhere." She heard the trembling in her voice, felt her knees threaten to buckle beneath her.

"Aye, that could be," Daniel John agreed quickly. Too quickly. "I'll have a look. She's probably nearby."

"But you can't be wandering about in the dead of night, not in this cold."

He looked at her. "And we can't afford to

lose Sadie, Mother. I don't think I should wait."

If the cow had been stolen, a few hours wouldn't matter, Nora realized with dismay. Still, she knew he was right; they had to try.

"If she's only wandered off, I won't be long. Sadie will come to the sound of my voice," he said uncertainly.

A nagging whisper somewhere deep inside Nora told her the cow had not wandered off. The theft of livestock, even in broad daylight, had been on the increase for weeks now, not only in Killala, but throughout all Ireland. People were doing whatever they must to survive. They had taken to eating horses, even dogs. A cow would seem a treasure.

She could see in Daniel John's eyes that he, too, held little hope of finding Sadie. But neither of them dared to give voice to their thoughts.

"Go, then," she said, averting her eyes. "But not too far. It will do us no good to find the cow if you catch your death in the searching."

He put a hand to her arm. "I'll find her, Mother. You go back inside now."

She nodded, still unable to meet his eyes.

Hugging her arms to her body against the cold, Nora stood, watching him start for the road. She turned once to look at the empty barn, then glanced around the yard.

She was suddenly struck by the memory of

Morgan's words when he had named off the requirements for relief distributions. No animals, he had said; no animals, no potatoes, and less than a quarter acre of land.

Well, then, it would seem we are now eligible for relief, she thought, nearly choking on her own bitterness.

The question was, would they live long enough to apply for it?

7

A Gaunt Crowd on the Highway

When tyranny's pampered and purple-clad minions
Drive forth the lone widow and orphan to die,
Shall no angel of vengeance unfurl his red pinions,
And grasping sharp thunderbolts, rush from on high?

RICHARD DALTON WILLIAMS (1822–1862)

Morgan spent the weekend at Frank Grehan's place near Ballina, working on a piece they were writing for *The Nation*, the journal of the Young Ireland movement. He had hoped a day or two away from the village might be just the tonic for his troubled thoughts about Nora and his own family. Instead, he spent an altogether dismal two days, wishing he had never come at all.

Why had he ever agreed to collaborate with the blustering, irascible Grehan anyhow? The man was more trying than ever, to the point that Morgan could scarcely wait to get away from him.

Grehan was an embittered man in his forties who lived alone in a gloomy, drafty old farmhouse. A loyal Young Irelander who fancied himself a radical and a revolutionary, he unfailingly turned a visit from an acquaintance into a political forum. Unfortunately, his acquaintance with the bottle went deeper than his knowledge of politics.

He had spent most of the weekend attempting to badger Morgan into assuming a more active leadership role in the movement, accompanying each argument with the statement that Morgan could "make a real difference."

Even as he ushered Morgan out the heavy front door, instead of sending him off with a friendly farewell, Grehan blasted him with still more rhetoric. "You think on it, Fitzgerald; you're ripe to lead. The movement is made up of mostly Protestants as yet, but your golden tongue and gift of reason can make the Catholic voice heard within the ranks at last."

Morgan ground his teeth as he reminded Frank that he was merely an out-of-work schoolmaster and a dilettante writer, not a politician. "And I have no 'Catholic voice,' as I have pointed out to you before. Why, neither Catholic nor Protestant would want to claim the likes of me, man. I'm a heathen in the eyes of both."

His attempt at levity went unnoticed. Grehan accompanied him out the door and into the yard, waist high with weeds. "The people are going to rise, Fitzgerald. It's in the wind, even now. Aye, there will be a rising, that's sure, and you should be one of its leaders."

With a great deal of firmness mixed with laughter, Morgan finally managed to free himself from his host's cloying grasp and take his leave. Hoisting his harp a bit higher, he whipped his cloak around his shoulders and started down the road.

The weather seemed grimly appropriate to his mood. Within moments he found himself in the midst of a savage storm of wind-driven, freezing rain and snow. Drawing his cloak a bit tighter around his throat, he ducked his head and turned his face toward Killala.

Despite the weather, he was glad to have escaped when he did. Had Grehan continued to press him, he might have lost his temper and revealed more of his personal displeasure with the "movement" than Firebrand Frank would care to hear.

An entire host of objections to the antics of Grehan and his bunch swarmed in his head like angry bees. He was particularly disgruntled about the new militant organization being formed out of the Young Ireland movement — the "Irish Confederation," they were calling themselves. He knew the plan. They intended to spread their influence by forming clubs in every city and town, whereby more and more pressure might be brought to bear on the British government. Repeal of the union between England and Ireland was one of their primary objectives, arguing as always that only absolute freedom could save their country from total destruction.

It sounded fine in theory, but in reality it had as many holes as a sieve. Oh, he knew well enough who Frank and his wild-eyed rebels had been listening to, all right: Fintan Lalor, a dark-natured, brooding recluse who had isolated himself on a farm in Queens County to agonize over Ireland's tragedy.

Lalor argued for a "moral insurrection," his premise being that only the rising up of tenants against their landlords would eventually free the Irish from England's chains. He used his considerable facility with words to incite farmers to withhold their rent payments until they were granted co-equal ownership of the land.

But Lalor's ideals would never be realized except by revolution: armed insurrection, not moral. And while he shared, with reservations, Lalor's contention that Ireland's only future lay in reclaiming her own lands from the British, Morgan knew beyond a doubt that these angry, "courageous" peasants were more figments of Lalor's imagination than fact. In reality, Ireland's farmers were dying in the ditches — frozen, starved, and decimated by disease. He found it incomprehensible that these raving visionaries could entertain the notion of an armed uprising by a starving, defeated people. Even a fool could see that the Irish peasantry were too enfeebled, too demoralized, and too broken to think of anything at all beyond survival. Moreover, it was commonly agreed that the famine had not yet reached its full horror; Morgan knew in his soul that a cataclysm of unimaginable proportions was yet to come.

With a failed potato crop for the second year in a row, the half-naked, poverty-stricken men and women who had managed to survive on the outdoor public works now had no employment at all. The public works were at an end; the workhouses were full and running over; thousands upon thousands of peasants were severely in arrears on their rents. To fall behind meant certain eviction, and to be homeless during this, the most severe winter in Ireland's memory, meant certain death.

Revolution, indeed! When a man had no food and no work, no health and no strength, no home and no hope — was such a man equipped for rebellion?

Morgan was convinced that before insurrection could even be considered, the people must be fed — fed and healed. Education, too, was vital. The Lord knew the Irish loved all manner of learning; but with years of their own Gaelic language forbidden and their schoolmasters and clergy in hiding, any traditional form of real education had gone by the wayside. In addition, there was the desperate need to end the hatred between Protestant and Catholic, which played a very real part in dividing the country.

We are forever fighting one another, Morgan mused bitterly, *the Irish against the Irish.* He could not help but wonder who, themselves or the British, had harmed the island most.

It was midafternoon before Morgan reached the edge of Killala. In spite of his heavy cloak, he was drenched and thoroughly chilled. So absorbed had he been in some lines for a new poem that he was jolted harshly back to reality by a sound like approaching thunder.

He whirled around. Cotter, the land agent, came bearing down on him from the west fork in the road, astride a foaming, wild-eyed stallion. Throwing a wall of mud and ice in Morgan's path, the agent wielded his riding crop like a lunatic. His heavy-jowled, bloated face was raw and wind-whipped. Below his hat, sparse, wet strands of red hair capped his ears.

The agent's small round eyes betrayed a meanness, an expression of bestial excitement that chilled Fitzgerald's blood. The man looked for all the world like a demon turned loose from hell's pit. Following him, also mounted, were the bailiff and two ruffians known to be Cotter's personal bodyguards. Running behind and struggling to keep up came a raggedy bunch of house wreckers, all brandishing crowbars.

Morgan leaped out of the way, twisting his ankle as he hurled himself into the slush-filled ditch to avoid being run down. Watching them charge by, fury slammed at his ribcage, and he raised a fist to their backs, wanting nothing so much as to hurl the lot of them into the bay. Instead, he could only stand unmoving in the ditch, stunned and impotent in his rage, watching as the mob came to a halt in front of Aine Quigley's cottage.

Anger gave way to sick horror as Morgan realized what was happening. Mass eviction. He had seen it before in Galway and Sligo, still carried the nightmare scenes in his mind. His stomach knotted and his breathing grew labored as he stood watching.

The Quigley place, sorely rundown and neglected, had not always been in such a sad state. Once the dwelling of Michael Burke's family, the large two-story house with its slate roof and tall, narrow windows had been one of the finest homes in the village. But according to Thomas, poor Aine had been at her wits' end for months now, trying to keep food in the bellies of her three small children after her husband died of pneumonia. The house had steadily gone to ruin.

There were three homes there at the turn in the road: Aine Quigley's, Sean O'Malley's, and, directly across from these two, the Gaffneys', all looking forlorn and uncared-for in the icy winter rain hammering down on them. Within the hour, Morgan knew with a terrible certainty, three families — two of them with children — would face death in a ditch.

For a long time he stood watching the scene unfold in front of the Quigley's, anger and outrage hitting him like waves. Finally he stirred. His feet were half frozen in his boots, his hands stiff from cold in spite of wool gloves. He lurched out of the ditch, starting in the direction of the wrecking crew.

With every step, the fire of his rage increased. A moan of physical pain escaped his lips as he stumbled, then lunged ahead. Nearly mindless now with fury, he charged through the icy slush on the road, as intent on his prey as a mad bull.

Nora stood in the middle of the road outside her cottage, tented beneath Old Dan's *bawneen* and wearing his boots as she searched the surroundings for a glimpse of Daniel. This was the third day straight the boy had gone looking for the missing Sadie. In spite of Nora's insistence that the cow was surely lost to them, he simply refused to give up; he had been out almost all morning in this terrible, freezing rain.

A noise made her turn back to look toward the opposite end of town. The sound came rolling up the road, an advancing roar of angry voices.

With the gloom of the day and the pouring rain, it was difficult to see much of anything, but she could look down the road and make out the Quigley house and one side of the O'Malley place. A crowd seemed to be gathered in front of Aine Quigley's — some on horseback, but most on foot. Nora stared for another moment; then, dropping the old man's work coat down to her shoulders, she quickly slipped it on and began walking.

She was over halfway down the road when Cotter, the land agent, came into view. He was sitting astride his big, dirty gray stallion, shouting orders to a group of men nearby. A sickening wave of foreboding engulfed her as she recalled a conversation she'd had with Aine Quigley only days before. Apparently Cotter had been threatening them with eviction for weeks. They had fallen behind with the rent some months before, and, according to Aine, only the fact that the agent had his unholy eye on Padraic's younger brother had kept him from turning them out before now.

The sick-minded land agent's attraction to young boys had been rumored in the village for years. Speculation had turned to outrage just last summer, however, when Dr. Browne's son let it slip to some of the lads that his father had treated young Fursey Lynch for "wounds" inflicted by Cotter.

An orphan boy from Kilcummin, Fursey Lynch had been given a place in the agent's barn, as well as his meals, in exchange for doing odd jobs around the property. Although the doctor's son had been vague about Fursey's "wounds," he let it be known that the lad's injuries were severe enough to keep him at Browne's house for nearly two weeks before his return to Kilcummin.

Aine Quigley, convinced that Cotter's leniency with their back rent hinged on his fascination for Padraic's brother, told Nora in hushed tones it was "the end for them," since the lad had left the village to live with an aunt in Ballina. "Cotter will turn us out without mercy now," she whispered to Nora, her eyes wide with fear. "And what will become of my babes, then? They won't last a day on the road!" Nora had done her best to reassure the distraught widow, but at the same time she feared that Aine was justified in expecting the worst.

A terrible dread welled up in her as she approached the Quigley house. She nodded a greeting to Mary Larkin, whose grim shake of the head indicated that the worst was about to happen. A silence had fallen over the group as she drew near, a strange, oppressive stillness, as if the entire assembly was waiting for someone to die. The faces of the people, both men and women, were lined with a mixture of fear and sympathy, disbelief and hostility.

Her gaze went from the bailiff, mounted on a scrawny brown horse, to Cotter, who sat scowling down at the crowd from his snorting gray stallion. It took her a moment to comprehend the significance of several raggedy-looking men standing near the horses, but when she did she nearly gasped aloud.

"Destructives," murmured a man nearby, as if voicing her dismay. Nora shuddered. These were the despised housewreckers, those who, after being evicted from their own homes, managed to survive by tearing down the houses of their neighbors for food or pay.

God have mercy, are they going to tumble Aine's house as well as turn her out? Nora wondered.

One of the local constables was reading off a list in a loud, imperious voice. Nora heard the names of the O'Malleys and the Quigleys called, then the Gaffneys. When no one appeared from any of the three cottages, Cotter spurred his horse forward, prodding the constable with his riding crop. Startled, the short, rotund man jumped, then took off running to the front door of the Quigley house, giving it three hard raps with his fist.

Nora's breath quickened with dismay when Aine appeared at the door. In her arms she held her youngest babe, a thin, fine-boned boy with hair the color of old ivory; two wee girls stood on either side of their mother. Every face, with the exception of the babe in his mother's arms, was pale with fright.

The constable started to speak, but Cotter went charging up the yard on his mount, his gruff voice drowning out the policeman. "Where's the man of this house?"

Nora could just barely hear Aine's reply.

"Why, my husband is dead, sir. More than four months past now." The woman's voice trembled almost as violently as the thin hand clinging to the doorframe.

Cotter turned to the bailiff, who was dismounting. "What have they got? Any animals?"

"A goat and a horse," the other man replied carelessly, handing over the reins of his horse to one of the housewreckers standing nearby. "They had a cow, but it seems it died on them in December —"

"The horse and the goat are dead, too, sir," Aine quickly interrupted. "We have no animals now, none at all."

"Well, your rent is in arrears, and since you've no way of paying it, you'll have to leave," Cotter ordered. "Get what you want from inside and get out. Now!"

Aine flinched as if the agent had struck her in the face with his riding crop. Wincing from the plight of her friend's pain, Nora instinctively took a step forward. She stopped when Cotter whirled around to eye the crowd that had gradually begun to close in.

"Stay back, the lot of you!" he bellowed. "You'd be wise to take heed of what is happening here. Any one of you behind in his rent — you'll be next if it's not paid in full when you're told!"

From somewhere in the crowd a woman cried out, and soon others began to weep with her. Aine Quigley, however, seemed resolved to fight. "Sure, and you can't mean what you say, sir! I've three small babes and not a coat among us. We've no food and no health! You'll be sending us to our deaths if you turn us out."

"Then apply for admission to the workhouse!" snapped Cotter, turning to glare down at the bailiff. "Get those men started at once! And you" — he wagged a finger at the bald-headed constable still in the yard — "see to the other tenant across the road."

A red-faced Sean O'Malley had come out of his cottage and now stood, his wife pressed behind him, halfway between his own place and Aine Quigley's. "There's no room in the workhouse, and well you know it!" O'Malley shouted at Cotter. "Would you have the woman and her babes die in the ditch before sundown?"

By now the crowd had again started to close their ranks and were gathering in around Cotter. Some of the women were still weeping, but the men's voices rose in an angry buzz that burst into a roar of fury when the destructives swung out and, dividing, began to swarm on all three houses.

"God have mercy on us!" wailed a silver-haired woman to Nora's left. "They mean to see us all dead."

Nora watched in horror as one of the housewreckers yanked Aine and the children away from the door and shoved them roughly out into the yard. Aine Quigley sent up the keening cry of the mourner as she watched her meager possessions being tossed out of the house into the mud and sleet. Pushing the babe in her arms at a woman nearby, she ran back inside, screaming.

The distressed murmurs of the watching crowd had swelled to a rumble of mounting fury when a roar rose up from somewhere behind them. Nora spun around with the others at the sound. Stunned, she watched Morgan Fitzgerald charging his way through their midst, his face livid, his eyes blazing.

Two of the housewreckers had just come out the front door, their arms filled with kettles and dishes. They froze at the sight of the fiery-haired giant tearing his way through the crowd, which was now parting to give him room.

One of the destructives shot a glance of alarm at Cotter, then scurried back inside the house. The other dropped the contents in his arms where he stood and took off running around the side of the yard.

They needn't have feared, for Morgan's objective was plainly Cotter. Stunned, Nora watched him charge the agent, who still sat astride his horse, his bloated red face a mask of incredulity. The wild-eyed stallion snorted, then reared with a force that sent Cotter flying. His riding crop sailed out of his hand and landed in the mud as he fell.

Morgan went for the agent, now lying on his back, feet up, in a pool of icy slush. Cotter was paunchy and awkward, no match at all for the frenzied giant towering over him. Grasping him roughly beneath his arms, Morgan jerked him upright and spun him around. The terrified agent squawked and let fly a string of oaths. Undaunted, Morgan lifted him into the air as if he were no more than a lumpy sack of potatoes. He held him there, feet dangling above the ground, arms flailing wildly as he faced the crowd.

Horrified, Nora could hear Morgan's words to the bug-eyed Cotter as he demanded, "*Call them off!* Get your riffraff out of that house, or I'll snap your cowardly spine, I swear I will!"

The agent's red face looked like a melon about to burst. He continued to rage and squeal as Morgan dangled him in front of the people.

At that moment the constable who had started for Michael Gaffney's place came racing across the road, his pistol drawn. He fired once into the air, then again. "*Put him down, Fitzgerald!* Release him at once or you're a dead man!"

Morgan swiveled to look, dragging Cotter around with him. As he pivoted, he set the agent rudely on his feet, but continued to grasp him firmly under the arms. Pushing Cotter in front of him as he went, he edged his way toward the policeman. "A grand idea, Constable! Go ahead, shoot! Shoot this devil and bless us all!"

A roar went up from the crowd, and several of the men now began to converge on the policeman. The man stood gaping for another instant, then lowered his gun and backed away.

Nora saw the other constable and Cotter's two bodyguards edge up behind Morgan's back. "*Morgan!* Look out — behind you!"

Morgan whipped around, dragging the agent as if the man were weightless. "Get back!" he warned, his face hard and determined. "His death will be on your heads, lads."

They halted, but didn't retreat, and

Morgan shouted again, "I mean it! Just give me an excuse, why don't you? Wouldn't I just love to snap his fat neck!"

Nora shivered in the hush that had fallen over the crowd as Morgan dared his attackers with a grim smile. Didn't the lunatic realize he was endangering not only himself, but all of them? Cotter would turn out the entire village for his madness!

"Well? Get on with it, then — him or me?"

The constables lowered their weapons, and the bodyguards took a few reluctant steps backward.

"I'll have the pistols on the ground, lads," Morgan demanded.

The policemen exchanged uncomfortable glances, but dropped their guns as he instructed.

A growl of rage exploded from Cotter. Morgan yanked him back against his chest, hard enough that Nora heard the man's bones snap as he cried out in pain. She cringed again, anger at Morgan and his mindless temper surging through her. The man he was threatening held the life of every person here in his very hands.

"Now, then, *Mister* Cotter — your honor, *sir,*" Morgan sneered, his mouth close to the agent's temple as he slurred his words in an exaggerated brogue, "you'll be after ending this little incident right away. Just send your boys along like good lads, and I'll turn you loose as well. We'll be having no more of this eviction talk today, if you please." His eyes went to the destructives. "But first, boyos, let's be putting the Missus Quigley's furniture back inside her house where it belongs."

"No!" Cotter twisted and squirmed, struggling in vain to free himself from Morgan's iron grip. "Stay where you are! Do you hear? *Stay where you are!*"

Nora's hand flew to her mouth as Morgan's grasp on the man tightened. Cotter shrieked, but Morgan merely pressed his mouth even closer to Cotter's ear and grated, "I think you'd best heed what I say, man, and heed it well. I have some lads of my own, you see, who are far more fierce than these miserable *spalpeens* of yours." One brawny arm locked under Cotter's chin. "Now here's the way it will be, unless you do as you're told: Some night very soon my men and I will come calling. We'll come while you sleep, and you'll not even know we're about." His voice hardened. "Until we've spread-eagled you in the yard and set you ablaze, that is."

The agent had stopped his squirming — indeed, he seemed to have stopped breathing. "Aye," Morgan finished smoothly, "you'll be ashes among the cow dung before anyone even suspects what has happened."

Cotter's eyes looked about to pop as Morgan tightened his hold on his throat. The agent frantically began to nod his agreement.

"Ah, so we understand each other then, your honor?"

Again Cotter wagged his head vigorously, tears tracking down his fat cheeks.

"Well, that's grand, then," Morgan said cheerfully, inclining his head toward O'Malley. "Bring me one of those pistols, Sean, why don't you? And perhaps you might want to hold on to the other one yourself."

The lithe, square-shouldered O'Malley didn't hesitate. He passed one pistol to Morgan, then leveled the other gun on the agent.

"All right, now," Morgan said evenly, releasing Cotter's throat to palm the gun. "We'll just be waiting until your lads put Missus Quigley's house back in order."

Morgan continued to hold Cotter firmly until all Aine's belongings had been returned to her cottage. Finally, he gave the agent a rough shove, pushing him toward his horse and training the pistol on him.

All eyes followed Cotter and the officials as they jumped on their mounts and started to ride away, their henchmen running behind them. Unexpectedly Cotter jerked his stallion around to face Morgan. "Know this, Fitzgerald," he grated out, his face flushed with hatred and humiliation, "this day you have signed your death ticket!"

An impudent grin spread over Morgan's face as he lifted his chin and cocked his head, but his eyes glittered as hard as ice chips. "That being the case, your honor, *sir,* you might do well to remember that *your* ticket is attached to my own."

The agent swore, then yanked his horse around and took off at a frenzied gallop. Behind him, the crowd of watchers broke into a militant cheer.

Nora stiffened, feeling her face grow hot as Morgan caught her eye and began walking toward her. She could sense the interested stares of her neighbors and wanted desperately to run.

"You saved my back, lass," he said quietly in the Irish. "I thank you for the warning."

Nora stared resolutely down at the frozen mire, not answering. Acutely aware of his eyes on her, she finally dragged her gaze up to meet his, encountering a faint glint of amusement that made her blood boil. His eyes went over her, traveling past Old Dan's worn, shapeless coat and her sodden brown skirt, down to her feet, lost in the old man's heavy boots.

His eyes met hers again and held. He said nothing; his smile said it all. It suddenly occurred to Nora how desperately woebegone she must appear to him, standing there like a drowned ragamuffin in the old man's clothes. Well, and what did she care *how* she looked to Morgan Fitzgerald?

Irked by his insolence, Nora snapped at

him. "You do know he's right, don't you? Not only has your madness signed your ticket to the gallows, but you've most likely sealed the fate of the entire village!"

His arrogant smile fled as he stood studying her face. When he finally spoke, his tone was guarded. "The fate of the village and all Ireland was sealed long before this day. If you did not know that before, then at least face the truth now."

"Just what is the truth?" she whispered savagely. "What, Morgan Fitzgerald, did you mean when you warned the agent about 'your lads,' as you called them? What is it you're hiding, with your wandering about and your gifting us with provisions from the Lord knows where and —"

Suddenly Nora stopped, shaking her head wearily. She dared not finish the question or play out her accusations to the end. There were some things, she realized with self-disgust, that were better left unknown.

When she looked up at Morgan again his eyes were hard, and for a moment Nora thought he was simply going to turn and walk away. Instead, he shoved the pistol into his belt, took her firmly by the arm, and started walking, pulling her along beside him. "Come along, Nora Ellen, I will see you home before you catch your death."

Mortified by his insufferable air of proprietorship, Nora tried to twist her arm free. Ignoring her, he merely tightened his hold and stepped up his pace.

Nora deliberately lowered her voice to avoid calling further attention to herself. "You haven't changed at all, Morgan Fitzgerald," she spit out bitterly, stumbling along beside him. "You still have more gall than sense."

He glanced down at her, not breaking his stride in the least as he gave her a measuring look. "And you, Nora lass, have not changed all that much yourself," he countered with just the faintest hint of a smile. "Yours is still a terrible beauty when you're vexed with me. Now, tell me, what were you doing out in this miserable weather to begin with?"

Nora flushed at his words. "I was looking for Daniel John."

She explained then about the stolen cow, being careful to conceal her feelings of desperation. "I told him to give it up, but he insisted on going out again this morning. The cow is gone for good. I know it, and I think he knows it as well."

"He feels as if he has to do *something*," Morgan replied softly. "With both Tahg and his granddaddy ill now, I imagine the lad is doing his best to take his place as the man of the house."

Startled at his perception — for she had already recognized her son's efforts to do just that — Nora glanced up at him. "Aye, I'm sure that's how it is with him." It made her heart ache to see her youngest trying so hard to become a man overnight. Fortunately for them all, the boy had always seemed far older than his years. True, he was a dreamer, but despite his fanciful imagination, he was a lad who could be counted on when he was needed.

"How is the old man?"

"Growing weaker by the day. He was still abed when I left the house." Nora's voice betrayed her worry. "I can't remember him ever lying in so late before." She paused, struck by a thought which she expressed, mostly to herself. "It seems that nothing is the same these days. Everything is changing. Even people."

Morgan looked at her, nodding slowly. "There are even more changes coming, you know. You'd do well to be prepared for them."

They had reached the front yard of the cottage. Morgan stopped and turned to face her, catching her hand in his. "Nora — I'm going to be gone for a few days, but before I leave I want to know that you've food enough to last until I get back. Especially now, with the cow gone, can you manage?"

Trying to ignore the sharp stab of disappointment she felt upon learning that he was leaving again, Nora nodded, avoiding his eyes.

With his free hand he caught her chin and

tilted it up, forcing her to meet his gaze. "I must know the truth, Nora," he said urgently. "I'll bring some more provisions with me when I come back, but I need to be sure you'll be all right until then. Don't lie to me, lass — your pride will not keep your family alive."

Stung by his words, Nora stiffened. She would *not* become dependent on him. She had no idea what he was up to, with this sudden *concern* for their well-being, but she must not allow herself to grow used to his presence in her life again. Morgan was quicksilver — unstable, unreliable, unpredictable. As for her pride, he was being entirely unfair. What he took to be pride was simply self-respect, and she thought he should have understood her need to retain what she could of it.

"Nora?" His eyes narrowed, challenging her.

"I — yes. We'll be fine."

Still he searched her eyes, as if he were trying to read her heart.

"Your concern is misplaced, Morgan," she said evenly. "Thomas and his children are your family. If you're determined to look after anyone, then see to *them*."

He let his hand fall away from her chin. "Thomas is a man grown," he said, drawing back slightly. "He takes responsibility for his own family."

"Well, it's not for you to take responsibility for *mine.*" Her words sounded more sharp than she'd intended. Still, she meant them. "We — will be all right," she said, gentling her tone a bit. "Truly, we will."

Morgan's eyes softened, a look Nora did not want to remember. "And that is all I'm wanting, Nora — for you and yours to be safe and well. Can you not accept that much from me, at least — that I still care for you?"

She could not look at him. She *wouldn't.* She would not look at him or listen to him or believe in him or feel anything at all for him. Not ever.

Mustering as impersonal a tone as she could manage, Nora fixed her gaze on a spot just past his shoulder. "Thank you . . . for what you did for Aine today, Morgan. It was very brave. I really must go inside now and see to Tahg and the old man."

She sensed that he was about to say more — something nasty, by the looks of his frown — but he held his tongue. His expression cleared as he gave a short nod and said agreeably, "Aye, and even more do you need to be getting out of those wet things."

She started to turn, but he reached out and put a hand to her arm. "Nora —"

She turned back to him.

"Tell Daniel John that I'll be back in a few days. Tell him I said goodbye."

She nodded, and started for the cottage.

Already she dreaded the look she would see in her son's eyes when he learned that Morgan was leaving again. But then he might just as well get used to doing without the man. Perhaps Morgan meant what he said, this time, about coming back in a few days, but that was only for now. The day would come — and soon, more than likely — when he would go wandering off again, not to be seen for months or even years. Morgan would never be — *could* never be — anything else but what he was. She must not allow Daniel John to believe, even for a moment, that the man would ever change.

And she must not allow herself to believe it either.

8

Winter Memories

All through the night did I hear the banshee keening:
Somewhere you are dying, and nothing can I do:
My hair with the wind, and my two hands clasped in anguish;
Bitter is your trouble – and I am far from you.

DORA SIGERSON SHORTER (1866–1917)

New York City

The snow that had begun at dawn increased with a vengeance throughout the day. Several inches already blanketed the city, and still it slashed relentlessly against the kitchen window facing the street.

Home from his watch and relaxing with his tea, Michael Burke propped his elbows on the table and stared down onto the street below. In the quickly gathering dusk, the snow wove a blowing veil about the gaslights, allowing the mean, cluttered streets to masquerade as a quaint, even charming winter scene. A flow of pedestrians hurrying home from work pushed urgently along, holding their caps as their coattails and scarves whipped sharply in the wind. Much of the garbage that bordered them on either side was disguised, distorted by flickering shadows from the snow swirling about the lamplight.

Michael checked his pocket watch; Tierney should be along soon from his after-school job at the hotel. Wiping a hand over the back of his neck, he yawned and glanced again at the newspaper on the table in front of him. He suspected much of his gloomy mood could be attributed to the *Tribune*'s front-page report of the troubles in Ireland. These days the papers were filled with accounts of the Great Famine, as they were calling it; indeed, it was a rare edition that carried no news of the mounting disaster across the sea.

Compassion for Ireland's plight seemed nationwide. Young as she was, America was a land with an enormous heart, a generous heart. Oh, there was no denying Tierney's frequent complaints about New York's resistance to the Irish. The hostilities were real enough, even among the Irish themselves. The Protestants continued to view their Catholic countrymen with contempt, just as they had back in Ireland, thinking them ignorant, superstitious peasants who were incapable of bettering their lot in life even if they had a mind to do so. Such disaffection for the "papists," some years past, had led to a number of Protestant Irish-Americans identifying themselves as "Scotch-Irish" to dissociate themselves from their Roman countrymen.

On the other side, the Catholic immigrants had transferred their native resentment of the normally wealthier and better educated Protestants to the same class here in the States. Distrust and bitterness fed the old antagonism, creating new rifts between the two groups. In addition, new barriers rose between the Irish and other emigrants, especially the Germans. The German Catholics, for example, found the Irish too grim and defeatist for their own energetic, practical religious beliefs, while the Irish thought the Germans somewhat naive and pompous.

Despite their differences, however, Americans simply were not a people who could ignore the large-scale suffering of an entire country, especially a country that had apparently been abandoned by her own "Mother England." Already meetings were being held — not only here in New York, but throughout the country — to respond to Ireland's needs.

Railways offered to carry free all shipments marked *Ireland*, and public carriers delivered at no cost all boxes going toward Irish aid. Relief committees throughout the nation hastened to put thousands of dollars and shiploads of food at the disposal of the Society of Friends — the Quakers — who were energetically organizing the United States' aid to Ireland.

Here in New York, Tammany Hall collected thousands of dollars, as did both Catholic and Protestant churches nationwide. "Donation parties" were held by all denominations, along with concerts and teas. Young ladies in private schools volunteered to make useful articles that could be sold for the benefit of Ireland. Jewish synagogues sent their weekly collections; a group of Choctaw Indians worked to collect an offering of $170; and in villages and towns all over America, women and children pooled their pennies and sent them to Ireland.

Such a flood of enthusiasm had swept the land that not enough ships could be found to transport the bounty. Aye, it was a grand thing that was happening, but it rankled Michael that it should require a disaster of such tragic proportions to unite his countrymen. Especially those who claimed to be Christians.

Michael sighed and tapped his fingers impatiently on the newspapers, then rose and went to stand at the window, looking up and down the street for some sign of Tierney. He, too, longed to do more in the way of donations, but he had already dipped deep into their small savings. Tierney, however, exhibiting his characteristic cleverness and knack for money raising, had organized a host of lads from school into teams, and among them they'd pestered a number of shopkeepers and tradesmen into donating generous amounts for the school's "Friends in Ireland" fund.

Those days Michael found himself thinking more and more of his own "friends in Ireland." Morgan and Nora were frequently on his mind. Back in November, when news reports of the famine had begun to pour across the sea, he had written an anxious letter to Morgan in care of his brother, Thomas. Each day that passed he watched with growing impatience for a reply.

Strange — after so many years and an ocean between them, his mind could still see the two of them clearly. Nora was now a woman grown, a wife and mother; yet it was difficult to imagine her as anything but a small, sober-faced lass with enormous sad eyes and the tiniest waist in Killala. He hoped she'd been happy with the husband she'd chosen; Nora deserved happiness, she did, for she'd had little enough of it as a girl.

As for Morgan Fitzgerald, he supposed *that* rogue could take care of himself well enough. Michael smiled at the thought of his old friend, with his harp and his poems and his roaming ways — and, always, his fatalistic but fervent love for Ireland. He was a vagabond, Morgan was. Ever the dreamer, he had been smitten with the wanderlust as a lad and seemingly never recovered.

The man was a puzzle of many pieces, one or two of which might never be found. Michael thought he had as much love for his homeland as any respectable Irishman, but with Morgan it was more than love of country. It was an obsession. He could still remember the great oaf's words to him when Michael had first told Morgan of his dream to see America, trying to convince him they should go together.

Backed up against a gnarled old tree, Morgan had stretched his long arms, locked his hands behind his head, and smiled that thoroughly impudent grin of his. "Ach, Michael, I could never do that, and you know it. You intend to go and never come back. I could never leave our Lady Ireland for good."

To Michael's way of thinking, Ireland was more the fallen woman than the lady, and he said as much.

Morgan had laughed, shaking his head. "Aye, she's a miserable island at that, but she's claimed me entirely, don't you see? There never was a woman quite so bent on owning a man as our *Eire*. She's a fierce and terrible mistress, I admit, and most likely she'll be my destruction. But beloved as she is to me, I could no more give her up than rip out my own heart."

Did Morgan still cling to his beloved, even

now? Michael wondered. He prayed not, for surely she would drag him to his death along beside her —

"Well, Da — I am here, but where are you?"

Startled, Michael jumped and whirled around to see Tierney standing just inside the door, grinning at him.

"Wool-gathering, it seems. I didn't even hear you come up the stairs."

Tierney tossed his gloves on a nearby chair, then hung his coat and cap on a peg by the door. A shock of dark auburn hair, wet from the snow, hung insolently over one eye. The boy's other eye was still dark from a mouse he'd incurred in last week's scrap with the Dolan boy.

The thought of Tierney's frequent fights brought a sour frown to Michael's face. "That eye is a grand sight."

The boy came to the table, his grin still in place. "Now, don't go starting on me, Da. What's for supper?"

"There's a pot of brown beans, and Mrs. Gallagher sent up a pan of corn bread. And I'm telling you again to quit calling me 'Da.' We're not living in Ireland — talk like the American you are."

"*Irish*-American," Tierney corrected, going to the stove to check the beans. "And you still say, 'aye,' you know. Can we eat now, Da? I'm starved."

"As you always are," Michael retorted, getting up from his chair. "Set the table and I'll fix our plates."

Tierney whisked around the kitchen getting the dishes out, flipping them carelessly onto the table as if they were unbreakable — which, Michael reminded him again, they weren't.

"Have you heard, Da? Eleven ships are sailing from here to Ireland tomorrow with food!" Tierney's voice was boyishly high with excitement, though more often than not these days it tended to crack with the gruffness of approaching manhood.

Michael nodded as he dished up a plate of beans and handed it to the boy. "Aye, and four more leaving from Philadelphia the day after. It's in the paper."

"Can we go to the harbor and watch them sail out? You're off duty tomorrow, aren't you?"

"I am, but need I remind you that you will be in school?" Michael shot him a stern look as he sat down across from him.

The boy shrugged and reached for the corn bread. "I won't miss that much. Not for just one day. Come on, Da — say we'll go."

"I will say a prayer if you'll hush long enough to listen." Michael glared at him, but the boy's tilted grin made him give over.

"Besides, I hate that school, and you know it," Tierney continued after Michael gave their thanks. "I wish I could go to the Catholic school."

"Catholics go to Catholic school."

"I know, and that's my point," Tierney muttered.

Michael put down his fork. "We are not going to have this conversation again, are we, Tierney?"

The boy shrugged, a gesture Michael increasingly disliked. "I will never understand why a lad born as a Protestant and raised as a Protestant has this cracked notion about becoming a Catholic."

"It's the Irish way," Tierney said, reaching for the butter.

"I said we weren't going to have this conversation again, and I meant it, boyo. But let me remind you of one thing: Ireland has bred a few Protestants as well as Catholics — myself, for one, and your mother as well, God bless her."

"I know that. But it's different here in New York. The other Irish kids are all Catholic; they think I'm some kind of freak. And I'm just about the only Irish kid in the whole school. All my friends on the block go to Catholic school."

"What *difference* does it make, Tierney?" Exasperated with the boy, Michael was far too tired and cross to be patient. "Christ is the same Savior to Protestant or Catholic — if they accept Him as such."

"Sure," Tierney muttered, pulling his mouth down in contempt. "And is that why the Catholics say theirs is the only church, and the Protestants say a Catholic church is no church at all — and anyone who disagrees with either one of them is a heathen?"

Michael drew a deep sigh and picked up his fork. "That's not the way with all Catholics or Protestants, lad," he said between bites. "The thing that matters is your heart, don't you see? I've told you about my friend back in Ireland, Morgan Fitzgerald?"

Tierney's face lighted up, and he nodded eagerly. Again Michael sighed. Morgan had become a bit of a hero to the lad, and he supposed he could blame himself for that. Tierney was charmed by all the tales of Morgan's exploits repeated over the years. Ah, well, perhaps he'd pay more attention to Morgan's words than those of his stodgy old dad.

"Well, Morgan was never entirely convinced that the Lord is all that interested in our church buildings and doctrines and religious symbols. He seemd to think the Almighty would be more concerned about *relationships:* our relationship with Him, and with one another as well. And do you know, Tierney, the longer I live, the more truth I find in my old friend's words."

The boy merely grunted, then shoveled another heaping spoon of beans into his mouth.

His eyes danced as he chewed. "Well," he said, swallowing, "when I'm grown and go to Ireland, I may not take to either church. Perhaps I'll look up old Morgan Fitzgerald and become a heathen, like him."

"Morgan is *not* a heathen — and will you stop with that foolish talk about going to Ireland!" Michael exploded, banging his fork down on his plate. "Why would you even think of it?"

He was unsettled by the way Tierney met his gaze without wavering. The boy's blue eyes, so much like his mother's, turned hard and cold. "You've always known that's what I want."

"Aye," Michael growled, "and never have I understood why! Ireland is a corpse. Can you not get that into your skull? She is dead and rotting above ground. There is nothing there for us, nothing for anyone except death. Why do you think I left it in the first place?"

If only he could help the boy to see what *he* had seen — the poverty, the defeat, the squalor . . . the *misery*.

"Morgan didn't leave," the boy said with a calm that fired Michael's anger even more. "He chose to stay and work to make things better."

"Morgan is Morgan — and perhaps a bit of a fool! Thousands upon thousands are fighting to get out of Ireland, to come here to America! They want what you already have

— what you seem to hold so cheaply. Doesn't it strike you as a bit odd that all those hordes of people are so anxious to leave behind what you seem to think is so grand?"

"I still want to go. I want to go because I'm Irish." The maturity and strength in the boy's voice chilled Michael.

"You're an *American*. And you should thank God every day for it!"

Tierney stared at him and, not for the first time, Michael felt a stirring of apprehension at the hooded, unreadable expression in his son's eyes.

Furious with the boy — and even more with himself for once again losing his temper with his son — Michael shoved his chair back from the table. "Eat your supper. Your foolishness has cost me my appetite. I'll be doing some reading."

He half-expected the boy to defy him; he did so often lately. But Tierney simply lowered his eyes and went on eating.

In the bedroom, Michael sank down onto the rocking chair that had been Eileen's. For a long time he sat there, unmoving, staring at the bed he had slept in alone for so many years. A longing for his wife welled up in him, bringing him close to tears. He had not missed her this much in a long, long time, and he suddenly felt a dreadful, cold loneliness. His wife was lost to him, and he was beginning to wonder if his son wouldn't one day be lost to him as well. He did not understand the boy — in truth, he never had — but that did not diminish his love for the lad. He only wanted . . . what? For Tierney to be like him?

Sure, and that was a joke. Tierney was like no one else — not himself, nor Eileen, nor anyone else that Michael could think of. Tierney was different. And it was a difference Michael did not understand, a difference that almost frightened him at times. What would the boy come to down the years?

He had such dreams for his son — for both of them. He wasn't going to stay a police sergeant forever; he had set his sights on Tammany Hall, had already made some contacts he believed would take him there. By the time Tierney was fully grown, he hoped to be in a position to help him become whatever he wanted to be. But the boy seemed to have no dream, no dream at all, except to be as . . . as *Irish* as possible. And what kind of a dream was that?

Michael closed his eyes, letting his head fall back against the cushion of the chair. Suddenly he wished he didn't feel so old. So old and so tired and so fiercely alone.

Da would never understand. He expected his son to share *his* dreams, not to have dreams of his own.

Tierney pushed his plate away and propped one elbow on the table, resting his chin in his hand. Well, he *did* have his dreams, and they had nothing at all to do with his father's.

It wasn't that he didn't love his da. Of course, he loved him, and he didn't relish making him sad. But he couldn't help the way he was nor would he change. Sometimes he wished that a man like Morgan Fitzgerald had been his father. He would have understood, would have encouraged his love for Ireland. Da never would. He loved New York and simply could not understand anyone who did not.

Well, *he* did not love New York — he *hated* it. He hated its filth and noise, its churning masses of people. He hated it most of all for the way the entire city hated the Irish.

Tierney got up, walked to the window and looked out upon the snow falling into the city night.

They'd keep us beggars if they could. In their eyes we're nothing but dumb animals, fit only for hauling the manure from their streets, killing their rats, ironing their clothes, putting out their fires — or policing their precious city.

Well, he wanted no part of this ugly place — he would *be* no part of it, not ever. He belonged to Ireland. In a way he couldn't begin to understand, in a way he could never have put into words, the country owned him.

One day he would go. He would travel the length and breadth of it, absorb it, merge with it, become one with it. Ireland was his home as New York could never be. Ireland was the mother he longed for, the bosom friend he craved, the missing part of his heart.

Somewhere in Ireland, Tierney Burke would find his destiny.

9

Evan's Adventure

Ill fares the land, to hastening ills a prey,
Where wealth accumulates, and men decay.

OLIVER GOLDSMITH (1728–1774)

London

Roger Gilpin was no gentleman.

Evan Whittaker had been in the man's employ only days before making that judgment, and now, eleven years of service later, his opinion had changed not a whit. Sir Roger could be incredibly crude in his manners and attitudes; he had a problem with spirits, and his behavior when he had been drinking ranged from disagreeable to intolerable. He seemed to delight in ignoring the authorities, insulting his contemporaries, and destroying his enemies — who numbered many. Even in the eyes of his few friends, he was often a bore. To his servants, he was thoughtless, bullying, and downright intimidating. Evan seemed to be the only soul in his employ to whom Sir Roger gave even a measure of grudging respect. More surprising yet, he seemed to have actually become somewhat dependent on his reserved, mild-mannered secretary.

Evan supposed he *was* nearly indispensable to his difficult employer. He didn't arrive at this conclusion by way of conceit; it was just the way things appeared to be, however inexplicable the reasons. It was a fact that he wasn't in the least intimidated by Sir Roger. He stood steady in the face of Gilpin's frequent storms of rage. Indeed, Evan's mother had always called him "unflappable," though his father had thought him hardheaded. At any rate, his phlegmatic disposition seemed immune to whatever cruelty Roger Gilpin had a mind to inflict.

Evan Whittaker was, in fact, the only employee who had ever remained at Gilpin Manor for longer than a year. The vulgar, self-important Sir Roger certainly did not inspire loyalty on the part of those who worked for him. Evan was an oddity, and perhaps that was a part of his appeal.

He had often been asked by his peers, and on occasion by one or more of Gilpin's acquaintances, why he *had* stayed with the difficult Sir Roger all this time. He had been offered a number of other positions over the years, and admittedly, he had considered leaving more than once. After careful thought, however, he always managed to talk himself out of the idea. His wages were outstanding, his living quarters more than comfortable, and he had grown used to the irascible widower.

Another possibility loomed in his mind, but he preferred not to dwell on it — it made him appear so *dull*, even to himself. Could he have become so complacent about his life and indifferent to the monotony of his days that he was unwilling to muster either the energy or the courage to make a change?

Of course, there *had* been a time when he would have welcomed an adventure. A shy, quiet youngster, he'd grown up as the only son — and a somewhat frail one, at that — of an aging clergyman in a small, depressed village near Portsmouth.

As a boy, Evan had been plagued by a dreadful stammer, mocked and ostracized by his peers in the schoolyard. His father had encouraged him to be brave and to trust God, and the lad had managed to obey at least half of his father's injunction. He learned to trust God, but the bravery never seemed to follow.

And so Evan retreated into his books. Only there did the young outcast find what he was looking for — adventure, romance, the opportunity, through his imagination, to become the swashbuckling hero of his dreams. There he did not stutter; there he was not ridiculed by pig-faced schoolboys; there, at last, he liked himself.

Evan Whittaker found his courage, and he found his faith. But he never seemed to find both in the same place.

Even now, in his mid-thirties, Evan had difficulty reconciling the two. He still read avidly, and his literary tastes remained very much the same. He *did* enjoy a good adventure novel about explorers or pirates, and he had no trouble at all imagining himself as the danger-defying hero, complete with a cape slung casually over his shoulder and a sword on his hip.

And Evan still trusted God. His faith, marked by a simple life of devotion, sustained him in his encounters with his ill-tempered employer and supported him in the mundane execution of his duties.

Have faith and be brave, his father had said. Well, Evan's life incorporated both — his heart rooted in the reality of Christ, his imagination caught up in the vast possibilities of fantasy.

Yet something was missing. When Evan allowed himself the luxury of thinking about it, he realized with a pang of regret that the two significant parts of his life had never merged. There was no bravery in his faith, no courageous acting out of his love for God. And there was no faith in the bravery of his imaginative heroism — no spiritual life beyond the sheer joy of adventuring with the fictional characters that populated his books.

Something, indeed, was missing. Somehow, somewhere, the two should have come together.

These days, however, he had little time for considering such philosophical imponderables; he had all he could do to keep up with his regular duties. This exasperating business in Ireland kept Sir Roger in a continual fit of temper, which in turn kept the household in a constant state of chaos. Evan invariably found himself with more letters to pen, more dinners to plan, and more frequent tantrums and bouts of rage to placate.

At the moment, Sir Roger was using Whittaker's presence in the library as an audience for his rage. And, as always seemed to be the case these days, the object of his wrath was Ireland.

"Killala!" Sir Roger spit out, pacing the length of the library. "I have never laid eyes on the squalid little pit — only *God* knows and cares where it is!"

His employer's reference to God made Evan blink and draw a tired sigh, for the man certainly had no acquaintance whatever with the Creator. "I believe it's located near a bay in western Ireland, sir," Evan offered, going on with his careful copying of the letter Gilpin had just dictated to George Cotter. "Very remote."

"I know *that!*" Gilpin snarled. Sir Roger had been pacing the room for the better part of an hour as he dictated. At last he stopped and turned to Evan, who lifted his eyes from the letter he was transcribing.

A tall, gaunt man with long legs, white hair, and large, slightly bulging eyes, Roger Gilpin never failed to remind Evan of an aging, frost-coated grasshopper. Indeed, "Grasshopper" was Evan's private name for his employer.

"I *asked* you your opinion of that fool Cotter's letter!" Sir Roger crossed his long, thin arms over his chest and fixed Evan with a baleful glare. "Well?"

Clearing his throat, Evan stared at the pen in his hand. "Ah . . . w-well, of course, the agent had no right . . . n-no right at all . . . to defy your instructions, Sir Roger." Knowing how annoying the Grasshopper found his habitual stammer, Evan now gave it free rein. "Ah . . . although I must s-say I can appreciate that an undertaking of this n-n-nature might well contain difficulties we haven't c-c-considered. P-perhaps, if m-mass eviction is the only feasible solution, we need to give the agent m-more time." Evan beamed a slightly vacuous smile at his employer from his chair at the desk.

"Oh, for pity's sake, man, can't you just say whatever you mean and stop that hemming and hawing?" Sir Roger's mouth thinned even more. "Can't you get that fixed somehow, that tic of yours?"

So now it was a tic. Only last week it had been a plague. Over the years the dreaded stammer had evoked such misnomers as "croak," "twitch," and "splutter." Perhaps the Grasshopper was mellowing.

"I'm sorry, s-sir, but I don't b-believe there's any . . . f-fixing for it." Evan did his best to look humiliated.

Sir Roger grunted and again began to pace. "Well, as to Cotter — he's supposed to be in charge out there! He's the land agent, and the land agent's job is to take charge of the tenants, isn't that so?"

Matching his words to his quickening pace, he spilled them out in a frenzy. "I don't pay him to let those shiftless freeloaders make a monkey out of him! Not that it wouldn't be easy enough to do — the man is a fool!"

After one more pass across the room, he stopped in front of the fireplace, where only a thin, feeble flame continued to fight its way between the logs. Reaching for the poker, Sir Roger began punching the fire back to life. When he straightened, he resorted to a mannerism Evan had always found oddly intriguing: after opening his mouth to a wide, gaping cavern, he snapped it shut with a smacking sound. *The Grasshopper*.

He now came back to the desk and picked up the letter from Cotter which lay near Evan's hand. "What were you able to find out about this — Fitzgerald creature?"

Evan shifted slightly on his chair, fastening his eyes on the book-lined wall across the room. Intense concentration seemed to relieve the stammer somewhat, and at the moment he thought it best to be precise. "Apparently, Morgan Fitzgerald is something of a . . . an enigma. Part p-poet, part vagabond, and p-part folk hero. He sounds f-formidable: big — very big — with an unruly m-mane of copper hair and, according to Quincy Moore, our c-correspondent, the 'strength of a Druid oak tree.' " Evan felt a delicious shiver wind its way down his spine; Moore's description could have been right from the pages of one of his favorite adventure novels.

Aware of Gilpin's impatient squirming but entirely unperturbed by it, Evan smoothed the sheet of vellum in front of him, aligning its four corners with those of the desk, just so. Then, fastening his eyes once more on the bookshelves — this time on the brass candlesticks — he continued. "Apparently F-Fitzgerald is a writer held in great esteem — a 'poet p-patriot,' Moore says." Evan glanced from the candlesticks to Sir Roger. "Ah . . . then there's the . . . association with the Y-Young Irelanders, as you know."

Sir Roger swore and again waved the letter in his hand. "The man is a common thug! He almost killed George Cotter!" He paused, then added sourly, "Not that it would be any great loss."

Evan bristled. Fitzgerald might be a great many things, but he was certainly no common thug. No, indeed. The man sounded anything but common.

Perversely enjoying his employer's agitation, Evan warmed to his subject, paraphrasing parts of Moore's letter as he went on. "Fitzgerald s-seems to be quite well known f-for his writings in the . . . *The Nation.*" Oh, dear, now he'd done it. Even the mention of the radical Young Ireland news journal was enough to set Sir Roger's teeth to rattling.

Hurrying on before his employer could let fly one of his florid streams of profanity, Evan explained, "Fitzgerald seems to be a highly . . . educated m-man. Until recently, he was best known for his p-poems and satirical essays, but it seems these days he's d-dipping his pen more and more into the ink of rebellion."

Sir Roger's eyes bugged out, and his mandible dropped down, presumably preparing for an expression of disgust, but Evan hurried on; he had saved the juiciest morsel for last and was not about to be denied his thunder. "As for this next observation: Moore stresses that it's p-purely rumor, although George Cotter is apparently convinced it's so."

The letter in Sir Roger's hand now crumpled as he clenched both fists and waited, his long, homely face set in a terrible scowl.

Evan drew a long, steadying breath and set

his gaze on the list of instructions he'd been copying. "It seems that for months now there have been . . . s-stories of a mysterious rebel leader and his men who are up to all manner of mischief in C-Connacht, especially in County Mayo."

Gilpin's eyes narrowed, and he looked to be in the throes of some sort of fit. "A *rebel leader?*"

"Yes. Well . . . Mr. Moore says these p-primitive folk in the west have a tendency to imbue their outlaws, as well as their heroes, with l-larger-than-life attributes, even supernatural traits. This rebel leader would seem to be a case in point. They c-call him the, ah, the *Red Wolf.*" A chill of delight gripped Evan as he uttered the name. What a *splendid* tale this was!

"Those who claim to have seen him, this . . . *Red Wolf* . . . say he and his marauders ride only at night. They say he has a head of curly copper hair and rides an enormous wild red stallion. Supposedly he and his men come charging down out of the hills when least expected, d-do their dirty work, and then simply . . . d-disappear back into the mountains and the mist." *Really, this would make the most wonderful novel . . .*

Realizing Sir Roger had asked him a question, Evan blinked, then looked up at him. "I'm s-sorry, sir?"

"I *said,* what *sort* of dirty work?"

"Oh — well, nothing too violent, actually. They've k-killed some cattle from time to time — a few head of yours, I'm afraid, Sir Roger. They steal grain, drive horses out of their p-paddocks, provide p-protection to men on the run — that kind of thing. The peasants adore them, it seems, because they drop . . . b-baskets of food at cottages throughout the villages and do other miscellaneous . . . good deeds for the poor unfortunates." Evan sighed. *An Irish Robin Hood, no less.*

"Is that all?"

Evan looked at him. "Well . . . yes . . . except that there are some, Cotter included, who suspect Morgan Fitzgerald of being this, ah, *Red Wolf.*"

Sir Roger actually growled — a choked, phlegmy rumble. For a moment Evan feared it might be the beginning of a seizure, but the Grasshopper was simply grinding his jaws in rage.

Leaning forward, Gilpin hurled the crumpled letter to the desk. "I want you to leave for County Mayo at once! At *once,* do you hear?" He made a jabbing motion with his head to the letter in front of Evan. "You'll deliver those instructions to Cotter personally, as my emissary!"

Wagging a long talon of a finger in Evan's face, he went on shouting. "And you'll stay in Killala until you see my orders carried out, do you understand? I want those . . . *creatures* . . . off my land and those . . . *bandits* . . . hanged!"

Good heavens, the man was *serious!* Evan squirmed. *He* — go to Ireland? Worse yet, to *Mayo?* Why, according to Quincy Moore the place was nothing more than a bleak, desolate rock pile, its inhabitants unwashed savages and wild men, most of whom still spoke some ancient, unintelligible tongue! *Furious fools,* Tennyson called them. Oh my, no — it was impossible!

"I'm afraid that's . . . quite impossible, Sir Roger," he said as firmly as he could manage. "I have a slight lung condition, you remember" — he cleared his throat — "and I understand the c-climate in western Ireland is abysmal. Besides," he hastened to add for good measure, "who would assume my responsibilities in my absence? My work load is heavier than it's ever b-been before." There. That should take care of *that.*

"You'll do as I say or your *work load,*" Sir Roger snarled, "will be considerably lightened. Considerably."

Evan lifted his chin in what he hoped was a gesture of defiance. "S-see here, Sir Roger —"

The Grasshopper was already hopping to his next thought. "Naturally," he said in a more conciliatory tone, turning his back on Evan, "you'll be generously recompensed for your travel expenses and your inconvenience. And of course, once you return you'll be due a sizable increase in wages." He paused, then turned back with a somewhat malicious smile to add, "And perhaps a vacation, as well, eh?"

Evan swallowed. He hadn't had a vacation in years. Perhaps the climate wasn't all *that* wretched. "A vacation, did you say?"

The Grasshopper showed his teeth.

"Think of it as — an adventure, Whittaker! Yes, that's it, an adventure! I should think a young, handsome fellow like yourself would be eager for a bit of travel and excitement."

Dear heaven, the man was actually patting him on the shoulder! Evan cringed. An adventure might be well and good, but he hardly thought a forced visit to Ireland qualified as such. Still, it *would* be a change of scenery. And there was the promise of a vacation . . .

"Well, if you're certain it's absolutely necessary —"

"Absolutely!" Gilpin boomed, thumping him solidly on the back. "This is excellent. You'll be able to give me a firsthand account of the famine conditions, as well."

Evan rose from his chair to avoid another bone jarring back pounding. "I thought Mr. C-Cotter and some of our other c-correspondents had already done that, sir. I'm sure they d-didn't exaggerate — the newspaper accounts c-confirm —"

"I should hope they didn't exaggerate!"

Gilpin gave a short laugh, crossing the room to the gleaming mahogany sideboard. He poured himself a drink from a crystal decanter and tossed it down in one enormous gulp. "For my part," he said, wiping his lips on the back of his hand, "I consider these potato blights heaven-sent. Yes, indeed," he went on, pouring himself another tumbler of whiskey, "a distinct act of Providence, I should think. So do Elwood and Combs and some of the other landlords at the Club. Why, it's the very solution to the Irish problem!"

He downed his drink, rolling the tumbler around in the palm of one large hand as he continued. "God knows we need to rid the land of those scavengers, and this famine has got them dropping like flies!"

Setting the tumbler down, he crossed to the fireplace, backing up close to it and clasping his hands behind him. "Cattle and horses, that's what we'll replace them with. It's Divine Providence, all right, Whittaker," he said, shooting Evan a pleased smile. "The Irish were starving anyway, dying of their own indolence. Why, the only thing those savages have ever known is poverty! They're too lazy, the lot of them, to turn an honest day's work. We landlords have to save ourselves before they bleed us dry! Once we get those *papists* off the land, we can turn it over to grazing and protect our investment in that wretched island."

From what Evan had read, not all the starving Irish were of the Roman Catholic faith, but he doubted that this fact would matter one way or the other to his employer.

"It's just as Trevelyan says," Sir Roger went on in a somewhat sanctimonious voice, "the Irish overpopulation and immoral character are altogether beyond our power to correct. Only God himself can deal with those idolaters. And it would seem that He is doing just that at last."

Trevelyan, assistant secretary of the treasury, had indeed seconded the Prime Minister's belief that the famine was the work of a benign Providence. And numerous members of Parliament seemed eager to echo that sentiment.

Evan wasn't entirely sure just what he thought about the Irish. But he was fairly certain that the God he knew would not share Roger Gilpin's attitude. He recalled his father — a clergyman for forty-odd years now — making a remark in one of his recent letters about the "suddenly pious Trevelyan is convinced that God has cheerfully set about starving to death thousands of infants and children, simply because their parents placed some statues in their churches."

Not being personally affected by the conditions in Ireland, Evan had given the matter little thought. Now, it seemed, he would have the chance — albeit unwelcome — to see for himself whether or not the devastation was, indeed, the judgment of God upon an idolatrous people. His personal theology led him to believe otherwise; he had never subscribed to the idea that Catholicism and true faith were mutually exclusive. But this was not the time to get into a controversy with his peevish employer.

Sir Roger roused Evan from his thoughts. "Well, then, it's settled! You'll leave for Killala right away. By the end of the week at the latest."

Evan forced an unhappy smile. "Yes, I suppose I shall."

"Good man." Sir Roger stretched up, poised on the balls of his feet, then dropped down. The Grasshopper preened. "Write up whatever papers you may need, and I'll sign them in the morning. Just be sure that Cotter understands there's to be no more delay — they're *all* to be turned out, with no exceptions! And if he doesn't do the job this time, I'll hire a man who *will!*"

A thought struck Evan, and he moistened his lips. "About this Fitzgerald person —"

"*Fitzgerald be hanged!* And I'll see that he is! Cotter says he has family there, in the village, and they're as destitute as the rest of the peasantry. Perhaps you can use them to bring Fitzgerald into line, eh?"

Evan nodded vaguely, chafing to get away from his employer. Sir Roger was quite a disgusting man, actually.

"Come, now, Whittaker, you needn't look so despondent! Perhaps you'll find yourself one of those saucy little Irish tarts to brighten up your trip. Make a man of you!" Gilpin gave his loud, abrasive laugh, obviously delighted with himself. "Just see that you don't bring her home with you. London has quite enough of them scurrying through the sewers as it is."

For a moment Evan feared the man was about to cross the room and slap him soundly on the back again. He edged his way to the door and, calling up an immense amount of self-control, managed not to bolt and run.

When at last he escaped the library, he went directly to the front door, dragged it open and stepped outside. Pulling in a long, cleansing breath of cold air, he willed the frigid wind to wash away the stench that seemed to have settled over him.

10

The Letter

And my heart flies back to Erin's isle,
To the girl I left behind me.

THOMAS OSBORNE DAVIS (1814–1845)

New York City

Not for the first time, Michael Burke found himself wishing for a uniformed police force. The idea of uniforms had been discussed and dismissed any number of times, mostly due to the men's fierce complaints. Many of the Irish lads, who comprised the majority of the total police force, were virulently opposed to the idea. Equating uniforms with the livery worn by English footmen, they remained adamant in their resistance to being decked out like "British lackeys."

From the beginning, Michael had disagreed, seeing the uniform as a means of gaining a bit more authority on the street. He was convinced that the instant recognition afforded by a uniform would automatically give a man greater influence, and thereby more control, among the rabble — at least a good deal more than their present copper badges could provide. From what he had seen in the streets of New York, Michael would have welcomed the edge of intimidation a mass of blue uniforms could effect.

He sighed and donned the blue woolen shirt lying on the bed, rubbing a calloused thumb over the copper badge affixed to his chest. For now, this makeshift uniform would have to do.

Michael headed for the kitchen, tucking in his shirttail as he went. Tierney, standing at the door, was just stepping aside to admit a stranger.

"Someone to see you, Da," Tierney said, studying the stranger with obvious curiosity.

"Sergeant Burke?"

Michael gave a short nod, taking in the stranger's appearance. Although he was dressed decently enough in the clothes of a working man, a furtive look filled the hooded dark eyes, and a hard set to his mouth immediately put Michael on guard.

"I've a letter for you," the man said without preamble.

Irish. There was no mistaking the accent.

Michael frowned. "Have we met, then?"

The man shook his head, volunteering nothing further as he pulled an envelope from his pocket and handed it to Michael.

"I was to see this safely into your hands,"

said the stranger. He paused, then added, "And I was asked to collect your reply as quickly as possible."

Michael recognized the large, untidy scrawl across the front of the envelope immediately. "Morgan," he said, surprised. "Morgan Fitzgerald."

The stranger gave a brief nod.

"But how — why the personal delivery?"

"I was told only that it's urgent, sir, and would you please send an answer back with me as soon as possible."

Michael studied the man's impassive face. "I didn't get your name."

The stranger met his gaze. "*Barry* will do. Do you think I could collect your answer by tomorrow, sir?"

Again Michael looked at the envelope in his hand. "You're going back to Ireland that soon?"

"Aye. I have some business to attend to in the city; then I'll be leaving."

"How is it that you know Morgan?" Michael pressed.

"I'm sorry, sir, did I lead you to think that? I don't actually know him at all. We have some mutual friends, you see, and when they learned I was coming over they asked me to deliver this for Mr. Fitzgerald."

Tierney had come to peer over his shoulder. "Aren't you going to open it, Da?" he asked eagerly.

Michael lifted his hand to silence the lad. "You say you need my reply by tomorrow?"

"If at all possible, sir. I need to get back straightaway."

"All right, then, I'll have it ready." Anxious now for the man to leave, Michael followed him to the door.

Tierney was at him again as soon as he turned around. "Is it really from your friend, Morgan, Da? Why do you suppose he had it carried by messenger?"

"It's from Morgan right enough," Michael said, ripping open the envelope.

Tierney hovered at his shoulder. "What does he say? Is something wrong?"

"Hush, now, and let me read it so we'll know."

As soon as he began reading, Michael realized the letter had not been written in answer to his own, mailed back in November. If Morgan had received it at all, he made no mention. Neither was it typical of the hastily scratched notes Morgan usually wrote; it was several pages long and written in a careful hand.

"Aren't you going to read it aloud, Da?"

Hearing the impatience in Tierney's voice, Michael shook his head distractedly. "It's too long. You can read it a page at a time as I do."

The further he read, the more disturbed he became. The news accounts he'd been following for weeks leaped to life through Morgan's vivid descriptions and uncompromising accounts of Ireland's tragedy. Michael felt as if Morgan were here, in this very room, telling him face-to-face of the devastation, the horrors that had fallen upon their country. All the ugliness he had heretofore only imagined became dreadfully real. And behind every line, he could sense Morgan's pain and his rage at his utter helplessness.

Handing the pages to Tierney as he finished each one, Michael's heart began to pound. The more he read, the worse it got. Morgan reeled off news about his own family and others Michael knew and remembered. *Nora . . .*

She had lost her husband — and her little girl! Dear heaven, her oldest son was failing, too? Michael realized he had moaned aloud for her pain when Tierney put a hand to his arm.

> The only hope for her at all is to leave Killala . . . to leave Ireland. While I know I'll have the time of it, convincing her to go, somehow I must find a way. Although Nora has not faced it yet, I doubt that Tahg, her oldest lad, will last until spring, and her father-in-law — do you remember Old Dan Kavanagh? — will most certainly be gone before then. If she does not leave, and soon, Michael, she will perish with all the others.

I have told her nothing of this yet, but with the help of some of my lads, I'm sure I can raise passage money for her and those of her family left alive, as well as for Thomas and his young ones, to come across. But I'll be needing some help, and that's where you come in, old friend, though what I'm about to ask is not an easy thing.

Curious, Michael frowned and scanned ahead, reading beyond the words of apology until he reached the next page.

And so, keeping in mind that you've been without your Eileen some years now, and remembering there was a time when you had a true fondness for Nora, I'm anxiously wondering if you could find it in your heart, Michael — you and Tierney — to take Nora and what remains of her family by then, into your home.

Stunned, Michael's eyes fastened on the last line for a long moment before Tierney's voice broke through his incredulity. Looking at his son, Michael hesitated, then handed him the page he had just read. His pulse skipped, then lunged and raced ahead as he went on with Morgan's letter.

The only chance I stand of making her

listen to reason is to give her the security of knowing someone will be there, waiting for her, when she arrives. In truth, what I am asking, Michael, is that you consider marrying our Nora . . .

Marry her? *Marry Nora?*

Michael's eyes went back over the words again, the blood roaring to his head.

I know there was a time when you had a great fondness for her, and with that in mind, I'm hoping an arrangement such as I suggest might not be entirely to your disliking.

By now I'm sure you're newly astounded at my always considerable nerve, but I must stretch your patience even further. Knowing Nora's infernal pride and insistence on propriety, I believe the only way she would ever entertain such an extreme idea would be if you were to write her yourself — just as if all this were *your* doing, rather than mine. Perhaps — and only perhaps — if she thought the need were more yours than her own, she might be willing to start a new life in America.

The room swayed around Michael. His mouth went dry, and his heart pumped wildly. But there was more.

You have a right to ask, and are wondering, I'm sure, why I do not wed Nora and bring her over myself. I cannot deny that I love the lass and have for most of my lifelong. But we both know it would be worse than folly for a woman like Nora to wed a man like me — even if she would have me, which I doubt. I can offer her nothing but a heart forever chained to a dying country. I cannot leave; besides, Nora deserves far more than the fool I am. And so I'm praying you will find it in your heart to make room for her and her youngest, Daniel John — and, should Tahg survive, him as well. I'm sure the old man would never leave, even if he should recover enough to travel.

I hope to secure passage for both families and perhaps raise some extra funds as well. I know the increased financial burden in this is no small matter.

In closing, I would ask that you send me a private answer by the lad who delivered this letter to you, and if, please God, your answer is yes, then send Nora a letter by him as well. I will see to it she never knows but what the idea was entirely your own.

If you must forgive me for anything, my friend, then forgive me for remembering your utter selflessness and your eager willingness to help others.

I thank you, and as always, I remain . . .
your loyal friend,

Morgan Fitzgerald.

Michael stared at the last lines of the letter for a long time. He felt oddly detached from his surroundings — lightheaded, isolated, weak. The only reality seemed to be the letter in his hand and the sound of his heart pounding violently in his ears.

When Tierney reached for the last page of the letter, prying it carefully from his father's fingers, Michael was only vaguely aware of releasing it. Finally he blinked and turned to look at his son.

The boy was gaping at him with a dazed look of disbelief that Michael was sure mirrored his own dumbfounded expression.

"What in the world are you going to do, Da?"

Numb, Michael stared at the boy. Then a thought struck him, jerking him back to reality.

"The question is, what are *we* going to do?"

Tierney stood watching him, the letter clutched in his hand. "What do you mean?"

Michael willed himself to think. "This affects you every bit as much as me, lad. We're talking about taking in an entire family — I can't make a decision like that alone." He stopped, swallowing down the panic swelling up in him. "Dear God, how can I make a decision like this at *all?*"

Silence stretched between them until Tierney finally broke it. "I still remember Mother. Does that surprise you?"

The boy's soft words caught Michael completely off guard. "Of course, you do, son. Tierney, no one is suggesting that Nora could ever take your mother's place, nor would she —"

Tierney shook his head. "I didn't mean that, Da."

Michael waited. "What, then?"

The boy looked away, embarrassed. "It's just that . . . sometimes I wonder if it wouldn't be nice, having someone — a woman —" He looked up, his face tight and pinched. "It might make it seem more like a home." His shoulders relaxed a little, and he released a long breath.

Michael's face must have mirrored the dismay he felt at the boy's words, for Tierney quickly tried to retract them. "I don't mean we don't already have a home, Da, nothing like that — I —"

With a small wave of his hand, Michael nodded. "I know. I know exactly what you mean, and it's all right. I've had the same thoughts myself, lad."

"You have? Honestly, Da?"

Again Michael nodded. Going to the stove, he set the kettle on for tea. Then he turned back to Tierney, who stood watching him, clenching and unclenching his hands.

"Da? What did Morgan mean — about your once having a — a fondness for Nora?"

Michael moistened his lips. He had not noticed before now the spurt of growth the boy seemed to have taken — he was nearly as tall as Michael himself — or the faint dusting of fuzz on his upper lip and cheeks, the newly angled lines and planes of his face. His son would soon be a man.

And so he would talk with him as a man. "Sit down, son. We'll have some breakfast, and I'll tell you about Nora . . . and how she was special to both Morgan and me. And then — then we must be deciding what to do."

Only then did Michael manage to admit to himself that he did not necessarily find Morgan's astounding request all that unthinkable.

Dublin

Two young men, both in knit caps and dock workers' jackets, waited in the darkness between the side of a warehouse and a pub on the wharf. It was late, past midnight, and the only light was a thin ribbon from the moon that barely managed to squeeze between the buildings.

The taller of the two was a year older than his companion and had dark hair and a hard mouth; he stood so still he scarcely seemed to be breathing. Hair the color of corn silk straggled below the cap of the smaller man, who was pulling nervously at his gloved fingers.

Neither had ever met Morgan Fitzgerald before tonight, but he was said to be a great steeple of a bearded man with dark red hair. They heard the sound of boots scraping the dock, and in another moment a dark, towering shadow loomed before them in the opening between the buildings.

"*I nanabhruid fen ama ge* —" the tall, cloaked stranger intoned by way of identifying himself. *My harp will sound a joyful chord.*

"*Gach saorbhile samh* —" Both men completed the greeting in unison. *For the Gaels will be free!*

Fitzgerald slipped into the space where they stood. "Any word yet?"

The fair-haired youth gaped at him openly, trying to get a better look in the dark, while the taller of the two shook his head. "None. But we've got your tickets. And some money."

The giant's copper hair could barely be seen in the shadows. His voice was oddly gentle for such a large man. "That's grand, lads. And what about the ship?"

The dark-haired man opened his coat and withdrew a small packet, handing it to him. "It's yours, sir. But we'll need a date."

The big man in the cape took the packet, and there was a hint of a smile in his voice. "You're efficient as well as generous. I do thank you. But as to a date, I'm waiting for a response to my letter. Your lad was to wait on it and return it himself?"

"Aye, sir. Those were his orders, and he's dependable."

Fitzgerald nodded. "Well, then, we'll simply go ahead with the plan. I'll have to trust my friend in New York to come through for me as I believe he will." He paused, running one hand down his beard. "Whether he does or he doesn't, I *must* get them onto that ship. Let's plan for the last weekend of March."

"Time enough," answered the dark-haired man without delay. "The ship is ready, as is the crew. The other passengers will be boarded before she sails into Killala Bay. One good thing, the weather should improve some by then." He paused, adding, "It's a small ship, sir, but American-built. Safer than any of those British coffins."

"I appreciate it, lads. It's my family — and others dear to me — who will be sailing on it."

The younger man spoke for the first time. "It's treacherous, sailing out of such a small harbor, sir."

He felt the big man's eyes on him and worried that he'd spoken out of turn.

But the voice in the darkness was kind when it came. "I know. But it's the only way, you see. There will be some going who are ill, if they last long enough to go at all. They will do well to make it to the bay, much less survive the trek to a distant port."

The youth was quick to reassure him. "Sure, and they'll be fine sailing out of Killala, sir."

Fitzgerald's heavy sigh filled the darkness. "If I can convince them to sail at all." After a brief lull, he said, "Well, lads, you can reach me through Duffy or Smith O'Brien for another day or so. Then I'll be starting for Killala — I dare not stay away any longer. You'll see that any message from New York reaches me there right away?"

"You'll be contacted just as soon as our man returns, sir. You can count on that," the dark-haired one assured him.

"Sir —"

The big man had turned to go, but stopped at the youth's voice, waiting.

"You've heard about O'Connell? They're saying he's a broken man."

Fitzgerald nodded and again sighed. "He has exhausted himself entirely."

"For Ireland," the youth said stoutly.

"Aye" came Fitzgerald's soft answer. "For Ireland."

The two men watched him disappear into the mist-veiled night. "He's not at all as I had pictured him," said the younger.

"How is that?"

"I expected him to be a somewhat — harder man. A bit loud and fiery, perhaps even gruff."

His dark-haired companion murmured agreement.

"Still, he calls himself a simple schoolmaster and a poet," said the youth.

"That he does," replied the older man. "But in County Mayo, they call him the *Red Wolf.*"

11

The Sorrowful Spring

For the vision of hope is decayed,
Though the shadows still linger behind.

THOMAS DERMODY (1775–1802)

March came to Killala with no song of spring, no hint of hope.

Ordinarily it was a month greeted with relief and lighter hearts. March meant the approaching end of winter and the drawing near of spring, the promise of warm breezes and planting time, the welcome escape from long months of indoor confinement and idleness. Soon the days would turn gentle, the evenings soft with the scent of sea and heather.

That had been March before the Hunger. Now the month arrived with the sobs of starving children and the endless clacking of death carts in the streets. Heralded by the lonely keening of those who mourned their dead and the shuffling footsteps of homeless peasants on the road, the winds of March moaned across the land with no respite from the winter's cruelty.

In every county, in every province, evictions were commonplace, starvation was rampant, and disease raged through village after village with the fury of a host of demons. By March the reality of an epidemic was undeniable. Fever hospitals dotted the countryside, but they were so few and so poorly equipped as to be almost negligible; the workhouses, too, were impossibly overcrowded and had long since closed their doors. The afflicted had little choice other than to suffer at home — if indeed they still had a roof over their heads — or to surrender their lives in a ditch by the road.

The Kavanagh household was no exception. They had depleted their paltry supply of food days ago, and with no cow or other stock to slaughter, they were facing imminent starvation. Nora had even found herself praying for Morgan Fitzgerald's return, in the far-reaching hope that he might bring another precious store of provisions with him.

Daniel John had gone outside just before midday to look for food — a futile effort, Nora knew only too well, and she had tried to dissuade him. The poor lad was trying so desperately these days to be a man, to be strong for them all, but there was nothing he could do. There was nothing *anyone* could do.

Her spirit had always been set against the wind, opposed to giving in to hardship or despair. But she had very nearly reached the point where she no longer had the strength or the desire to drag herself through another hopeless day. Were it not for her sons and the old man needing her so desperately, she could easily lie down and welcome death.

But they *did* need her, and as long as they did she could not give up. She sat watching them now, her ailing son and father-in-law. Daniel John had helped her move his grandfather's bed into the alcove next to Tahg's so she could more easily attend to the two of them at once. They were both sleeping, Tahg fitfully, his forehead furrowed with pain as he shivered beneath the threadbare blanket. Old Dan lay somewhere in the shadowed place where he'd been for days, waiting for the angels to come for him. Except for the heaving of his sunken chest, he moved not at all.

Nora leaned her head back, closing her eyes against the painful sight of their misery. Not for the first time, she was stirred by anger and resentment at the thought of all that had been taken from the old man and his descendants. This was *his* land, after all, his and that of his ancestors before him. Ever since the youthful Eoin Caomhanach — the first John Kavanagh — had fled to the west after Cromwell's invasion, this land had been worked and farmed by the Kavanagh family. Driven across the country like cattle fleeing from a storm, those early refugees from Cromwell's cruelty had learned to make the best of the land as they found it.

But over the years, history repeated itself, and the people of Killala, like those throughout all Ireland, found themselves plundered and stripped of all they owned, reduced to the station of destitute serfs upon their own land.

At a moan from Tahg, Nora's eyes snapped open. Dragging herself up from the chair, she gave her head a moment to clear, then went to wipe a trail of blood-tinged spittle from Tahg's chin. His face was white, with that awful transparency that seemed to reflect the dim light of the room. In spite of the cold — for there had been no turf to burn for days now — his skin was hot and damp with unhealthy perspiration.

The pain in her head throbbed fiercely as she tended to Tahg. Turning to Old Dan, she tucked his blanket more closely about his shoulders, then braced her hands on either side of his wasted body to steady herself. Straightening, she gasped as a hot wave of nausea washed over her. Her ears were ringing, the room spinning. She grabbed for the bedstead, but missed.

She fell, tumbling slowly at first, then faster and faster toward a deep, dark pit. Again she reached out, clutching at something, anything, to break her fall. But it was too late. The pit yawned and widened, sucking her into a dizzying whirlpool of darkness, then hurled her into oblivion.

* * *

Daniel hadn't intended to go so far; certainly he had not thought of ending up here, on the hill where the land agent lived.

But he had promised himself not to return to the cottage until he'd found some sort of provisions for his family. Tahg was so terribly ill, as was Grandfar — and lately Mother looked nearly as weak and sick as they did. He had to get help for them all — he simply *had* to!

Now, after searching for more than two hours and finding not even a rotten old turnip, he stood staring up at the bleak gray house of the agent, attempting to muster his courage. Perched almost at the very top of the hill, it was a grim, ill-kept block of a place, square and ugly and battered by the Atlantic winds. It stood there in all its drab coldness, glowering down on the village as if to mirror its occupant's contempt.

In spite of his earlier promise to himself, Daniel shivered, longing to turn back. But he knew in his heart that this might be the one place he would find food — food that could very well mean his family's survival. And so he began to walk, hesitatingly at first, then with more purpose.

About a quarter of the way up, he stopped to read a notice tacked up on a fencepost. It was the same warning he'd seen in numerous places throughout the village. Thomas Fitzgerald had said the stranger in town had nailed up the notices, the one sent from London by the Big Lord. Gilpin's lackey.

The tenantry on Sir Roger Gilpin's estate, residing in the village of Killala and surrounding manor, are requested to pay into my office on the 30th of March, all rent and rent in arrears due up to that date. Otherwise summary steps will be taken to recover same.

It was signed by the agent, *George Cotter.*

Daniel wanted to rip the notice from the post and burn it. No one in the village — including his own family — was in a position to pay the rent.

Anger and fear churned together inside him, making his empty, bloated stomach cramp even more. Clenching his hands into tight fists, he resumed his trek up the hill with more determination. He passed a stone fence that followed a wild thicket up to the stables, and, farther up, a rough-hewn storage barn. It was a forlorn, wild-looking property that appeared to have had no attention for years. The buildings were in need of paint, the weeds overgrown; and paper and other debris littered the yard.

Out of breath, his chest heaving from the effort of the climb, Daniel stopped. Partially concealed by a tumble of overgrown brush, he stood unmoving, taking a long, careful look around his surroundings. Satisfied that nobody was about, he broke into a run, heading toward the back of the house. As soon as he came around the side, he spotted a large bin and some barrels, but they were dangerously close to the door. He crouched, again scanning his surroundings.

The backyard led straight into the woods with a path leading off to the right, toward the stables. There was no one in sight, no sound from the house. With the wind whipping his face, he broke toward the barrels near the door.

He made it as far as the nearest barrel when he froze, paralyzed by the sound of approaching hoofbeats.

A horse snorted, and somebody shouted, *"Halt! You — stay where you are!"*

Daniel whipped around to see the agent bearing down on him on his enormous gray stallion. Behind him, on a black mare, sat a small, slender man with fair hair and round spectacles. He was dressed like a gentleman, and Daniel knew at once this must be Lord Gilpin's man from London.

Instinctively, he stiffened, bracing himself for the blow he was sure would come.

Cotter drew his horse to a sharp halt, and the other man stopped beside him. The agent's eyes were blazing, his face flushed and slick with perspiration. In his upraised hand he held a riding crop.

"What the devil are you up to, you little nit?" he shouted, waving the crop in Daniel's direction. "Thinking to rob me, is that it?"

Daniel tried not to shrink beneath the agent's fierce gaze. His tongue seemed glued to the roof of his mouth, and his heart threatened to explode, but he stood his ground, waiting.

Cotter looked as slovenly as he was rumored to be. Stains spotted his coat and a tear showed in one sleeve; he was unshaven and appeared to need a wash.

Daniel's only thought was to run, and he did lunge forward. As if the agent had anticipated his move, Cotter turned the big stallion's lathered body sideways to block him.

"Stay where you are, you thieving little wretch! I want your name!"

Daniel opened his mouth, but the words wouldn't come. He swallowed, trying again. "Daniel . . . Daniel Kavanagh."

"From the village?"

"Aye, sir."

"How many more of you are hiding in the bushes?" Cotter glanced toward the woods.

"None . . . none, sir. I'm alone." Daniel's heart was hammering crazily, and he feared that, in an instant of terror, he was going to humiliate himself by breaking into tears. But he fought for a deep breath, seeing something in the agent's eyes that said it would go even worse for him if the agent sensed his fear.

"Well, then — what are you doing here? Have you come to steal or to beg?"

"I — neither, sir." Shame crept over Daniel as he tried to explain. "I was hoping you wouldn't mind if I helped myself . . . to some of your leavings."

Cotter's lips turned up in disgust. "You thought to steal from the garbage? What are you, then, a rat?"

Angered, Daniel refused to shrink from this bleary-eyed man. "No, sir," he muttered harshly. "I am simply hungry. As is everyone else in the village."

The agent leaned forward on his horse, his small, glazed eyes boring into Daniel. "Well, then, perhaps you'd like to beg," he sneered. "Any lad hungry enough to eat a man's garbage should certainly be humble enough to beg, I would think."

Daniel stiffened, blinking furiously against the tears threatening to spill from his eyes. He looked at the younger man on the horse beside Cotter, surprised to see him studying the agent with a look of open contempt.

"Who are your people, boy?"

Daniel's gaze returned to Cotter. A faint shift in the agent's tone made him wary. Cotter's anger seemed to have faded; in its place was another expression that sent a ripple of uneasiness coursing through him.

"My people? My da was Owen Kavanagh, sir, but he's dead now. My mother's name is Nora, and I'm called after my granddaddy, Dan Kavanagh."

"And how many more nits at home?"

"Just my brother and me, sir," Daniel replied grudgingly. "My little sister died of the fever."

Cotter rubbed the side of one hand across his stubbled chin. "And you're hungry, is that it? You and your family?"

Daniel gave a curt nod, bitter that the agent would feign ignorance of the widespread starvation in the village.

"Lazy, too, I'll wager," Cotter sniped, leaning forward still more.

Daniel was struck by a roaring wave of rage, and with it a sudden desperate wish to be a man grown. A big man, as big as Morgan, so he need not stand here and be disgraced by this disgusting, loathsome creature. For the first time in his life he knew the intense, almost debilitating desire to harm another human being.

"But perhaps you're not as lazy as some, after all, eh?" the agent was saying. "At least you had the industry to go in search of food."

Daniel frowned, puzzled as to what Cotter was getting at. "I'm not lazy, sir. I'd work if there were work to be had."

The agent straightened a bit, giving Daniel a long look of appraisal. "You'd welcome a job, would you?"

"Aye, sir," Daniel said uncertainly. "It's not that I haven't tried to find work."

Cotter smiled, but the smile only increased

Daniel's apprehension. Something lay behind the look that he did not understand.

"What's your age, boy?"

"My — I'm thirteen, sir."

"Mmm." Cotter went on studying him carefully. "You're old enough, I suppose. None too strapping, though you're tall for your age. Are you strong enough for hard work, do you think?"

Daniel now began to feel a surge of hope. "Oh, I'm that fit, sir! I could do any work I set my hand to."

Again the agent stroked his chin, and Daniel squirmed inwardly under his keen inspection. He felt as if every inch of his frame was being measured. Even as his hope increased, his stomach knotted. There were stories about the agent, murmured stories and accusations about some terrible, unspeakable aberration in his nature that was only spoken of in whispers . . .

"I suppose there's always work to be found around this place for a boy who is fit," Cotter proclaimed loudly, jarring Daniel out of his uncomfortable thoughts. "How soon could you start?"

He was offering a job! The ground tilted beneath Daniel's feet, and his legs went weak with relief.

Forgetting the rumors, dismissing his feelings of uncertainty, Daniel answered him quickly before the man had time to change his mind. "As soon as you'd want, sir! Today, if you wish."

Cotter slapped the open palm of his hand with the riding crop. "Good enough. I'll give you bed and board and a fair wage."

Bed and board? "I — I wouldn't have to stay here, would I, sir? I can come up in the mornings just as early as you like, and stay late in the evenings, but —"

The agent's eyes narrowed, and his mouth thinned to a tight line. "If you work here, you stay here. I need somebody I can count on, day or night."

Daniel's mind reeled. His mother couldn't do without him, couldn't manage Tahg and Grandfar on her own. But the money — he *must* take the job!

His eyes went to the fair-haired man, who was studying him with an expression that startled Daniel. *Pity.* The man was staring at him with open pity.

Daniel looked away, pretending he hadn't seen. He lifted his chin; he wanted no pity, least of all from an *Englishman*.

"All right, sir. I'll have to go home and tell my mother, but I'll come back whenever you say."

Cotter twisted his mouth to one side, raking Daniel's face with his eyes. "See that you're back before sunset this evening." He raised a hand, pointing a finger warningly. "If you're *not* back when I say, you need not come at all, do you mind? I'll find a boy I can *depend* on."

Daniel nodded, eager now to get away and tell his mother the good news. As soon as Cotter waved him off, he bolted around the side of the house.

He ran all the way down the hill, ignoring the cramps in his stomach and the burning pain in his chest.

Sure, and I do thank you, Lord . . . I can't tell how much it means to know you're looking after us after all . . .

He couldn't wait to see his mother's face, to see relief in her large sad eyes instead of the ever-present fear that lately seemed to grow darker and darker. Perhaps she would be able to smile again. It had been so long since he had seen her do more than force a thin smile for Tahg's sake.

Reaching the bottom of the hill now, he slowed and started down the road toward home. Despite his exhaustion and dizziness, he knew a sense of hope and expectation he had not felt for a long, long time.

Suddenly, in the midst of his relief and excitement, he recalled something he'd overheard Sean O'Malley say to Morgan the night of Timothy's wake:

"Sure, and I'd go to work for the devil himself, Morgan, would it put food in my family's bellies again."

At the time, Daniel had caught his breath

at the man's blasphemy. Now, he could only try to ignore the possibility that he might be about to do what Sean O'Malley had only threatened.

She was coming to. Morgan quickly rose from the chair, bending over her as she attempted to focus her eyes in the dim light from the lantern.

"Nora?" He had covered her with his cloak and now tucked it more snugly under her chin.

A large bruise discolored her left cheekbone, just below the small cut near her eye. Her hair had come loose from its pins, and he moved to smooth it away from her face. She watched him through heavy, dull eyes.

"How do you feel?" he asked her, taking her hand.

She blinked, her eyes still uncomprehending.

"You must have blacked out. I found you on the floor."

She squeezed her eyes shut, then opened them again. "My head . . ."

"Aye, I expect it hurts." Again he stroked her hair back from her forehead, and turned to tug the chair closer to the bed.

Suddenly her eyes widened, and she tried to lift her head from the pillow. "Tahg —"

"Tahg and the old man are both all right," Morgan quickly assured her, putting a hand to her shoulder until she dropped her head weakly back onto the pillow. "You must rest, now. Just lie still."

He sat down, taking her hand between the two of his. "I got worried when nobody came to the door, so I came inside to check on you. You gave me quite a fright, lass." *Frightened him out of his wits was what she did.* "Nora . . . how long since you've eaten?"

She turned her head away.

"Nora?"

Keeping her face turned from him, she gave a small, weak shrug beneath his cloak.

"I've brought food, Nora," he told her. "Enough for several days." When she still made no reply, he went on. "Did you hear me, lass? As soon as Daniel John comes in, we'll have something to eat. Where is he, by the way?"

At last she turned back to him and spoke. "He went looking for food. He's not back yet?"

Morgan shook his head. Guilt lay heavy on his heart. He should never have stayed away so long. The small, forlorn figure beneath his cloak was little more than a ghost of herself. He shuddered involuntarily as a memory of the young Nora flashed across his mind. Gone were the laughing eyes of her youth, the vibrant energy of her nature. The raven tresses that had shone in the summer sun hung lank and graying around her ashen face.

Cheekbones jutted above sunken hollows, and her deep gray eyes were darkly shadowed. He had known a moment of total, blood-chilling panic when he found her slumped on the floor beside the old man's bed, looking for all the world as if the life had left her body.

Well, he would not leave her again. From this time on, for as long as she remained in the village, he would be here, too, to take care of her.

Without thinking, he lifted her hand and brushed his lips across her knuckles. "It will be all right, *ma girsha,*" he murmured. "Everything will be all right, you'll see. But you must continue to fight for a little while longer."

As if she had not heard him, she turned her face to the wall. "I just want it finished," she said woodenly.

He lifted his head, frowning at the defeat he heard in her voice. "No," he said firmly. "You must not allow yourself to think so. You have to fight, Nora."

Slowly, she dragged her gaze back to his face. "Fight?" A low moan of bitterness escaped her. "For *what?*"

He rose from the chair, and, bending over her, pressed his hands into the mattress on either side of her shoulders. "For your sons. For yourself. For *life,* Nora. You must fight for life."

She closed her eyes as if to block out the sight of him, and he was struck anew by the frailty of her fine, delicate features. Dear God, she was so small, so thin and weak!

"Nora — look at me."

Her eyes opened, and he saw the unshed tears. Stabbed by the fear and misery in her eyes, he dropped down beside her and scooped her up his arms. "Cry, lass . . . it's all right to cry . . . cry it out . . ."

She made a small, choked sound and allowed him to press her face against his chest. "I'm so *afraid,* Morgan," she whispered against him. He felt her shoulders sag, then begin to shake. "I know it's wrong . . . I should have more faith. But I'm so frightened all the time. I try not to show it to the others, but I'm . . . terrified, Morgan . . . *I'm terrified* . . ."

The dam of her grief and fear burst then, and Morgan felt a spasm of shudders wrack her fragile body. As he held her, he tried to will some of his own strength into her.

After a long time, she turned in his arms, her face damp, her eyes haunted and glistening. When he saw a look of uncertainty, then embarrassment, steal over her features, he tightened his embrace before she could free herself.

She stared up at him. "I — I'm sorry . . . I can't think what —"

"Shhh, none of that," he said firmly, resisting her effort to slip out of his arms. "Nora, listen to me, now. As soon as the boy comes in, we'll have some supper, and then we'll talk. There's something I need to tell you, and I want Daniel John here when I do."

"What?"

"It will keep," he said, drinking in her face and her hair tumbling free over his arm, cherishing this rare, precious moment of holding her again, if only to comfort her. "We must get some food into you before —"

"Mother?"

They broke apart at the sound of Daniel John's voice, calling out from the kitchen.

Morgan got to his feet. "In here, lad."

The boy's eyes were large with excitement as he came charging into Nora's bedroom. "Mother, wait till you hear my news! I —"

He stopped, his eyes going from Nora to Morgan. "Morgan? What is it? What's wrong?"

"Your mother has had a fall, lad."

Nora extended her hand to the boy, and he hurried to her side to grasp it.

"Are you all right?"

"It's nothing," Nora assured him. "I — I fell, that's all, and Morgan found me. I'm perfectly fine. Now, what's this about your having news?"

Daniel John straightened, still holding her hand. Morgan thought the boy's enthusiasm seemed a bit strained, but there was little doubt as to his eagerness to tell Nora.

"I have a job!" he announced. "A real job."

Nora's hand went to her mouth. "A *job,* Daniel John? But how —"

Smiling at her surprise, the boy nodded eagerly. "Didn't I tell you things would be getting better for us soon?"

"That's grand news indeed, lad," Morgan said carefully, sensing the boy's forced cheerfulness. "And what is this job you have found for yourself?"

Daniel John blinked, hesitating for only an instant. "I'm going to be working for the land agent," he said, not looking at either Morgan or his mother. "I start tonight."

12

Night Voices

Borne on the wheel of night, I lay
And dream'd as it softly sped –
Toward the shadowy hour that spans the way
Whence spirits come, 'tis said:
And my dreams were three –
The first and worst
Was of a land alive, yet cursed,
That burn'd in bonds it couldn't burst –
And thou wert the land, Erie!

THOMAS D'ARCY MCGEE (1825–1868)

Sprawled indolently in a tattered armchair, Cotter smirked at Evan over his tumbler. "You look a mite green, Whittaker. Was our tour of Sir Roger's holdings a bit much for your delicate sensibilities?"

Evan simply shook his head, unwilling to expose what he privately thought of as his "sentimentality" to anyone as coarse and unfeeling as Cotter. His normal reserve was so shaken he did not have the energy to dissemble, so he could only keep silent.

For hours, his head had been hammering

with a fury that threatened to prostrate him — indeed it *had* made him violently nauseous for a time. The hour's rest he'd taken late in the afternoon had done little to ease his misery. At the moment, he was only vaguely aware of the agent's drunken rambling, which had been going on for the better part of the evening. His mind still reeled from the ghastly scenes he had witnessed earlier in the day, and he felt a desperate need to flee the room, knowing he needed both time and solitude to absorb the day's events. No matter how much he might wish to avoid doing so, he had to confront his rioting emotions.

Never in his wildest imaginings could he have conceived the succession of horrors he had encountered in this suffering village. Dante's nine levels of hell seemed little more than a glimpse of the misery of Killala. Within hours, the nightmarish experience had engulfed him, reaching deep into his spirit to pierce some dark, undiscovered depth, touching and altering something vital to his very being. Instinctively, he knew he would never be quite the same man he had been before today.

Across from him, Cotter downed another long pull of whiskey, then nodded to himself. "They're a disgusting bunch, eh? Live like pigs and die like dogs. The esteemed Sir Roger will be well rid of the lot of them, wouldn't you say?"

Evan didn't miss the way the agent slurred his employer's name as if it were an obscenity. He was appalled by this dull, slovenly creature, and could scarcely believe that Roger Gilpin continued to allow him to manage his properties. For his own part, he had all he could do to remain in the same room with the man.

A sudden thought of the comely boy with the soulful blue eyes struck Evan, and he found himself greatly relieved that the youngster had not returned to the agent's house that evening. Watching Cotter when they'd first encountered the boy, Evan had sensed something in the agent's rapacious stare that had both sickened and alarmed him. Only now did he identify the man's glazed, oddly feverish expression as one of undeniable lust.

Most likely the boy's failure to show up accounted for the agent's foul mood. As the evening wore on, Cotter had grown increasingly surly, until now, intoxicated and hostile, he no longer made the slightest attempt to be anything less than offensive.

"To my way of thinking, we can't turn them out fast enough," the agent muttered, seemingly as much to himself as to Evan. "Worthless bunch of savages."

His patience about to snap, Evan fought to keep his voice even. "I-I'm sure," he said, "that when I r-report to Sir Roger the extreme circumstances of his tenants, he will d-do the Christian thing and d-delay all scheduled evictions." Even as he voiced the words, Evan knew he was attempting to convince himself as much as the agent.

"At any rate," he added more firmly, "I shall send a letter to London immediately t-to apprise him of the conditions here."

Cotter uttered a short, ugly laugh and straightened a bit in his chair. "Oh, he knows the conditions here well enough! Why do you think he chose to turn the lot of them out when he did?"

Evan looked at him. "Wh-what, exactly, do you mean?"

Cotter stared at his near-empty glass for a moment, then lifted his eyes to Evan. His smirk plainly said he thought the younger man a fool. "You saw it for yourself, did you not? Those poor devils are in no shape to defend themselves! Why, they're starved to the point of death. They'll not be lifting so much as a hand for their own protection. Sure, and we won't have to *force* them out of their squalid huts — we'll simply let the death cart driver *drag* them out! Oh, yes," he said, grunting out a sound that might have been amusement, "old Gilpin knows what he's doing well enough."

Evan could feel the sour taste of revulsion bubbling up in his throat, and he had all he could do not to choke on his own words. "Nevertheless, Sir Roger has not seen the circumstances of his tenants for himself. I shall spare no details of their plight."

Cotter fastened a bleary-eyed, contemptuous stare on him, all the while rooting inside his ear with his little finger. "How long have you worked for Gilpin, Whittaker? Ten years or more by now, I shouldn't wonder."

"Eleven," Evan replied coldly.

The wide gap between the agent's upper front teeth seemed to divide his mouth in half each time he flashed his insolent grin. "Well, then, you can't possibly believe for a shake that the old goat has so much as a hair of charity in his soul. You needn't defend him to *me,* man. Haven't I been working for either him or his black-hearted father for nigh on twenty years by now? I know full well what a devil he is."

Evan rose from his chair, disturbed as much by his uneasy awareness of the truth in Cotter's remarks as by the agent's crude disrespect. "Mr. Cotter," he said stiffly, placing his empty teacup on the scarred table beside the chair, "I hardly think it p-proper to discuss our employer in this fashion. Besides, I find myself quite exhausted, and I still have to write to Sir Roger. If you don't mind, I'll retire to my room now."

The agent's only response was a distracted smirk and a drunken wave of the empty tumbler in his hand.

Steeling himself not to run, Evan held his

breath as he crossed the dimly lighted room. So unsteady did he feel, so furiously was his stomach pitching, he feared taking a deep breath lest he disgrace himself by losing his dinner in full view of the leering agent.

The initial shock of Daniel John's announcement about Cotter's job offer had finally waned, although the boy's frustration was still evident. It had taken an hour or more of argument among the three of them, no lack of pleading on Nora's part, and, finally, a few stern words from Morgan, but eventually they'd managed to talk without shouting at one another.

The bedroom was swathed in deep shadows, lighted by only one squat candle. Nora sat ashen-faced on the edge of the sagging bed, watching her son, wringing her hands worriedly. Daniel John stood as fixed as a rock in the middle of the room, his fists tightly clenched, his eyes sullen.

Morgan's own emotions were scarcely less turbulent. Upon learning of Cotter's attempt to lure the lad into his employ, a fresh surge of hatred for the degenerate land agent had roared through him. Even now, his temper was still stretched tight as an archer's bow.

"*Whatever* possessed you to go to the hill in the first place?" He hurled the question at the boy more sharply than he'd intended, immediately aware that his anxiety was making him unreasonable.

From his rigid stance in the middle of the room, Daniel John met Morgan's eyes without flinching. "Hunger," he said evenly. "I only went as a last resort. I had looked everywhere else I knew for food, and found none. The big house seemed the only possibility left."

"And Cotter came upon you by surprise."

The boy nodded.

"And offered you a job."

"He did."

"Which you accepted without conferring with your mother first," Morgan said, making no attempt to soften the rebuke in his tone.

Daniel John lifted his chin. "I thought my having a job would please her." He paused, then added defensively, "At the least, I thought it might save us."

"Oh, Daniel John, I still can't believe you did such a foolish thing!" Nora exclaimed, pushing herself up off the bed and making an effort to stand. "To resort to *stealing?* You know that is wrong; it is *sin!* And to think that you might have been shot!"

"And is it less sin to watch my family starve while that pig on the hill wallows in his greed?"

The boy's quiet retort made Nora pale. Seeing her sway, Morgan grabbed her.

"Nora! Here, sit down; you're entirely too weak to be up yet." Carefully, he helped her onto the chair beside the bed before turning back to Daniel John.

"Your mother has told you that you must not take Cotter's job, lad, and she is right. You have heard the stories about the agent, have you not?" When the boy made no reply, Morgan pressed. "Well?"

"I — rumors, is all," Daniel John muttered, looking away.

"No, and they are not *rumors!*" Morgan closed the distance between them to snatch the boy roughly by the shoulders. "There is all too much truth to the tales, and you'd do well to mind what you have heard. Cotter is a sick, depraved man — don't be thinking you're a match for the likes of him!"

Daniel John surprised him by twisting free. "I can take care of myself!" he burst out. "And I still say it's foolish to turn down such a job when we're starving to death!"

For an instant Morgan's own temper flared, but just as quickly he banked it. "Now, you listen to me, lad. The subject is no longer up for discussion — your mother has said you're not to go back on the hill, and that is that. If you need any further explanation as to why Cotter was so eager to get you under his roof, the two of us will go outside and I'll explain it to you more clearly. But for now I want your word that you will obey your mother."

He winced at the desperation in the boy's eyes. No longer a child, yet not quite a man, the lad looked like a young animal caught in a trap. Morgan could almost feel the conflict raging within Daniel John.

The boy stared at him another moment, then turned to Nora. "And what are we to do, then, Mother? What choice do we have?" His voice sounded thin and childlike, and Morgan yearned to pull the boy into his arms and somehow shelter him from all the ugliness hovering just outside the cottage walls.

His mind went to the letter he had written Michael. With every day that passed, his impatience grew. He had been so sure that this time when he returned to Killala, he would come with a letter in hand. The ship was to be in the bay in a matter of days; he must broach the subject of emigration to Nora before much longer, or it would be too late entirely.

He cast a look at Daniel John. Even as lean and coltish as he was, with his long arms and legs, and his shoulders crowding the seams of his shirt, there was no denying that he was growing into a winsome, grand-looking lad. God only knew what that demented animal Cotter might yet try to get the boy into his clutches. He would not be stopped by one failed attempt. Not Cotter. He had tried once, and he would try again, perhaps something more devious or even dangerous next time.

His eyes went to Nora. Dear Lord, she was so terribly weak, so frail! Just to look at her and see the way she had failed made him heartsore. No wonder the boy had been driven by desperation.

Daniel John's question, asked for the second time, roused Morgan from his grim musings. "Mother? What choice do we have? What can we do?"

When Nora did not answer, Morgan made his decision. Clenching his fists, he looked first at the boy, then to Nora. "You can leave Ireland," he said at last, making no attempt to gentle his words. "There is that choice, and it would seem the time has come for the both of you to give it serious consideration."

Daniel John's eyes grew large with surprise, and Nora gasped aloud. Deliberately avoiding their gaze for the moment, Morgan turned and walked toward the blanket-draped opening of the room. Keeping his back to them both, he stopped just short of the threshold. "Daniel John, I want you to come help me with the meal while your mother rests. We will have something to eat, and then we will talk."

Saying no more, he turned, feeling their astonished eyes on his back.

The night's rest for which Evan so desperately longed refused to come. He lay on his back, as rigid as a paralyzed man, his eyes frozen on the ceiling in the darkness. Only in the vaguest sense was he aware of the musty dampness of the room, the faint clinking of glass downstairs where Cotter, he assumed, still sat drinking.

After a time he felt himself falling into a gray, trance-like state between wakefulness and sleep; he seemed to dream, yet remained dimly aware of his surroundings. Against his will, he again found himself walking the streets of Killala, streets lined on either side by the frozen dead. Once more he saw himself surrounded by entire families of corpses. Parents and grandparents, young children and infants lay heaped like worthless rubbish in ditches along the road — skeletons clad only in thin rags, many entirely naked.

A silent scream froze in his throat as some unseen, determined force urged him back inside the same dark, cold cabin he had visited earlier that day. Once more he was made to breathe the fetid stench of fever and death. There, in the same corner, lay the emaciated corpse of a small child; beside it, the wild-eyed, filthy mother, totally devoid of her senses, crouched on the floor, weeping and shrieking some unintelligible plea. The gaunt, mute man who might have been either young or old was still hunched close to his wife, watching her with blank, unfeeling eyes.

Outside, sprawled on the road, were the leavings of a dog's carcass, its near-frozen remains being consumed by a woman and three small children. Off to one side a voiceless procession of half-dead townsmen trudged by, seemingly blind, or at least indifferent, to the gruesome scene.

Against his dream-drugged will Evan continued to travel through the hideous labyrinth of the day. Staring in numb helplessness, he watched a young mother, obviously half-starved and ill with fever herself, drag the lifeless body of her little girl outside their cottage and leave it, partially covered with rocks and straw, in the open yard. Starting back to the door, she stumbled and fell, then lay unmoving only feet away from the improvised grave of her dead child.

Cotter appeared at his side — only this Cotter seemed more demon than man. With a gaping black hole where his mouth should have been and the yellow, soulless eyes of some other-world fiend, he grinned and gestured that Evan should come along with him.

Evan's stomach heaved, and he tried to pull free of Cotter's claw-like hand on his arm, but the creature urged him across the road to a hovel, familiar in its wretchedness. A neglected one-room cabin with a dunghill at the door and a sloppy mud floor inside, it looked to be abandoned. Its only furnishings consisted of a dilapidated bedstead with some straw and a tattered blanket tossed across it, an empty iron cooking pot, and two rickety wooden boxes. Five cadaverous children clad only in paper huddled near the crumbling hearth, while the father, ragged and barefooted, lay in a stupor on the bed. The dead mother had been left to herself on a soiled pallet near the cold fireplace.

Cotter pushed him outside, cackling. *"What did I tell you, eh? They live like pigs and die like dogs!"*

Back on the wet, ice-glazed road their horses were forced to halt and wait while a death cart passed by. It was filled with corpses tied in sacks, heaped on top of one another in random piles.

"Nowadays they mostly tie them up in sacks or sheets and dump them into the pits as is," Cotter explained in a voice that echoed with indifference. *"Else they use a false bottom casket, so's they can dump one corpse out before going for another. We've long since run out of coffins, you know."*

The children terrified Evan most. Not the weak, helpless children he had encountered throughout the day; these were nightmare children, vengeful, malicious sprites who clawed at his face and dug at his eyes until he thought he would surely die from the horror. As if performing some dark, macabre dance, they spiraled through the chambers of his mind, fleshless wraiths not quite alive and yet not dead.

He recognized them for what they were:

obscene, horribly mutated effigies of those innocents he had observed earlier in the day. But those children had neither cried nor spoken; indeed, they had made no sound at all, but simply stared in vacant despair and utter helplessness, as if biding their time until the death carts would stop for them. With their partially bald scalps, cavernous eyes, and deep facial lines, they had appeared to be wearing death masks. Even more terrible was the peculiar growth of soft, downy hair sprouting from their chins and cheeks, giving them the chilling look of ancient little monkeys.

Caught in the midst of the nightmare children twisting and writhing all around him, Evan felt himself hurled from one to the other as he was swept faster and faster into the depths of their tormented frenzy. He tried to cry out, but his throat seemed paralyzed by terror. Panicked, he turned to Cotter for help. But Cotter was gone, absorbed by the churning darkness just outside the ring of children.

Small hands grabbed for Evan, stuck to his skin, covered his mouth and stole his breath. They were chanting something in voiceless whispers . . . taunting him, threatening him, warning him . . .

"God, help me!"

Evan shot bolt upright in bed, terror-stricken by the sound of his own strangled cry. For a long time he couldn't move, could scarcely breathe. Huddled beneath the blankets, chilled by his own clammy skin, he trembled so violently that he shook the entire bed. He was wide awake, but unable to see anything in the thick, damp darkness of the bedroom.

Yet even now he could not escape the children. In the black silence of the night, their sunken, horror-filled eyes continued to accuse him as they took up the chant of Cotter's complaint:

"We've long since run out of coffins, you know . . . We've long since run out of coffins."

13

A Starless Night

Was sorrow ever like to our sorrow?
Oh, God above!
Will our night never change into a morrow
Of joy and love?

LADY WILDE [SPERANZA] (1820–1896)

Nora's cottage was hushed, the silence in the kitchen thick and strained.

It had been over two hours since they shared the meal. The candle on the table had burned nearly to the bottom, but there was still a dim light from the fire Morgan had built out of a half-rotted log and some old copies of *The Nation*. The only sound to be heard was an occasional lapping of flames against wood and the low, mournful wailing of the wind outside.

Morgan sat across the table from Nora, watching her stare into the fire. She was still wrapped in his cloak and appeared almost childlike beneath its weight. He was again struck by the alarming pallor of her skin, even dappled as it was by the soft glow of firelight.

She had not met his eyes for what seemed an interminable time, but merely sat, wooden and silent, almost as if she had forgotten his presence.

Moments before, Daniel John had retreated to his room — most likely, Morgan suspected, because he was unwilling to face the possibility of another argument. The heated exchange that had broken out between Morgan and Nora earlier had obviously upset the boy — and it had lasted the better part of an hour before finally being halted by a strangled fit of coughing from Tahg.

Tahg. Morgan could not help but wonder what was keeping the lad alive. He had reached the point in his illness where he would often become extremely agitated, sometimes even incoherent, after a seizure. Morgan had seen it before with lung fever; the afflicted would panic and begin to thrash about with a kind of savage energy before collapsing once again into a stupor. This time it had taken both him and Daniel John to hold the boy down while Nora worked to cool his skin with wet cloths.

Mercifully, he slept now; Morgan hoped that Daniel John might, too, although he thought it unlikely. What with the events of the day and the commotion of the evening, he feared the boy would find little peace this night.

This was not the way he had wanted it, not at all the way he had planned for it to be. He had hoped that his first mention of emigration would come only after a comfortable length of time spent in preparing Nora and her family to face the truth: that leaving Ireland was their only choice if they were to live.

Had there only been more time, perhaps he might have talked them around to the idea with some degree of calm and common sense. As it was, however, he had more or less been forced to hurl the suggestion at them with no warning at all. Their reactions had been predictably stormy.

At first Daniel John had responded with little more than bewildered amazement, saying nothing. Later, though, Morgan realized the lad's aloofness had only been the precursor to a kind of dazed confusion. Even when the boy left the room and ascended the ladder to his bed in the loft, his stiff movements and glazed stare were unmistakably the mannerisms of one who has been badly stunned.

Nora, however, had been far more vocal, exhibiting a feverish kind of anger, protesting every point Morgan attempted to raise with a vigor he would not have expected, given her frailty. Finally, unwilling to risk her collapsing again, he deliberately broke off the conversation, urging her to at least consider the possibility he had raised.

He had left the cottage then, on the pretense of foraging for more wood. When he returned, he found her as she was now, silent and unyielding. At first he assumed her withdrawal to be the result of anger with him and his "daft ideas." He had taken his time poking up the fire, then looking in on Tahg and the old man — both were sleeping — before finally coming to draw up a chair opposite her. Only after several moments had passed, moments during which neither of them spoke, did he see her lips moving faintly and realize that she was praying.

He took this to be a good sign. If she was praying, then she must also be thinking. Could he dare to hope that the Lord might be his ally in all this? Certainly he had thought to do his own praying about things, but given the sin-stained condition of his soul, why should he think any prayer of his would reach heaven?

Now, as he watched the firelight play over her face, memories of the young girl she had been filled his thoughts unexpectedly. Without warning, a crest of longing rose deep inside him, a wave of remembrance of lost joy so powerful and poignant he nearly moaned aloud. He *did* turn his face away so that he could no longer see the gentle curve of her cheek, the graceful line of her throat, and the softly pursed lips moving ever so faintly in petition.

Oh, Lord, I must not let her see . . . even suspect . . . the burden of love I still carry for her. There are times I ache to tell her the truth, to gather her into my arms and plead with her to love me again as she once did, to be mine for whatever time we might be able to steal together. Oh, God, for once help me turn a deaf ear to my own selfish desires and make me mindful instead of Nora's good . . .

Aware that she had been praying — or at least making a numb attempt at it — Nora felt a sudden rush of guilt when she realized that she could scarcely recall her words. How long, she wondered, had she been sitting here, mouthing vain repetitions and meaningless pleas?

Forgive me, Lord. I cannot think . . . I simply cannot think . . .

She glanced over at Morgan, who sat staring into the dying fire as if oblivious to his surroundings. Something about his profile caused Nora to scrutinize him. Was it the uncharacteristic sag to his heavy shoulders, a slackness to his face she had not noticed there before? Surprised, she saw that there was an unkempt look about his appearance, and that in itself was enough to make her inspect him all the more closely. Careless as he might be about the company he kept or the manner in which he spent his days, Morgan had never been untidy or neglectful of his person. Tonight, however, an air of resignation seemed to hang about him. His always-unruly curly hair was messed — was that why she had not noticed until now the thick brushing of silver at his temples? Even his clothing looked rumpled and worn — and so did Morgan. Faint webs fanned out from the corners of his eyes, deep grooves bracketed his mouth, and his usually bronzed complexion had grayed with the distinct shading of fatigue.

An unexpected, irrational stirring of sadness rose in Nora at the realization that, like herself, Morgan was growing older. Just as quickly she chided herself for her foolishness. She and Morgan were the same age, after all — neither of them chicks any longer after thirty-three years. Besides, considering the dissipated life some said the man had led, he actually looked quite fit.

As if sensing her appraisal, Morgan turned, smiling at her. Inexplicably, Nora felt a sharp stab of pain at the tenderness reflected in that smile.

"Tell me, *ma girsha,*" he said, "how is it that I've become an old dog while you've remained but a pup?"

Nora caught her breath at the way he seemed to have read her thoughts. " 'Tis not a dog you've turned into, or so I've heard," she stammered, "but a wolf. A *red* wolf," she added pointedly.

When he did not reply, she continued to

challenge him. "Did you think you would not be found out? Who else could it be? 'Tis said that the leader of this mountain gang of bandits is a 'huge tower of a man with wild red hair and an even wilder red stallion.' Connacht's own *Robin Hood,* they call him."

Morgan lifted a questioning eyebrow, saying nothing.

"Oh, I know about England's outlaw-hero well enough!" Nora snapped, irritated that he seemed bent on ignoring her accusation. "Was it not your father himself who taught me, at the school?" Her mouth thinned with indictment. "Daniel John knows, too. And aren't you setting a fine example for him and the other children in the village, leading them to believe that it's righteous to steal so long as it's for a good purpose? Sure, and haven't we seen the results this very day of such thinking?"

"Who else knows?"

"And is that all you will say for yourself, then — *who else knows?*"

"In the village. Who else in the village knows?" he repeated impatiently.

"There is talk. Did you think there would not be?"

He made a scornful, dismissing gesture with his hand. "There is always talk. I can't recall you being one for village gossip, Nora."

"And is that all it is, then? Village gossip?"

A shrug was his only reply.

A chill went over Nora, and she drew a shuddering breath. Until now she had only suspected the truth. In spite of believing him to be capable of the thievery and rebellion attributed to the notorious outlaw, a part of her had managed to resist the idea. Perhaps a foolish, lingering fidelity to their childhood friendship and young love had made her want to keep his memory unsullied. But the steady green gaze he leveled on her forced Nora to acknowledge what she had tried to deny for so long: Morgan Fitzgerald was indeed *an mhac tire rua*. The *Red Wolf*.

A sudden torrent of anger surged through her, and she leaned toward him. "*Why*, Morgan? How did you come to such a thing? You with your fine education, your brilliant mind, your poetry and songs — how could you throw it all away as if it had no meaning and turn into a — a common *outlaw?* Is it the political business, then . . . this Young Ireland movement? Is it that?"

Morgan drew in a long breath, expelling it slowly. Shaking his head, he answered, "No. Oh, most of the lads are of the movement, I suppose, but the movement has no part in this business. That is one thing, this is another. No," he went on in a weary voice, rubbing the back of his neck with one hand, "this is about hunger. And survival. The survival of our families — our villages."

Nora stared at him with dismay, awareness

gradually dawning. "That is where the food comes from," she said, watching him. "The supplies you bring into the village — to *us* — the medicine for Tahg, the money you said would pay our passage to America —" Appalled, she stopped. "Oh, you foolish, foolish man!" she cried. "Don't you realize the destruction you are bringing down upon your head? They will *hang* you! Don't you care at all?"

Morgan's gaze never wavered as he reached for her. Feeling the warm, unyielding strength of his large, calloused hands closing over her own, Nora stiffened and tried to draw back. But Morgan held her firmly, leaning across the table, thrusting his face close to hers, so close she felt herself trapped by his eyes. "Do *you* care, *asthore?*"

My treasure. The old endearment from their youth brought scalding tears to Nora's eyes.

"Do you care, Nora?" he repeated softly, bringing her hand to his face and laying her palm against his bearded cheek.

Panic seized Nora at his touch, the unexpected softness of his beard against her hand.

"Well, of course, I care," she said, averting her gaze from his. "I would hardly want to see any man on the gallows."

"Even a fool like me?" he prompted, a tender touch of amusement in his voice.

"Indeed." She could not look at him.

"Nora?"

Unable to stop herself, she met his eyes, and the enveloping warmth she encountered there — an entire tide of feeling — was achingly familiar. Familiar, and somehow frightening.

Nora's mouth went dry, her heart rocked, and for one mad moment no years of pain stood between them. She was a girl again, and Morgan her hero-lad. Startled, she squeezed her eyes shut to close him out. But when she opened them again she found him staring at her with a searching look that seemed to hold a myriad of questions. And in that brief, suspended breath in time, a knowing passed between them, an awareness that long-ago hopes had languished, but not died, that young love had paled, but not entirely fled.

And then it was gone.

He released her hands and rose from the chair. "I should go now," he said roughly. "But will you promise me to think, Nora — really think — about what I have suggested to you this night? You must be the one to make the decision; you are still the mother, and responsible for the safety of your family."

When Nora would have interrupted his admonition, he lifted a hand to stop her. "Remember, now, you need not worry about funds to pay your passage. As I told you, a number of passages are already paid, and a ship is on the way." He hesitated, and for just an instant Nora caught a sense that he wanted to say more — indeed, was withholding something from her.

But his gaze quickly cleared, and he said firmly, "I will help you get Tahg and the old man . . . if he's still living . . . to the pier. And I'll see to your food supplies as well, getting them boxed and loaded onto the ship. The only thing that will be left for you to do is to pack the few personal things you may have need of."

He looked away, then started for the door. Without warning, Nora was struck by the suspicion that Morgan was not so much concerned for their welfare as he was desperately eager to be rid of them. He had clearly gone to a great deal of trouble to make sure they would have no excuse for *not* leaving.

Why hadn't she realized before now that they had become a burden to him? Of *course,* he would be anxious to see them out of Killala! For some unfathomable reason — a stroke of uncharacteristic Christian conscience, she supposed — he had assumed a kind of guardianship for her and her family. Clearly, he now had second thoughts, could scarcely wait to pack the lot of them off to America.

A sharp thrust of disillusionment tore at her heart. "How very neatly you have arranged my life for me, Morgan! I don't suppose it even once occurred to you that you might be assuming too much!"

Her voice trembled with humiliation and anger as she continued to rail at him. "I can't think what possessed you to feel responsible for me and my sons, but I can assure you it's entirely unnecessary. Whether we do or we don't choose to leave Ireland is none of your concern, you see. We will manage, and you're not to fret yourself about us another moment."

Morgan had nearly reached the door, but now he whipped around to face her, his eyes flashing a warning. Closing the distance between them in two broad steps, he hauled her up from the chair, his large hands completely engulfing her shoulders. "You can be the most *infuriating* woman!"

When Nora made no reply but simply stared up at him, he scowled and uttered a groan of frustration. "Can you not get it through that stubborn head that I'm only trying to help you?"

In truth, Nora seemed unable to do anything more than gape at him, wide-eyed. His immense frame filled the room, his burning eyes seared her skin, and for one wild instant she thought he might shake her soundly. But after another long moment his hands went limp and the fire in his eyes died away. Releasing her, he turned and, without another word, stalked out of the cottage.

Staring after him, Nora drew in a ragged breath. She glanced down, vaguely aware that she was still wrapped in his cloak. She started to call out to him but stopped, knowing he wouldn't hear. Numbly, she lifted the corner of the rough, heavy frieze of his cloak and brought it to her face. The scent of winter, woodsmoke, and the vast outdoors flooded her senses; hunched over in weakness and regret, she moaned aloud.

"*Mother?* Mother, are you all right?" Daniel John's alarmed voice behind her made Nora straighten and turn.

He came to her at once. He was in his nightclothes, and Nora knew from the pinched look of concern and anguish on his face that he had heard at least a part of the argument between her and Morgan.

"I'm fine, son," she said in an unsteady voice. "But why are you not sleeping?"

He shook his head. "There's too much to think about."

Nora studied his young face, lined too soon with the cares and burdens life had thrust upon him. Putting a hand to his arm, she said gently, "Still, you must rest, Daniel John."

"Mother . . ."

Nora waited, taken aback, as she often was lately, by the change in her youngest son: his soaring height, his spreading shoulders, the sharpening angles and planes of his long, handsome face, so like his father's. He was only thirteen — almost fourteen, she reminded herself — but soon the last trace of boyhood would be gone, exchanged for the mantle of a man.

So quickly gone, that wondrous time of childhood, when worries were the responsibility of grown-ups, when dreams seemed more real than life itself, and almost as precious. Would Daniel John ever find time for his own dreams? Or was he simply to make the leap from child to man with nothing to bridge the distance? Indeed, she sometimes wondered if her son had *ever* been a child. Always, he had seemed older — stronger, wiser, more mature than many of the other children. Had she made him this way with her ever-increasing dependence on him?

"Mother, can we talk?" His tone held an urgency that pulled Nora back to their surroundings.

"I thought . . . now that Morgan is gone . . . we could discuss what he — what he suggested."

She looked at him. "About leaving Ireland?"

He nodded.

" 'Tis late, Daniel John," Nora reminded him feebly, knowing herself to be too weak, too exhausted and . . . wounded to handle anything further this night.

He peered into her face. "Yes," he said finally. "All right, then. I don't want to tire you. But will you just answer me one thing, Mother?"

"Of course, son. If I can."

"Do you — do you think perhaps Morgan might be right? He seems so determined that we leave Ireland. Do you agree with him, that emigration is our only hope of survival? Are things truly that desperate, Mother?"

Unable for the moment to meet his searching eyes, Nora looked down at the floor. She wasn't at all certain exactly *what* she believed. At least for now, she seemed incapable of getting beyond the degrading suspicion that Morgan merely wanted to unburden himself of them in the easiest way possible. Why couldn't he simply have realized from the beginning how vastly unsuited he was for the role of benefactor? It would have been so much better for them all.

She could not stop her anger from spilling over. "Of course not!" she snapped out. "He's only making things sound worse to frighten us into doing what *he* has decided we *should* do!"

Daniel John stood staring at her with an expression that was both puzzled and hurt. "I . . . I don't think Morgan would do that, Mother. He's not like that, not a bit."

Suddenly irritated with the boy's adoration for the man — which Morgan clearly did not deserve — Nora proceeded to tell her son exactly what she thought to be the truth behind his hero's professed concern for their welfare.

14

Choices and Wishes

Day and night we are wrapped in a desperate strife,
Not for national glory, but personal life.

JOHN DE JEAN FRAZER (1809–1852)

Early the next morning, Morgan stopped at Nora's cottage with an axe and a cart, explaining that he was on his way to fell a tree and asking if Daniel John wished to come along.

The two walked and climbed for nearly an hour before stopping halfway up a steep, dense hillside. They stood appraising a medium-sized elm tree and a smaller beech for firewood.

Although it was a cold, damp morning with mist bleeding down the hill, the sky was clear; indeed, it looked as if the sun might actually be about to shine upon Killala for the first time in weeks. Looking down on the village from this far up, its streets veiled by the shimmering mist, Daniel could hardly believe it was teeming with death and disease. The bodies heaped along the road weren't visible from up here, nor were the beggars, those few still able to stumble through the town. But here and there a ragged tunnel of smoke from a torched cottage rose to meet the mist in a grim reminder that the Reaper of Death was still on the prowl in Killala.

And, as always, silence reigned — the terrible, ominous silence, somehow more agonizing than actual cries of human misery. Even here, far above the town, the unnatural silence of the famine seemed to hover. Other than the occasional snap of a twig underfoot or the brushing of branches in the light morning wind, the same awful stillness that permeated the entire village shrouded the hill.

Morgan finally broke the silence. "The beech will do best," he said decisively, slipping out of the cloak he had retrieved only that morning. "We can be done with it faster, and it will burn just as long."

Daniel nodded shortly, not looking at him. Feeling ill at ease in Morgan's company was a new experience for him, and a distressing one. The harsh words spoken in haste the evening before seemed to have raised a wall between them. He had spent a long, restless night trying to sort out an entire parade of troubled feelings, not the least of which was humiliation.

Their argument over Cotter's job offer had

provoked the first sharp words Morgan had ever uttered to him, and the scene had left Daniel feeling ignorant. He resented being scolded like a wee wane. Even if he *had* been foolish in going to the agent's house, he would have expected Morgan to understand the desperation that drove him there, rather than reprimanding him for it.

As for Cotter — certainly Daniel had heard the tales about the land agent. But what Morgan — and his mother as well — seemed bent on ignoring was the fact that Daniel was no longer a child. If he had not thought himself up to handling a weak, dull-witted man like Cotter, he wouldn't have agreed to accept the job in the first place.

Morgan's unexpected rebuke had been bad enough, but even more disturbing had been the abrupt, uncompromising manner in which he had forced upon them the subject of emigration. Obviously, he had upset Mother a great deal; the bitter, scathing things she said after Morgan left the cottage had been painful, painful and impossible to believe.

Her accusation that Morgan wanted only to be rid of them had gone straight to Daniel's heart, piercing like a bandit's knife. When he attempted to protest on Morgan's behalf, she had ignored him. "Morgan is a man after living for himself — and himself alone!" she'd snapped. "And for his precious Ireland, of course! He cares for nothing else and never will. Why, he's even managed to coax Thomas and the children to go along with this daft scheme! Sure, and won't he be as free as a sea bird, once he gets the lot of us onto a ship?"

Despite his own conflicting emotions, Daniel still thought his mother's allegations unfair. Both she and Grandfar had always accused Morgan of being selfish and irresponsible, indifferent to the feelings of others. But Daniel had never seen him in that light. Admittedly, Morgan was a solitary man — perhaps even a bit peculiar, as some in the village insinuated. He was lonely, often melancholy, at times even aloof. But never uncaring — especially with Mother. He had seen the way Morgan sometimes looked at her when he thought nobody was watching . . . as if she were a rare and precious jewel, a treasure to cherish. Daniel could not put a name to the expression that came over Morgan's face, but there was no mistaking the endless depth of caring there.

And yet, if Morgan *truly* cared, would he be so determined to send them away? To emigrate might mean they would never see one another again, after all; Mother said Morgan had no intention whatsoever of leaving Ireland, not now, not ever. If he had any real affection for them, would he be quite so eager to set them on their way to America?

America. The word had once been magic to

Daniel. Often he had dreamed of visiting the liberty-loving young country. Like Morgan, he doubted that any true Irish heart could help but be stirred by the tale of America's struggle for independence from the British.

But how could Morgan think Daniel would want to *stay* there? Didn't he understand that he wasn't the only one who loved Ireland? Wasn't this *his* country as well as Morgan's? Killala, the mountains — the entire island — this was *home*. Everything he'd ever known and loved was here. Did Morgan think he could simply turn his back on it, leave and forget it altogether?

"Daniel John? Are you going to help me?"

Morgan's voice yanked him out of his troubled thoughts. He whipped around and, without thinking, blurted out, "Morgan — I don't want to go! I don't *want* to leave Ireland!"

Clearly taken aback, Morgan stared at him a moment before answering. "Of course you don't want to leave, lad," he finally said, his voice quiet. "You think I do not know that?"

"Then why did you even bring it up? You saw how weak Mother is! All you did was upset her!" Daniel's earlier hurt and confusion parted to make way for a growing wave of doubt. "Is it true, then, what Mother thinks — that you simply want to be rid of us?"

Morgan stood leaning on the axe, his eyes

hooded. "Your mother said that, did she?"

Miserable, already wishing he had held his silence, Daniel turned away without answering.

Behind him, Morgan's voice was soft and oddly uncertain. "And you, Daniel John? Is that what *you* think?"

Daniel John swallowed, feeling torn and bewildered and even a little frightened. "I don't know," he muttered, still keeping his back to Morgan. "I don't suppose I know *what* I think anymore."

And how could he? Morgan thought with despair. *He is but thirteen years old. A boy, not a man. A boy who has lost his father, his little sister — and is now losing his grandfather and older brother as well. And as if that were not enough to crush the spirit out of him, here am I, suggesting that he forsake his home and his country in the bargain. Of course he does not know what to think, except perhaps that his life has become a tale of madness, a cruel and heartless jest.*

"Mother was right, you know." Daniel John finally turned to face him when he spoke. "Even if we were of a mind to leave, it would be impossible. Tahg cannot walk — he scarcely even speaks anymore. And Grandfar —"

Morgan nodded. "Yes, lad, I know," he said, trying to be gentle. "Your granddaddy is dying. And I am sorry, Daniel John, deeply sorry." He paused. "But can you not understand, lad, that it is only because I don't want to see you and your mother die as well that I'm trying to make you face reality — face it and do something about it?"

"You know Mother will never be able to bring herself to leave!" the boy argued, his voice breaking for an instant in his frustration. "Not only because of Grandfar and Tahg." He paused, as if debating as to whether he had the right to say what came next. "Mother . . . Mother would be afraid, Morgan. Why, she'd be terrified, don't you see? She's never been farther than Ballina in her life! Her entire world is here, in Killala."

Again Morgan nodded, unable to dispute the lad's insight about his mother. Yes, of course, Nora would be frightened. Hadn't he known all along that fear might prove to be the one obstacle he could not overcome? Everything else was within the realm of possibility: money for passage, a ship, even the hope of a livelihood once they arrived. But what to do about Nora's fear?

Wasn't that the reason he had counted on Michael's willingness to help? His hope was that having somebody to depend on, somebody *familiar,* once they reached the States would make all the difference for Nora.

Ah, Michael, Michael, why haven't you answered me, man? Have I hoped for too much, after all?

"Morgan?"

The boy seemed to be looking everywhere else but at him. "If . . . if *you* were to go, Mother might not be so frightened. It would make all the difference if you were with us. I don't believe she considers me any protection at all — she still thinks of me as a child, you know."

Stricken, Morgan groped for an answer; it was a question he had not anticipated. Not that he hadn't already thought of the possibility. In the event that Michael did not answer his letter, or if he answered but was unwilling to help, he had considered accompanying Nora and the others across, then returning once they were settled.

But the timing could not be worse. The new Confederation was planning a rising — a plan doomed to failure before it began. How else could it end but in defeat? Their army would be made up mostly of hungry men and starving boys, with any number of wild-eyed fanatics thrown in who had no real conception at all as to what they were fighting for. An army of starving peasants and visionaries was hardly a match for the mighty British Empire.

Despite his conviction that defeat was the only possible outcome for such an undertaking, however, Morgan could not bring himself to turn his back on Smith O'Brien. His friendship with the leader of the Young Ireland movement — and hence the leader, albeit a reluctant one, of the planned rising — made it impossible for Morgan to walk away. Besides — as Smith O'Brien had pointed out to those members like Morgan who tended to be less radical — a few cool heads might help to temper the heat of the rebellion's real fire, the impassioned militant, John Mitchel. This strong-willed son of a Unitarian minister could not be a more dramatic contrast to O'Brien, a reserved, Protestant country gentleman; yet the two had somehow managed to engulf themselves and the entire movement in a gathering storm that could explode into open rebellion at any time.

Because of his friendship with O'Brien, Morgan had promised his pen — and his men — to the Young Ireland movement, and hence the rising. He would not renege. He was committed.

But was he not also committed to the boy who stood across from him, staring at him with entreating eyes? And to the lad's mother?

Nora. *Dear God, don't make me choose between her and Ireland again. I made my choice once, and I have lived with it. But, please, God, not again . . . not again . . .*

Raking a hand through his hair, he looked away, turning his gaze toward the mountains. "Daniel John, please try to understand. I am deeply involved in some things right now that I must see through to the end. I have committed myself to a plan, and to some people, and to leave Ireland at this time would be akin to betrayal."

Unexpectedly, the boy nodded and said, "You're talking about a rising."

Morgan shot him a surprised look. "What do you know of a rising?"

"I've heard Grandfar talking," Daniel John said with a shrug; "him and the other men in the village. And at meeting some weeks ago we were warned about such a possibility. The speaker said we should have no part in it." He stopped, managing a small, bitter smile. "As if anyone in the village has the strength left to take up arms."

He lifted his eyes to Morgan's, his expression sad but knowing. "I'm sorry, Morgan," he said quietly. "I shouldn't have said what I did. I understand why you can't go."

Morgan took a step toward him with the intention of explaining himself still further, but Daniel John shook his head. "No, really, it's all right," he said in a choked voice. "I do understand, at least I think I do, how it is with you . . . how it has always been. It's as if Ireland has absorbed your very spirit, made you a part of her."

Morgan had never loved the lad quite so much as he did at that moment. He thought his heart would surely explode as he laid his hands lightly on the boy's shoulders, saying, "Aye, it is as you say. But do you also understand, lad, that though it is a different kind of love, it is no greater than my feelings for you and your mother?"

Daniel John gave a short, stiff nod, averting his eyes. "Aye, I do know that, Morgan. I have always known."

The ache in Morgan's heart swelled. "Then know this as well, lad: I would never, ever, wish you or your mother separated from me. It crushes me to even think of it. But what I *do* wish is for you to live, Daniel John — to live and have a chance for a good life, a better life than this suffering island can ever offer you."

Daniel John looked up at him, and Morgan saw with dismay that the boy's eyes were filled with tears. Impulsively, he caught him in a brief embrace, then held him away. "You are growing up quickly, lad," he said, still holding him loosely by the shoulders. "And you will grow to be a fine man — a *great* man, I am thinking."

The boy flushed, but Morgan went on. "You have a noble, heroic heart, Daniel John. You will do your mother proud." He stopped, searching for the words to express what he so desperately wanted to say. "There is something I want to tell you, lad, and no matter what may happen in the days and years to come, I pray you will always remember it." He tightened his grip on the boy's shoulders, regarding him with pride and approval. "If I had ever had a son, Daniel John, I would have been pleased had he been a lad like you, exactly like you. Many is the time I have wished you mine."

For a silent moment they stood so, each searching the gaze of the other. Suddenly, Daniel John threw his arms about Morgan's neck and clung to him. "Go with us, Morgan!" he choked out, the words muffled against Morgan's shoulder. *"Please! Go with us!"*

Morgan held him tightly, squeezing his eyes shut against the pain. Obviously, none of this was going to be as simple as he had hoped.

TWO

SONG OF SILENCE

The Waiting

The Lord himself has scattered them;
he no longer watches over them.
The priests are shown no honor,
the elders no favor.
Our eyes failed,
looking in vain for help;
from our towers we watched
for a nation that could not save us.

LAMENTATIONS 4:16, 17 (NIV)

15

Night Watches

For where is Faith, or Purity, or Heaven in us now?
In power alone the times believe – to gold alone they bow.

RICHARD D'ALTON WILLIAMS (1822–1862)

Cotter sat alone in the large, drafty front room, nursing his whiskey along with his rage.

He had spent most of the day fuming about the Kavanagh boy, plotting his revenge on the thieving little rat. He was vaguely aware that night had fallen. The darkness around him was relieved only by the low fire across the room, which had almost burned itself out. A candle had been flickering earlier, but when the draft from the ill-fitting windows snuffed it out, he hadn't bothered to light it again.

He was completely alone in the house, except for Whittaker, who had secreted himself in his room upstairs immediately after supper. Cook had returned to her cottage in the village after the evening meal; and since the latest in a succession of housekeepers had quit only last week, there were no other domestics presently on the grounds.

From time to time Cotter shot a furious glare at the ceiling, angrily willing the milksop Englishman in the room above to feel the heat of his wrath. For the most part, however, he merely sat, sprawled drunkenly in his chair, drinking and cursing. Sometimes aloud, more often to himself, he cursed Daniel Kavanagh, his family, and the useless inhabitants of the village.

As for the boy, that impudent *gorsoon* would pay, he would. He could not imagine what had possessed the young pup, pretending to be so eager for a job, then defying him deliberately. Well, he would rue his insolence, and soon. Tomorrow the foolhardy young buck would find out the hard way that he could not afford to flout George Cotter's authority.

The agent tossed down the rest of his whiskey. Aye, tomorrow young Kavanagh would learn to his misfortune the consequences of rebuffing those in authority. Indeed, many of the disrespectful savages in this squalid village would have themselves a taste of their agent's authority tomorrow.

Mastery was the thing, he concluded with a self-satisfied smirk. Mastery, not mercy. The English dandy upstairs liked to run on about mercy. Well, Whittaker would also be learning soon enough that mercy had no place in this hellhole. Power was the thing that got the job done — *British* power. The power of the British landlord.

He laughed aloud. To these ignorant Irish peasants, what other power was there?

Upstairs, on his knees, his head resting on clasped hands atop the bed, his brow beaded with perspiration, Evan Whittaker pleaded with his Lord.

He pleaded for control over the hot anger coursing through him, an anger fueled by disgust and targeted at Cotter, yet somehow directed at his own homeland at the same time. He found it incomprehensible that one people could devastate another in such a way, with such blatant inhumanity and indifference. The question that had confronted him, nagged at him all day, was how a nation like England, perceived as a nation of greatness and nobility by other lands throughout the world, could simply turn its back on a starving country — a country from which they had drawn huge quantities of grain, produce, cattle, and manufactured goods for years. The accusation that they were allowing the Irish to starve to death was no longer a point of debate; a number of Protestant churchmen throughout both countries had begun to add their outraged protests to those of the Catholic clergy, confirming what had been, up until a few months past, merely rumor and insinuation. Facts were facts, and Evan no longer attempted to deny the truth. But what dumbfounded him most was the arrogant detachment, the glib ease with which they had condemned this suffering island.

Why?

The question had been on his lips for hours, and he still had no answer. But it seemed to him that at the heart of England's unmerciful treatment of the Irish, there had to be something larger than neglect, more significant than bigotry. Or did he only cling to that assumption because he could not bring himself to accept the fact that his own country had condemned an entire people out of greed? Greed and apathy.

And so as he prayed for an ebbing of his anger, as he pleaded for mercy and divine intervention in the lives of the suffering Irish, he prayed for God's mercy upon his own land as well, for England and her hardened heart.

So intent was Evan upon his supplications that the noise below scarcely penetrated his awareness. When it came again, he raised his head to listen.

He heard the sound of breaking glass, then a low, guttural roar, followed by an instant of silence. Evan held his breath, waiting. After another moment came a high-pitched shriek, then an explosion of laughter.

The sound of madness.

Evan shuddered, swallowed against his fear, then squeezed his eyes shut. Clasping his hands even more tightly, he bowed his head and returned to the Quiet, to the secure shelter of his Hiding Place.

The letter from Michael came that night.

Morgan was sitting at the kitchen table, fiddling with a piece of writing by a young medical student in Dublin, a member of the Young Ireland movement named Richard D'Alton Williams. Williams wrote for *The Nation* under the *nom-de-plume*, "Shamrock." He was a talented lad who on more than one occasion had asked Morgan to critique his poems. Tonight, however, he was finding it difficult to concentrate on Williams' work, in spite of its usual excellence.

It was late, past midnight. The children had been in bed for hours. Thomas, his shaggy hair falling over his forehead, sat nodding and dozing by the fire. Earlier he had been reading from the Scriptures; his large hands still held his Bible securely in his lap.

Pushing his pen and paper aside, Morgan rose to go and wake his brother lest he topple from the chair. He was halfway across the room when someone pounded on the door. Morgan jumped, and Thomas awakened with a startled grunt.

As soon as he opened the door and saw the young, sober-faced Colin Ward, he knew that at long last he had his reply from Michael.

A diminutive, wiry lad, Ward wore an eye patch to cover his missing left eye, lost in a brawl on the Dublin docks. At the moment he appeared half-frozen and nearly exhausted. Morgan urged him inside, but the youth refused to sit down and rest.

"No, thank you, sir. I'll take but a moment to warm myself, and then I must be off to Castlebar. I have one more delivery yet tonight."

Reaching into a pouch on a rope tied about his waist, he pulled out a large, thick envelope and handed it to Morgan. "Here you are, sir. All the way from New York City — and safe and dry at that, though it has passed through many hands, I should imagine."

His heart pounding, Morgan reached for the envelope with one hand while squeezing Ward's shoulder with the other. "I cannot thank you enough, lad. I had almost given this up."

Morgan glanced at the hefty envelope, pulling in a sharp breath of anticipation when he saw that it was addressed in Michael's hand. So impatient was he to open the letter he had to make an effort not to be rude to Ward. But he need not have worried, for the lad seemed as eager to be gone as Morgan was to read his letter. After a brief introduction to Thomas and a few observations about O'Connell's failing health and Smith

O'Brien's troubles, Ward started to leave.

Morgan saw him out, then turned to Thomas.

"So it has come," his brother said, watching Morgan with the first spark of interest he had exhibited since Catherine's death.

Morgan nodded. He had told Thomas of the letter to Michael, omitting his proposal regarding Nora. So far as his brother was aware, Morgan had simply contacted his old friend to ask assistance for his family in matters of lodging and employment.

"Go on, then," Thomas said, returning to his chair. "I am as anxious as you to hear his reply."

Standing in the middle of the kitchen, Morgan opened the outside envelope, his hands trembling when he realized it contained two separate letters, each in its own sealed envelope. One was addressed to him, the other to Nora.

Putting aside for now the torrent of emotions surging up inside his chest, he ripped open the letter addressed to him. He read in silence for a moment, his eyes scanning the words quickly but thoroughly.

As he had hoped — hoped and half-feared, he admitted to himself — Michael declared himself willing to do what he could to help Nora and her family, as well as Thomas and his children. Though it was not an overly long letter, it was warm and plainly sincere. The decision, Michael said, had not been his alone, but had been made only after much prayer and lengthy discussion with his son, Tierney.

> We are agreed that Nora should come to us, along with those family members who manage to survive the terrible events you have described. And so I have written a separate letter to Nora, as you so insightfully suggested, to make an honorable proposal of marriage, explaining that I greatly need the companionship of a wife, and that Tierney even more needs the mothering influence and nurture she could provide.
>
> I have tried my best, Morgan, to be entirely sincere and convincing. In truth, I do fervently pray that Nora will come. I am not exaggerating when I say that Tierney and I need her, but in all honesty I might never have come to this realization if you had not written when you did. While I have attempted to build a good life for the both of us, I fear it is often a somewhat lonely life; I know the boy, to say nothing of myself, would benefit greatly from Nora's presence.

Not only was he in full agreement with Morgan's suggestions, Michael went on to say, but he was enclosing some money inside Nora's letter, "just in case additional funds might be needed once her passage is paid."

Bless the man, he had even gone so far as to inquire into employment opportunities for Thomas before writing, saying he thought he might have "something lined up for him by the time they arrive."

As Morgan neared the end of the letter, he was feeling a bit better about things — at least until he came to Michael's closing remarks, which seemed to leap up off the page as if to challenge him.

> It's entirely true, of course, that when we were young, I was that mad for Nora. Yet, although I did ask her to accompany me to America as my wife, I was never fool enough to hope she could care for me in any way other than as a friend. We both know that she never saw me apart from your shadow, and I was never so blind as to be unaware of your love for her as well. That being the case, I must ask you, man: Are you absolutely certain this is how you want things to be?

Ah, no, Michael, this is not the way I want things to be! Were I a different man and this a different time, I would make Nora mine in a shake, if she would have me.

Dragging his gaze back to the letter,

Morgan continued to read.

> Please know, Morgan, that by raising this question I am in no way attempting to renege on anything, but am only trying to be absolutely certain you realize what you are doing. If you are indeed convinced, then know this: If we do this thing, if Nora agrees to come to me and be my wife, then it will be for the duration.
>
> What I mean to say is that, if you bid her goodbye once, you will be saying goodbye forever. For I will commit my heart to her — and what is left of my life — in an attempt to give her whatever happiness is within my power to give. Do not think that if you should have a change of heart at some time in the future I will simply step aside to make way for you, for indeed I will not.

Morgan gave a small, grim smile, for he could not help but remember Michael's tenacity, once he made a decision.

> So consider your feelings well, old friend, for there will be no going back. That done, if your decision still stands, then do your utmost to convince Nora to come to me, and to come quickly. Do not let her delay and die in Ireland. Convince her to come now, before it is too late. And

I thank you, Morgan, for your trust, for I know in my heart that by doing this you are giving up the only thing you have ever truly loved besides that wretched, dying island. . . .

For a long moment, Morgan continued to stare at the pages in his hand, though he knew Thomas was growing impatient. He felt a cold, desolate hole begin to open somewhere deep inside him, and for a moment the image of Nora's wounded, fearful eyes froze in his mind with a pain he thought could not be borne.

At last he lifted his eyes from the letter to meet Thomas's questioning gaze. "You are going," he said quietly. "It is all arranged. Your fares are more than paid for, and Michael has even explored some job possibilities for you. And it would seem —" He faltered, then managed to go on with forced cheerfulness. "It would seem that he intends to ask Nora to marry him when she arrives. Perhaps that is the very thing that will finally convince her to go."

Thomas's eyes on Morgan were grave and searching as he slowly got to his feet. "I'm thinking it should not be Michael Burke asking Nora to be his wife. You have loved that lass since you were a boy."

Shaking his head, Morgan made no attempt to answer. Instead, he deliberately changed the subject. "You can be ready soon, you said."

After another long look, Thomas nodded. "Aye, there's little enough to pack." He paused, again searching Morgan's face. "It's grateful I am to you, brother, for making this possible. You have kept us alive for weeks now, and it would seem that once more you are saving me and my children. I owe you much. But won't you at least give thought to going with us? I know —"

Morgan interrupted as if he had not heard. "I will count on you, Thomas, to be a help to Nora — assuming I can convince her to go."

"She is still resisting, then?"

Morgan uttered a short, dry laugh. "Adamantly. I am hoping Michael's letter will help to bring her around."

"You said the other night when we first talked that things were set, with the ship."

"Aye. It should be in the bay anytime now. Possibly as soon as the end of this week."

Thomas said nothing more for a moment, but Morgan could see that he was troubled. "What is it, then? You're not having a change of heart?"

Thomas shook his head. "No, none of that. But I cannot help thinking of that coffin ship that sailed from the bay last year," he said, raking a hand down one side of his beard-stubbled face. "I'm not worried for myself, you understand. It's the children."

The *Elizabeth and Sarah* to which Thomas referred had sailed from the bay the past summer only to lose forty-two of her passengers to death during the voyage. Morgan had learned from one of the Young Ireland men in Quebec that the ship had actually broken down and had to be towed the rest of the way into the St. Lawrence.

"That ship was greatly overloaded with passengers and understocked with provisions," Morgan reminded Thomas. "You will be going on a much finer ship — an American vessel. They're far better constructed and more ably commanded, in addition to being much faster than the British vessels. My men arranged this especially for my family, Thomas; they promised to do their best to secure a safe, fast ship. I understand your concern, but —"

Thomas put up a hand to stop him. "I'd not be much of a father if I did not fear for my children's safety. But risking their lives on a voyage across the Atlantic still appears to be a far safer venture than keeping them here to die in Killala."

Morgan was relieved at his brother's good sense. If only he could convince Nora to see things the same way. "I will go to Nora first thing tomorrow morning," he said, carefully folding the pages of Michael's letter and tucking it back inside the envelope. "You will get the children ready as quickly as possible?"

"Aye, they will think it's a great adventure, no doubt." Thomas's expression darkened. "Perhaps it will even help to ease their grieving for their mother."

With a distracted nod, Morgan lay the envelope on the table. He was weary, almost aching with fatigue and a somber sense of impending loss. Yet he knew he would manage little sleep this night.

"You should get some rest, brother," Thomas said, his own eyes red-rimmed and heavy. "It is late."

"You go on. I want to work a bit longer on Williams' poem."

After Thomas left the room, Morgan continued to stare at the envelope on the table for a long time. Finally, he sighed, and, cupping the candle's flame with the palm of his hand, snuffed it out.

Still he could not bring himself to move, but merely stood like a cold marble statue in the darkness of his brother's cabin.

The breaking of his heart was now complete.

16

So Many Partings

Famine and plague, what havoc have ye made?
And was it thus that stalwart men should die?

JEREMIAH O'RYAN (1770–1855)

Old Dan drew his last breath early the next morning.

An icy rain had returned during the night, and even now, long past dawn, its gray chill seemed to drape the entire cottage in gloom. Sensing that the old man's death was imminent, Nora had sat by his bed most of the night. When at last she heard the death rattles in his throat, she rose and went to call Daniel John in from the kitchen.

"You will want to say your goodbyes to your grandfather now, son," she told him gently. "He will soon be gone."

With anguish in his eyes, the boy parted the curtain and entered the alcove. Nora followed, waiting at the foot of the bed as Daniel John slipped in between Tahg and the old man. Tahg was awake — one of his increasingly rare lucid times — and lay watching as his brother took their grandfather by the hand.

"Can he hear me, do you think?" Daniel John asked, not taking his gaze from the unconscious old man.

"Only God knows," Nora answered. Tortured by her son's grief, she put a hand to her throat, swollen painfully with unshed tears.

In the silent shadows of the alcove, Tahg suddenly reached out a thin, white hand to his brother, who turned to look at him. "I'm sure he hears," Tahg said in a strained whisper. "Tell him for me, too, Danny. I can't —" He broke off when a fit of coughing stole his breath.

Daniel John's eyes filled as he stared at his older brother for a long moment. Finally, he nodded and turned back to Old Dan, then began speaking in the Irish.

The ache in Nora's heart grew fierce as she listened to her son's last farewell to his grandfather. He thanked him for the countless sacrifices he had made for the family, acknowledging the noble memory, the legacy of love and goodness and integrity Old Dan would be leaving behind.

"I will do my best . . . to be true to your name, Grandfar . . . to bring honor to you. I will remember for all my life that the name of Daniel Kavanagh is one to wear with pride."

Nora sobbed aloud as the boy bent to kiss

the old man's sunken cheek. She had said her own goodbyes earlier that morning, but God help her, it was still hard to let him go. Dan Kavanagh had been the only father she had ever known, and in truth he had treated her as his own flesh and blood. She could not imagine this cottage, which he had built with his own two hands — or, for that matter, life itself — without him.

For the next hour, the three of them kept their vigil, praying together, then mourning together when it was finally over. Both boys cried, and Nora felt it was a tribute to their da that they were able to do so. Owen had raised both his sons to be strong in heart and tender in spirit. He had been a fine father, Owen had, as fine a father as a husband, and she missed him deeply, especially at times like these.

Before she realized what she was doing, she found herself wishing that Morgan would come. Just as quickly, she despised herself for her own weakness, for she knew it was his *strength* for which she longed, not merely his presence.

She was so tired, so utterly exhausted. The very thought of having to deal with yet another death overwhelmed her to the point of desperation. But deal with it she must, and right away, especially with Tahg so ill; he must not have to lie there, in a bed alongside his dead grandfather, for any length of time.

Obviously, she could not send for Morgan. After their words two nights past, she was certain he was as bent on avoiding her as she him. He had been noticeably ill at ease the day before, when he'd stopped by the cottage for Daniel John. No, Morgan would not be coming round again soon — if ever.

On the heels of this thought came a fierce longing for Catherine Fitzgerald. Nora herself had never laid out a body. Catherine had tended to the pitiful wee babe who had been stillborn, between Tahg and Daniel John. When Owen died, Catherine laid him out, and she had been there again for Ellie. But now Catherine was gone, and this time Nora was on her own. She would not ask Daniel John to help; she simply couldn't. The boy was still only thirteen, not yet a man grown. And this was his grandfather, after all — he should not have to do what it was *her* place to do.

What she *would* do, however, was to send him for Thomas Fitzgerald. Thomas had promised that when the time came he would make a coffin for Old Dan. It would be a simple one, of course, for they had only some scrap wood and part of an old table she had saved with this day in mind. But at least the old man would not be dropped into the ground from one of those awful hinged "trap coffins" used by the death-cart drivers. Dan Kavanagh had been a man of great pride and dignity before the Hunger had stripped most of it away, and Nora was immensely grateful to Thomas for offering to spare her father-in-law the final humiliation of a pauper's grave.

There would be no wake, of course, and this distressed her. The old dear should have had a proper mourning. For years Dan Kavanagh had been treated to the respect and confidence of the entire village. Why, he was one of the very oldest residents, he was. In the old days, he would have been a tribal chieftain. His ancestors dated back to the time of Cromwell's invasion, when the young Eoin Caomhanach — John Kavanagh — had fled across the island to Connacht rather than risk exile to Barbados.

Still, there would be no wake. The few villagers who might yet possess the strength to make their way to the cottage had all they could do to see to their own families. Besides, with the fever now on the rage throughout the district, few were willing to risk public gatherings, even to show respect for the dead.

There was nothing to do but lay out the old man in private and see to it that he at least had a proper burial. *Thank God for friends like Thomas,* she thought with a deep sigh. She would send Daniel John for him right away.

Morgan dumped an armload of wood next to the fireplace, then went to the table to drain the last of his tea. Replacing his empty cup, he picked up the envelope containing the letters and, after giving it a long look, tucked it securely inside the pouch tied at his waist.

This morning he would deliver Michael's letter to Nora. It must be done now, before his foolish feelings allowed him to delay any longer. He had spent most of the night at odds with himself, sleeping hardly at all as he mulled over and over again what lay ahead. By dawn he had almost managed to convince himself to simply keep quiet about the letter. He would take Nora and the others across, to the States, and once they arrived he would —

He would do *what?* The lack of an answer to that question ultimately forced him to face the utter absurdity of his plan. Unless he were willing to stay in America and build a life together with Nora — and why would he even imagine she would have him? — then there was no conceivable reason to go with her.

He squatted down to punch up the fire, putting aside his foolish thoughts. Thomas was going, and Michael was waiting; Nora would be perfectly fine. The best thing for her — indeed the *only* thing, if she was to find the happiness she so deserved — was for her to marry Michael Burke. He was a grand lad, a veritable rock of a man: sober, hard-working, ambitious, a man of unimpeachable integrity. And hadn't he already committed himself to Nora's happiness? He would give her a new life, a good life in America. In addition, he could provide Daniel John opportunities the likes of which the boy would never see here in Ireland.

He would take the letter to Nora this morning. Then the only thing remaining would be to convince her to *go.*

He would never see her again, never again feel his heart melt from the warmth of her huge gray eyes or hear her soft, uncertain laugh or touch the silk of her raven hair . . . Daniel John would be lost to him as well . . . He would not see him grow to manhood, would not be allowed to feed his hunger for learning, share his dreams, encourage his music. So much would be lost to him, so much . . .

But so much would be *gained* by *Nora,* he reminded himself, straightening. And that would somehow have to make his own loss bearable. Besides, who could say he would not see her again? He could always pay a visit to the States.

But by then she would be another man's wife.

He uttered a sharp sound of disgust at himself. Had she not been another man's wife for years? It was time for him to stop playing the fool for the woman and get a grip on himself.

Squaring his shoulders, he crossed to the table and sliced off a crust of bread, chewing it without really tasting it. Little Tom came trudging out from his bed just then, and, as always, ran to Morgan, climbing him as he would a tree.

Morgan scooped the little fellow the rest of the way up, hoisting him onto his shoulder. He was scarcely out of didies, this one, but already the stunned, morose look of the Hunger was on him. His enormous green eyes — as green as Morgan's own — held, instead of a childish glint of fun, the faintly suspicious, watchful stare of a stray pup trying to gauge an unpredictable master's intentions.

Yet this wee wane was healthier by far than most of the other children in the village. *Pity those little ones,* Morgan thought grimly, *who had no outlaw uncle to fill their bellies.*

"Your sisters are still asleep?" Morgan asked the tyke in the Irish. As he most often did with his own family, he spoke the ancient language, determined that the children should grow up entirely at ease with the original tongue of their people. Morgan loved the language, and because he knew himself to be one of the last remaining Gaelic poets and writers, he was determined to do his part in keeping this much of their heritage alive. As long as their language survived, perhaps there was hope that all things Irish would not perish under Britain's colonization.

The little boy nodded and put his arms around Morgan's neck in a tight hug.

"Say the words, Tom," Morgan demanded.

"They are sleeping, Uncle Morgan," the little boy replied in the Irish.

"Ah, then to you is appointed the privilege of waking them," Morgan said, grinning at his nephew as he swung him down to his feet. "You have my permission to tug their ears, if that's what it takes. Just a tiny tug, though; you must not hurt them. Girls are very tender, don't forget." Swatting the little boy lightly on his bottom, he stood and watched him go trundling off to the back of the cottage, where his sisters slept.

"And what is he about so early?" Thomas asked, rubbing the sleep from his eyes as he entered the room.

"I thought it might be well to wake the lasses. There will be much to do over these next days, and they could be of help to Nora, as well."

"Johanna, perhaps," Thomas agreed solemnly, tucking his shirttail inside his breeches. "Katie is that weak, though; she seems to tire with the least effort."

Fear lurked in his brother's eyes, and Morgan didn't wonder at it. He, too, had seen the frailty of his eldest niece. Katie had a blotched, feverish look about her. The girl had never been a sturdy child, and lately she appeared even more wan, almost wraith-like. Morgan suspected the lass had long been plagued with a heart malady; she seemed to gasp for her breath with the slightest exertion and never appeared to feel entirely well.

"Little Tom can help," Morgan said reassuringly. "He's growing fast, that one."

Thomas's expression cleared somewhat. "Aye, he'll be a brawny lad. He's the stoutest of the three. Catherine used to say the boy was —"

He stopped at the sound of a rap on the door, immediately followed by Daniel John's voice. "Thomas?" Pushing the door open a bit, the boy stuck his head inside.

Thomas motioned him in. "What are you doing out so early in the day, lad?"

Entering, Daniel John looked from Morgan to Thomas. "It's Grandfar," he said quietly. "He . . . he is gone. Mother said I should ask if you would come."

"Of course, lad," Thomas answered without hesitation. "Of course, I will come. Let me just finish dressing and wake the girls so they can see to Little Tom."

Morgan went to the boy and clasped his shoulder. "When, lad?"

"An hour ago, no more."

"I will come with Thomas," Morgan said, "if you want me to, that is."

Daniel John nodded soberly. "Please."

"When does your mother want the burial, do you know?"

"This afternoon. Since there can't be a wake, she thought it best for Tahg if we had the burial right away. That is," the boy added, "if Thomas can get the . . . the coffin ready soon enough."

Morgan nodded, squeezing Daniel John's shoulder. "We will help him. Your mother is right — it will be best this way." He paused, aware of something more than grief reflected in the lad's eyes. "You're troubled about the lack of a wake, is that it?"

The boy nodded. "I know it can't be helped. But I wish there could be . . . *something* for him. Something special, you know." For an instant his eyes brightened. "Morgan, do you think —" He stopped, looking uncomfortable.

"What, lad?" Morgan prompted, turning the boy toward him.

Daniel John looked up at him uncertainly. "I know that you and Grandfar were not friends," he said, his voice faltering for an instant, "but . . . I thought if you could write something . . . a poem that would be just for him . . . it might somehow make the burial more special."

It pained Morgan that the boy would be so reluctant to ask. "I had great respect for your granddaddy, Daniel John," he said quietly. "As it happens, I would consider it an honor to write a lament for Dan Kavanagh."

Daniel John smiled, his gratitude boyishly transparent. "I do thank you, Morgan. I know Mother will be pleased as well."

The thought of Nora reminded Morgan of

the letter he had yet to deliver. Old Dan's death had created still another delay. For just an instant he was relieved, then felt ashamed of his selfishness. At this point, every delay only served to tighten the net of peril around Nora and his own family.

This evening, then. This evening, after the burial, he *must* give her the letter. He simply did not dare to wait any longer.

17

A Most Unlikely Hero

And to him, who as hero and martyr hath striven,
Will the Crown, and the Throne, and the Palm-branch be given.

LADY WILDE (1820–1896)

At three-thirty that same afternoon, Evan Whittaker arose from another intense hour on his knees before the Lord, and began to pace. Cracking his knuckles, chewing his lip, he walked the floor from one end of the room to the other, trying desperately to decide what he should do — what he *could* do.

Evan had always considered himself a tolerant person. He had adopted his father's philosophy that even the best of men had their flaws and the worst of men could be expected to have at least one redeeming feature, if not more. Consequently, he thought he was reasonably objective and forbearing with his fellowman. That had been his father's way, and over the years he had conscientiously striven to make it his own.

Of course, Father had never met George Cotter, and by now Evan heartily wished he could say the same. After spending the better part of a week in the scurrilous agent's company, Evan was forced to admit that thus far he had been unable to find a single redeeming feature in the man. Bearing with the agent's "flaws" was turning out to be a monumental challenge.

Cotter seemed determined to force this eviction business, despite every attempt Evan made to delay things. Until less than an hour ago, he thought he had managed to stall the agent from carrying out Sir Roger's original demand to implement mass eviction. Insisting they wait until their employer had an opportunity to reconsider his instructions, Evan had almost managed to convince himself that once Sir Roger learned the dire nature of his tenants' plight, he would indeed grant them at least a measure of mercy.

This afternoon, however, Cotter belligerently announced that, one, he had his orders; and, two, Evan was "only a secret'ry and not the one to be telling him his job." Thus, he would proceed to carry out Sir Roger's original instructions that very afternoon — and he would start with the family of that "heathen Fitzgerald." If the outlaw was lodging with his brother, as was rumored in the village, he would soon find himself without a hiding place.

Evan was aware that Thomas Fitzgerald had only recently buried his wife, and that he and his three children were just barely surviving in some godforsaken hillside cabin. Moved by feelings of pity he chose not to analyze, he met the agent's brash announcement with as much cunning as he could muster, attempting to gain a temporary grace period for the ill-fortuned family. Only by convincing Cotter that Thomas Fitzgerald offered the best chance of apprehending his outlaw brother was Evan finally able to delay the Fitzgeralds' eviction another day.

Cotter seemed to take a great deal of delight in Evan's discomfiture, fixing him with a glare of contempt and a threat: "This being your idea and all, Whittaker, you can handle the Fitzgeralds yourself; I have a number of others to attend to today and tomorrow. Why, you may turn out to be the very man who brings down our infamous *Red Wolf*," he added with an ugly laugh. "Oh, and speaking of that good-for-nothing marauder," he went on, "I've asked the magistrate to see to a warrant for Morgan Fitzgerald's arrest as soon as possible. I'm having some *Wanted* posters prepared, offering a three-month rent extension to anybody who gives information leading to his capture."

Angered by the man's insolence, Evan had ventured to remind Cotter of the limits of his power. "Th-that is presumptuous and n-not at all within your authority!"

"Ah, but I am entirely within my authority!" Cotter shot back. "Didn't you bring me Gilpin's instructions yourself? 'Get this Fitzgerald outlaw locked up,' " he said, quoting Sir Roger's letter, " 'and use whatever means necessary to do so.' " He paused, shooting Evan a look of smug triumph.

Evan attempted one last argument, but Cotter merely scowled and wagged a meaty finger in front of his face. "You just handle the brother! I'm way behind schedule now in carrying out my duties, thanks to you and your simpering, and I'll not delay any longer!"

Thus Evan prepared to leave for Thomas Fitzgerald's cabin, ostensibly to question the man about his brother before serving an eviction notice on him. What Cotter did not know was that Evan also intended to warn Fitzgerald that his notorious brother was about to become a hunted criminal.

Pacing the floor, Evan admitted to himself that, while his sympathy for Thomas Fitzgerald might be understandable — the poor man was newly widowed and making every effort to save his small family — his concern for the man's fugitive brother was something else. Morgan Fitzgerald was, by all accounts, an outlaw. He flagrantly defied the authorities, flaunting his lawlessness by wandering in and out of the village whenever he chose.

Still, Evan felt some sort of incomprehensible bond to the man, a strong enough affinity that he was intent on warning him of Cotter's vengeful plan to do him in.

Outlaw or not, the *Red Wolf* had undeniably managed to save a number of lives, and had done so without wreaking any known physical harm on those in authority. A few discreet conversations with some of the villagers had revealed not only an overwhelming sense of gratitude, but no small amount of admiration for the Irish raider. Apparently he had become a kind of folk hero to much of Mayo's populace — understandable, Evan thought, considering the way the outlaw and his men continued to risk their own skins in an effort to save the people from annihilation.

Evan could not deny that he found the tales surrounding this local legend intriguing. The *Red Wolf* was no ordinary, brutish scoundrel. The mixture of adulation and intimidation he seemed to inspire argued that he was anything but ordinary and certainly far from brutish.

In addition, Evan grew increasingly convinced that it was not Roger Gilpin's orders that had brought him here, to Killala, but rather the leading of the Lord. He was here for an entirely different purpose than the unpleasant tasks Sir Roger had assigned to him. As he prayed he sensed a whisper in his spirit: he was to be, in some inexplicable manner, *responsible* for Morgan Fitzgerald, perhaps for others in the village also.

He stopped pacing to adjust his flawless cravat and smooth his waistcoat. Suddenly, he felt somewhat foolish, wondering if he could possibly be allowing his penchant for melodrama, a suppressed longing for adventure, to cloud his normally sound judgment. After all, Morgan Fitzgerald *was* an outlaw, an *Irish* outlaw who was likely to be a vulgar, swaggering sort and not at all kindly disposed toward anyone reckless enough to present him with a warning about his freedom.

Especially if the bearer of such bad tidings happened to be an Englishman.

Still, there *was* that inner sense of responsibility for the man — indeed, for this entire village — which continued to pervade his being every time he prayed. It had to mean *something*.

Fogging his eyeglasses with his breath, Evan cleaned the lenses with an immaculate handkerchief, then carefully settled them over the bridge of his nose. His headache was returning with a vengeance, and he longed to simply collapse on the bed and forget about the *Red Wolf*, George Cotter, and Killala. Instead, he sighed and collected his legal case and gloves from the scarred, wobbly desk, then opened the bedroom door and left the room. Evan was halfway down the long, dim hallway when his attention was caught by raised voices coming from downstairs, at the front of the house. He recognized Cotter's surly tone, but there were others — two, he thought, both gruff and coarse — which he assumed belonged to the agent's roughnecks. Evan was not one to eavesdrop, but he could not help but overhear Cotter's words.

What he heard made his heart thud to a stop, then begin to race. Drawing back, he stood, unmoving, listening.

"That's what I said!" Cotter snarled. "*Kavanagh. Daniel Kavanagh.* You're to nab the young scoundrel and bring him here, just as soon as you can lay your hands on him! He bargained with me," the agent went on in an outraged whine, "and agreed to take a job days ago. Why, I paid the deceitful *gorsoon* a day's wage already! He will work it off or go to gaol! He'll find he can't steal from *this* landlord without paying a dear price for it!"

Evan nearly choked at the blatant lie. He had witnessed the entire encounter between Cotter and young Kavanagh, and there had been no exchange of money. Of that much he was certain.

Holding his breath, he took a step backward, concealing himself in the shadows. The replies of the other men were muffled, but Cotter's loud voice boomed all the way up the stairs.

"You just be sure and have him here by this evening! Tell the mother that her son is a thief, and if she doesn't want him in gaol by dusk, she'll send him along with you. If they refuse to cooperate, turn them out on the spot." He let go a high-pitched laugh. "They'll be out by nightfall anyway, but that's for our ears only, until later. You just bring me the boy!"

Rage hit Evan like a massive blow. He had all he could do not to go flying down the steps and attack the besotted land agent. But Cotter was still giving orders, so Evan steeled himself to stand and listen, intent on learning all he could. He could almost see the odious man's slick, fat face and self-satisfied smile as he went on with his instructions.

"You collect the bailiff and the police right away — take care of the evictions in the Acres first, before you go to the Kavanagh shanty. And mind your orders, now: no extensions, and no exceptions!"

There were some brief, muffled words from the other men, then, "I don't want to hear about widows and orphans, you fool! My orders are to turn out anyone more than three months in arrears, and to turn them out at once! *Burn* them out if you must, what do I care? At any rate, their filthy huts are to be torched before evening! The fever is rampant out there!"

Evan stood, scarcely breathing, his mind scrambling to take in what he had just overheard. Dear heaven, the man was a lying blackguard! He was going to have that boy picked up like a common criminal and then throw his family out in this ghastly weather, not to mention all the other poor souls who would suffer the same fate.

Stunned and weak, Evan swallowed hard, then began to back up toward the bedroom. Once inside, he quietly closed the door and leaned against it, trying to think.

He must *do* something, of course. But *what?* Cotter had his ruffians and a number of armed police at his command. And, to make matters worse, he had legal authorization from Sir Roger for what he was about to do.

Evan turned his fury inward for a moment. Like a fool, he had handed over Sir Roger's signed instructions to the agent when he first arrived. All Cotter had to do was wave the orders under the nose of the bailiff and the police, and they would comply with whatever the agent demanded. As for those thugs who had been ordered to lure that poor unsuspecting boy up here, they were probably paid well enough that they would go to any lengths to satisfy Cotter's whims. It would be the Kavanagh boy's word against the land agent's, a foregone judgment against the youth.

Tossing his gloves and legal case onto the desk, Evan crossed the room and sank down onto the bed. For a long moment he could do nothing but stare at the floor in frustration.

Finally, he turned to the bedside table, picked up his Bible, and opened it.

What can I do, Lord?

He was only a frail, stammering Englishman who knew nothing about bravery except for what he read in adventure novels. He did not understand these people, none of them — Cotter, his toughs, the suffering villagers. Nor did he understand or even care about this wretched island. He had never in his life felt so isolated, so alone. What was one man against an entire army of wickedness?

His eyes fell on the open page, and the words leaped out at him: *A king is not saved by his great army; a warrior is not delivered by his great strength . . . the eye of the Lord is on those who fear him, on those who hope in his steadfast love, that he may deliver their soul from death, and keep them alive in famine.*

Evan squirmed, clutching the open Bible more tightly. "I'm hardly cut out for the . . . business of deliverance, Lord, and even if I were, I wouldn't know where to begin. B-besides, I'm really not a bit stout — my lungs, you remember — and while I'm not altogether fearful, I suppose it's fair to say that I *am* somewhat t-timid about certain things. Oh — and of course you know that I st-stammer in the most disconcerting way, especially when I'm . . . tense or nervous . . ."

He fidgeted, flipping through the pages

aimlessly. At last his fingers stopped, and he looked down again.

Then the Lord said to Moses: "Who has made man's mouth? Who makes him dumb, or deaf, or seeing, or blind? Is it not I, the Lord? Now therefore go, and I will be with your mouth and teach you what you shall speak."

"Lord, p-perhaps this isn't important . . . but wasn't it Aaron who actually ended up d-doing most of the talking for M-Moses? Besides, I'm afraid I don't quite understand what it is, exactly, you want me to do. I wouldn't even kn-know where to start."

Evan drew a deep breath and shut the Bible. The words rang in his mind — not audibly spoken, but very clear: *Your ears shall hear a word behind you, saying, "This is the way, walk in it," when you turn to the right or when you turn to the left.*

"Lord . . . the th-thing is," Evan objected, "ah, well . . . this is Ireland, you see, and I'm . . . an Englishman, and, well . . . you know how they feel about us . . . I'm not at all sure I have any credibility whatsoever with these people."

Have we not all one father? Has not one God created us? Why then are we faithless to one another?

"But, Lord, wouldn't I be betraying my employer? As much as I d-dislike the man, I've worked for Roger Gilpin for years, and he does . . . trust me to carry out his instructions."

Should you serve the wicked and love those who hate the Lord? Choose this day whom you will serve, Evan . . . choose now.

"Lord! Lord, I . . . I chose *you* years ago! Nothing can change that, not ever." Evan moistened his lips. "But I still don't see *how,* Lord —"

Not by might, not by power, but by my Spirit.

Evan squeezed his eyes shut and waited in self-imposed darkness. He didn't want to do this — he wasn't even certain he *could* do it, and yet something pushed him on. Something had always been missing in his life; he loved God, but his faith had never been tried in action. Now, as he sat in silence, a calmness began to wash over him. He felt as if he were in the center of a dark tunnel: from both sides light advanced toward him, at last converging where he waited.

The light flooded into him, illuminating not his surroundings, but some hidden inner reservoir of his own soul. From the deep recesses of his memory, Evan's mind recalled the words, *"Who knows if you have come to the king's court for such a time as this?"*

He drew a deep breath, and in his own exhaled sigh, he heard his father's familiar voice: *"Trust God, and be brave."*

At last Evan opened his eyes. Replacing the Bible on the table, he got up from the bed and went to the desk, once more collecting his legal case and gloves. He was amazed at the peace that filled him, relieved that he seemed to know what he must do. Not *how* he was going to do it, at least not yet. But for now, it was enough to know that he must act, and that God would be with him when he did.

The nasty business at the Fitzgerald cabin would have to wait, he decided, opening the bedroom door. First, he must find a way to thwart the capture of Daniel Kavanagh.

18

Dan Kavanagh's Lament

In all my wanderings round this world of care,
In all my griefs – and God has given me my share –
I still had hopes, my latest hours to crown,
Amidst these humble bowers to lay me down.

OLIVER GOLDSMITH (1728–1774)

Death had become so much a part of every day in the village of Killala that the passing of yet another soul went more or less unnoticed. Still, there were those who claimed that a number of dark portents had warned of Dan Kavanagh's approaching demise.

Old Mary Larkin, for example, claimed to have seen a *badhb* — the crow symbolizing death — hovering near the Kavanagh cottage late in the afternoon. And Judy Hennessey, who grew more and more demented by the day, insisted that she had heard the *banshee* — the female angel of death — wail her eerie song just past midnight. When her mother-in-law pointed out that only family members or others in close relationship to the dying could hear the white-robed phantom of the night, Judy snapped back that as one of the Kavanaghs' nearest neighbors she guessed she knew what she'd heard well enough.

In truth, however, the only event that might have drawn attention to yet another death was the fact that the deceased was being buried in a proper coffin after a traditional procession; someone had even thought to toll the church bell in advance of the mourners.

When the word finally circulated the village that it was Old Dan Kavanagh on the way to the graveyard, a few heads nodded wisely, as if to imply that you could expect it of the Kavanaghs to observe convention, even during a time of widespread disaster. Didn't they always do things according to the old ways? To some, the family's strict adherence to tradition might hint of excess pride, but most of the townspeople would have disagreed. The Kavanaghs were an old, established Christian family, early settlers in Connacht and a well-respected name in the village for generations. If it was their way to observe the proprieties, who, then, should be denouncing them for it?

The cold rain that had begun that morning and continued steadily throughout the day was considered by all to be a good omen for a burial. A few villagers still strong enough to walk the distance to the graveyard joined the funeral procession — some in remembrance of kindnesses done by Dan Kavanagh, others out of affection for Nora and her family. It was a grim, blood-chilling sight, this mourners' march. Gaunt and hollow-eyed, some scarcely clothed or at best wrapped only in thin rags against the rain and driving wind, they tramped in silence along the traditional route to Killala's graveyard. Ill and doomed and defeated, they looked like a macabre parade of the walking dead on their way to a mass burial service of their own.

In this poor, sad village, as in hundreds of others all across Ireland, the graveyard was filled to overflowing. Only those farsighted persons who had in better days secured their plots were still laid to rest in the traditional burial site. Improvised graves marred the entire town — indeed the whole countryside. Roadside ditches, backyards, hillside slopes, even the shore by the bay hosted makeshift coffins, or corpses wrapped in sacks or papers. Open pits into which corpse after corpse had been tossed and heaped, one upon the other, were simply covered over with a thin layer of dirt. Cabins where fever and disease raged were most often knocked down, then torched, turning them into funeral pyres.

Priests could no longer keep up in their efforts to administer last rites; indeed, many were dying in large numbers themselves, a consequence of exhaustion and giving up their own food to feed their parishioners. The Protestant clergy, though the numbers of their fold were fewer, also felt the sting of frustration in their attempts to comfort the sick and perform a seemingly endless number of funeral services. Roman and Protestant clerics served side by side in the beleaguered fever hospitals, where suffering and death provided a natural focus for unity.

There were never enough gravediggers. Frail, emaciated survivors excavated the graves for their loved ones; in their weakness, they dug scarcely deeper than they might have for potato plants. Tombstones were no longer given a thought. A pile of stones or a piece of cloth on a stick were the only monuments erected to mark the countless unknown graves.

Once recognized as a land of vigilant, painstaking respect for the dead, Ireland's growing apathy seemed a terrible and piercing commentary on the country's present wretchedness. But on this day of further loss in Killala, there was grief. Even the mist-shrouded, ancient round tower appeared to mourn and weep over the suffering village, much as Christ must have sorrowed over Jerusalem.

Daniel stood at the graveside in the rain, watching them bury his grandfather. The rough-hewn, simple coffin Morgan and Thomas had hastily constructed was lowered into the grave the same two men had dug. A few shawled women drew nearer to commence the ancient keen.

The traditionally silent funeral procession had followed the coffin to Killala's graveyard, laying Grandfar to rest with simple prayers, some reading of scripture and, finally, a wonderful Irish lament that Morgan had written. But Daniel offered the final tribute to his grandfather's memory. Strumming the Kavanagh harp in the way of the ancient harpers, which Morgan had taught him, he began to play and sing the lament that had been passed down through generations of Kavanagh men. Originally written for *his* grandfather by Eoin Caomhanach, the piece had been preserved from the seventeenth century; for almost two hundred years it had concluded the burial services of male members of the Kavanagh clan.

Daniel had always felt a strong sense of kinship with the ancestor who had composed the lament. After losing his entire family to Cromwell's bloodthirsty soldiers when he was only fourteen years old, Eoin Caomhanach had been forced to flee his lifelong home in Drogheda for the unknown, untamed western coast of Ireland. Today, that special affinity seemed even stronger. Both had lost precious family members; both had been placed in the position of lamenting a beloved grandfather. And, like Eoin, Daniel knew that soon he, too, might be forced to leave his home for the uncertainty of an unknown land.

Pain stabbed his heart, and it took all the will he could muster to keep his voice from breaking as he fixed his eyes upon his grandfather's grave and began to sing.

"My harp will sing across the land,
across the past and years to be.
No loss or grief nor death itself
will still its faithful melody."

Daniel faltered only once, but at the touch of Morgan's hand upon his shoulder, he caught a long breath and went on:

"To sing the presence of a God
who conquers even exile's pain —
Who heals the wandering pilgrim's
wound
and leads him home in joy again."

At the end of the ceremony, Thomas shoveled an ample amount of thick, wet clay over the coffin, finally placing the spade and shovel on top of the grave in the form of a cross. Daniel led his mother away, with Thomas at her other side and Morgan following closely behind. Along with the rest of the mourners, they turned and set their faces against the cold, rain-swept wind and started for home.

Daniel wondered as they walked if Grandfar could see them from heaven. Was he aware of how much they already missed him? Somehow he hoped that the old man had heard Morgan's moving lament at the graveside and had been pleased with it. In heaven, of course, Grandfar's bad feelings toward Morgan would have been wiped away by now, but Daniel still wanted him to know the respect Morgan had paid him.

On the wordless march toward home, Daniel prayed — for his grandfather's peace, for the "blessed rest of heaven" for which the old man had so often yearned.

I pray that Grandfar is with you already, Lord . . . that he's resting his head on a giant pillow of a cloud, as he used to speak of doing, and that he's feasting on the beauty and grandeur of heaven.

He could almost hear his grandfather's deep, gruff voice as he spoke of the place prepared for him:

"Sure, and don't I hope that the mansion the Lord has built for me is a snug, warm place where these old bones can be thawing out at last? It won't matter at all whether it's grand in any way, just so long as it's warm. Not that I'd mind a table heaped with some meat and potatoes as well . . ."

Daniel was struck by a fresh wave of loneliness for the old man who had been as much friend and companion as grandfather to him throughout his years of childhood. With Grandfar gone and Tahg naught but a shadow of himself, it was officially up to him to assume the role of head of the house.

In truth, at this moment he felt shamefully young and filled with fear. It struck him again that everything he had ever trusted in or counted on was being ripped away from him, one piece at a time. His da, now Grandfar — even Tahg, ill as he was — all were lost to him.

And his home: Was that to be his next loss? His home, his village, his country?

The questions that frequently assailed him these days once again came hurtling through his thoughts, questions he could not seem to avoid, no matter how much they distressed him. When this nightmare of death and destruction finally ended — if indeed it ever *did* — would there be anyone . . . or anything . . . left that he cared about? Or was this, as some in the village seemed to believe, the end of all that they loved, perhaps even the end of the world?

Again rose the awful possibility that God had abandoned the island entirely. That being the case, there was indeed no hope, no hope at all, left to any of them.

And if there were no hope, even the few

who might manage to survive would be just as well off dead. Grandfar himself had said that life without hope was no life at all.

Daniel was only now beginning to understand what his grandfather had meant.

On his way into the village, Evan was so engrossed in his anxious thoughts that he was almost upon the odd, straggling procession before he actually became aware of them.

He reined in his horse and sat watching their dispirited approach. Huddled and shivering in their wet, ragged clothing, they appeared to be coming away from the graveyard, even though Cotter had made it sound as if formal burial services were a thing of the past.

Leaning forward on his mount, Evan's attention was quickly caught by a tall, thin youth at the front of the procession. The boy had an ancient-looking wire-strung harp slung over one shoulder, and appeared to be supporting the small, black-clad woman at his side, as if she were too frail to stand alone. Both were thoroughly drenched from the soaking rain.

Apparently sensing Evan's eyes on him, the boy slowed his pace, then stopped and lifted his head.

Daniel Kavanagh.

Evan caught his breath. He had not expected to encounter the boy like this, in the open, surrounded by people. He darted a glance at the woman, whom he took to be the lad's mother. But who was the gaunt, graying fellow at her side? Hadn't the boy told Cotter that his father was dead?

Young Kavanagh now tipped his chin even higher. A wary glint, just short of defiance, hardened the boy's expression, and Evan caught a glimpse of the same quiet, unbending courage he had sensed in the youth that day on the hill behind Cotter's house.

Evan's gaze left the boy to scan the crowd, locking almost at once on a man standing just behind young Kavanagh and his mother, towering over them like some sort of threatening guardian angel. Again his breath caught in his throat, and his entire body began to vibrate with a blend of fascination and dread. Unable to tear his gaze away from the copper-haired giant, Evan fought to regain his wits.

The man was a mountain in frieze, a colossus decked in a homespun cloak and worn leather boots. Swallowing hard, Evan found himself staring into the most intense, dangerous green eyes he had ever encountered, and he knew at once he was looking into the face of the notorious outlaw-patriot, Morgan Fitzgerald.

The *Red Wolf*.

19

An Encounter on the Road

A fighting-man he was . . .
A copper-skinned six-footer,
Hewn out of the rock,
Who would stand up against
His hammer-knock?
A goodly man, A Gael. . . .

JOSEPH CAMPBELL (1879–1944)

The Irish giant's intimidating size, the thick, wild russet hair tossed wetly about his head, and the full bronze beard perfectly mirrored what Quincy Moore had written of him. Fitzgerald's features were neither coarse nor heavy, as Evan had anticipated. Indeed, had it not been for the terrible scowl fixed upon his face, the man might have been considered almost handsome in appearance, if a bit rustic.

Evan now became aware that the entire procession had stopped where they were on the side of the road, and that all eyes were fixed on him in a combined force of open hostility. Still he found it impossible to drag his gaze away from the giant, who seemed determined to annihilate him with his blazing stare. The man stepped out in front of the boy and his mother as if to shield the two of them with his body, and his size was such that he almost totally concealed them both.

Up until this moment, Evan had viewed the stories about the Irish brigand with a mixture of intrigue, skepticism, and a certain sense of excitement. Confronted with the legend face-to-face, however, he was struck by a reaction he could not have anticipated. To his surprise, his mind now registered a distinct quake of panic.

Not only was the rogue even larger in life than the tales told about him, but a carefully controlled energy seemed to emanate from him, a power that, while temporarily under restraint, threatened to break loose at any instant. The big man's obvious calm and ease of posture suggested, if not actual arrogance, at least absolute confidence; yet Evan sensed an inferno blazing inside the man, constrained only by sheer force of will.

For a moment the granite-faced Irishman simply stared at Evan as if he were no more than an irritating toad. When he finally did move, he took only two broad steps, then stopped, his eyes traveling slowly up the height of the horse until they came to rest on Evan's face.

Evan steeled himself to meet the man's patently contemptuous stare, praying he wouldn't stammer. He cleared his throat and took a deep breath before speaking. "Good . . . day to you, sir. My name is —" He stopped, determinedly pushing the words from his mouth. "Whittaker. Evan Whittaker."

The man's cloak had fallen open, revealing a harp similar to the boy's riding high on one shoulder, and what appeared to be the handle of a pistol tucked into the waist of his breeches. The Irishman again stepped forward, this time coming close enough that he could easily have reached up and yanked Evan from his mount if so inclined. It did not escape Evan that one hard tug from that hammer of a hand would most likely break his arm, and for a moment he had all he could do not to lash his horse and go tearing off down the road.

Despite his apprehension, however, he had to admit that coming upon both Fitzgerald and the Kavanagh boy together seemed too propitious an occurrence to be written off as mere chance. If this were God's way of providing him a means of carrying out His will, he could hardly afford to retreat out of cowardice.

The giant stood in menacing silence, his eyes shooting out a blast of disgust strong enough to make Evan flinch. Driven by an increasing urgency, he reminded himself that the chap was a poet, a back-country schoolmaster — not an armor-decked warlord. Best not to dwell on the unsettling fact that he was also reputed to be a revolutionary and an outlaw — an *armed* outlaw.

"A-a—am I correct in assuming that you are M-M-Morgan F-F-Fitzgerald?" Evan felt his skin heat as the humiliating stammer now exploded full-force.

A murmur behind Fitzgerald was silenced with a slight lift of the giant's hand. Again his contemptuous expression pinned Evan in place. The green eyes narrowed, the wide, generous mouth thinned to a slash, and finally the big Irishman spoke. "I am Fitzgerald. And what is that to you?" he countered in a voice deadly in its quiet.

Feeling increasingly threatened, Evan groped to maintain a calm of his own. "As I said, my n-name is Whittaker." He paused, waiting.

"Aye. The *Englishman*."

An entire history of contempt echoed from those quiet words, and Evan thought he would never again feel quite the same about himself. His hands went clammy inside his gloves, and the knot in his throat swelled to a fist. "I . . . really must t-talk with you right away, Fitzgerald." Hesitating, he then added, "And . . . the boy as well."

The fire in Fitzgerald's eyes now died, to be replaced by a glacial stare. "And what boy would that be?"

Evan managed a stiff nod in Daniel Kavanagh's direction. The Irishman's bearded chin seemed to slide forward and lock in place as his voice turned even softer and more menacing. "Now what possible business could the Big Lord's lackey have with an ignorant Paddy like myself and a poor village lad?"

Evan swallowed with great difficulty, but refused to let the man goad him. "I assure you, it's im . . . p-portant. For you *and* the boy."

"Ah, indeed."

"Is there s-somewhere we could talk alone?" Evan pressed. "You m-must believe me, it's for your own good."

"Oh, of *course* it is," Fitzgerald answered. His tone was openly mocking, but a warning still lurked in his eyes.

Evan's exasperation with the man overcame his caution. "N-now see here, F-Fitzgerald, you're in t-terrible jeopardy, as is young Kavanagh! It would b-be to your advantage to hear me out."

Fitzgerald's expression darkened, and when he spoke the mask of the cynic had disappeared. "Have a care, man. This is not the day to be dallying with me."

Evan could no longer contain his frustration. "For the love of heaven, m-man, I'm not *dallying* with you! I'm t-trying to save your neck! And the boy's as well!"

He cringed as Fitzgerald's ruddy complexion paled with fury, but he also thought that at last he might have penetrated the stubborn Irishman's guard. The man turned away for a moment, saying something in the barbaric tongue Evan recognized as Gaelic. Immediately, the mourners began to move, a few at a time, continuing their doleful march down the road. Only the boy, his mother, and the craggy-faced man at her side remained.

Young Kavanagh suddenly moved, starting toward Fitzgerald, who motioned him off with an upraised hand and a firm shake of his head. Again, he muttered something in their unpronounceable language, and the boy stopped, leveling a dark, furious frown on Evan.

Turning back, Fitzgerald searched Evan's face with narrowed eyes for a long moment. "You'll understand if I seem to question your interest," he said in a voice as deep as a drum roll. "It's a new thing for me entirely, you see, having an Englishman concerned for my well-being."

Searching frantically for just the right words to break through Fitzgerald's antagonism, Evan pulled in a deep, steadying breath.

Oh, Lord, please take this abominable stammer away, at least for the moment, so Fitzgerald won't think me such a joke. I can't possibly be of any help to him or the boy if he won't even take me seriously!

Vaguely recollecting that the heroes in his favorite adventure novels always tightened their jaws when faced with a challenge, Evan now clenched his own. Facing his adversary with rigid resolve, he decided to go right to the heart of things. "I thought you should know that Cotter's bully-boys will be at the Kavanagh cottage before evening," he said, trying to keep his voice low enough that only Fitzgerald could hear. "They, ah . . . they have orders to collect the boy and take him to Cotter on . . . on the pretext that he was paid a day's wages he never earned."

"That's a *lie!*" His face contorted with rage, Fitzgerald reached to lay a hand on the mare's neck. "The boy owes that blackheart nothing! *Nothing!*"

"I understand that," Evan quickly assured him, flinching at Fitzgerald's abrupt movement. "I'm telling you what I heard, nothing else."

Evan shuddered in spite of himself at the fury that seemed to shake the big man's powerful frame. The quiet voice cracked like a whiplash, and fire leaped in Fitzgerald's eyes. "And how is it that you know what Cotter and his rabble are up to?"

"I overheard them. His two thugs are supposed to assist with some evictions in the — the *Acres* — then come back to town and pick up the boy. They're to take him directly to Cotter," Evan explained. He was vaguely aware that his stammer had fled as his words came tumbling out in a rush — confirmation, perhaps, that God was indeed enabling him.

Fitzgerald started to speak, but Evan stopped him. "That's not all," he said, pressing his lips together nervously. "I'm . . . supposed to be serving an eviction notice on your brother even now. He and his family are to be out of their dwelling by tomorrow morning."

Evan felt almost driven now, engulfed by a need to deliver all the sordid facts into Fitzgerald's hands as quickly as possible. "As for you," he went on, "you'll be arrested the minute they catch sight of you. Cotter's putting out *Wanted* posters all over the village, and there will be a warrant for your arrest issued yet today, if there isn't one already. You *must* get away!" He paused, then added urgently, "And the boy — he dare not return to his home!"

Fitzgerald took a step back, measuring Evan with suspicious eyes. "What are you about, man? What, exactly, is your game?"

The blunt question stopped Evan for only an instant. "We can't afford to waste time sparring about my motives! In truth, I . . . I'm not at all sure I understand them myself. You'll simply have to trust me."

A sharp, ugly laugh exploded from Fitzgerald. "You are an Englishman," he said, as if that explained it all.

Evan bristled. "I am also a *Christian.*"

"Aye," Fitzgerald bit out, his tone thick with scorn. "As was Oliver Cromwell."

Grinding his teeth to keep from screaming at the man, Evan challenged him. "I thought perhaps *you* might be a believer."

Fitzgerald lifted an eyebrow in feigned surprise. "Ach, and could a Paddy be a Christian like yourself?" he drawled. "Ah, no, we're but cowherds and bogmen, don't you know? Heathens, every last mother's son of us."

Evan was taken aback by the faint light in Fitzgerald's eyes, which seemed to alter his entire appearance. The militant chieftain had suddenly taken on a lively, if sardonic wit.

Flustered by the quicksilver change in the man, Evan snapped defensively, "You are wasting precious time, Fitzgerald! It was my understanding that you have . . . some concern for the Kavanagh boy; certainly you must have a care for yourself. Will you do nothing to save your life and his?"

"You have not answered my question," Fitzgerald said, his expression turning hard as he dropped the exaggerated brogue. "Why are you doing this? You *are* Gilpin's man, are you not?"

By now Evan was feeling decidedly peevish. His chest ached from the miserable wet weather, his nose was dripping, and his backside was sore from spending a great deal more time on horseback than he was used to.

Moreover, he was out of patience with Fitzgerald's mulishness. "I am Roger Gilpin's secretary!" he snapped, gripped for a moment by a coughing seizure. When he could again speak, he added, "I'm employed by the man. That doesn't necessarily mean that I . . . agree with all his methods."

Fitzgerald said nothing, but merely crossed his arms over his spacious chest and gave Evan another long, studying look.

Forcing himself not to shrink beneath the Irishman's fierce glare, Evan chose his words carefully. "Quite frankly," he said, "I'm not at all certain my employer would approve of Cotter's conduct. That man is utterly despicable! And I know he's lying about the boy, because I was there that day when he offered young Kavanagh a job. There was no money exchanged — none at all." He paused. "As for what he intends to do with *you* —"

Something glinted in Fitzgerald's eyes, and Evan faltered. The man *was* an outlaw, after all; who was to say he wouldn't shoot him on the spot if he didn't like what he heard?

"Cotter believes you to be . . . ah, I believe the name he used was . . . the *Red Wolf*. In addition," Evan continued cautiously, "you seem to have . . . threatened him at some time, I take it? He makes no secret of his hatred for you."

Fitzgerald seemed thoroughly unruffled about his own peril. "You say Cotter's men will be back in the village by evening?"

Relieved that the man finally seemed to be listening, Evan nodded eagerly. "You *must* get yourself and the boy out of sight! Do you have a place where you can go?"

Ignoring his question, Fitzgerald raked a hand down one side of his face in a gesture of frustration. "You're sure Thomas — my brother — has until morning before he's turned out?"

Evan nodded. "Supposedly because the bailiff and the bully-boys have their hands full with other evictions this afternoon. Frankly, I believe Cotter is giving your brother some notice on purpose, hoping to flush you out of your hiding place. He thinks you're staying there, at least part of the time. I imagine he's expecting you either to try to stop the eviction or, at the very least, to delay it." He paused, then added pointedly, "He's determined to see you hang."

"And I'm just as determined that he won't," Fitzgerald said absently, casting a sweeping gaze around their surroundings. "So, then, it would seem we have only tonight to get ready to leave."

"You must find a safe place for yourself and the others," Evan urged. "They'll tear the village apart looking for you."

"My family will be leaving for the States soon — there is a ship coming any day. Until then, I know of a place where we can stay."

"You're going with them to America, I hope?"

Fitzgerald shrugged. "Who knows what I will do?" he said cryptically. "In the meantime, there is a place where we can go." He paused, fixing Evan with a studying look. "And you will come with us."

Startled, Evan hurried to protest. "Now, see here, I can't —"

"You will come with us," Fitzgerald repeated in a tone that left no room for argument. "I may need you. First, however, we must hide Daniel John, then get Tahg and Nora away from the cottage. That will take some doing, I fear."

"Tahg? Who is Tahg?"

"Daniel John's elder brother. He is ill. Mortally ill." Fitzgerald turned a bitter look on Evan. "There are many in the village just like him — one night on the road will kill them all."

Evan gripped the horse's reins more tightly. "I'll do whatever I can to help move him."

Fitzgerald waved him off. "It's not that at all. I could carry the lad with one arm, he's that frail. But to take him out in this cold rain . . ." His words died away, unfinished. For a long moment he stood in silence, tugging mindlessly at the wet hair at the back of his neck as he stared off into the distance.

"Fitzgerald?" Evan waited until the

Irishman turned to meet his eyes. “Once Cotter realizes he’s been thwarted, you can expect that he’ll be wild. He’ll stop at nothing to get the boy. I think he’s obsessed.”

“He’s a devil,” Fitzgerald said.

“But a dull-witted one,” Evan pointed out.

Fitzgerald looked at him, then began to nod, slowly. “Aye, there was a great deal of sense left outside his head,” he answered dryly. “What is your point?”

“That your wits and mine should be more than enough to foil him.”

Fitzgerald studied him for a moment more. “How far are you willing to go with what you’ve started, man?”

“What do you mean?”

“I mean that you may be able to save some lives here,” Fitzgerald replied, his gaze steady. “But only if you’re willing to risk your soft position with Gilpin and perhaps your English honor as well.”

Uncertain as to what the man was getting at, Evan nevertheless nodded, waiting.

“There’s no more time for talk,” Fitzgerald muttered, still peering into Evan’s face. “Just answer me this, for once you commit yourself, there can be no turning back. You say you are a Christian; but which is more dear to you, Evan Whittaker — your Savior or your Saxon neck?”

For a long, silent moment Evan felt himself turned inside out, as if his very soul were being laid open to the burning eyes of his inquisitor. And in the same moment he somehow knew that the answer to Morgan Fitzgerald's piercing question was even more important to Evan himself than it was to the Gael.

He shut his eyes, allowing his spirit a moment of quiet before he answered. Then he faced Fitzgerald with a level look of his own. "I should imagine that I value my . . . *Saxon neck* quite as much as you do your stubborn Irish hide. But not so much that I would ever betray my Savior." He swallowed with some difficulty, adding, "I shall do whatever I can to help rescue you . . . and those who are dear to you, Fitzgerald. You have my word on that."

As Evan watched, a slow, wondering light seemed to soften and gentle the big man's face, a light so faint Evan almost thought he might be imagining it. But, no, the warmth rose in Fitzgerald's eyes, a glow that somehow hinted of approval. And without ever questioning why this brash Irishman's affirmation should matter in the slightest, Evan found himself basking in its warmth.

"By all that is holy," Fitzgerald said quietly, his great leonine head thrown back as the rain slashed his face, "it would seem that I have found myself an Englishman with a noble heart. Now, *there* is a wonder for us all."

Evan flushed. He knew himself to have been saluted by this great tower of a man, and he savored it.

"All right, then, Whittaker," Fitzgerald said, still examining Evan as if he were some sort of a rare oddity, "let us get on with it. We have much to do, and from the looks of you we'll need to do it quickly before you catch your death. First, though, we need a plan as to how we can hold off Cotter's thugs until I can get some of my lads and an extra horse or two down from the hills."

"I'm still the official emissary of their landlord," Evan pointed out. "I should think I'm more than capable of managing those roughnecks." Even as he spoke, he was hoping he sounded more confident than he felt.

Fitzgerald permitted himself a ghost of a smile. "Aye, somehow I think you can."

"Before anything else, though," Evan said urgently, "we *must* get young Daniel hidden away."

Fitzgerald nodded. "He can go with Thomas for now."

"Good. But I'm afraid Mrs. Kavanagh needs to come with *us*. Things may get unpleasant if Cotter's toughs show up, but with her help I believe I can get rid of them."

"Give me a moment," Fitzgerald said with a short nod. Turning, he walked off, tossing out a stream of Gaelic to the others as he approached.

Not long after he reached them, the Kavanagh lad shot a look of disbelief in Evan's direction, while the woman's face went white with visible alarm. Only the tall, haggard-looking man next to her appeared unshaken as Fitzgerald went to him and, gripping his shoulders, began to speak. Seeing the two men together, Evan immediately noted the resemblance. Evidently, this gaunt, sad-eyed man was the brother he had been ordered to evict. Feeling suddenly ill, he was struck by a fresh blow of guilt for his years of association with Roger Gilpin, and renewed shame for himself and his country.

The woman and the boy continued to stare, first at Fitzgerald, then at Evan, with incredulous, frightened eyes. He attempted a lame smile of reassurance, but his face quickly froze in the effort. Seized by a sudden wave of uncertainty, he fought down a surge of panic. These people despised him, as well as everything he stood for; in their eyes, he was the enemy, a man to be feared and shunned. What had ever possessed him to think he could gain their trust, especially within such a short period of time? There was no earthly reason, even if they were to accept his *willingness* to help, that they should trust his *ability* to help. For that matter, there was no earthly reason why *he* should trust *himself!*

Still, it wasn't *himself* he was trusting, any more than it had been an *earthly* reason that had brought him this far. *Trust God,* his father had said. *Trust God, and be brave.*

Less than an hour later, Nora sat rigidly on a chair in her kitchen, struggling to accept the fact that her entire life was about to change.

The whirlwind in which she found herself seemed to be gathering strength. What had started when they encountered the Englishman on the way back from the graveyard had continued to build until she thought she would go mad from fear and confusion.

First, Morgan had sent Daniel John rushing off with Thomas, offering no more than a hurried explanation about getting the boy "out of Cotter's reach," and a reminder to "use the space beneath the cabin if it's needed" — whatever *that* meant.

Scarcely a heartbeat later, he scooped Nora up and set her squarely on the horse with the Englishman, ordering them to take the back road around the village to her cottage, that he would meet them there "in a shake."

All the way down the road the Englishman mumbled what sounded like words of apology and reassurance, but Nora had been far too distraught and bewildered to catch more than a few bits and pieces of his British blather. The only thing she *had* understood was that Cotter meant to abduct Daniel John, and this was enough to take her to the very edge of hysteria.

By the time they reached the cottage, she was trembling so violently she thought she would fly to pieces before Whittaker could get her off the horse. She went through the motions of tending to Tahg, doing her best not to let him see her terror, but she was aware of the lad watching her with uneasy eyes, as if he sensed something was wrong. When she mumbled a hurried, awkward explanation about Whittaker being a "friend of Morgan's," the boy stared at her incredulously but offered no argument.

During the entire time she busied herself with Tahg, Whittaker hovered nearby, peering at her through those odd little spectacles of his as if he feared that any moment she might run screaming from the cottage. As soon as Morgan arrived, the two of them closeted themselves in a corner of the kitchen, doing a great deal of muttering and nodding, virtually ignoring her.

Now, leaving Whittaker in the back of the cottage, Morgan crossed the room to pull up a chair and sit down, facing her. Nora had all she could do not to shout at him. For a moment he simply searched her eyes, saying nothing. Then, drawing a deep sigh, he reached for her hand, seemingly mindless of the way she immediately knotted it into a tight, unrelenting fist.

"Nora, I am sorry," he said, studying her. "I would not have yanked you about as I did had there been more time."

Nora stiffened, glaring at him. "Why are you listening to that *Englishman*, Morgan? What is he doing here, in *my* cottage, telling us what to do?" She was aware that her voice was shaking as hard as the rest of her. "Does he not work for the landlord himself?"

Morgan was still in his cloak, and with his free hand he reached now to shrug it off, letting it fall over the back of the chair. "Believe it or not," he said, sliding his harp off his shoulder and placing it carefully on the table, "he is trying to help us. In truth, he means to save our lives."

"You are cracked!" Nora exploded. She heard the shrillness of her voice, tasted the fear that caused it, but she could not stop. "And since when do you heed the words of an Englishman, Morgan Fitzgerald?"

Morgan smiled grimly and nodded. "Aye, it is an incredible thing, I admit. Still, I believe the man, Nora. He is risking a great deal to help us. But listen to me, now," he said, his expression sobering, "there is more that you must know, much more than I had time to explain before. Did Whittaker tell you anything at all," he asked quietly, "about the evictions?"

"Evictions?" His expression was inscrutable, but something in the way he watched her made Nora sit stock-still, unable to breathe. "What evictions?"

Dragging in a long breath, Morgan enfolded both her hands between his. "Nora," he said gently, "you will have to be very strong. What I have to say is not easy."

Squeezing her hands, he seemed to choose his words with great care. He spoke in a quiet, level voice of the horrors to come — of their imminent homelessness and what Nora could only view as their approaching doom.

When he was done, she began to rock back and forth, trying mindlessly to still the shaking of her body. "God help us," she whispered, and then again, "God help us, what are we to do?"

"We are going to get you and Tahg out of here as quickly as possible," Morgan said grimly. "You and the boys will stay at Thomas's cabin for a few hours. Later tonight, I will take you to a place in the hills where you will be safe until the ship for America comes."

Nora felt her face crumble with fear and disbelief. "Are you *daft?* Tahg cannot leave the cottage!"

He gripped her hands even more tightly. "He *must* leave, lass. There is no other way."

Nora twisted, trying to tug her hands free, but he held her. "*No!* No, you are mad!" she burst out. "It would *kill* him to be taken out in this weather, after all this time and him so ill. Sure, and you must see that, Morgan — Tahg would *die!*"

In spite of his hands gripping hers, she managed to pull herself up off the chair, still wrenching in vain to twist free. Morgan, too, shot to his feet, catching her by the shoulders. *"Nora, listen to me!"* he shouted, his eyes burning into hers as he held her. "There is nothing else we can do! They will tumble the place down around your head if you resist. *Then* what will become of Tahg? You can't think he would survive *that!*"

Nora stopped struggling, her mind finally beginning to register the awful truth in his words.

His grip on her shoulders relaxed only slightly. "Hush now, and hear me out, *ma girsha,*" he said, his voice dropping to a low, soothing tone. "There is a way out of this, after all. But you must mind what I say."

She shook her head in hopeless protest. "Do not try to deceive me, Morgan," she choked out brokenly, no longer even trying to stop the tears. "You know as well as I that nothing can save us now! 'Tis the road for us . . . oh, God help us, how will we manage? What am I to do with Tahg?"

"Stop that!" His voice cracked like a whip, and he shook her soundly. "You must not give way, do you hear me? I will do all I can, but you must keep your wits while I am gone."

"Gone?" The word struck her like a blow.

He nodded, watching her closely. "Only

for a short time — an hour, perhaps two. I'm going to bring some of my men down from the hills, with extra horses. They will help us to get away."

"But Tahg —"

He slid his hands down her shoulders to grip her forearms. "There's a cabin where we're going. Tahg will be warm and safe until the ship arrives."

Nora gaped at him. "But what of Cotter's men while you're gone? What if they turn us out before you get back?"

His hands tightened on her arms. "You'll be all right until I return with the lads. Whittaker is going to make certain of that. In the meantime, you must get some things together for you and the boys. Pack only what you need — no more. When I come back, you must have Tahg ready to leave, and yourself as well. Can you do that, Nora? Whittaker will help you."

When she hesitated, trembling, he pulled her to him. Dipping his head to make her meet his relentless gaze, he cupped her face between his hands. "You will be all right, lass, I promise you. I will let no harm come to you or your sons, but you must do your part. And you must not give in to your fear."

Nora closed her eyes. Her head was pounding, her mind reeling.

"Nora? Look at me."

She opened her eyes, slowly dragging her

gaze to lock with his. Still framing her face with his hands, he again spoke her name. "Nora . . . you used to trust me, do you remember, lass?"

Nora could not answer, but merely nodded, all the while allowing his eyes to hold her captive.

"Can't you trust me again, *ma girsha?* At least once more? For the sake of your life, and that of your sons, Nora? Please?"

She searched his eyes, still unable to allow herself to hope. Yet he seemed so determined . . . so sure.

"Nora?"

Slowly, she nodded, unable to wrest her eyes from his.

"There's my good lass," he said, his voice softening to a hoarse whisper, his gaze brimming with an old, familiar fondness. "It will be all right. You will see."

At the unexpected touch of his lips on her forehead, Nora caught her breath sharply. She stood unmoving as he tipped her face up to look at him. "I will go now," he said, his eyes searching hers, "and fetch our English hero. First, though, you must promise me that you will do whatever he might ask of you while I am gone."

When she would have protested, he touched a finger to her lips. "Nora, impossible as it may be to comprehend, I know in my heart that Evan Whittaker is a good man, an honorable man. And a clever one as well, if I'm any judge. For now, we will simply have to trust him."

He held her gaze until she finally gave him a small, uncertain nod of assent. Then, with seeming reluctance, he released her, picked up his cloak and harp, and hurried out of the room.

Moments later, behind the cottage, Evan watched the small mare Cotter had given him to ride sag as Fitzgerald swung himself up on her back.

"How long will it t-take you?" he asked, convinced the little black mare could not carry so heavy a burden for very long.

"Two hours at the most — one is more likely," Fitzgerald replied, raking Evan with a measuring stare. "It's not far, but I'll be stopping at my brother's on the way out of town. To make sure Daniel John is safely hidden, and to have a word with Thomas about what to do should Cotter's thugs decide to come calling."

Evan was uncomfortably aware that he was being appraised. He sensed that Fitzgerald, if not actually having second thoughts about his trustworthiness, was at least making one last attempt to reassure himself.

"You saw how frail she is?" he asked Evan abruptly.

"Mrs. Kavanagh? Yes, I did. I told you, I

shall help her however I c-can. If she w-will allow me to help her, that is," he amended.

Still delaying, Fitzgerald glanced up at the rain-heavy clouds. "We will need bedding for Tahg — several layers, if she has it. I'll try to borrow one or two cloaks from my lads as well." He paused. "You are absolutely certain you can turn away Cotter's men?"

Hooding his coat over his head, Evan fidgeted impatiently. He was going to have the most ghastly chest cold after all this came to an end — if indeed it ever *did* come to an end. "Yes, yes, of c-course, I'm certain," he reassured Fitzgerald, ignoring the immediate twist of doubt that followed his words. "You really *m-must* go now! You dare not be caught here!"

"Aye, I am going," the other man answered, starting to turn the horse.

Both of them jumped at the distant sound of hoofbeats. Fitzgerald whipped around, shooting a startled look first toward the road, then back to Evan. "It's too soon! What are they doing back in town —"

Panicked, the blood pounding in his ears, Evan stared at him. "Get *out* of here!"

Fitzgerald slanted him one last warning look as he yanked the mare around. "If anything happens to her or her sons," he bit out in a murderous voice, "you are a dead man!" Hauling up sharply on the reins, he tore off in a frenzy across the field, throwing rocks and splattering mud as he went.

At that moment, Evan knew with absolute certainty what he had only suspected before: *Fitzgerald was in love with the Kavanagh woman!*

His mouth went dry. Pressing the knuckles of one hand to his forehead, he groaned aloud. Fitzgerald was not the kind of man to make idle threats; of that, Evan had no doubt. And now that he was aware of the real motivation behind the big Irishman's actions, he knew with chilling conviction that his own life depended on his being able to save Nora Kavanagh and her sons.

The drumming sound of approaching horses was growing louder by the second. Evan watched Fitzgerald's back for an instant more before hurrying around the side of the cottage, cringing as the deep, sludge-filled ruts sucked his feet down and filled his boots with cold, muddy water.

He shuddered, more from desperation than cold, and went back inside. As yet he had no idea what he was going to do to turn Cotter's bully-boys away.

But he must do *something*. There was too much at stake for him to fail. *Lives* were at stake.

Lord, I don't know where to start . . . Please show me the next step to take . . . help me not to fail these people. Lord . . . help me not to fail you.

20

The Wind Is Risen

Many times man lives and dies
Between his two eternities,
That of race and that of soul.

WILLIAM BUTLER YEATS (1865–1939)

The Fitzgerald cabin was cold and dank. There was plenty of wood left from Morgan's recent trip to the hills, but Thomas had ordered them not to light a fire. "We'll not be wanting to call attention to ourselves in any way," he explained. "We will keep warm by packing for the journey. There is much to do this night."

Daniel admired Thomas for the way he had risen to this most recent crisis. Many of the villagers considered Morgan's brother a dull, plodding man, albeit a kindhearted, honorable one. Through the years-long friendship between their families, however, Daniel had come to know Thomas Fitzgerald as a quiet, orderly individual, unswervingly devoted to his God, his family, and his friends, in that order.

The two brothers were more alike than was usually perceived, especially in their mutual love for the land. While Morgan's passion was more inclined toward Ireland's culture, her history, and her always questionable destiny, Thomas found his fulfillment in working the land itself, coaxing it to yield its maximum bounty. Despite their differences, both men shared a basic bond with all that was Irish and a common instinct to preserve it.

At the moment, Thomas was showing keener instincts than most of the townspeople would have credited him with. As soon as he shoved Daniel safely inside the cabin, he set him and the children, including Little Tom, to preparing for their forthcoming "adventure." Deliberately fueling their excitement about the voyage to America, he assigned each of them specific jobs, encouraging their efforts with occasional words of approval. In the midst of a dilemma that might well spell ruin for them all, he still managed to convey a sense of expectation to his children for what lay ahead, reminding them that God was very much a part of this, as He was all things.

While the silent Johanna and wee Tom helped their father to pack the most essential of their meager belongings, Daniel and Katie worked hurriedly to collect the few remaining bottles of Catherine's homemade medications and herb ointments. Opening the wooden box that held her midwifery instruments, they emptied its contents onto the kitchen table, replacing them with precious containers of medicine, as well as vinegar, soap, needles, and dressings.

While they worked, they talked sparingly, speaking in low, strained voices. Mostly they watched one another with anxious eyes. Daniel was more than a little worried by Katie's appearance. In spite of the food Morgan had managed to provide, she appeared to be failing at an alarming pace. She was wretchedly thin, so slight her bones seemed to protrude through her skin, all sharp angles and knobs; she wheezed with every breath, as if the slightest movement required great effort.

He tried his utmost to be cheerful as they worked, making frequent efforts to reassure her. But his own mounting anxiety about his family, combined with a nagging whisper of guilt, made it nearly impossible to keep his mind on what he was doing. While Morgan had not pointed a finger of blame, Daniel knew he had set something in motion during his ill-fated encounter with George Cotter. Apparently, his actions were going to exact a dear price from them all — and for that he was deeply grieved and ashamed.

"Daniel John?" Katie's soft voice tugged him back from his troubled thoughts, and he looked over at her.

"What did you mean when you said Cotter had made your mother's decision for her?"

Forcing a note of brightness into his voice, Daniel replied, "Just that she can't very well refuse to go to America now, since after today we'll have nowhere *else* to go."

Katie tucked a small vial of ointment in between some dressings. "But you don't really want to go, do you?" she asked.

Daniel shrugged, avoiding her gaze. "This is not the time to think of what I want or don't want," he replied. "From what Morgan told your da, we'll either go to America or go on the road."

"I never thought it would happen to *us*," Katie said in a choked voice. "I suppose I've always thought that somehow Uncle Morgan would *keep* it from happening to us."

Her eyes seemed enormous as she stared into the distance, biting her lip. Daniel fumbled for words that might ease the haunted look about her, but his own throat was treacherously swollen. "Your uncle Morgan has done all he could, and more," he said lamely. "At least our passage is paid, and our families will be crossing together."

"But Uncle Morgan *isn't* going," said Katie dejectedly, dragging her gaze back to his. "And nobody seems to understand why."

"I don't suppose anyone but Morgan could understand that," Daniel said. "He is tied to

Ireland in a special way, a way that only he can fathom. It's almost as if his heart is somehow . . . chained to the land itself."

"I — I really don't want to go either, you know," Katie said in little more than a whisper. Clutching at the knuckles on both hands, she added, "I suppose I'm afraid."

The woeful expression in her large green eyes told Daniel this was no time to play the brave man. "To be sure, I might be a bit afraid, too."

Her quick, grateful look made him glad he'd been honest. "Are you, Daniel John? Truly?"

He nodded. "I am. But I'd rather be afraid in America and have some hope for a future than to stay here in Killala, and have to be afraid every day of dying on the road. That would be a harder thing, I am thinking."

As he spoke, he absently touched the harp on the end of the table. The sight of the ancient instrument that had been passed down through so many generations made him wonder if his youthful ancestor, Eoin Caomhanach, had also suffered this same unmanly fear at the idea of leaving his home for an unknown land.

Katie seemed to consider his words. "It helps me to know that you will be going with us," she said with her usual directness. "I'm sure I won't be quite as frightened with you there."

Daniel wished he shared some of her confidence in him. He didn't think he'd ever been quite this frightened, except perhaps the day Cotter had caught him trying to loot the agent's garbage barrels.

"Daniel John . . . why is this happening?"

"What do you mean, Katie?"

"The Hunger. So many people starving and dying, losing their homes — I don't understand. Doesn't God care about us at all anymore?"

Staring down at the open box in front of him, Daniel shifted from one foot to the other. He had no answers for Katie, none for himself.

When he made no reply, she continued. "I once heard your mum tell mine that maybe God had placed a curse on Ireland," Katie remarked gravely. "She said the Hunger might be His way of punishing us for our sins."

Daniel looked at her. Her eyes were glazed, her skin a waxen white. Even as they stood there, scarcely moving, he could hear her laboring wheeze. He wished for a cheerful answer to give her, but could think of none. His mother often spoke of punishment and sin, and he was aware that she believed Ireland to be suffering the hand of God's wrath. He wasn't at all sure he agreed with her — at least not altogether. He still had a problem with the thought that a God who loved enough to send His own Son to die for depraved sinners would just as easily punish innocent babes.

At times even Grandfar had seemed to chafe at his mother's grim comments, actually scolding her upon occasion for such "talk of doom." His da had known best how to deal with what he called her "dark moods," had always seemed to know instinctively when to tease, when to cajole, or when to simply leave her alone until the despondency passed.

"Is that what you believe, Daniel John?" Katie asked, snapping him out of his thoughts. "That we are cursed by God?"

Slowly, Daniel shook his head. "No, in truth I don't," he said, feeling a faint nudge of guilt, as if he were somehow betraying his mother. "Da used to say it was England who had cursed us, not God."

"I never knew a country could curse another country," said Katie skeptically.

"It's more that they condemn us, I should think. By keeping us slaves on our own land and taking the very food out of our mouths — food we have grown ourselves — they've condemned us to poverty and hopelessness."

Closing the lid of the medicine box, Katie looked at him thoughtfully. "You sound just like Uncle Morgan."

Daniel gave her a faint, sheepish smile. "Well, in truth, they are his words, not mine."

"Why do the English hate us so, Daniel

John?" she asked abruptly. "They don't even know us, not really. How can they hate us so fiercely when they don't *know* us?"

Daniel looked into the dead fireplace. "Morgan says it isn't so much hate as indifference."

When he turned back to her, Katie was staring at him with a blank, uncomprehending look.

"It's as if they don't consider us — *worthy,*" he tried to explain. "We're not so much human beings in their estimation as we are . . . beasts. Animals. They believe us to be wild and ignorant savages that must be kept in our place. They've always held that Ireland belongs to them, you see, not to the Irish. They colonized a part of it, and so as far as they're concerned, they have every right to do whatever they please with their own land."

"But it's *not* their land, it's ours!"

"Aye, Katie, but what we look at from one side, they look at from the other — and neither they nor we are seeing the entire picture."

"That sounds like Uncle Morgan, too," she said testily, running her hand over the top of the wooden box.

Daniel shrugged. "What do *you* think?"

She gave him a long, burning look. "I think," she replied fiercely, "that I *hate* England! It's an evil country entirely."

Tying a rope around the box to secure it,

Daniel glanced over at her. "I don't know that an entire country can be evil," he said carefully. The last thing he wanted, with her feeling so poorly, was an argument, but she was obviously cross with him.

"Well, people *can* be evil," she countered, "and I think the English people must be very evil indeed!"

"Sure, and the English have no sole claim on wickedness, lass." Thomas had crossed the room and now stood at the end of the table, watching the two of them. Bracing both hands on the back of a chair, he added quietly, "Evil abounds wherever the old, sinful nature rules the heart, and many are the places throughout this world where that is the case, Ireland being no exception. You both must know by now that only our Lord can change hearts, and change them He does, Katie Frances. Even English hearts, at that."

Katie shot him a skeptical look. "That may be so, Da," she muttered grudgingly, "but soon there will be neither good nor evil folks in Ireland. They will all either be dead or gone to America."

Daniel felt a chill skate down his spine. There was no denying the bitter truth of her words. He was grateful when Thomas ended the exchange, calling everyone to gather around the table for a time of prayer.

Hearing Thomas Fitzgerald pray was much like listening in on an intimate conversation between good friends, Daniel thought. Thomas never so much seemed to talk *to* the Lord as to talk *with* Him. So forthright, so earnest were his words — and so frequent his silences — that at times Daniel found himself trying to imagine what the Lord might be saying in response.

At the moment, however, he was finding it nearly impossible to keep his thoughts focused on Thomas's prayer. The day had simply been too much. He felt as if he had been swept up in a rolling ball of thunder, a storm hurtling faster and faster toward destruction. He was almost ill with fear: fear for his mother, for Tahg, for Katie and her family — and for Morgan. It was a new kind of fear, an overwhelming, cloying sort of terror that seized both his mind and his body and held them prisoner. He had never felt quite so young and utterly helpless in his life.

". . . Aye, preserve our young, Lord God, that they might have many tomorrows to live for you . . ."

As Thomas's quiet words finally penetrated the turmoil in Daniel's mind, he willed himself to listen, to focus his attention on the simple but fervent prayer being lifted up. Gradually, his pulse stuttered and slowed to a normal beat. Catching a deep, steadying breath, he now added his own silent assent as Thomas went on praying.

"Guard us all and see us safely through this

night and the days to come, Lord. Protect Nora and young Tahg and the courageous Englishman who is risking himself to help us. Shelter Daniel John and all the rest of us as well in the shadow of your love, and see us safely to your appointed destination. And, as always, Lord God, I pray for the soul of my brother, Morgan, who has not yet recognized the fact of his love for you or the depth of his need for you, but who is, without even knowing it, a man much like your chosen prophet, the sorrowful Jeremiah, whose great heart was broken by his own country. . . ."

Surprised, Daniel's eyes shot open. Moved at the look of intense pleading on Thomas's good, plain face, he found himself wondering if Morgan had any idea at all how very much his brother loved him.

Then he thought of Tahg, and quickly added a fervent prayer for his *own* brother. He was convinced that Tahg, more than any of the rest of them this night, would need the merciful intervention and protection of a loving God.

The silence inside the Kavanagh cottage was broken only by the sound of anxious breathing. Nora had heard the horses ride up, followed by the muffled sound of men's voices. Evan had no time for anything more than a whispered warning to the widow to stay close to her ailing son, advising that it might be good to "hover over him and allow her maternal concern to show, as instinct might indicate."

Instinct had indicated nothing at all to *him* as yet, and he was uncomfortably close to panic. Glancing across the bed of the barely conscious boy, he met the gaze of Nora Kavanagh. Her morose gray eyes were wide with fear, and her hands had caught the bedding in a death grip. Given the terrors this woman had endured, Evan wouldn't have been at all surprised if she had shattered into a fit of hysteria.

From the first, Nora Kavanagh had struck him as a timid, weary woman whom life had beaten down one time too many. Lovely as she was — for she possessed a winsome beauty that even the ravages of the famine had not been able to destroy completely — she nevertheless bore the appearance of one wholly exhausted, physically and emotionally depleted. Moreover, she gave off a sense of unmitigated despair, much like a cornered animal whose only choices ran to a hunter's gun or a trap.

Evan had not missed the fact that her eyes darkened with suspicion each time she so much as glanced in his direction. There was no telling what she might do. That uncertainty, added to his own impending panic, made Evan wish, at least for an instant, that he had never heard of this wretched village or its inhabitants.

He looked at young Tahg Kavanagh and

was immediately ashamed of his own cowardly selfishness. Pity coursed through him as he took in the boy's smudged, sunken eyes, glassy with fever and heavy with weakness. The youth's skin was waxen and pale, except for an angry flush blotting his cheeks.

"What will we do?"

Nora Kavanagh's slightly shrill question made Evan straighten and pull in a deep breath. "I will answer the d-door," he said, clearing his throat. "You . . . stay with your son and just . . . say n-nothing." He stopped, then added, "I believe I, ah, would perhaps feel somewhat b-better about things if I knew you were p-praying while I'm . . . talking with these fellows."

"Mr. Whittaker?"

Evan darted a startled glance at the boy. It was the first time he had heard him speak, and the lad's voice was little more than a hoarse whisper.

"I . . . will pray, too," young Tahg managed to say, moistening his parched lips. "I can still . . . pray."

Unexpectedly, Evan's eyes filled, and he blinked. Nora Kavanagh bent over her son, bringing her lips close to his ear to whisper an endearment and give his shoulder a gentle squeeze. When she straightened, Evan thought the fear in her eyes might have abated, just a little. "Yes, we can do that much, at least, Mr. Whittaker. Both Tahg and I will be praying."

Evan was surprised and reassured to see her struggling for — and seemingly gaining — her composure. "Th-thank you, Mrs. Kavanagh. It helps me to know that."

Just then a furious pounding began at the door. Evan and Nora locked eyes for another instant before she sank down onto the chair beside her son's bed. Gently tugging the boy's hand out from under the bedclothes, she clung to it, saying softly, "We are praying, Mr. Whittaker . . . we are praying."

Feeling oddly bolstered, Evan nodded and started for the door, then stopped. Turning, he checked the curtain to be sure both the woman and her son could be seen from the kitchen.

After a hurried stop at Thomas's cabin, Morgan had left the village by the back road. Now he sat his horse, looking down on the village from the crest of the hill one last time.

A deadly quiet covered the hillside, the only sounds being the horse's snorting and the rain dancing off the tree limbs. He could still make out Nora's cottage, though at this distance the horses in front scarcely looked real, more like tiny brush strokes on a painting.

But they were real enough, all right, as were the thugs to whom they belonged.

Morgan was aware of his own labored breathing — not from exertion, but from his burden of dread for Nora and others. Now that he was out of Whittaker's presence, he wondered what had possessed him to set such store by the man. What had he done, leaving Nora and her ailing son to the questionable protection of a frail-looking Englishman who was a stranger to them all? How had the thin, bespectacled Saxon managed to inspire his confidence and capture his trust so quickly? He had left everyone he loved at the mercy of this slight, stammering Britisher who had no reason at all to care one way or the other whether they lived or died.

And yet Morgan had sensed that Whittaker *did* care, and cared a great deal. He shook his head as if to rid himself of the sudden doubts that threatened to stop him in his tracks. He had done all he knew to do, and in truth the Englishman was the only hope they had.

Something stirred within him, and he recognized it reluctantly as fear. He did not frighten easily, for the very fact of his size and its effect on others had made it easy to assume a certain invulnerability over the years. Without ever meaning to, he had long ago relegated fear to the distant fields of childhood.

But this was different. This present dryness of his mouth and racing of his heart had nothing at all to do with little-boy terrors or childish nightmares. This was the very reality of fear — close-up, tangible fear for the only people in his life he really cared about, the only people in his life who cared, at least a little, about *him*. It was a fear borne of his own helplessness, for when all was said and done he was only a man, even if a bit larger and stronger than most. A man vulnerable, with limitations and weaknesses and all too little hope.

How long has it been since I have prayed? he wondered abruptly. *Really prayed, with a desperate heart and a longing soul . . . and enough faith to send my pleas heavenward?*

Years. Years of wandering and doubting, years of bitterness, denial, and an unrepentant spirit. Years of ignoring God because he was sure that God had chosen to ignore him.

And yet something inside him was rising up and fighting for a voice, fighting to cry out, to be heard, to make its pain known.

Fighting to pray.

He yanked on the reins so savagely the little mare squealed and reared up, then surged forward as if to free herself of the wild giant on her back.

"Oh, God!" Morgan roared, his face locked in a fierce grimace of agony as he galloped furiously into the slashing rain. *"God! Do you remember me? After all this time and all my sin, do you even know my name? Does Morgan Fitzgerald still exist for you?*

"Do you see me, do you see my people? We are Ireland, God! Do you remember Ireland? Do you?"

21

A Gathering of Heroes

O brave young men, my love, my pride, my promise,
'Tis on you my hopes are set.

SAMUEL FERGUSON (1810–1886)

Evan turned for one last look at the mother and her son before opening the door. It was a touching scene, he thought, reassured. The woman leaned across the bed, clinging desperately to the boy's hand as if she feared he would be taken from her any moment; the boy lay still and quiet, his eyes closed, his sunken cheeks stained with angry red.

Despite the fact that he knew the boy's eyes were closed because he was praying, Evan felt a chill of eerie premonition trace his spine. There was a macabre reality about the vignette, the boy's apparent lifelessness, that sent a huge lump surging to his throat.

The mother was weeping. For some reason, the sight of her tears caught him up short, although why that should be, he had no notion; if ever a woman had reason to weep, surely Nora Kavanagh did.

Turning toward the door, he attempted to swallow down his panic and effect a visage of calm.

Lord, use me . . . free me of my fear and make me . . . adequate.

Dragging in one enormous steadying breath, he threw the bolt and swung the door open. An armed policeman and Cotter's two brutish bodyguards stood scowling at him. Behind them stood half a dozen or more men, all with crowbars.

Evan stiffened, but granted them not so much as the blink of an eye as he nodded formally. "Gentlemen?"

The bigger of Cotter's toughs stepped up and put a hand on the doorframe. "What are *you* doing here?" He was a decidedly unpleasant creature, Evan considered, with his skin deeply pitted from pox scars and a nose so far off center it appeared almost deformed.

Returning the man's contemptuous appraisal, Evan replied, "I was hoping to find Thomas Fitzgerald here," Evan replied coldly. "I have e-eviction orders to serve on him."

"Well, sure and you won't find him *here!*" the thug growled with disgust. "The Fitzgerald hut is down the road."

"I . . . am quite aware of that," Evan said coldly. Praying they would not take note of his horse's absence, he hurried to add, "Fitzgerald was not at home. Cotter m-mentioned the families were close, so I thought perhaps I m-might find him here." He shot a meaningful glance toward the invalid boy and his mother, then shook his head with a sympathy he did not have to pretend. "Helping out with the b-boy, you know."

The hateful stutter was out of control again. Most likely that accounted for the blistering stares of disdain both ruffians now fastened on him. Still, if the despised affliction worked to divert their attention, perhaps he could bear it with more grace. Obviously, he was nothing more than a lame joke to these burly barbarians, and that just might work to his advantage.

"I say," he ventured now with affected anxiety, "this Fitzgerald chap . . . he's not the outlaw his b-brother is, is he?"

The two thugs exchanged looks, then grins. "Ah, no," said the bigger of the two, "not a bit. Thomas Fitzgerald is just a slow-witted farmer is all. But," he added with a sneer, "you'll not want to be close by if his renegade brother turns up, Whittaker! He'd have you for dinner, he would!"

All the men laughed, even the constable. It was just as Evan thought: In their eyes, he was a milksop — somewhat comical, highly contemptible, but utterly harmless. So much the better. He would play his part to the hilt.

Thinking fast, Evan leveled his eyeglasses

over his nose. "Ah, good, at least I d-don't have to worry about *him!*" he burst out with feigned relief. "More than likely, he won't b-be b-back in the village before tomorrow."

The big bully with the pockmarked face abruptly sobered. "What's that you say?" he snapped, his eyes narrowing to mean slits. "What do you know about the outlaw?"

"Well, I d-don't know *anything,*" Evan said guilelessly, "other than what's rumored in the village. Somebody saw this . . . M-Morgan Fitzgerald ride out of town earlier." Again Evan dropped his voice to a whisper and leaned toward the men. "Supposedly, he's g-gone to a nearby town for supplies," he said slyly, "but if he's as sweet on the wo-woman as they say, I'd be inclined to b-believe he's gone to fetch a surgeon for her son. The boy's dying, you know," he said, pursing his lips and clucking his tongue. "So sad, isn't it?"

"What town? Did they say what town?"

"Town? Oh yes, I b-believe it was, ah, B-Ballina. Yes, that was it. B-Ballina."

The two men again locked gazes. With an air of conspiracy, Evan motioned them outside the door, then followed. "Do you think that's where the other b-boy is?" he questioned in a hushed tone. "The one you're supposed to, ah, fetch for Cotter? He's certainly n-nowhere around *here.*"

The shorter of the two men, who had hair the color of old rust and an incredible number of ginger freckles on his face, jumped on Evan's remark. "The younger brat? He's not here, then?"

"Oh no," Evan answered, widening his eyes. "I inquired after him, knowing of Cotter's . . . interest. No, he's not here."

"Where did the woman say he is?"

Evan made a small dismissing motion with one hand. "Her? Poor soul, she can't t-talk at all, she's simply d-devastated. Her son is dying, you know." For emphasis, he leveled an icy look of rebuke on the man.

The big man studied him. "You're sure the outlaw is headed for Ballina? That's what you heard?"

"Well, I can't be *certain,*" Evan said haughtily. "All these Irish names sound alike to me. But, yes, I b-believe that was the place. B-Ballina." *Oh, Lord, forgive me . . . I know most of this isn't true, not at all, but I simply don't know what else I can do.*

The rusty-haired man turned toward his companion. "He's probably right about the younger boy. The brat's forever tagging after Fitzgerald when he's in the village. If they're together, we could take the both of them at once. That should be worth a dear bonus, wouldn't you say?"

The taller, meaner-looking of the two shook his head. "Our orders is to empty this place tonight."

"Aye, and our orders were first and foremost to deliver the Kavanagh *gorsoon* to Cotter! You know him well enough to know which job will please him most, presenting him with both the boy and that devil Fitz-gerald, or tumbling some worthless widow from her cottage."

Evan saw his chance and pressed it. "Oh, I say, you're n-not thinking of evicting the woman *tonight,* are you?" He reached to straighten his eyeglasses. "Oh, that won't do at all! Why, Sir Roger would have a stroke if he knew we had tossed a widow and her dying son out into the cold! Oh, dear, n-no! I simply won't hear of it."

The big man glowered at him. "It's not for you to say. It's for Cotter."

Squaring his shoulders, Evan fixed the man with a freezing glare. "B-Begging your pardon, but George Cotter is only an *em-ployee* of Sir Roger Gilpin. And *I,*" he bit out precisely, "am Sir Roger's *assistant,* and I'm telling you that you will *not* evict this woman to-tonight. N-not if you want to continue in the employ of Gilpin estates."

The two men exchanged long looks. "I think we ought to go directly on to Ballina," said the freckle-faced man. "We're wasting time here."

"We may do that," agreed the other, "but if his honor doesn't mind, we will first have us a look inside." The man's eyes were hard with an unreadable glint.

Evan could almost feel the perspiration fighting to break out along his forehead. Did he see malice lurking behind those small gray eyes? Had he, in his haste and his nervousness, given himself away somehow?

Please, Lord, get them out of here quickly . . . please . . .

"Why, of c-course," he stammered, stepping aside to allow them entrance. "You'll want to dry out a bit before going on, I'm sure."

The big man motioned to the others in the yard that they should wait, then followed his rusty-haired cohort inside the cottage. They stopped in the middle of the kitchen, their gazes sweeping their surroundings until they spied the woman and the boy within the alcove.

Evan shot her a look, but it went unheeded. It was also unnecessary, he saw at once. Nora Kavanagh was clearly up to what was expected of her. Her eyes were fastened on her son as she wept copious tears, shaking her head over and over in gesture of desolation. She dragged her eyes away from Tahg only once to glance at the men standing in her kitchen, immediately breaking into loud sobs as if the very sight of them had triggered a fresh outburst of grief.

"As I said," Evan murmured discreetly, "the b-boy is in a terrible way. He'll be gone before n-nightfall, I should imagine." With a flash of inspiration, he added, "I say, you Irish *do* t-take on in this sort of thing, don't you? She's b-been wailing like that ever since I got here."

With obvious resentment, the freckle-faced man shot him an angry glare. "You think it be unnatural to grieve over a dying lad? Your own, at that?"

Feigning indignation, Evan bristled. "Certainly n-not! But you *do* have so many, after all. I suppose I didn't expect . . . well, you know . . ."

The other man twisted his lip in disgust. "Aye, I do know." Turning to his tall, broad-shouldered partner, he snapped, "Come on, then. It's Ballina for us."

The big man with the bad skin studied the mother and her son for what seemed to Evan an interminable time before giving a short nod. "Aye, we're off, then. But mind," he said, scowling at Evan, "if Thomas Fitzgerald shows up here, you question him good. If he has word of his brother and the boy being anywhere else but Ballina, send a message by the bailiff. We'll leave him in the village, just in case. Or would you rather he stay here, should there be trouble with Fitzgerald?"

Evan's mind raced. "Why should there be t-trouble? I'm simply going to serve his papers and be off. He has until tomorrow to leave; I'm certainly not g-going to wait around here until morning. No," he said firmly, "there's no need for anyone to stay. If Fitzgerald d-doesn't show up before long, I'm going back to Cotter's house, where it's warm."

Both men gave him one more long look, then stalked impatiently out of the cottage. Evan waited until the entire dastardly crew was safely out of the yard and back on the road before shoving the door closed and bolting it. He leaned against it for a moment, his eyes squeezed shut.

Forgive me, Lord, for lying as I did. I just couldn't think of another way.

After a moment, he opened his eyes to find Nora Kavanagh still weeping. Taking a deep breath, he crossed the room, going to stand at the curtained alcove. "You were splendid, Mrs. K-Kavanagh," he said with total sincerity. "You are a very b-brave woman."

She glanced up, staring at him almost as if she had only then become aware of his presence. Tears continued to spill over her cheeks, but she said nothing.

The boy finally broke the silence. "And you . . . are a very brave man, Mr. Whittaker. My mother and I . . . we both thank you."

Feeling too awkward to reply, Evan glanced away. "Well, now," he said briskly, "if you'll just tell me what to do, I shall help you with your packing, Mrs. K-Kavanagh. I suppose we should get b-busy with it, since Fitzgerald said he would be returning soon."

The woeful look she turned on him made Evan long to comfort her. Clearly, the poor woman was only a step this side of utter collapse. But once more she rallied and, pulling herself up off the chair, brushed her lips across the boy's cheek. "Aye," she said wearily, leaving her bedside vigil, "let us have done with it, then."

Evan had never seen such raw, exposed pain in another human being's eyes as he encountered when Nora Kavanagh passed by him to enter the kitchen.

Pat Gleeson had been Cotter's bodyguard for nearly six years, long enough to know that the agent turned vicious when foiled. The memory of Cotter's rages helped him make his decision.

Turning to the man on the horse beside him, he said bluntly, "We'll stop at the Fitzgerald hut before heading for Ballina."

Sharkey, a short, muscular man with a nasty streak, shot Gleeson an impatient glance. "For what? You heard what the Britisher said."

Ignoring Sharkey's irritation, Gleeson said, as much to himself as to his companion, "Something about that stuttering little fop puts me off. He may be Gilpin's man, but I don't trust him." Turning his horse, he gave a sharp jerk of his head to indicate Sharkey should do likewise. "We'll just have ourselves a look," he said. "I'll not be easy unless we do."

Sharkey glowered, but turned his horse, signaling the men behind them to follow. "That one has never trusted a soul in his entire wretched life, I'd wager," he muttered under his breath. "Pity he cannot see that not all men are as deceitful as himself." His scowl deepened, as did his impatience, when a sudden blast of rain let loose from the clouds, a downpour that drenched them all within seconds.

"Men, Da!" Katie cried, peering out the small front window. "Men on horses are coming!"

Thomas was hoisting a trunk to his shoulders and had it halfway up in the air when Katie called her warning. Setting it to the floor, he hurriedly pushed it beneath the bed where the Kavanagh harp had already been safely stored.

Morgan had feared that Cotter's toughs would come to check out the cabin. Thomas's mind raced, trying desperately to remember his brother's exact instructions.

"Katie Frances, did you mind what I told you? About what you are to say to the men if they ask questions about me or your uncle Morgan — or Daniel John?" Without waiting for her answer, he jerked his arm toward the small deal table in the middle of the floor.

"Hurry, boy!" he whispered harshly to Daniel. "There is no time!"

The lad scooted the table off its platform bottom, and Thomas quickly eased the wooden plank away so they could lower themselves into the hole it concealed. As soon as Daniel dropped down, out of sight, Thomas looked at his wide-eyed daughter and warned, "You'll not forget to replace the plank and the table, lass?"

She shook her head, but Thomas still hesitated, worried for the stark look of fear on her face. "It will be all right, *asthore.* Try not to be afraid — God is with us."

Katie nodded, biting at her lower lip. "I know, Da."

With a short nod, Thomas turned to the other two children. Using a hand language Morgan had helped him to develop, he once more reminded Johanna to take Little Tom to the back bedroom, and to stay there until the men were gone.

As soon as the children left the kitchen, he followed Daniel into the hole. Total darkness enveloped him the instant Katie slid the table back to its place. The black pit was actually a tunnel that led a distance away from the cabin; he and Morgan had started it over a year ago. When Morgan was in the village, he helped with it, but Thomas had done most of the digging himself, he and the two girls. In the beginning, he had used it as storage for their precious extra food supplies. Later, when the food was gone, he'd continued to tunnel, always with the thought at the back of his mind that Morgan might someday need a hidey-hole nearby; he had never expected to be hiding in it himself.

In the thick, unrelieved darkness, he could not see the boy at his side, but he was aware of Daniel John's trembling. Lifting a hand, he fumbled until he found the lad's shoulder.

"God help us, Thomas," the boy murmured.

"God *will* help us, Daniel John," Thomas replied, silently praying a psalm of refuge even as he voiced his reassurance.

When Morgan found the mountain cabin empty, he almost panicked. Only the leavings of some stirabout and bread crumbs gave him hope that the lads could be found close by.

He was soaked all the way through his cloak to his skin, his hair dripping down over his shoulders, but he took no time to dry off or warm himself. Gathering some blankets from the back room, he crashed out the door, hurriedly tugging the small mare around to the back of the cabin to a rude lean-to deep in the woods.

As soon as he entered the shed, the immense red stallion tethered at the back began to snort excitedly. Morgan crossed to the horse and soothed him, speaking the Irish.

He saddled him quickly, tossing the blankets across his broad back, then tied the mare to a lead rope.

"Aye, I have missed you, too, Pilgrim," he murmured, making a soft clicking noise with his tongue between his teeth, which immediately quieted the big stallion. "But tonight we will ride together again."

Leading both horses from the shed, Morgan silenced Pilgrim with a sharp warning as the stallion began to fight the mare's presence. After checking the lead rope, he swung himself up into the saddle. "So, then, where are the lads, Pilgrim? Where have they gone, eh?"

He thought he knew. Two priests and a country clergyman had thrown up a tent near Kilcummin, where they aided those on the road with what food and remnants of clothing they could collect. The lads made a practice of helping them out in any way they could, going down in the evening once or twice a week to drop off a bit of this or that, as well as to lend a strong back where needed.

The smudged tracings of hoofprints in the mud proved him right; at least they had headed in that direction. He had counted on finding the men at the cabin, and he resented the need to spend precious time running them down. He knew his anger was unreasonable, his impatience unjustified, but he was bone tired, anxious, and growing more apprehensive by the moment.

His mind went to those he had left behind in the village. Try as he would, he could not imagine the frail, mild Whittaker facing down Cotter's bully-boys. Even less would he allow himself to entertain the consequences of Daniel being discovered at Thomas's cabin before he could get back.

Suddenly the sound of hoofbeats and tree limbs brushing together made him look up, startled. Colin Ward and the other five lads galloped out of the woods toward him, hailing him as if he'd been gone for a month; Morgan actually gasped aloud with relief.

He yanked Pilgrim up short, waiting. "I need the lot of you in the village," he bit out when they reached him, wasting no time on a greeting. "Bring in any extra horses we have from the woods and ride as hard as you can." His eyes went over the six men, resting on the biggest of them all. "Cassidy, you meet me at Nora Kavanagh's cottage, with at least one extra horse. The rest of you go to my brother's cabin — go down the back road, and make sure you're not seen. Cassidy and I will meet you there." He paused, then added, "We will be bringing my family and the Kavanaghs up here this night."

"*All* of them?" questioned Cassidy, his heavy black brows drawn together. "The children as well?"

Morgan looked at him. "All of them," he

said. "The children especially."

He saw the men exchange glances. As briefly as possible, he explained, giving them only a hurried sketch of the events that had taken place that day. When he had finished, Cassidy spoke without hesitation. "We will get them out, Morgan."

The others nodded their assent, and Morgan drew a long breath. "Remember, we must not be seen. If we are taken, it will mean disaster for them all."

"We will not be taken," Colin Ward announced in a hard voice. Morgan knew from past experience that the young man with the black eye patch had the courage legends were made of and wits enough for two men. Just hearing Ward's reassurance made him feel easier.

"The other horses are nearby," said Ward, nodding toward the small mare on the lead rope. "Why don't you send that one with us, sir? She'll only slow you down."

Morgan quickly released the mare, handing her off to Ward. Cassidy parted his way through the other riders, pulling his horse up sharply beside Morgan.

With a short nod, Morgan turned his horse, and together he and the burly Cassidy started down the mountain for Killala.

22

Undertones

We are fainting in our misery,
But God will hear our groan.

LADY WILDE (1820–1896)

The two rough-looking men burst into the cabin as soon as Katie cracked open the door. Flinging it aside, they shoved her backward into the kitchen with such force she cried out.

The bigger of the two, the one with the scarred skin and mean-looking eyes, glared at her. "Where is your da, girl?"

"He's not at home right now, sir," Katie finally managed, nearly choking on her own voice. She was trembling, not from the cold cabin, but from fear.

"Well, and where *is* he, then?" grated the same man.

Katie's mind groped for just the right words, knowing that what she said and how she acted might be terribly important to her da and Daniel — indeed, to them all. "I'm . . . not exactly sure *where* he might be, sir. Just that he's away for now. I'm sure he won't be gone long, though."

Both men continued to pin her in place with their cold, threatening stares, but it was the big man with the heavy shoulders and cruel eyes who questioned her. "And what of your uncle, then? Morgan Fitzgerald?"

Katie swallowed hard but forced herself to meet the man's gaze. "My uncle Morgan, sir? Sure, and I don't know where he is. He doesn't live here with us, you know."

"We hear otherwise," pressed the second man.

His face was peppered generously with freckles, his mouth seemingly trapped in a permanent frown. Still, he acted a bit less gruff than his companion, so Katie fixed her eyes on him as she spoke. "Oh no, sir! Uncle Morgan stops for a visit now and then, he does, but he never stays for any length of time at all."

The freckle-faced man raked a hand through his straight red hair. "Are you satisfied at last, Gleeson? Can we get on with it now?"

Ignoring him, the big man swept the cabin with his eyes. "Who else is here with you, girl?"

Katie's heart lurched, then raced. She could not shake the image of her da and Daniel huddled in the dark pit below the cabin. "Who else, sir?"

His eyes on her were hard and impatient.

"Aye," he snarled, *"who else?"*

Katie was certain the trembling of her chin must be apparent to both men. "Only my younger sister and wee brother, sir. Johanna is putting Little Tom to bed. My mum is dead, you see."

Katie held her breath. The man finally gave a short nod. "Check in the back!" he snapped. The freckle-faced man let go with a violent oath, but made his way across the room toward the rear of the cabin.

Seconds later he returned with Little Tom, clinging tightly to the hand of Johanna, who was white with fear. The big, burly man shot the same questions at Johanna as he had Katie, but the girl simply stared at him with huge, frightened eyes.

"My sister cannot hear or speak, sir," Katie quickly explained. "She has no way of knowing what you want."

He looked at her, then again at Johanna before turning to his partner with a scowl. "We will go now," he said shortly, starting for the door, then stopping. "Let us hope that you are telling the truth, girl," he said roughly. "It will go hard for your da and your entire family if you are lying."

He watched her closely, as if he half expected her to deny everything she'd said. Her heart pounding, Katie met his eyes with as level a look as she could manage.

As soon as the two men were out the door,

she rushed to throw the bolt. Turning, she sank back against the door, staring at Johanna, waiting until the fierce trembling of her legs subsided enough that she could finally cross the room and move the table away from the hidey-hole.

Evan would never have believed he could feel such monumental relief at the sight of two outlaws. When Fitzgerald and the great brawny creature called Cassidy first edged themselves through the back door of the cottage, he could have fallen at their feet in welcome.

Fitzgerald's first move, of course, was to see to Mrs. Kavanagh. Evan found himself surprised and quite touched to see the gentleness which the Irish giant afforded the small, pale widow. It occurred to him, watching Fitzgerald's courtly tenderness with the woman, that this big, heavy-chested Gael was at heart, if not in breeding, a consummate gentleman.

When Fitzgerald quizzed him briefly but thoroughly on his handling of Cotter's thugs, Evan once again encountered a glint of approval in the Irishman's gaze.

"You have my thanks, Evan Whittaker," Fitzgerald said quietly across the boy's bed. "You are a brave man."

He turned his attention to Tahg. "We will make you as warm and as comfortable as humanly possible, lad," Fitzgerald said in a gentle voice, taking the boy's frail hand and bending over him. "This will not be an easy thing for you, Tahg. But it is necessary."

His eyes shut, Tahg nodded. " 'Tis all right, Morgan. I understand. I'm only sorry to be such a burden . . . making everything so difficult —"

The boy's mother choked out a protest, but it was Fitzgerald who, bracing a huge hand on either side of the boy's thin shoulders, silenced him. "I'll not be listening to such foolishness from a man grown," he said with a stern frown. "There is no burden about it. Once we get you into some warm wrappings, you will ride out of here on Pilgrim's back, and that will be that."

Evan would have thought Tahg Kavanagh to be beyond enthusiasm of any sort, but the boy's eyes shot open and actually appeared to brighten. "Pilgrim? Is that your horse, Morgan? Is he a stallion?"

"He is," replied Morgan, straightening, "and as hard-headed and cantankerous a great brute as you are likely to find trampling Irish sod. Now, then," he said briskly, "let us get you ready for your journey."

The boy gave a weak nod. "You are going, too, Morgan?"

Carefully freeing Tahg's arms from the bedding, Fitzgerald looked at him. "Well, of course, I am going. Would I set you on old

Pilgrim by yourself?"

Tahg shook his head. "No . . . I mean, you are going to America with us, are you not?"

Fitzgerald stopped his movements for only an instant, his wide mouth straining at a smile. "Not this time," he said, quickly adding, "perhaps later."

Tahg tried to push himself up. "But, Morgan, you *must* go! You dare not stay here, in Killala, after —"

Fitzgerald brought a finger to his own lips. "We will save our talking for later, lad. For now, we must hurry; there is little time."

With obvious reluctance, the boy sank back onto his pillow, remaining silent as both Fitzgerald and Cassidy worked to wrap him, first in Morgan's heavy frieze cloak, then in several layers of bedding. Throughout the entire process, the boy followed Fitzgerald's movements with a mournful expression and pain-filled eyes.

Watching him, Evan felt certain that a part of the pain in young Tahg's gaze was, for a change, not entirely physical.

23

As the Shadows Advance

Through the woods let us roam,
Through the wastes wild and barren;
We are strangers at home!
We are exiles in Erin!

FEARFLATHA O'GNIVE (c. 1560)
[TR. SAMUEL FERGUSON]

The road from Nora's cottage to Thomas's cabin at the edge of town spanned only a short distance, but tonight it seemed an endless trek. Indeed, Morgan felt as if he had been riding for hours.

His heart was stretched tight enough to crack. How long had it been since he'd last drawn an easy breath? Not since hoisting Tahg onto Pilgrim's back, that was certain. Instinctively, he tightened his embrace around the boy, snugly wrapped in several layers of bedding. Even so, Morgan felt the lad's trembling, heard him utter a soft moan with Pilgrim's every step.

The rain had stopped. Other than an occasional errant cloud moving across the face of the moon, the night sky was beginning to clear. He looked ahead. Nora was riding with Cassidy, with Whittaker just behind them on the extra roan. The horses took the wet, rocky hillside at a slow walk. Even Pilgrim, ordinarily a daredevil, had tempered his impatience, as if aware of the need for caution.

Morgan had fallen a ways behind the others, but in the faint spray of moonlight he could see them clearly. Too clearly. Although relieved for Tahg's sake that the rain had ended, he would have preferred the safety of cloud cover. Still, they should soon be well concealed by the fog drifting down from the mountains.

Despite the fact that the wind was cold and he wore no cloak, perspiration ribbed the back of his head, trickling down his back beneath his shirt. Anxiety. The thought of the ordeal ahead, and all that could go wrong gripped him with dread. And yet there was nothing he could do but go on.

And so they rode into the night, like prisoners already condemned to the gallows. Their only hope of survival lay in the hands of a God who seemed to have forgotten their very existence. A God who was absent.

Morgan's gaze traveled down over the hill, to the ancient round tower, then back to the night sky with its faintly shadowed moon. Lately he had found himself brooding over this . . . *absence* of God. Was it a fact? And, if so, did that *absence* somehow signify the *presence* of something else? Something evil?

All through history, it seemed that a common seed of evil sprouted its corrupt fruit, the spoiled and worthless crowding out the healthy and good. Civilization was much like the potato blight, he thought: As long as the plants blossomed prettily, grew healthy and strong in the sun, they were taken for granted but not really prized for their value. It was only after the pestilence struck, blighting the leaves and seizing the roots, finally wiping out an entire country's livelihood, that the worth of the now destroyed crop was finally realized.

With a shudder, Morgan pulled Tahg closer, as if to shelter him and will him to survie. To endure.

If only the good can ever hope to supplant the evil . . . if only what is innocent can ever hope to uproot the defiled, then what hope was there for this wasted island? The best of Ireland was dying or fleeing . . . What would be left behind to bloom in Ireland for a future day?

Oh, God . . . what would be left?

Daniel watched through the jagged tear in the paper-covered window. Any instant now he hoped to catch a glimpse of Morgan and the others.

Behind him, the dim room was crowded. Boxes bound with rope, one large trunk and a smaller one, three sacks of miscellaneous items — all were heaped randomly in the middle of the floor. Morgan's men were there, three of them; the other two had slipped out of the cabin earlier to scout the village and watch for Morgan as he brought his charges across the hill.

"You'll not see them coming until they're at the door." Katie had edged up beside him. "They will come down on the other side of the hill, not around the front way."

Daniel nodded, but continued to peer out into the moon-dusted darkness. "I know. It's just that I thought they would be here by now."

She touched his arm. "They will come soon, Daniel John. Uncle Morgan will see them safely here."

He looked at her then, managing a smile.

"Aye, he will that. Sure, there is nowhere safer to be than under your uncle Morgan's protection." Still studying her flushed, thin face, he added, "You did well tonight, Katie, turning Cotter's men away from the cabin as you did. You were brave."

She shook her head. "I did not feel brave, I can tell you! I was frightened out of my wits! I still can scarcely believe I didn't ruin things for us all by breaking down like a cry baby."

"Well, you didn't," he said. "And besides, *feeling* brave isn't the same as *being* brave, you know. It's how you behave that counts the most, not how you feel —"

They both heard the sounds at the side of the cabin at the same time — the low murmur of voices, the wet slap of hoofs in the mud. Daniel caught a glimpse of his mother as she rounded the corner of the cabin, then Morgan.

"It's them!" he cried, motioning to Katie to throw the bolt.

Morgan came in first, carrying Tahg in his arms like a baby in its wrappings. Daniel's mother and a big, gruff-looking man with a barrel chest came next, followed by the Englishman.

Without stopping, Morgan inclined his head to Daniel, motioning him to follow as he carried Tahg directly to the back of the cabin and eased him onto the bed. Daniel started to loosen the bedding from around Tahg's face, stopping for a quick embrace from his mother. When she began to fuss over Tahg, he moved aside to give her room.

As the blankets dropped away from Tahg's face, Daniel choked back a gasp of dismay. His brother's eyes were pinched shut, his lips cracked and tinged a milky shade of blue against the stark white of his skin. For a moment his heart stopped at the terrible thought that his brother was dead.

Finally Tahg began to cough. His eyes fluttered open, and Daniel caught his breath in relief. Glancing across the bed at Morgan, however, his relief immediately died. Morgan's eyes were fixed on Tahg with a grim, watchful expression. As if sensing Daniel's gaze, he looked up. Their eyes met, and in that instant Daniel knew with a stab of anguish that Morgan held no hope at all for Tahg's survival.

Instinctively he took a protective stance closer to his brother. Tahg looked up, moistening his parched lips in a weak attempt to smile. "Danny . . ."

"Aye, Tahg, I am here," Daniel said quickly, putting a hand to Tahg's thin shoulder.

"Are we ready, then, Danny?"

"Ready, Tahg?"

His brother gave a small jerk of a nod. "Aye . . . are we ready to go to America?"

Daniel stared at his brother, his throat tightening even more. "Aye, Tahg, we are almost ready at last."

Again the older boy nodded. "We must . . . we must convince Morgan to go with us, Danny . . . tell him . . . tell him he must go, too . . ."

It was the fever talking, Daniel knew. And yet he could not help but look across the bed to Morgan, who avoided his gaze by staring resolutely at Tahg.

"Do not wear yourself out, lad," Morgan said, his voice gruff. "We will soon be leaving for the mountain. You must save your strength for yet another ride."

Tahg's eyes rolled out of focus, then closed, and Daniel knew that he had once again drifted off to the place the fever took him.

Two miles outside of town, Pat Gleeson reined in his mount so sharply the stallion reared on his haunches and pawed the sky. Snorting, the horse hit the ground hard as he came down. Beside him, Sharkey pulled up his own horse with an oath. "What do you think you're doing, you —"

Gleeson sat his horse with his brawny arms braced straight out, his hands knotted tightly on the reins. "Where was the Englishman's mount, do you suppose?"

Sharkey stared at him as if he'd taken leave of his senses.

"Whittaker's *horse!*" Gleeson demanded impatiently. "Where was it? And why was he so intent on hanging about the widow's cottage — and not evicting her, eh?"

His partner twisted his face into a grimace of disbelief. "What do I know — or care — where the Englishman's *horse* is? What kind of madness is on you now?"

Gleeson didn't answer. Thinking hard, he sat staring into the night with fixed eyes and a growing certainty.

"Come on," he said, turning his horse, "we're going back."

Again Sharkey swore. "What's wrong with you, man? It's the boy and the outlaw we want, not some slow-witted farmer or widow woman! I should think —"

"Well, *don't* — you haven't the mind for it! Now, *ride!* We are going back!"

Without another word, Gleeson squeezed his legs against the stallion's sides and took off at a mad gallop.

Sharkey hurled a stream of evil epithets at him as he tore off, but after an instant spurred his mount and followed.

They had the cart nearly loaded and hitched to one of the extra horses when the sound of approaching hoofbeats came tearing out of the night. Crouched down on one knee to tighten a wheel, Morgan raised his head to listen, then lunged to his feet.

O'Dwyer and Quigley had returned from their scouting mission around the village. Waiting, Morgan wiped the oil from his hands onto his trousers.

"Is all quiet, then?" he asked the fair-haired Quigley as the men reined up in front of him.

The words were hardly out of his mouth when young Quigley blurted out, "The ship is in, sir! It's coming into the harbor now!"

For a moment Morgan could only stare at them, his brain refusing to take in what they had said.

"An American packet, it is," spluttered the

red-faced O'Dwyer with a huge grin. "A small one, but it looks fit."

"The ship is in." Morgan tested their news on his own lips. "You are certain?"

Daniel John walked up just then, staring wide-eyed, first at Morgan, then at the men on horseback. He started to speak, but Morgan stopped him with an upraised hand.

"Oh, there's no mistaking it," O'Dwyer assured him. "There's a green silk hanging from the steerage deck, just as we were told! Aye, it is your ship, right enough. There will be no need to head for the mountain this night," the man went on. "We can take your people directly to the pier."

Disoriented by this unexpected turn of events, Morgan's mind groped to change directions. "Tonight? But will they let them board tonight, do you suppose?"

O'Dwyer's grin turned sly. "Sure, and we will convince them to do so."

"Mind, we can't afford to take any more risks than are absolutely necessary," Morgan cautioned. "Especially with an ailing boy on our hands. We dare not have him jostled about or lying in the cold."

"The lass did say that most of the agent's thugs had started on for Ballina," Quigley reminded him. "That should leave only the bailiff and Cotter himself. It's not likely the two of *them* would give us any grief."

Morgan nodded vaguely. It was beginning

to make sense. Indeed, it occurred to him that their chances were now better than they might have hoped, with Cotter's bodyguards and the constables out of the picture. Still, he could not feel altogether easy with their circumstances — not yet. It seemed too smooth, and it had been his experience that when things appeared too smooth, trouble was often lurking nearby.

"All right, then," he said, still apprehensive as he scanned their thickly shadowed surroundings. "We will get them ready to go at once. You men will need to give us all the guard you can, in front and in the rear." He paused, glancing at Daniel John, who stood listening to the exchange with a mixture of excitement and uneasiness in his eyes.

Returning his gaze to O'Dwyer and Quigley, Morgan continued. "We cannot be stopped," he said quietly. "No matter what happens, we cannot be stopped. We *must* get them aboard that ship."

"Morgan, *you* dare not be seen!" O'Dwyer exclaimed. "They'll have you on the gallows by dawn if you're caught! Let us take the ailing boy with us, and you go on to the mountain!"

Shaking his head emphatically, Morgan dismissed the suggestion with a wave of his hand. "I will see them aboard that ship first."

"But if you are spotted, man —"

Again he cut O'Dwyer's protest short. "I

must go back inside. Stay here and keep watch while I tell the others."

Beside him, Daniel John put a hand to his arm. "Morgan —"

Morgan looked at him, then shook his head. "We have said what is to be said, lad. Come with me now. Your mother will need your help."

The boy studied him for another moment, then dropped his hand away.

Thomas was just coming out the door with another box as they approached. "This is the last of it, except —"

He stopped in mid-sentence, his eyes going from Morgan's face to Daniel John's.

"The ship is in," Morgan said without preamble. "There is no longer a need to go to the mountain. We will ride directly to the harbor instead."

His brother stared at him. A combination of surprise, regret, and long years of unspoken feelings hung between them.

"Put that in the cart, Thomas," Morgan said quietly, gesturing to the box. "We are leaving at once."

Still Thomas hesitated, his eyes going over Morgan's face. At last he gave a small nod and took off down the mud-slicked path, loping awkwardly toward the cart that held his meager belongings.

Morgan watched him for a moment, then turned to the boy. "Let us go and tell the others," he said quietly. "The waiting is over."

The waiting was over . . . and still he had not given Nora the letter — Michael's letter . . .

Now she would have no privacy for reading it — yet read it she must. As yet she did not know that on the other side of the ocean help was waiting.

Ah, well, there was no more opportunity to choose the proper moment. He would have to give her the letter before they left the cabin, let her read it wherever and whenever she could — after they boarded the ship, if need be. At least she would leave Ireland with the assurance that she would not be without security, without protection, once she reached the States.

Michael, Michael, she is coming. Be there for her. Be good to her, old friend . . . be everything to her that I could never be . . .

It was a rare night that George Cotter was still sober by eleven o'clock; tonight was such an occasion. So great was his anxiety that the two drinks he had downed earlier might just as well have been water. So when Harry Macken, the bailiff, appeared at his door in an obvious state of agitation, Cotter was alert enough to make sense of the man's ranting.

"There is a ship in the bay! I saw it myself!" Macken exclaimed, brushing past Cotter.

"What are you raving about?" Cotter

snapped as he stepped aside to let him enter. Closing the door, he turned to face the excited bailiff. "And what are you doing *here?* I thought you were with Gleeson and Sharkey."

Worrying his hat between both hands, the hatchet-faced Macken scowled. "I *did* go with them — at least, that is, until they left for Ballina. They felt I should stay behind in case Fitzgerald turns up back in the village."

"Ballina?" Cotter's head began to throb. "What do you mean, they left for Ballina? Make sense, man! Are you saying they have not found the boy yet?"

Macken shook his head. "Your Mr. Whittaker seems to think that Fitzgerald and the Kavanagh boy are on their way to Ballina, that they won't be back until tomorrow at the earliest."

"Fitzgerald *and* the Kavanagh boy?" Deep inside Cotter's belly a fire flared to life, adding even more agony to the already hammering pain in his head. "Gone to Ballina?" he choked out.

"Aye, so the Englishman claims to have heard. Anyway, Gleeson and Sharkey took the others and started out. I was headed home and saw the ship making anchor. I thought it best to make you aware of it right away."

"I know about a ship!" Cotter snapped, leaning toward the bailiff. "Gilpin himself paid for a number of passages, just to get the rabble off his land." He stopped, rubbing the stubble on his chin with an unsteady hand. "What kind of ship does it look to be?"

Macken shrugged. "It flies the Stars and Stripes. It's not such a big vessel, though. Mid-sized, from what I could tell in the fog."

"Stars and Stripes?" The tremor in Cotter's hand grew worse. "An *American* ship?"

Macken nodded. "Aye, it was that, I'm sure."

Enraged, Cotter let out an oath. The passages Gilpin had paid for were booked on a *British* vessel!

Cotter's mind raced. Hatred boiled up inside of him, hatred for the outlaw Fitzgerald and for the sniveling young scoundrel who was obviously depending on the bandit for protection.

"You said the Englishman told you about Fitzgerald and the boy —" he burst out suddenly. "Where did you see him? Where was Whittaker?"

Macken lifted a quizzical brow. "Why, at the widow's cottage. He was waiting for Fitzgerald's brother."

"Why there?"

As Macken explained, Cotter's fury rose. He stared at the bailiff for a moment. Abruptly, he turned, going to the closet under the stairway. "Wait — I'll need my coat."

Macken stared at him. "Your *coat?* Where would you be going at this time of night?"

"To the harbor, that's where!" Cotter shot over his shoulder. "And you are going with me!"

They thought him a fool, that was clear enough. Fitzgerald, Whittaker, even the boy — they thought him too dull-witted to see past their traitorous scheming.

Well, they would find out their mistake soon enough. He would show them that George Cotter was not nearly the fool they liked to think.

Killala slept as the American packet drifted into the harbor. Here and there a dim flicker of candlelight could be seen behind a cabin window, but most of the village was shrouded in fog and darkness. Even the sluggish, tarnished waters of the bay were black now, except for the reflected wash of moonlight around the ship.

Nobody in the village would have suspected that escape lay just beyond the weathered, drab buildings near the bay. Nobody would have dreamed that deliverance waited at the end of the pier. It would have made little difference if they had, for the few remaining residents of the village with health enough to travel would have had no money for passage to America.

The packet had already dropped anchor and now rocked gently in the waters, her silhouette forlorn in the fog-wrapped moonlight. Waiting in the deserted harbor, shifting silently in the dead of night, the lonely ship might have been one of the ghost vessels from the old tales repeated by the fireside in better days. Draped in mist and distorted by shadows, she was eerily quiet, except for an occasional creak or groan from the hull. Even the ocean beneath her seemed to whisper, as if reluctant to disturb whatever presence might wait above.

She was small but fully rigged, with three masts and a graceful, apple-cheeked bow. Sturdily constructed and buoyant in appearance, she was not a new vessel by any means. A seasoned cargo ship, she had originally been built to carry cotton and corn eastward, iron and machinery westward. These days she carried emigrants — mostly Irish — to North America.

She was the *Green Flag*, and only her crew knew that she was not all she might appear to be.

24

Flight of Terror

The last may be first! Shall our country's glory
Ever flash light on the path we have trod?
Who knows? Who knows? for our future story
Lies hid in the great sealed Book of God.

LADY WILDE (1824–1896)

Leaving Thomas's home was almost as painful for Nora as leaving her own. Spartan and plain as it was, the small cabin echoed with memories: the sound of Catherine's soft humming in the kitchen as they worked together, the children's laughter and the men arguing politics beside the fire, the long waiting throughout the night of wee Tom's birth . . .

God in heaven, how many goodbyes can a heart survive before it is broken beyond repair?

She sat on the edge of the bed beside Tahg, studying the dimly lit cabin as if to memorize it. They were ready to leave. The ship was in, most of their belongings loaded in the cart, the candles extinguished, all but one. Whittaker was holding the door to let the children file outside with some small bags and boxes. After a moment he followed them out, leaving Nora alone with Tahg and Morgan.

Still wrapped in his bedding like a babe, Tahg lay drifting in and out of his feverish dreams. Watching him, Nora stroked his arm beneath the rough wool blanket. His face was pinched and bloodless, white as a winding sheet except for his spotted red cheeks; his eyes were closed, his long, dark lashes edging lids that looked swollen and bruised. One thin hand clutched the bedding, and she reached to enfold it gently with her own.

He had never been strong, her eldest son. Even as a little boy he had appeared frail and delicate, tiring easily for no apparent reason. Could he possibly survive this night . . . and the nights to come?

Oh, merciful Lord, help my son. Wrap love and strength around him like these blankets, and protect him from the dangers of this night . . . protect us all from the dangers of this night . . .

"I will bring the boy and his mother," she heard Morgan say to the burly man who had just stepped up to the door. "Keep a close eye on the children."

The man nodded, leaving the door ajar as he left.

"Nora?"

She looked up. Morgan had come to stand in front of her, a wool blanket tossed carelessly about his shoulders like a makeshift cloak. His face was lined with worry and fatigue, his eyes somber. He was holding something in his hand — an envelope.

"I should have given this to you before now," he said, "and did intend to. But one thing or another kept happening. Now" — his voice faltered, and he glanced away for an instant before going on — "now there is no time left. You will have to read it after you're aboard."

He seemed awkward, uncertain; a rare thing for Morgan. Nora's eyes went to the envelope in his hand.

"This is for you," he said quietly, pressing the envelope into the palm of her hand and closing her fingers around it. "It's from Michael."

Nora stared at him, then glanced down at the envelope in her hand. "Michael?" she repeated, frowning in confusion as she read her name on the front of the envelope.

He nodded. "Aye, our Michael. Michael Burke. I have written him much of the Hunger and the sad state of things across Ireland."

"But why is he writing to *me?*" Nora gaped up at him. "And how . . . why did he send it to you?"

Raking a hand through his hair, Morgan looked everywhere in the cabin but at her. "I received a letter as well," he said, turning away to stand at the window. "When I last wrote to Michael, I told him I hoped to convince you to make the voyage with Thomas and the children. He is simply offering to help you get settled, once you arrive. I . . . I imagine your letter is much the same as mine."

When he turned to face her, his expression had brightened, though it seemed to Nora that his tight smile was forced. "He has done well for himself, Michael has, being a policeman in New York City. He knows people — he'll be a great help to all of you."

Nora stared blankly at the envelope. "He still remembers us?"

"Did you think he wouldn't?" Morgan interrupted, crossing the room. "Michael was a good friend, still is. But tuck the letter away for now, Nora. We dare not delay our leaving any longer. After you're safely aboard the ship, you can —"

"Morgan!"

The harsh cry came from the large, powerfully-built Cassidy. He stood framed in the open doorway, his face taut and white. "Riders coming! From the east!"

Morgan seemed to freeze, but only for an instant. Uttering a choked groan, he spun around, swinging Nora into his arms. "Take the lad with you!" he shouted to Cassidy, jerking his head toward Tahg's motionless form on the bed.

The brawny Cassidy scooped Tahg into his

arms, hastily pulling the bedding about the boy's face.

By the time they reached the road, the others were already mounted, waiting. As Morgan swung Nora onto his own stallion's back, she saw Daniel John with Whittaker, astride the small mare.

"Get those children out of the cart!" Morgan shouted to his men. "Ward — bring the little boy here! Daniel John — get off the mare! I want you on a horse to yourself, up here with me and your mother! One of the lasses can ride with Whittaker. *Hurry!*" He swiveled then to Cassidy, and together they anchored Tahg securely on the big man's albino mount.

A youthful-looking man with an eye patch ran up and plopped Little Tom into Nora's arms, immediately trotting off. Even as she attempted to soothe the whimpering child, Nora quaked with fear. As if sensing his rider's panic, the big stallion threatened to shy. Snorting, he lashed out with his forefeet, quieting at once at an angry command from Morgan, who was frantically tossing some of the heavier tools over the side of the cart as an anguished Thomas looked on in despair.

Nora realized she was still clutching the letter from Michael in her hand; with trembling fingers she now tucked it down inside the front of her dress. Waiting for Morgan to return, she sat shivering at the feel of restrained power in the enormous creature beneath her. So long of leg and broad in girth was the red stallion that she could almost imagine she sat upon one of the giant steeds of ancient legend.

When Morgan finally swung up into the saddle behind her, she choked out a deep sigh of relief. Again the horse snorted, tossing his mane, but Morgan quickly settled him with a sharp litany in the Irish, hauling on the reins to turn him around. "Ride hard and keep your heads," he bit out, meeting the eyes of his men one by one for an instant. "We must not be stopped!"

He paused, turning his mount even more in order to appraise the caravan he would lead. "Ward," he said, jerking his head toward the youth with the eye patch, "you and Quigley stay behind. Do what you can to delay them. Stop them altogether if you can! We need time!"

He yanked the horse around, and the stallion reared as if to expel some of his excess energy. Coming down, he pawed the ground, then tore off down the road in a fury.

The wind smacked at Nora's face, sucking the breath out of her. Terrified, she felt her heart slam hard against her chest and begin to race wildly, mimicking the frantic rhythm of the thundering hoofbeats beneath her. She caught Little Tom against her in a smothering embrace, praying for divine protection as they flew over the mud-slicked, deeply rutted road.

From behind, Morgan's big arms locked her in a vise. She could feel his labored breathing at the back of her head. Just the thought that Morgan was rattled was enough to parlay her own fear into panic, but she fought it down. She must not pass her terror on to the child in her arms.

It was a ride straight out of a ghastly dream, a nightmare flight of horror through the fog-fingered darkness. The treacherous highway seemed to leap up like a snake as they pounded over it, while on either side trees strained their naked, gnarled branches toward them. The fog thickened as they neared the bay, wrapping its dank, cloying tendrils around both horse and rider until they were all but lost from one another's sight.

As they rode, Nora's blood chilled with a sense of evil all about them. She imagined the arms of the rag-clad corpses along the road reaching out, groping upward in a macabre attempt to pluck them from their horses, forcing them to join the roadside legion of the dead. It seemed for all the world as if the very pit of hell had opened, spewing its horde of demons into the fog to run them down. She could almost smell the stench of sulphur at her back.

The night seemed filled with the sounds of

their desperation. Lathered horses pounded and snorted, anxious men lashed them to an even greater frenzy. Amid the smothered sobs of the children, Nora was certain she heard Tahg moan from somewhere behind her.

Suddenly wee Tom made a sharp cry, and Nora realized she must have clutched the boy too tightly in her terror. Quickly she dipped her head to murmur a comforting word in his ear, squeezing her eyes shut for an instant.

"There, ahead!"

At Morgan's cry, Nora's eyes snapped open. Directly ahead of them, at the far west end of the harbor, lay a three-masted ship bobbing gently in the bay waters. Draped in fog and silhouetted against the pale, moon-lit sky, the aging vessel looked like an eerie apparition.

A mixture of relief and alarm welled up in Nora at the sight of the ship. This was their goal, then, the end of the road. It might just as well have marked the end of her world. The very ground was being torn from under her feet. Any moment now she would be hurled into a vast unknown as dark and unfathomable as the great Atlantic itself.

Tears scalded her eyes as she glanced at Daniel John. His face set straight ahead, he leaned far forward on his brown-and-white horse, his eyes locked on the ship ahead.

"Morgan! They come!"

It was the youth with the eye patch, the one called Ward. He came roaring up through their ranks, his horse lathered and wild-eyed.

"*Cotter's men!* They are coming through the village! Riding hard!"

As soon as they reached the pier, Morgan hurled himself down off the stallion, swinging Nora and Little Tom onto the ground.

Immediately he turned to yank Daniel John from the mare's back, giving him a firm shove toward Nora.

"Stay with your mother!" he ordered, meeting Ward as he dismounted.

The youth was clearly shaken. "They were too many!" he exclaimed, his face ashen. "They got past us! Quigley was shot — he is dead!" He stopped, wiped the back of his arm over his mouth, as he gasped for breath. "They are right behind us, Morgan! You must get away before you're taken!"

Except for Thomas and Johanna, who were still coming with the cart, the others had arrived and were dismounting. Now they gathered in close to listen.

Cassidy grabbed Morgan's arm. "Ward is right! For the love of heaven, man, get yourself out of here! We will see to your people!"

Morgan shook him off without a reply, then sent both him and Ward off to join the others.

For a moment, Nora could not think beyond the horror of the young Quigley lad, murdered on their behalf. Her gaze abruptly flew to Morgan, who had pulled his pistol free from his waistband and stood, waiting anxiously for Thomas.

Only now did the full extent of his sacrifice for his family — for them all — strike her. It could just as easily be *Morgan* lying back there in the mud, his life forfeited for their sake.

Hiking Little Tom against her shoulder, she clutched at Morgan's arm with her free hand. "He is right, Morgan! You *must* come with us! It's the only way! Sure, and you will hang if you stay here!"

He looked down at her, briefly covering her hand with his, his eyes searching hers as if to read her heart. "Believe me, *ma girsha,* you will never know just how much I *want* to come with you." He lifted his hand to her cheek.

They stood in silence for another moment. *Weariness. So much weariness filled those eyes that had once laughed and danced with the reflection of her love for him.*

Gradually a ribbon of fog wound its way between them, momentarily clouding their faces before drifting off over the water. Finally, with obvious reluctance, Morgan dropped his hand away. Taking Little Tom from her arms, he started off to help Thomas, who had just arrived with the cart.

Nora watched him go, his great, broad back bent as if straining beneath a formidable weight. For the first time in a long time she sensed the conflict in his soul, the fires that drove him. A terrible sorrow gripped her, a rush of loneliness to which she could give no name.

God in heaven, I do not want to leave him . . . how can I leave him so? He will be alone entirely . . . without Thomas . . . the children . . . Daniel John. Without me . . .

She forced the thought from her mind with the bitter reminder that Morgan did not need her or anyone else. Hadn't he lived his entire life as if to prove that very fact?

Once the cart was unhitched, Morgan returned with Daniel John and Cassidy, who was again carrying Tahg in his strong arms. Grasping Daniel John's hand, Morgan pressed it to Nora's, joining them. "You must go now! Cotter's men will be on us any moment. It will not do for them to see you, especially, Daniel John. Thomas has all the passages," he said, glancing toward the ship. "You've only to go aboard. Cassidy will carry Tahg on for you."

Nora followed his gaze. A few shadowed figures had begun to appear on the lower deck, ghostly in the swirling mist. Some now started down the gangplank while others remained on the deck.

"The crew," Morgan said. "They will help you board." He paused, then urged her again, "Please, Nora — you dare not wait any longer!"

Their eyes met and held one last time. His gaze was hooded, distant. Nora felt as if a great chasm had opened between them.

"I will try to come aboard before you sail, to say goodbye," he said gruffly. "If not —" He stopped, looked at her, then at Daniel John, abruptly pulling them both into his arms. "If not, know that I will keep you both forever in my heart. There will never be a time when you are not with me."

Daniel John's eyes brimmed with tears, and Nora thought she would strangle on the knot of grief in her throat. Just as she would have made a last attempt to change Morgan's mind, the moment was shattered by a panicky shout from Thomas.

"Morgan! They are here!" His son in his arms, his little girls on either side of him, Thomas came lumbering toward them. In the distance behind him came a band of shouting men on horseback.

Morgan shoved Nora and Daniel John toward two of his men, yanking his pistol free as he spun around. "Sullivan, O'Dwyer — get everyone aboard! *Now!*"

Cotter's men came charging up, reining in their mounts just short of the pier.

"Go!" Morgan roared, shooting a look over

his shoulder as he feverishly herded Thomas and the children onto the pier.

Somebody fired a shot. Horses shied, screaming and rearing. Morgan's two men lunged into the midst of the emigrants, frantically driving them toward the ship, shouting at the crew to help.

Gripping Daniel John's hand, Nora began to run. She looked back to find Cassidy, saw him coming right behind them, Tahg locked securely in his arms. Suddenly Nora stumbled, wrenching her ankle. She cried out, and Daniel John caught her around the waist, then pulled her onto the gangplank.

Halfway up, she looked back. Her last sight of Morgan saw him striding resolutely toward Cotter's men, his head high, his pistol aimed.

25

To Stand With the Gael

Shall mine eyes behold thy glory, O my coun-
try?
Shall mine eyes behold thy glory?
Or shall the darkness close around them, ere
the sunblaze
Break at last upon thy story?

FANNY PARNELL (1854–1882)

Frozen by indecision, Evan teetered on the end of the pier, just outside the ragged line of emigrants hurrying toward the ship. He watched them in their race to get aboard for only a moment before turning and going back the way he came.

With three of his men diverted at the ship and Quigley dead, Fitzgerald was left with only the youth called Ward and Blake, a thin man with graying hair and a sharp edge of flint in his eyes. These three now stood together a short distance away from the entrance to the pier, guns leveled at Cotter's men.

The two rough-looking bodyguards, Gleeson and Sharkey, along with the constable, had already dismounted and stood glaring angrily at Fitzgerald and his men across the slight rise of muddy ground that sloped between them. At their backs waited half a dozen others, still mounted in an undisciplined row, like ill-trained troops reluctant to attack.

Evan was unarmed, but he felt a need to at least stand with Fitzgerald. Moving cautiously, he went to stand almost directly behind the three Irishmen. Just as he did, Fitzgerald stepped out, his pistol aimed directly at the head of the biggest and most brutish of the two bodyguards.

His voice was deceptively soft, laced with an unmistakable threat when he spoke. "You are outnumbered, Pat. You'd do well to be off with your lads right now while you still can."

Gleeson glanced over his shoulder at the line of men mounted behind him, then turned back to Fitzgerald and said pointedly, "I think not."

"Then think again," Fitzgerald said quietly. "One of my lads is worth three or more of those poor *goms*. That is no secret to either of us."

"Don't be a fool, Fitzgerald! Whatever daft scheme you and that traitorous Englishman have cooked up, it is over and done with now! You and the boy are coming with us, so flush him out and be quick about it!"

Gleeson was waving his gun in every direction, his eyes as unfocused as those of a drunken sailor. Swallowing nervously, Evan moved up a step, then another, edging over to the side of young Ward.

Fitzgerald was smiling — a terrible rictus of a smile that brought a chill to Evan's blood. "Ah, Pat, just drop your pistol, why don't you? Else I will have to drop *you* and leave my men to finish off the rest of your lads while your dust is still settling. Be the good fellow, now, and lay down the gun. We both know you never could shoot straight enough to hit the side of a barn. You're next to blind, and that's the truth."

It did seem to Evan that Fitzgerald and his men had the others at a distinct disadvantage, despite the fact they were outnumbered. The men still on horseback looked to be the very dregs of the village — paid housewreckers, most likely — and, as best as he could tell, unarmed. The constable, a pawnchy, seemingly timid soul, was brandishing his pistol in a palsied hand, but if he managed to wound anyone at all, Evan felt sure it would be entirely by accident. As for Fitzgerald and his men, they all had weapons, and Evan felt certain they were more than adept at using them.

Yet something in the eyes of the two named Gleeson and Sharkey made the back of his neck prickle. *Hatred.* The kind of mindless, depraved hatred that seemed to have no purpose beyond destroying the object of its malice. They would kill Fitzgerald simply because they were paid to kill him, never mind that he was one of their own countrymen, and a patriot at that.

Unexpectedly, the constable made a stab at asserting his authority. "Now, see here, Fitzgerald," he said lamely, "you're deep enough into the stew as it is! You are a wanted man! Throw down your weapon and deliver up the Kavanagh boy before this goes any further. To persist will only bring more grief upon your family and you!"

It was the wrong thing to say; Evan knew it at once. He had already seen Fitzgerald's fierce protectiveness for his brother and family, his unshakable resolve to ensure the safety of his loved ones. Watching him now, Evan sensed the rage shuddering behind every taut line of that powerful frame.

The burning green eyes seemed to bore a path right through the constable's weak bravado. "Well, then, if my hanging is already assured," Fitzgerald said, his voice hard, "I see no reason for further caution, do you? Ah, perhaps you'd step just a bit closer to Gleeson and his comrade, constable — in case I'm forced to deal with the three of you at once."

The policeman blanched, hesitating. Fitzgerald's deadly smile remained locked in place, and after another moment the constable stumbled backward, lowering his gun and finally dropping it to the ground. Immediately the man shot a furious glare at the backs of Gleeson and Sharkey, as if this entire debacle were their doing.

"Thank you, constable," Fitzgerald said with that same icy calm. "Now, Pat, if you and Mr. Sharkey there will oblige me by doing likewise, all you lads can still manage a night's sleep in your own beds."

When Gleeson and Sharkey made no move but simply stood, glaring at him, Fitzgerald glanced at Ward, who gave him a brief, answering nod. With faultless timing and before anyone knew what was happening, they shot the pistols from the hands of the other two men.

Murder in his eyes, Gleeson started to lunge, curbing his charge when Fitzgerald raised the gun and aimed it steadily at the man's head. "I will not miss, Pat," he said quietly. "We both know that I will not miss." He stood waiting, as still and as implacable as a mountain. At the same time, Ward sprang across the rise and collected both weapons.

Gleeson cursed Fitzgerald with an obscene oath but dropped back. Beside him, Sharkey now raised his hands in the air, shaking his head as if to indicate he was finished with it all.

Watching them with the keen eye of a

hawk, Fitzgerald nodded slowly. "Aye, that's better. Now, then, you may get back onto your horses and take yourselves off to your home and hearth fire. But carefully, lads," he warned, his voice tightening, "very carefully."

Seconds passed, during which the two men cast surly looks at each other. Behind them, the rank of mounted men sat deadly silent, as if holding a collective breath. Finally, their faces set in grudging defeat, both Gleeson and Sharkey began to back away, then turned and stalked off to mount their horses. Gleeson gave the reins a vicious snap, shouting to the others to follow as he spurred his horse hard and galloped off like a man possessed.

Moments later — though it seemed hours — Evan was still struggling to catch a steadying breath. Shaking his head a little to clear it, he leveled his eyeglasses on the bridge of his nose with an index finger. "Well," he said pointlessly, then again. "Well, that would seem to b-be that."

Fitzgerald turned to him with a faint, grim smile. "And what did you have in mind by sticking around here, Mr. Whittaker? Were you planning to plead for my life if it became necessary?"

Evan twisted his mouth with distaste. "I thought to d-do just that, if you really want to know, though the idea of groveling to those . . . heathens made me almost ill."

"Don't you realize at all the fix you are in, man?" Fitzgerald asked with a wondering frown. "By now you are as much a priority on Cotter's hanging list as I am."

"Oh, I kn-know that well enough, of course," Evan replied. He was only too well aware of what he had done to himself, had been aware of it since the moment he made his decision to go against Cotter. "I suppose I was hoping *they* didn't know it yet."

His eyes glinting with tired amusement, Fitzgerald put a hand to Evan's shoulder and started toward the pier. "Walk with me, my friend. We will go on board to say a proper goodbye."

With the moon hidden behind a thick bank of clouds, it was difficult to make out anything other than shadows on the ship. As they started down the old, sagging pier, Evan was keenly aware of being dwarfed by Fitzgerald's towering shadow. He realized, though, that he was no longer intimidated by the Gael's impressive size. The big Irishman now treated him with respect — indeed, had called him "my friend"; and the warmth behind his manner somehow served as a vast equalizer.

Fitzgerald stopped for a moment, drawing in a long sigh of exhaustion. "So, then, Whittaker, what do you do now? Go back to England and seek different employment? Or will you try to mend things with Gilpin?"

Evan felt something warm begin to swell inside him, and he knew before the words ever left his mouth that they were not altogether his own. "No, I really d-don't think I'm meant to go back to England. At least n-not yet."

Glancing down at him, Fitzgerald lifted a questioning brow. "What, then?"

"I suppose," Evan replied uncertainly, "I suppose I m-might just as well stay here for now. Perhaps I could be of some assistance to you and your men?" he posed hopefully.

Fitzgerald shot Evan a look that plainly questioned his sanity. "You can't do that, man! Why, Cotter would have a noose around your neck before sundown tomorrow! You're mad to even think it! Go and get on that ship, why don't you? There are extra passages paid in full — use one of them for yourself! You've more than earned it."

Boarding the ship had already occurred to Evan. He had some money with him, more saved, and indeed he had always wanted to see the States. But something in him was loathe to leave Fitzgerald just yet.

What, Lord? What more can I possibly do for this man? He's obviously dead set on braving it out here in Ireland.

"What about *you?*" he blurted out, turning to face the big man at his side. "You've a p-price on your head, your family and . . . and friends . . . will be gone — what would keep *you* here now?"

Fitzgerald looked off into the bay, delaying his answer. When he finally spoke, his tone was vague and infinitely weary. "Madness, some would say, and I'm not so sure but what they would be right." He stood, facing the ship, his magnificent head lifted slightly to the sky as if he had in mind any moment to fling heavenward a myriad of unanswered questions. One long-fingered hand absently chafed the ragged neckline of his improvised cloak, the other clenched and unclenched at his side in a kind of mindless rhythm.

Watching him, Evan caught a fleeting glimpse of one of the medieval clan chieftains: a provincial Irish prince, perhaps, with a torn woolen blanket for his royal robe and an elusive veil of fog for his crown. A prince who ruled a ruined kingdom in which his own dying populace was breaking his heart.

"I wed myself to an island," Fitzgerald was saying, tugging Evan back from his thoughts as they resumed walking. "For better or for worse, she is mine. There are changes on the wind, things coming, to which I am committed, both for country and out of loyalty to friends. I will stay," Fitzgerald said quietly, "because I must. More than that, I cannot explain."

They were almost at the ship. A raw, wet wind was whipping up again, and Evan shivered, both from the sting in the air and from the aura of fatalism he sensed in Fitzgerald's manner. He smelled the brackish waters of the bay, felt the heavy gloom and dread of this night closing in, threatening to engulf him.

A few scattered crew members were milling about on the decks and along the wharf. Looking toward the steerage deck, Evan could just make out Fitzgerald's brother and the others standing in a line, as if waiting to be shown where to go. Ship lanterns, combined with thin wisps of moonlight, haloed the dull waters of the bay, washing both him and Fitzgerald in a dim, wavering glow.

Fitzgerald lifted a hand to those on deck, then stepped onto the broad wooden gangplank. Impulsively, Evan caught his arm, stopping him. "I *wish* I could help you!" he choked out, meaning it with all his being.

Fitzgerald turned, raking Evan's face with a searching look. "Do you mean that, *mo chara* . . . my friend?" he asked quietly. "Because you *can* help me."

"Of course, I m-mean it! You've only to tell me how."

"If you really want to help me, man, then get on board that ship with my family! It breaks my heart every time I think of the fear they must be feeling, *will* be feeling throughout the days and weeks ahead. Thomas and Nora — they know nothing of cities, of strangers . . . of the world. They are innocents." He paused, then added grimly, "And both of us know, do we not, what evil the world is capable of wreaking upon the innocent?"

Evan stared at the man, seized by the burning, desperate appeal in his eyes.

Is this it, then, Lord? Is this what you want me to do?

Almost at once, filling his heart, illuminating his thoughts, the answer came. "All right," he said quietly, turning to stare at the ship. "I will go."

"Do you mean it?" Fitzgerald pressed Evan's hand with a dangerously tight grip. "You will go with them? Look after them?"

"As if they were m-my own," Evan replied softly, knowing in his heart that, in a way he would never understand, they had indeed become his own.

Stepping up onto the deck, Fitzgerald continued to grip Evan's arm. "You are a rare man, Evan Whittaker, a truly good and noble man." He paused, giving a small nod. "And a brave one as well."

Evan uttered a short, dry laugh. "I am anything but b-brave, Fitzgerald. Most of my life, at least, I have been the m-milksop Cotter believes me to be." Evan pulled in a long sigh. "No," he said, shaking his head, feeling inexplicably sad, "I am not b-brave."

"No coward would do what you have done

this night, Whittaker, certainly not for a family of strangers. Only a man with a heroic heart."

"You are wrong about that, my friend," Evan said softly. "Only a m-man with a *changed* heart, a captured heart."

Fitzgerald stared at him quizzically. "I do not believe your heart has ever required changing, Evan Whittaker. I believe it has always been good and brave."

"My heart is the heart of a *c-coward!*" Evan bit out, making no attempt to mask his self-contempt. "Until this past week, the only courage or daring I've ever known, I managed to experience from reading adventure novels! No," he protested, unwilling that Fitzgerald should see him for anything other than what he was, "only the yoke of Christ gives my heart any goodness or worth whatsoever."

Fitzgerald's eyes narrowed skeptically, and Evan hurried to explain. "Christ said to shoulder His yoke, to take His b-burden and learn from Him. But when I first accepted that burden and said yes to His yoke, I did not dream I was agreeing to help bear the burden of the entire world — a burden that includes the suffering of all mankind, throughout the ages."

He paused, gratified by Fitzgerald's intent expression. Growing more and more aware of the Lord's loving desire to communicate with this hurting, complex man, Evan stopped to wait on his Savior's leading.

When it came, even *he* was surprised. "I think, Morgan Fitzgerald, that you have tried in your own way to d-do exactly that . . . to take on the burden of your entire country, your people, and help them bear their suffering. But in doing so, you have neglected — even rejected — the very p-power that would enable you to withstand such an infinite, insufferable burden."

He was listening. He was hearing. At least for this brief moment, the Lord finally had Morgan Fitzgerald's attention.

Evan put a hand to the Irishman's brawny arm, felt the muscles tense beneath his touch. "When I was just a boy, my father told me, 'Trust God, and be brave.' I always thought I trusted God, but I never had it in me to be brave." He paused. "Now, I think I understand. When I finally trusted God fully, to lead me as He wished, the bravery followed."

Evan looked intently into Fitzgerald's eyes. "The two are connected, don't you see? In trusting God, I ultimately found the courage to do His will. And you, Morgan Fitzgerald —" He took a deep breath, then rushed to his conclusion. "Perhaps in being *courageous,* you will ultimately find your way to *trusting* God."

Evan paused, amazed at his ability to speak to this Irish giant so directly. "My friend, you are a very b-big man, a strong, powerful man. But even *you* are not man enough to bear the pain of a nation, to carry the burden of an entire people, unless you in turn allow Jesus Christ to hold *your* heart and carry *you*."

The silence that hung between them was crowned with Fitzgerald's unvoiced questions and Evan's unanswered prayers. To Evan's surprise, the other man did not appear offended; on the contrary, the big Irishman was watching him with a look of keen interest and something else — something Evan thought might have been regret.

"Fitzgerald . . . if I go with your family as you have asked . . . if I d-do that, will you promise to do something for *me?*"

The Irishman's eyes grew even narrower, and Evan hurried to assure him. "Actually, it's not for me. It's for *you*. But it will give me a certain peace if you agree."

Fitzgerald's nod was grudging, his blanket-cloak falling back from his shoulders as he crossed his massive arms on his chest.

"All I ask," Evan said quietly, "is that you take the time to think about what I've said . . . about your burdened heart, and what Christ can do with it."

"He owned my heart once, when I was a lad," Fitzgerald said tightly. "These days He has no use for it. It is far too worn and tarnished."

"God is not put off by tarnished hearts, my

friend. The only kind of heart He cannot use is one of stone that can no longer be broken." Evan swallowed down his compassion for the look of utter pain that now passed over the Irishman's face. "Fitzgerald, I do not know very much about you — not very much at all. But this much I *do* know — your heart has most assuredly not turned to stone."

He paused. He could see the other man struggling to conceal whatever tide of emotion was assailing him, but he made the decision to plunge ahead and finish what he had begun. "A man like you, empowered by a God like ours, would be a formidable instrument of change. For your people, for your nation — perhaps even for other nations. I believe with all my heart that God intends to shake you. I don't pretend for a moment to know how, but I believe He means to have your attention . . . and your heart . . . and that one way or another, He will. Be warned, Morgan Fitzgerald, for the Ancient of Days and the Shepherd of your soul is in pursuit of you . . . *and there is no hiding from Him.*"

26

One Last Goodbye

But alas for his country! – her pride is gone by,
And that spirit is broken which never would bend.
O'er the ruin her children in secret must sigh,
For 'tis treason to love her, and death to defend.

THOMAS MOORE (1779–1852)

Morgan sent his men off the ship as soon as he went on board. "I want you to split up," he said. "Tell Ward and Blake to ride to Cotter's place and wait for me there. I'll be along shortly." When Cassidy would have interrupted, he waved him off. "You knew we would settle with Cotter. That is for later. For now, the rest of you go back up the road and stand guard while you wait for me. Gleeson and the others could always change their minds and turn back, you know."

The emigrants were still waiting on the steerage deck when Morgan went aboard. He found Nora crouched in a dim corner, huddled over Tahg, who lay quietly where

Cassidy had placed him; both little girls and wee Tom sat one on either side of her. Daniel John, his knees pulled up to his chin, was perched close by, leaning against a stack of boxes as he watched two rough-looking sailors arguing in front of a rusted porthole. A few feet away, at the railing, stood Thomas and Whittaker, gazing out at the pier.

Morgan intended to have a look at their quarters below, before leaving, but for now it was more important that he see Nora alone. Watching her, crouched there in the shadows with her ailing son, he hesitated, then touched her lightly on the shoulder. "Nora?"

She looked up, and he caught her hands, raising her to her feet. "I want to talk with your mother," he told Daniel John. "Stay here with Tahg until we return."

Guiding her amidships, he sought an isolated corner and led her to it. "We've only a moment," he said. "I should be getting off soon, and I still want to see your quarters before you sail."

There was just enough reflection from the ship's lanterns that he could see her face. Her eyes were enormous, glistening in the shadows as she stared up at him.

Morgan was all too aware of her fear. Taking her hand, he lifted it to his mouth and pressed his lips to it. "It will be all right, *ma girsha,*" he said, lowering her hand but holding on to it. "Truly it will. I know this is a hard thing, but it is the *right* thing, for all of you. I do believe that with all my heart."

Looking down at their clasped hands, Nora said in a voice that was little more than a whisper, "Sure, it might not be quite so hard a thing if you were going with us, Morgan."

He winced. Releasing her hand, he tilted her chin upward, forcing her to meet his gaze. The anguish in her eyes made him want to weep.

"Morgan, please. It's not too late."

Gently, he pressed a finger to her lips to silence her, sadly shaking his head. "Hush, *macushla*. We will not spend these last few moments arguing with each other. There has already been enough of that."

He had not expected her to cry. When he saw the tears spilling over from her eyes, he caught her to him and held her. "Nora . . . ah, lass, don't, please don't. You will unman me . . . you are tearing me to pieces."

She stunned him entirely by flinging her arms about his neck, crying, "Morgan, go with us! *Please* — go with us!"

His heart aching, he eased her away from him just enough to frame her face between his hands, to lose himself in her eyes one last time. "A part of me *does* go with you, will always be with you. Ah, lass, I could never forget you; don't you know that by now? But won't you at least try to understand, for my sake? If ever you loved me, even a little, please try to understand why I must stay."

Weeping openly now, Nora clung to him. "I have *always* loved you, Morgan! Always! Even with Owen, there was a part of me that still belonged to you!"

As soon as she uttered the words, she put a fist to her mouth as if to stop them, too late. Seeing her dismay, Morgan tried to soothe her, but instead only seemed to make things worse. Now she sobbed even more furiously. "God *forgive* me! I should never have said such a thing to you."

She was destroying him. With a soft moan, Morgan buried his face in her hair, fighting back his own scalding tears. "I am a great fool, Nora, but loving you as you deserved to be loved would have taken so much more than I had to give. Loving you, I would have lived for you, rather than for what I have always known my destiny to be. Forgive me, sweetheart," he whispered into the damp warmth of her hair. "Forgive this fool."

Blinded by his own unshed tears, he gave in to his heart, surrendering the last remaining part of the love he had tried all these years to withhold from her. He kissed her, despising himself for all the joy he had lost, all the years he had wasted, yet all the while knowing she had been better off without him.

She amazed him by kissing him back, fiercely, desperately. He felt his heart fall away, completely shattered. Dragging his mouth from hers, he gripped her shoulders, pleading with his eyes. He dared not hold her a moment more or he would never leave the ship. "We must get back," he murmured with regret, setting her gently away from him.

Unable to face the desolation in her eyes, he looked away for an instant. "Your passages are paid and your belongings have been loaded, so you are ready." Groping for something to ease the pain of the moment, he faced her again. "Did I tell you, our friend Whittaker has decided to go with you?"

"Whittaker?" she said, wiping at her eyes with both hands. "Whittaker is going to America?"

Morgan forced a smile. "Aye, that he is. So you will have the benefit of his considerable wits at your disposal for whatever you may need. He is already half in love with you, you see, so whatever you want, sure, and you've only to ask."

When his teasing failed to bring the hoped-for smile, Morgan lifted his hand to brush away a strand of hair clinging to her temple, then bent to kiss her lightly on the cheek. "Go with God, *Nora a gra,*" he said, strangling on the words. "And know that the best part of my heart goes with you."

"Touching, Fitzgerald. Touching, indeed. In truth, your heart will be the only part of you going anywhere at all — now or ever."

Nora screamed and Morgan, stunned,

pulled her with him as he whipped around in the direction of the voice.

Smiling an ugly, vengeful smile, George Cotter hauled himself through the open doorway of a nearby hatch, the bailiff on his heels. Each was holding a gun.

Daniel heard his mother scream and scrambled to his feet, his heart pounding like a wild thing as he tore around the corner.

He saw them at once, standing toward the middle of the ship — his mother and Morgan, held at gunpoint by two men. The gunmen's backs were toward him, but it took only an instant to recognize Cotter and Harry Macken, the bailiff.

Whittaker and Thomas ran up alongside him, but Daniel could not take his eyes from the scene amidships.

"Get *back,* boy!" Whittaker ordered in a harsh whisper. "You must not let them see you!"

Daniel stared at the Englishman with incredulity, his pulse thundering in his ears. "How did *they* get aboard? Where are Morgan's men?"

Whittaker shook his head in frustration. "The men are already gone — I saw them leave." He paused. "As for how those two got aboard, I doubt a bailiff would have much difficulty talking his way onto a ship docked in a harbor under his jurisdiction."

"We must *do* something! They will kill them both! *What can we do?*"

The three of them looked on in horror as Morgan, facing them, pushed Daniel's mother behind his own large body and then stood, one hand lifted as if in warning, the other at his waist, close to his pistol.

Thomas put a restraining hand on Daniel's arm. "They won't hurt Nora, lad — it's Morgan they —"

He jumped, as did Daniel and Whittaker when Cotter shot his gun into the air. Morgan threw up both hands, as if in surrender.

Daniel could just make out the taut mask of rage contorting Morgan's face as he stood, hands raised, legs spread, facing Cotter and Macken.

Alarmed, he saw his mother step forward, moving up to Morgan's side.

Thomas tugged at his arm, whispering urgently, "Come, lad! Go back to your brother and stay there! If they see you, it will only make things worse!"

Daniel, only vaguely aware of Thomas's plea, was intent on figuring a way to help Morgan and his mother. At that moment, two sailors rounded the corner near the hatch where Cotter and the bailiff were standing. Daniel's hopes rose, but only for a moment. The crewmen stopped short as Macken turned his gun on them and motioned them toward the hatch, where they quickly disappeared.

As soon as the sailors backed down the hatch, Cotter again demanded they produce Daniel John. Lowering his gun, he leveled it directly at Morgan's heart. "You will turn over the boy, Fitzgerald, or I will kill you — right after I shoot the mother, that is." He glanced at Nora with a malevolent smile that made Morgan ache to smash his face in.

"No!" Nora cried, clutching Morgan's arm, staring at him in terror. "Morgan —" She broke off and turned back to Cotter. "My son isn't here!" she cried. "He's still back in the village —"

Morgan cringed. She was rambling, and he feared she would try something foolish. His mind racing furiously, he gripped her arm.

"You will watch her die, Fitzgerald," snarled Cotter. "Is that what you want?"

Morgan's brain boiled in rage and uncertainty. Never had he felt such hatred. Were it not for Nora, he would take his chances and go for both of them, never mind the guns.

Suddenly Nora twisted free of his grasp. *"No!"* she screamed wildly, flying at Cotter. *"You'll not have my son!"*

Morgan gaped in horror, then snaked out his arm to stop her. Too late. He lunged, charging forward. Now he had her, yanked her back, shoved her hard behind him.

Suddenly a wave of shouts came rolling toward them. His head shot up to see Daniel John and Thomas barreling up the deck, followed by Whittaker, all three charging madly into their midst.

Cotter whipped around, his gun flailing. Seeing him, Thomas flung one long arm out, knocking Daniel John to the right, toward the railing and out of the way.

At the same time, Whittaker rushed toward Macken. The bailiff aimed his gun at the Englishman, fired, and missed.

Seeing his chance, Morgan shoved Nora toward the railing and Daniel John. Pulling his pistol as he spun, he hurled himself at Cotter.

Too late, he saw the agent raise the gun and aim it toward Thomas.

"*No,* Thomas, stop!" Morgan shouted, throwing himself at Cotter.

Cotter fired once, then again as Morgan tackled him.

Thomas had begun to run the instant Daniel John broke loose. He had never been slow, but now he prayed wings for his heels as he went roaring up the deck, shouting like a madman in hopes of diverting the armed men from Nora and Morgan, slowing only enough to fling Daniel John out of the way.

His mind registered the sight of Morgan grabbing Nora, pushing her away, toward the railing. For an instant Thomas thought he did fly as he flung himself toward Cotter.

Then a hot, jagged pain pierced his chest, stopping him in mid-flight. Amazed, saddened, he felt himself drop from the sky.

As he fell, he cried — first, his brother's name, and then his Savior's.

Mad with rage and horror, Morgan saw Thomas fall, then Whittaker. With a thunderous roar, he yanked Cotter away from his brother's body, downing him with one vicious blow to the head, then another before finally putting a bullet through his chest. The agent's gun went spinning crazily across the deck and into the bay.

Morgan turned. Whittaker lay huddled on the deck, his face a grimace of pain, blood gushing from between his fingers as he clutched his upper left arm.

For a fleeting instant Morgan glanced from Whittaker to his brother's still form, sprawled on the deck, blood pouring from the gaping hole in his chest. An ancient blood-beast reared up inside him. His lungs exploded with a murderous scream, and he hurled the full force of his powerful frame at Harry Macken.

The bailiff was already backing away, stumbling and waving his gun in midair as he went. Morgan closed the distance between them in two great leaps. He sprang, throwing himself on the bailiff's back, knocking Macken's pistol from his hand with a fierce blow.

The bailiff was down, spread-eagled on his back and jabbering wildly. Morgan pinned him in place with one huge hand splayed in the middle of his chest, raised the gun in his other hand and leveled it at the bailiff's head.

He stared at the wailing man beneath him, saw the spittle running out of the side of his mouth, the tears of terror pouring down his cheeks. Cursing him, he tossed his own gun onto the deck and began to batter Macken with his bare hands.

It wasn't enough. Yanking him up from the deck, he started to slam the nearly unconscious man up and down on the deck, hard enough to shatter his spine.

All the while the monster inside him raged, urging him on, whipping him into madness.

It took three sailors to pull Fitzgerald off the bailiff, barely in time to save Macken's life.

Evan looked on in sick horror as Fitzgerald, torn free of the man he would have killed, stretched to his full height, raving. More awful still was the slow look of devastation that settled over his face when he turned his wild-eyed gaze upon his slain brother, still sprawled grotesquely at his feet.

Weak as he was from the gunshot wound in

his upper arm, Evan could only make a feeble attempt to comfort the grieving Irishman before dropping to the deck in a near-faint. Nora Kavanagh and the boy, Daniel, did their best to get through to Fitzgerald, but there was no reaching him. Throwing them off, he flung himself across his brother's body, then lifted the dead man into his arms and clutched him against his chest. There he remained, rocking his slain brother, his stunned, vacant stare fixed on nothing.

Those close by could just make out the soft muttering that fell from his lips like tears that had found a voice.

"Why, Thomas . . . *why? Yours* was the life worth saving, not *mine* . . . not mine . . . why did you do it, brother? Why?"

Almost an hour later, some of the crew returned with a magistrate and two constables. It took every man of them, plus a number of sailors, to pry the stricken, dazed Fitzgerald from his brother's body and clamp his legs in irons.

When it was over, both Thomas Fitzgerald and Cotter lay dead, Macken injured almost past reviving.

The authorities arrested Morgan Fitzgerald, as well as Ward and Blake, who were captured while waiting for their leader outside Cotter's house. The other three Young Irelanders got away.

Evan wept with Nora Kavanagh and young Daniel as the police led Fitzgerald off in irons. The Gael spoke not a word as he stumbled into the night, his shoulders sagging, his great head bowed. Evan had all he could do to keep the devastated young widow and her son from bolting from the ship and running after him. He eventually managed to restrain them only with the reminder that the three orphaned children would desperately need their help.

Long past midnight, Tahg Kavanagh died, before the ship ever set sail for America.

THREE

SONG OF FAREWELL

The Passage

My harp is tuned to mourning,
and my flute to the sound of wailing.

JOB 30:31 (NIV)

27

Erin, Farewell

The minstrel fell – but the foeman's chain
Could not bring his proud soul under;
The harp he loved ne'er spoke again,
For he tore its chords asunder;
And said, "No chains shall sully thee,
Thou soul of love and bravery!
Thy songs were made for the pure and free,
They shall never sound in slavery!"

THOMAS MOORE (1779–1852)

A day had come and gone, and soon it would be dawn again. They were now twenty-four hours away from Killala. A full day separated from home. A lifetime removed from all that was safely familiar.

They had set sail just before daybreak, stealing as silently and smoothly out of the bay as the mind drifts from the edge of wakefulness to a dream. Indeed, to Daniel the *Green Flag* did seem more dream than fact. As soon as he realized they were weighing anchor, he felt himself suspended in a web between reality and illusion. He knew where he was and where he was going, and yet he felt as if at any moment he might awaken in his own bed at home.

He had done his utmost to commit to memory one last view of Mayo's wild, forlorn coast, the sheltering mountains, the immense, heavy sky, the dark waters of the bay, the round tower. But at the last moment there had been such confusion, so much panic and commotion, he could only turn his back on the harbor and stumble to his quarters with the others.

Afterward, he had felt the most terrible dread that he was leaving behind something infinitely precious, something essential to his very being. It was more than the anxiety of being uprooted, more than grief for all he was losing. Throughout the sleepless night, the dark shadows of foreboding deepened, engulfing him, overwhelming him. He felt as if a piece of his heart had been torn from his body and hurled overboard into the sea.

Now he sat on the hard edge of his bunk, staring into the darkness of the steerage quarters, absorbing the sounds and smells of the ship — all unpleasant. It was still dark outside the four small portholes, and almost as dark inside, amid the rancid, filthy bunks. Only two lanterns swayed from the wooden ceiling to shed a dim light on their crowded quarters.

Above the constant creaks and groans of

the aging hull droned a steady wailing from passengers who had boarded at other ports before Killala. Much louder were the breathless, agonized moans of those suffering from seasickness. From at least half a dozen bunks came the unmistakable sound of retching. The very walls seemed to ooze dank, foul odors, saturating the air itself with despair.

Daniel's stomach pitched suddenly, then settled. He glanced in his mother's direction, two aisles across, but the coarse jute curtain separating the women's quarters from the men's had been pulled almost all the way closed. He could catch only a glimpse of her berth. He hoped she was sleeping, hoped even more she would not dream.

His gaze now came to rest on Whittaker, in the bunk beside him. The Englishman lay unmoving, eyes closed, his breathing shallow. His arm had been tended by the ship's surgeon, a Dr. Leary, a tall, gruff man who seemed kind enough, though he fairly reeked of the pungent odor of whiskey and tobacco.

The berths were unbelievably small and crowded — pine shelves with iron bedsteads connected to the beams. They were less than the width of the back of a man's coat, yet each bunk housed at least four people. Daniel, Whittaker, and Little Tom had been assigned a berth already occupied by a widowed farmer from Galway, while Daniel's mother shared hers with the two Fitzgerald girls and a surly young woman named Alice.

Daniel gripped his knees with his hands, staring down at the floor. He still felt somewhat dazed, oddly detached from his present surroundings. Like a sleepwalker wandering through a house crammed with unfamiliar occupants, he was aware of his fellow passengers only as they hindered his freedom of movement, not with any real awareness of their individual needs or misery.

There had been no true goodbyes for them — no final farewells, no pipes to play them off, no women to keen for their going. Tragedy had set the wind at their backs. Death had been their valedictory, grief their song of farewell.

Even now, hearing the groaning of the ship's timbers, the mournful bleat of a fog horn, the echoing cries of misery from other voyagers who lay suffering in the depths of steerage, Daniel felt a strangely painful need, an aching urgency to say goodbye, to *separate* himself from all that had gone before this moment. He was seized by an inexplicable longing to make a final farewell to the small whitewashed cottage in which he had been born and spent his childhood, to the ancient round tower upon which he had focused so many of his questions and dreams — and, of course, to Morgan, who had sacrificed the one thing he prized most — his freedom — in order to guarantee theirs.

His eyes traveled down to the foot of his bunk, where he had placed the Kavanagh harp. Despite the fact that his brother had seldom played the ancient instrument, by rights it had belonged to Tahg, as the eldest son. Now it fell to Daniel to preserve it and the long history of tradition that went with it. The sight of the well-loved instrument should have been comforting, he supposed, if for nothing else but its familiarity and ties to the past. But at this moment he could find no comfort in the harp, or in anything else.

Instead, he found himself wondering what had become of *Morgan's* harp, and the thought made the fist of grief in his throat swell even more. Morgan's harp, his hefty box of writings, his few worn books — all had been tucked inside the saddlebags across Pilgrim's back.

A new thought struck him now, bringing a flood of hot tears to his eyes: What would become of *Pilgrim?* Nobody else could ride that great beast, nobody other than Morgan, who, though he ranted and raved at the animal, was fiercely attached to him.

He did not know which pain pierced most deeply — the loss of Tahg and Thomas to death, or the loss of Morgan to Ireland. Each stab of sorrow seemed to rip at a different part of his heart.

God, help me . . . help me to get past my own

pain so I can help my mother, be a source of strength to her, and to Katie and Johanna and wee Tom. God, help me to be a man . . .

Nora had known loneliness as a child — the pain of rejection, the shame of being the daughter of the village strumpet, hungry and ragged and unloved. But never had she known the loneliness, the emptiness of spirit that seized her now.

Over the past months she had forced herself to move through one tide of grief after another, staggering, stumbling through her own agony without ever completely surrendering to it. Tahg's illness, his dependence on her, had been enough to keep her going.

Now Tahg was gone, and she suddenly found herself not only paralyzed by the enormity of all she had lost but, for the first time in years, unneeded. There was no longer a loving husband depending on her, no wide-eyed little girl, no ailing father-in-law, no bedridden son. She still had Daniel John, of course, but he didn't need her, not really. He was healthy, would soon be a man grown, and already was showing the first stirrings of independence.

So much change, so much loss. Family, home, even country — gone. Friends, too. Catherine . . . Thomas . . . Morgan —

She would not think about Morgan . . .

But she could not stop the thought of

Thomas — dear, good, kindhearted Thomas, who had ever put his family and friends before himself, even to the point of sacrificing his own life for his brother. They had buried him at sea, along with Tahg, only hours after the ship left the bay. Somehow Whittaker, weak as he was, had convinced the ship's captain to allow it, thereby sparing them all the agony of leaving their loved ones behind to lie in unmarked graves.

That alone was a great deal more concession, Nora was certain, than would ultimately be afforded Morgan Fitzgerald.

Again she tried to shake off the thought of him. Odd, how the sound of his name still pierced her heart, even now. Should it not have made a difference, she wondered dully, finally hearing from his own lips that his love for her had been as real, as impossible to deny as hers for him? Shouldn't it have helped somehow, made things easier?

No, no, of course it made no difference. He was lost to her, as good as dead. They would hang him, that much was sure. They would lock him inside an airless cell, and that in itself would all but kill him. Then they would hang him and toss him into a common pit on the bog.

And hadn't the man done everything but lead himself there by his own rope?

Oh, Morgan, Morgan, you fool! Was it really worth it all, now that it is over? Was it worth the death of your brother, the death of your honor . . . and our love? Was it worth your life, Morgan?

Gone — everything was gone, torn away from her one piece at a time, like old fabric heedlessly rent and discarded. Daniel John was all she had left, and even for him she could not stir herself to feel, to care again.

She heard him come up beside her bunk, sensed his troubled gaze on her back. But she lay still, eyes closed, unwilling — unable — to encounter the sorrow she knew she would see in that haunted blue gaze. Her own pain would not allow her to face his, and so she pretended to be asleep. She was his mother, and undoubtedly he needed her comfort; but she had no comfort to give him, not now.

Nora felt his light, uncertain touch on her shoulder, but she didn't move. After a moment, he released her, his boots kicking the sawdust on the floor as he walked away.

She opened her eyes and watched the two sleeping girls across from her. Katie's face was flushed and pinched in sleep. She lay huddled close to Johanna, whose dark red hair fell in wild tangles about her face. Only now did it strike her that the girls were orphans. God in heaven, what would become of them and Little Tom? What would become of them all?

She should be weeping. How could she *not* weep, mourning her son, her friends? How could she feel — *nothing?* Her heart seemed a dark, frozen pit, empty of all human feelings, even pain.

At the very least she should feel guilt. God had withdrawn His blessing from them, that was clear. Aye, He had removed everything — His blessing, His Spirit, His love — everything but His wrath. It was just as she had long suspected: He was punishing them for their sin. Punishing *her*.

Oh, she *had* sinned, and in such vile ways! She had been conceived in sin, raised in sin, then gone on to compound it all by withholding a part of her heart from her husband, wantonly allowing her thoughts at times to drift from that good man to Morgan and their foolish, childish love for each other.

And Tahg. Perhaps Owen had been right all along, accusing her of favoring their eldest son over and above the other children. She had not seen it, but Owen had. God had seen. God could not be fooled; He knew her heart.

Now only Daniel John was left to her, and yet her heart was too empty, too dead to take him in.

Her hand went absently to cover her heart as if to see if it were still beating. Through her dress she touched the envelope Morgan had given her, surprised for an instant to discover it there. She had forgotten the letter entirely.

Michael's letter. Morgan had insisted she read it as soon as possible. She thought about it for a moment, then let her hand fall away.

What did a letter matter now? What did *anything* matter now?

Later. She would read it later.

Evan was doing his best to reassure the worried boy, but obviously his efforts were having little effect. Still, he persisted. "I'm sure she'll b-be all right, son. You must give her time, however. She's had a t-terrible loss, she's utterly exhausted, and still st-stunned from it all. It may take some time before she's herself again, so you must be patient with her."

Sitting on his side of the berth, young Daniel gave him a morose look. "You do think she's all right, then? Physically, I mean? You don't think she's ill?"

"Ill?" Evan tried to consider his reply with care, but his shoulder was burning with such a vengeance he found it almost impossible to concentrate on anything but his pain. He was beginning to question what, exactly, that bleary-eyed surgeon had done to him.

Shifting from his back to his right side, he grimaced with the effort. "No, of course not, though she will undoubtedly require your close attention. Your m-mother seemed somewhat . . . frail to me, lad, even before tonight's tragedy. The combination of grief and fatigue, added to her already weakened physical condition — well, it was simply t-too much."

Pushing himself up onto one elbow, Evan watched the boy. "To be p-perfectly frank, Daniel, I believe your mother has endured enough to devastate even a p-person in splendid health. She was weak to begin with, and so it's only natural that she would be . . . d-distraught . . . perhaps somewhat disoriented for a time."

His head bowed, the boy nodded miserably. "I wish I knew what to do for her." He looked up, and Evan winced at the frustration and pain in those magnificent eyes. "She — she doesn't seem to want me near her, you see."

Evan stared at him with dismay. "Oh, n-no, son, you mustn't think that! Why, your mother is utterly *devoted* to you — that's as evident as can be. No, I think she has simply . . . withdrawn. Just for now. She's had more than enough to crush her spirit: losing her home, your brother, seeing Thomas Fitzgerald slain so brutally . . ." Evan shook his head, his words dying away.

"And Morgan," the boy choked out. "The way they took him off — it grieved her something fierce, did you see?"

Evan felt a lump swell in his own throat at the thought of his last sight of Morgan Fitzgerald, clamped in irons like a common felon, his back bent in defeat. "Yes, yes, I saw," he said. With a deep sigh, he rolled over onto his back, keeping his face turned toward the boy.

"I never knew . . . before last night," Daniel murmured, staring down at the floor, "that Mother cared so about Morgan. More often she acted as if he were naught but a nuisance when he came round. They always seemed to argue, they did." He paused, and Evan sensed his confusion. "But she must have counted him as a real friend, after all. I thought — I thought she would fly apart when they took him away, she was that shattered. She did care, much more than I knew."

Evan looked away. "Yes, yes, I'm sure you're right," he said softly. "And Fitzgerald cared greatly for your mother and you, as well."

He had cared enough to risk his life, indeed to give up the freedom he prized, even *more* than life. *Dear Lord, have mercy on that valiant man . . . he may have done some wrong things, Lord, but his heart struggles to do right, it truly does . . . have mercy on him, Lord . . . have mercy on his tortured soul . . .*

Seemingly lost in his own thoughts, Daniel lay down. Soon his eyes closed, and his breathing grew deep and rhythmic with sleep. Evan, however, remained wide awake. The muddled Dr. Leary had indicated he might be "somewhat uncomfortable" for a day or so; obviously, the man had been right.

He did hope the rheumy-eyed surgeon wasn't representative of the rest of the ship's crew or its facilities. Fortunately, the captain seemed efficient enough, if uncompromisingly cold. Evan wondered about the stiff-spined Captain Schell. He was a disturbing sort of man, defying every preconceived notion Evan had ever held about brawny, adventuresome sea captains. The novels he read most often portrayed ship commanders as large and loud — brash, beefy characters who barked out their orders in a decided brogue and were rarely if ever clean-shaven.

The enigmatic Captain Schell, however, was neither brawny nor brash, and his beardless face appeared to have been waxed, so smooth and tight was the skin. There *was* just the slightest hint of an accent in the man's precise speech — Germanic, Evan thought — but it only served to strengthen the overall impression of quality education and unquestionable authority. The only flaw in Schell's otherwise marble-smooth skin was an ugly red slash of a scar carved almost the entire length of the left side of his face, from temple to jawbone.

The scar drew immediate attention, but not so much as the strange pale blue eyes that bored through round-rimmed spectacles. Those eyes seemed to mock the object of their attention one moment, only to freeze into a glacial stare the next.

Still, the man had surprised him twice before they ever set sail — first by remaining adamant in his refusal to delay weighing anchor when the authorities would have detained the ship, and again in his ready willingness to provide a burial at sea for the Kavanagh lad and Thomas Fitzgerald.

Neatly uniformed and precise in behavior, the captain seemed a stark contrast to the ship he commanded. Evan had read about the superiority of American vessels over British ships. That information, plus the knowledge that Fitzgerald himself had arranged for these passages, had led him to believe that conditions would be, if not luxurious, at least clean and comfortable.

Accommodations on the *Green Flag* were neither. Had Fitzgerald observed firsthand the immature crew — most appeared to be mere youngsters, a fact that Evan found unnerving — and the crowded, squalid conditions in steerage, he would undoubtedly have removed his family from the ship with all haste.

He supposed he might be judging the ship too quickly. He really hadn't seen much of it, after all, having spent the last twenty-four hours in this abominable, rancid bunk. And things always looked bleak when lying flat on one's back. At any rate, he couldn't afford to allow conditions around him to affect him too greatly. He sighed. With this miserable gunshot wound in his arm, it was going to be difficult enough to keep his word to Fitzgerald about looking after his loved ones;

fretting over the ship's accommodations would only make things more difficult.

Besides, no matter how unappealing their circumstances aboard the *Green Flag*, they could not help but be vastly superior to what Fitzgerald must be facing just now.

The unsettling image of the great Gael caged in a remote Mayo prison cell was enough to drive Evan off his bunk. Staggering from the hot pain in his shoulder, he sank to unsteady knees and began to pray.

For the first time in his life, Morgan was confined to a place where he could not see the sky, could not open the door and walk out a free man. God knew he had earned himself a cell — more than once, if truth be told. The real wonder was that his lawless and careless ways had only now caught up to him.

The gaol in Castlebar was a miserable hole, a dark, dank room reeking of vermin and unwashed bodies and years of mold. A filthy blanket tossed over a lumpy mattress of straw served as a bed, a bucket as a privy. There was no window, no chair, no water pitcher. The only sound was an occasional scurrying of a rat making its way from one corner to the other.

Morgan could not stand upright, nor could he take more than four broad steps from wall to wall. Had there been any furnishings he would have tripped over them, for the darkness was almost totally unrelieved, save for the palest wash of light from a candle outside in the corridor.

At the moment he sat on the edge of the mattress, his elbows propped on his knees, his head supported by his hands. He was neither fully awake nor quite asleep; his bad tooth throbbed just enough to keep him from getting any rest. It occurred to him for an instant that there was a dubious irony in a man plagued by a toothache when about to be hanged, and he smiled grimly to himself in the darkness.

He heard the jingle of keys and looked up with no real interest as the gaoler opened the door to allow Joseph Mahon entrance.

"I'll be just outside, Father," said Cummins, the gaoler, waiting for the priest to enter the cell. "You've only to call if you need me. Have a care with that one — he's big and mean clear through."

Mahon came the rest of the way in, his arms filled with some packages and Morgan's harp.

"Morgan," he said with a nod, coming to stand near the bed. "How are you, lad? Here, I've brought you clean clothes. And some of your things from your saddlebags. They said you could have them."

In the shadows, Morgan noted that the priest was as lean as sorrow, his long, narrow face drawn and hollowed out, his silver hair thinned to a web across his skull. The Hunger exempted no man, not even a man of God.

Morgan thanked him for his things, laying them at the head of the bed.

"So, Morgan, what is this they are saying you have done? 'Tis a real fix you've gotten yourself into this time."

Morgan patted the mattress beside him, and the other man sat down. "Aye, I'm in trouble for sure, if they've sent the priest," he said. "With things that bad, it's not likely I'll have time enough for the books, Joseph."

"You needn't play the *googeen* with me, Morgan," the priest said quietly. "We have known each other too long for that."

Morgan turned his gaze to the floor, disconcerted by the man's undisguised sympathy.

"I came to see if there is anything you need," said Mahon. "And to tell you how sorry I am about Thomas. Your brother was a good man, a truly good man."

"What have they done with him, do you know?" Morgan asked, cracking the knuckles of both hands.

"They allowed me to go aboard and administer the last rites. He was then to be buried at sea." Mahon paused. "Along with the Kavanagh lad — young Tahg."

Morgan lifted his head to face the priest. "Tahg?"

Mahon nodded. "He died before they sailed."

Morgan stared at him for a moment, then again cupped his head between his hands, digging at his beard with his fingers. "Oh, God," he whispered. "Oh, God, how much more?"

"You at least have the peace of knowing Thomas died in a state of grace," said the priest.

"Thomas *lived* in a state of grace," Morgan bit out.

"Aye, more than most," agreed Mahon.

"And just see his profit from it."

"We do not live a godly life for profit, lad, but to the glory of our Lord. Your brother would have been one of the first to testify to that."

Morgan said nothing, involuntarily drawing away when the priest reached to touch his arm.

"Morgan, you are a tormented man. Let me help you."

"Help me?" Morgan jerked to his feet. "What, then? Shall I confess to you, is that what you'd have me do?"

"Ach, if only you would."

"You know I have never believed in that way."

"Then confess to your *Savior,* Morgan. Sure, and you still believe in Him, I would hope."

"Are you saying I don't have to go through *you,* then, Joseph? Strange words for a priest."

"Do not mock me, Morgan. I only came to help, and to tell you of your brother."

Morgan unclenched his hands, splayed them on his knees. "Aye, I do know that," he said with a sigh. "And it was kindness itself for you to come, Joseph. You are a good man. You have done much for my family and for the village."

"Morgan, 'tis no secret to you and to my people that I myself have questioned certain tenets of the church from time to time. I've never been the one to say that every word handed down from Rome is divinely given."

"That's so. I think you must be as much a renegade of the cloth as I am of the law, Joseph," Morgan said, managing a thin smile.

In truth, he greatly admired the slight, aging priest. The man had poured himself out for the villagers year after year, spent himself completely, never complaining, with not a thing to show for it other than the stoop of age and an occasional kiss on the hand.

"Well, then, reject the church if you must, but for the sake of your soul, lad, do not reject our Lord. He does know what He is about, even if we cannot see it."

Unwilling to subject himself to a theological discussion, Morgan ignored the priest's caution. "Did you see the others when you went aboard, Joseph? Thomas's children . . . Nora?"

Mahon shook his head. "They wouldn't let me below decks. I was allowed only a moment with Thomas, they were that eager to set sail." He stopped and clasped his hands together in his lap. "Morgan — for what it may be worth, I understand what you did last night. Cotter would have killed you if you had not got to him first. You and perhaps several others as well."

Morgan shook his head. "Have no illusions about what I did, Joseph. I went mad, and that's the truth. I would have murdered George Cotter even if he hadn't shot my brother; more than likely I would have killed him even if he had no gun. And no doubt I would have finished off poor old Macken as well, had they not pulled me off him when they did." Rubbing his jaw against the pain of the aching tooth, he went on. "No, the truth is that something inside me tore loose, changed me into more beast than man. But don't ask me to repent of killing the agent. God himself could not convince me that George Cotter deserved to live."

Wringing his hands, Mahon studied him. "That is not for us to decide, Morgan. We cannot know why God chooses to give life to some or withdraw it from others. But one thing I do know: There is an entire well of hatred and bitterness in you, lad, that must be emptied if you are ever to find your way back to the Lord." He drew a shaky breath. "Morgan . . . you know they will hang you."

Morgan looked at him. "Aye, they will."

Mahon seemed flustered by his directness. "You must not die with all this hatred on your soul, Morgan, and with such . . . lawlessness, such sin. Please, at least let me pray with you."

Morgan saw in the priest's face what he had seen in few others: a pure, selfless compassion and concern for another human being. It should have moved him, but in truth it only made him sad. "Don't waste your efforts on me, Joseph," he said, turning his back to the other man. "There are too many others in the village who need you. Save what strength you have for them. I deserve the hanging they are going to do, and we both know there is no stopping it."

Behind him, Mahon's quiet words sounded unexpectedly stern. "Do not let your brother's death be in vain, Morgan! Even worse, do not let our *Savior's* death be in vain."

Morgan felt a muscle near his right eye twitch. When he turned, the priest had risen to his feet and stood watching him.

"Say what you mean, Joseph."

"Thomas loved you to the point of despair, Morgan," the other man said firmly. "He agonized over you — over your soul. The man literally stormed the gates of heaven for your return to God's arms, time after time, year after year, never once conceding that his efforts might be in vain. And at the end —" Mahon stopped, but his gaze never wavered. "At the end he died in order that you might live. Sure, I do believe that you owe Thomas's noble memory at least a prayer in your own behalf."

Angry at the man's intrusion into his grief, Morgan scowled, opening his mouth to shoot back a caustic reply.

But the priest ignored him. "God in heaven, lad, do you not see it, even *now?* Your brother's unselfish death, our Savior's sacrifice on the cross — both were for *you*. Thomas died to spare your flesh, but our Lord died to spare your soul. Morgan, Morgan," the priest said, shaking his head sadly, "you belonged to Him once. Why have you turned from Him all these years? Let Thomas's final gift to you be your way back to the Savior!"

Steeling himself against the storm of emotion battering at his heart, more mindful than ever of the ache throbbing against his jaw, Morgan again turned his back on the other man. "I am not up for this, Joseph," he said unsteadily. "I know what you are trying to do, and I know you mean well. But I ask you to leave me. Please."

There was silence for a moment, then the

sound of Mahon's weary footsteps scraping the stone floor as he came to stand beside him. "I will go, then, Morgan. But I want you to know that I will do whatever I can to change some minds. I will go this very day to speak with the authorities."

In reply, Morgan gave only the ghost of a knowing smile. Finally, the priest gave his arm a light squeeze, hesitating another moment before calling the gaoler.

"I will come if you need me, Morgan. Night or day, I will come. You've only to call."

Morgan nodded shortly, waiting until the priest was gone before crossing the room and sinking down onto the mattress. Idly, he began to finger through the things Mahon had brought: some worn books, a stack of poems and articles for *The Nation*, a clean shirt and pants. At last his hand went to the harp. He lifted it, placed it on his lap, and sat staring at it for a long time.

Finally, his face twisted with pain and rage, he began to yank at the strings, pulling them free one at a time until all dangled brokenly.

Then he stood, and with an agonized cry ripping up from the very center of his soul, gave the useless instrument a fierce toss, hurling it against the stone wall of the cell.

It fell to the floor with a voiceless thud.

28

Changes and Challenges

O wise men, riddle me this:
What if the dream come true?
What if the dream come true? and if millions unborn
Shall dwell in the house that I shaped in my heart. . . .

PADRAIC PEARSE (1879–1916)

New York City

Michael Burke stood staring at his reflection in the bedroom mirror, a practice to which he was not ordinarily given. Lately, however, he had become increasingly concerned about his appearance.

At the oddest times and in the most unlikely places he would catch himself trying to measure just how much he had changed in seventeen years. It embarrassed him, caused him no end of impatience with himself, to realize that this recent preoccupation with his looks had been brought on entirely by the unsettling question of how he might appear to

Nora after so long a time.

This morning he felt neither pleased nor displeased by the image staring back at him, only anxious. Walking a beat, chasing the pigs from city streets, and running at least one gang member to the ground every day kept him fit and lean enough. And there was more than one advantage in not being a drinker; his middle was as trim as it had been the day he sailed out of Killala Bay.

A few lines in the face could not be denied, mostly about the mouth, which, according to Eileen, had always been a bit grim at best. Ah, well, at least his hair was still thick and dark, though lately some silver had begun to peep through here and there.

He leaned a bit closer to the mirror in order to inspect his face more thoroughly. After Eileen's death, he had considered growing a beard, or at least a mustache. Now he decided it would be best to remain clean-shaven — at least until Nora had had a chance to get used to him again.

If she came.

Unwilling for the moment to dwell on whether she would or would not make the journey to America, he began to comb his hair. The room reflected in the mirror caught his attention — a small room, too small, and too drab entirely. Somehow Eileen had managed to fill it with color and freshness, but her cheerful influence had long since faded. He had changed nothing since her death, yet the room did not appear the same at all. The ruffled curtains and pillows she had made, the coverlet she had quilted, the rough pine she had faithfully waxed — it was all the same, yet altogether different. The iron bedstead needed polishing, the vanity was scratched and dull, and the curtains hung as limp as a cow's tail on a hot summer's day.

He frowned at himself and the bedroom in the mirror. It was a faded, dull room, in sore need of a woman.

And that's what I've become, he thought. *A faded, dull man in sore need of a woman.*

He pulled back from the mirror and went to stand by the window. If Nora were coming, she might well be on her way, even now. According to the messenger who had come for his return letter to Morgan, the ship was to sail from Killala some time near the end of March. That being the case, they could arrive in New York as early as the end of April or the first part of May. It would take at least five weeks, perhaps longer, depending on the type of ship and the weather. Some of the packets were said to be crossing in as little as thirty days. His own voyage had lasted for nearly six weeks; his seasickness, however, had made it seem far longer. It had been a miserable time, despite his youthful excitement at the adventure that lay before him.

Unless Nora had changed greatly, he doubted she would be excited. Frightened, perhaps, and even resentful at having to leave her own Ireland for a strange land, but not excited. Nora had never been one for adventure or change, had ever held back when it came to daring the unknown.

Why, then, was he so foolish as to think she would marry him?

Perhaps because he wanted it so — wanted it selfishly, to fill his emptiness, ease his loneliness. But he *could* help her and her boys, after all. The flat might not be much, but it *had* to be better than what she was used to in Killala. He knew the cottages in the village well enough: even the best of them boasted only dirt floors, patched windows, and turf fires. Besides, now that he had the promise of a promotion, he might soon afford a better place in a nicer neighborhood. Just because he worked Sixth Ward didn't mean he had to live here forever, especially with a wife and a family.

Until this moment he had not admitted to himself how very much he *wanted* her to come, how greatly he was anticipating it. And it was not an anticipation he would have felt for just *any* woman. No, it was *Nora* he could not get out of his mind, shy Nora from Killala whom he longed to see.

Oh, Lord, if she is on that ship, bring her safely to me. It's a terrible journey at best, and to a shy lass like Nora it will be a torment. Give her the courage to leave, Lord, and then give her the stamina to survive the crossing. I'll be good to her, I promise I will . . . I'll do all that I can to make her glad she came —

"Da?"

The bedroom door came flying open as Tierney charged into the room. Michael sighed. The boy never walked, it seemed, could only run or leap or trot; indeed, sometimes he seemed to fly.

"I thought we recently had us a talk about knocking before bursting into someone's room," Michael said. He had to force a frown, for this morning his spirits were too high for more than a token sternness.

His son grinned at him, as if sensing his good humor. "Don't fret yourself, Da. Once your Nora arrives, I promise I'll knock before I come crashing into the bedroom."

Now Michael *did* frown. "That'll do, Tierney! Don't be fresh. And she is not 'my Nora'!"

"Not yet," Tierney shot back, still grinning as he plopped down onto the bed. "So, then, d'you think they are coming?"

"There's no way to know that."

"But if they do come, you think Nora will marry you, right?"

Uncomfortable with the boy's scrutiny, Michael turned back to the mirror and pretended to straighten his collar. "And how would I know the answer to such a foolish question? No man can say what a woman will do."

"Mmm. Well, I hope they come. And I hope she marries you. But then, I'm sure she will, since she already knows what a fine fellow you are."

Pleased, Michael exchanged grins with him in the mirror, then turned. "You really mean that, don't you, Tierney? You *do* want them to come?"

"Sure I do, Da, I've already told you so. It'll be grand! You'll have a wife, and I'll have myself a brother. Well, perhaps not a brother," he said, folding his arms over his chest, "but at least a friend from Ireland. I can't wait to ask him all sorts of questions!"

"Nora has two sons, Tierney," Michael reminded him.

"Oh, I know," the boy put in quickly. "It's too bad about the older one. He must be very ill."

Michael shook his head. "Aye, it sounds so. But we can continue to pray for the lad, you know."

"Sure, Da. Listen, I've got news!" He stood, and Michael saw now that his face was flushed with excitement. "I'm to have a raise in pay, starting next week. That'll be a help if we're to take on a new family, won't it?"

"Why, that's fine, son, just fine," Michael said, crossing the room to make up the bed.

"Help me with this, won't you? And before you tell me more about that raise, I'll hear your reason for coming home so late last night."

Tierney talked as he worked. "Mr. Walsh stopped by and asked me to stay over a bit — that's when I found out about the raise."

"Walsh himself talked to you? Isn't that a bit unusual?"

Tierney flung the coverlet up on his side, then smoothed the pillows. Walking over to the bureau, he picked up the previous day's newspaper and, rolling it into a tube, began to tap it against the palm of his hand. "He told me he's pleased with my work — *greatly* pleased, he said. So, starting next week, I'm to handle the desk until eleven."

Michael straightened, frowning. "That's too late for you to be out, Tierney. Too late entirely. You have your schoolwork to do, and you must get your sleep as well. Besides, what's the man thinking of, giving a boy your age such a responsible job?"

"He knows I can do it," Tierney said, color rising to his cheeks as he slapped the paper harder against his hand. "He trusts me, you know."

Michael could not argue with that, not in good conscience. Tierney *was* responsible, at least when it came to his job.

The lad had always seemed older than his years; at times his maturity worried Michael, for he wanted a normal childhood for his son. More than likely Walsh had seen that same maturity, and he could hardly fault the man for that. It would not do to have the boy think he was criticizing him for being dependable.

"Tierney, understand, son, I am glad Mr. Walsh thinks so highly of you, but —"

"Come on, Da," the boy interrupted, tossing the newspaper back onto the bureau. "You know I don't have to put in all that many hours to get my grades. Even if I did, that's just another advantage to the job: I can mind the desk and study at the same time. Mr. Walsh said so, said I can do whatever I please just so long as I don't neglect the desk."

"Tierney —" Michael stopped, uncertain as to how to phrase his reservations. "Mind, now, I think it's grand that you've done so well, and I'm proud to hear that you're appreciated. It's only that I don't want you getting too tight with Patrick Walsh. There is plenty of talk about the man, and not all of it good; I've told you that already. I've heard questions raised all too often about the nature of his businesses — and the legitimacy of them."

Tierney scowled. "You've also told me I should never mind gossip," he bit out. "And I *won't* listen to it about Mr. Walsh! It's jealousy talking, that's all. He's smart and ambitious, and he's good to those who work for him, which is more than you can say about most of the other swells in this city."

"That may be true," Michael countered, "but you must admit, it's a rare thing entirely for an Irishman to make his mark in New York at all, much less in only a few years, as Walsh has. I'm only saying that you should have a care, Tierney, that's all."

The boy's casual nod told Michael he would remember his caution no longer than it took to repeat it. "Sure, Da, I'll be careful. But I'm telling you, you've nothing to worry about with Mr. Walsh. Anyway, guess what else? I told him about Thomas Fitzgerald, how he'd be needing a job and a place to stay, and he said if he's any good at all at gardening, he just might have a place for him. His present man is going west next month, so he'll be needing somebody to replace him. There's even a gardener's cottage on the grounds — he has a grand estate on Staten Island, you know. And that's not all," the boy went on, his words spilling out in a breathless rush. "He also told me he has some extra work for me some Saturdays if I want it, up at his house. Odd jobs, he said, but he'll pay me well."

Michael regarded his son with troubled eyes. Something about Patrick Walsh's easy generosity bothered him. Irishmen in New York City nearly always fell into one of two categories: Either they remained unemployed, or they worked at low-paying, undesirable jobs that "respectable" citizens refused to touch. Yet Patrick Walsh had managed to become a wealthy, successful businessman in only a few years. He owned at least half a dozen boardinghouses near the docks and in other low-rent districts, plus a couple of nicer hotels farther uptown. There was no telling how many saloons belonged to the man, no figuring how he had wangled his way into the political establishment at Tammany Hall. The fact that Walsh seemed to enjoy wealth, influence, and respectability — all uncommon to the Irish in New York City — made him immediately suspect in Michael's mind.

Still, he hated to spoil the lad's news. "Just remember what I've told you, Tierney — have a care. Things — and people — are not always as they seem. Now, then," he said, shoving his hands down deep into his pockets, "I've some news for *you*. It seems that I am up for assistant captain."

Tierney crossed the room in three broad strides to grab Michael by the shoulder. "But that's *grand*, Da! Is it definite, d'you know?"

"Well, nothing is certain until it's announced, but I was told by Captain Hart I should expect it."

"And you deserve it! You're one of the best they have, and it's time they were knowing it!"

Surprised at this rare affirmation from his son, Michael beamed at him. "So, then, it would seem that we will both be getting a raise in pay. Perhaps this is a sign from the Lord that we are indeed about to expand our family."

"Could be, Da, could be," Tierney said negligently, reverting now to his usual non-committal manner as he moved to check his own appearance in the mirror. "You'd know more about that sort of thing than I would." He started for the door. "I must be off, or I'll be late. Are you leaving now?"

"Not yet, but soon. I have to go in a bit early today. Price and I are to escort some ladies from one of those benevolent societies into Five Points later this morning."

Tierney made a face, and Michael nodded in agreement. The thought was enough to dampen his cheerful spirits. Like every other policeman on the force, he dreaded the notorious Five Points slum with a vengeance.

"Why in the world would a bunch of rich old ladies want to venture into *that* place?" Tierney asked, starting for the door.

"Well, with some, of course, it's little more than curiosity," Michael answered, following him out of the bedroom. "Others, I suppose, truly want to help, but mean to see where their money will be spent before making any sort of commitment."

Tierney gave a small grunt of disgust. "I

doubt they'll much like what they see."

"Their intentions are more than likely the best," Michael replied with a sigh, going to the stove to put some water on for tea. "But they've no idea — none at all — what they're letting themselves in for."

"I'll wager they won't be staying very long once they get a close look at the place. I'm going now, Da."

Michael turned around, watching him shrug into his jacket. "Mind, don't be late again tonight. I'll pick up some pork on the way home and we'll have us a meal together for a change."

"Right." Halfway through the open door, Tierney stopped and turned back. "Say, Da, I've been wondering, have you given any thought to where you're going to put all those people once they get here? There's quite a bunch of them, after all."

Michael stared at him, then gave a brief shrug and a lame smile. "Aye, I have given a great *deal* of thought to it, but so far I've not come up with any answer."

"Ah, well, we'll work it out. The lads can bunk with me, and of course you and Nora will share a room —" He stopped, shot Michael a rakish grin. "Once you're married, that is." Before Michael could add a word, he went on, his expression all innocence. "We'd better hope that Thomas Fitzgerald and his family get a situation soon — otherwise it could get a bit crowded around here."

He waved, then bolted out the door, leaving Michael staring after him.

Michael carried his tea to the kitchen table and sank down onto a chair, looking around the room. The boy had a point, one that had already given him a sleepless night or two.

Where *was* he going to put all those people if they came? Especially Thomas and his little boy and lassies?

Tierney seemed willing enough to have Nora's lads share his room, though they'd be severely crowded in that wee hidey-hole. And Nora . . .

He found himself reluctant to think about Nora at the moment. More than likely she would not even consider marriage for some time. She had been widowed for only a few months, after all. And, even if they should happen to wed right away, for the sake of propriety if nothing else, he mustn't think she'd be ready for marital intimacy right off. Why, they didn't even know each other anymore. Anything more than a marriage in name only was highly unlikely for a long, long time. He did not know quite how he felt about that, nor was he willing to examine his feelings.

Meanwhile, he was still faced with the problem of providing housing for as many as seven additional lodgers in a three-room flat. The Irish in New York were used to bundling up together — Michael had seen as many as six or seven families in one room many a time. But he'd like to be able to give them all a bit more than just a roof over their heads and a place to eat and sleep.

His heart began to race again, a common occurence these days. Worry, he supposed. Worry and nervousness and perhaps even a bit of fear. His life might well be about to change in a most significant way.

He raked both hands down his face, then propped his elbows on the table and rested his head atop his folded hands.

All I can do is trust you, Lord — trust and make the little I have available to the rest of them. I know you'll work it out for us, Lord, and work it out for the best, so help me to stop worrying and show a bit more faith in your providence.

29

A Visit to Five Points

They shall carry to the distant land
A teardrop in the eye,
And some shall go uncomforted –
Their days an endless sigh.

ETHNA CARBERY (1866–1902)

The ladies under the protection of Michael Burke and Denny Price had made a good show up till now of containing their horror and controlling their shock. Michael knew from past experience, however, that their hard-won composure would not survive the next stop on their tour. He could only hope that one of them had brought along some smelling salts.

This was at least the fifth group of society women he had escorted through the gutters and garrets of Five Points. He supposed it had never occurred to a one of them that New York's finest might have a few other things to do besides conducting private tours through the most infamous slum in the city. Apparently, the thought had eluded Chief Matsell and Mayor Brady as well. Otherwise, this foolishness would have been stopped long ago.

The results of these silly excursions were always the same, never amounting to anything more than a few offended sensibilities. At least two would faint, and a fresh sense of hopelessness would convince the well-intentioned ladies that, indeed, they could do little for the poor wretches trapped in Five Points — unless, of course, they happened to be willing to invest the rest of their lives and a considerable chunk of their wealth into providing a whole new way of life for the entire populace. Those who knew the district best — its inhabitants, the police, and a few priests — would be quick to agree that only a dedicated team of strong hearts and even stronger backs could ever hope to make the slightest difference in this place.

Today's half dozen ladies had thus far seen only the fringes of the notorious slums, but already they had to stop and collect their nerves before going on. Watching them, Michael had to admit that this group seemed a bit different than most — more observant, less frivolous, and, he thought, genuinely devastated by the misery they encountered.

At the moment they stood clustered about Denny Price, who was doing his best to brace them a bit with some Irish charm and futile reassurances. Denny *was* a charmer, all right, handsome enough that the women could not resist him, and as clever as he was good-looking. This was one of those times, however, when Michael found his partner's charm somewhat thin and the women's smiling response to it a bit grating. Five Points never failed to have a negative effect on his disposition.

Leaning against a wooden fence, his grim gaze left the women long enough to scan the area where so many of his countrymen lived in unrelieved misery. Although the district was inhabited by refugees from other countries, the Irish comprised the bulk of its population. Indeed, it seemed the only place in New York City — other than the police force — where the Irish were entirely welcome.

The brightness of the morning did nothing to disguise the gloom of the slum. In fact, it seemed strange to Michael that the sun did actually shine on Five Points. Its deceptive, cheerful warmth could almost tempt the unaware into believing this was just another neighborhood, housing its share of good and bad residents going about the normal business of living.

Michael knew better. Five Points was an abomination, possibly the habitat of more vice and wretchedness than any other one place on earth. Even the sun's cleansing, nourishing rays must surely die the very moment they touched its contaminated soul.

It had not always been so. Standing on the

site of a low, swampy pond, the area had been a fairly decent residential community until about 1820. But the landfill hadn't been properly packed, and gradually the buildings began to sink into the swamp, their doors tearing free of their hinges, their facades crumbling. The more respectable families moved on to better parts of the city, and the destitute Irish moved in. The entire district had long ago degenerated to a breeding ground of drunkenness, crime, and depravity.

Five Points was so named because of the five streets that emptied themselves into the center. The slum lay only a short walk from Broadway's center of wealth and elegance, another moment from City Hall. From where Michael now stood, he could look directly onto the small, triangular courtyard at the center of the point where the streets converged, a park-like place dubiously named "Paradise Square." This was where the ladies in his party had congregated, casting uncertain glances at their surroundings.

There was not a redeeming feature to Five Points, not one. A maze of dilapidated, rotting buildings with patched and broken windows, its commerce consisted of grog shops and brothels in abundance. The neighborhood was populated by brutal men with vicious eyes, squalid, dispirited women, and filthy, neglected children in rags whose mothers were often drunk right along with the fathers — though in many cases, of course, there *were* no fathers.

With no proper sewage or garbage disposal, the alleys teemed with offal and trash. Both the streets and the buildings constantly reeked from the stench of animal and human waste, kerosene stoves, and whiskey. Beneath the dank cellars and fetid garrets ran dozens of underground passages connecting blocks of houses on different streets, affording ideal getaway routes for the hardened criminals who drifted in and out of the district and certain death for anyone else foolish enough to enter.

The place was the terror of the police force and every decent citizen who was aware of its existence. Home for entire gangs of gun-fighting Irish, thieves, and murderers, it also housed rampant disease and utter hopelessness. Buried in ignorance, filth, pestilence, and poverty, Five Points was a pool of concentrated, unchecked evil. And at the heart of it all stood the predominant landmark of Five Points, the ugly, infamous building to which Michael and his partner were about to escort the unsuspecting ladies.

The Old Brewery.

Lurking in the square, ringed on one side by "Murderer's Alley," the old Coulter's Brewery building had long ago been converted into a multiple dwelling. It was a veritable monstrosity of a place — mustard-colored, sagging, hideous as a misshapen toad. It squatted in defiance of all decency and authority, the acknowledged headquarters of corruption and perversion for all to see.

Michael hated the very sight of the place. Every trek through its diseased passages brought on nightmares, and he knew tonight would be no exception. His stomach heaved at the thought of what waited inside, but the ladies would not consent to forego their exploration of this most disreputable of the slum's many dens of corruption.

Wanting only to have it over and done with, Michael sighed and detached himself from the fence, heading toward Price and the women. "Ladies, if you insist," he said with a somewhat rude jerk of his head in the direction of the building.

Ignoring at least three sets of raised eyebrows, Michael parted their numbers and started across the square. With himself in front and Price bringing up the rear, he resolutely marched them straight toward the Old Brewery.

If human misery and degradation could be measured, Michael thought, then certainly the weight of it within these walls would be enough to sink the city into the ocean. Over the years, any number of journalists and social chroniclers had attempted to depict the stark horror of conditions inside the Old Brewery. All had failed, for indeed there was a point at which raw evil could not be described, only — to the observer's peril — seen and felt.

Such was the iniquity running rampant throughout the Brewery's dark, winding passageways. Michael led the way with a lantern in hand, cautioning the ladies to have a care where they stepped. "The whole of the building is rickety and unsafe," he warned, parting two drunks sprawled at the bottom of the steps.

A spur of annoyance nipped at him as they made their way up the tottering stairs and started down the hall. He found something almost obscene in these well-dressed, impeccably coiffed uptown ladies injecting their presence into the squalor and hopelessness of this place. What, exactly, did they think to see or hope to accomplish?

The boards creaked and groaned in protest as they moved along the hallway. Almost in unison the women lifted their skirts to keep their hemlines from touching the begrimed floor, all the while casting apprehensive glances into the darkness around them.

Great mounds of what appeared to be filthy rags lay in heaps against the wall, but as they passed by the rags would stir, then attempt to rise, revealing the pathetic forms of human beings, both Negro and white. In the dim glow of the lantern, dozens of half-naked children could be seen cowering or playing in the shadows.

Too cross by now to make any concession toward the ladies' delicate breeding, Michael could not resist pointing out a patched section of floor just ahead. "That place was dug up a while back," he informed them, "after finding some of the boards sawed free. There were human bones underneath — the remains of two bodies." He stood aside, waiting for the women to tiptoe around the area, their faces pale and taut as they minced away from the shabby repair job.

His sense of decency overcame his petulance, however, when he realized the sounds coming from a dark alcove just to their left were those of a couple taking their pleasure right there in the hallway — a common enough occurrence in this pit of immorality. With a deft pivot to the side, he managed to divert the group's attention to himself by swinging the lantern and pretending to stumble as he hurried them past the alcove.

A few of the rooms were open to view, the doors either ajar or ripped from their hinges. They passed by one, slowing almost to a stop at the sight of three elderly women inside, all lying on a bed of filthy rags pushed into a corner. Each appeared to be feeble and emaciated. Across the room two other women, these younger, sat at a dilapidated table crowded with whiskey bottles and what looked to be the remains of several meals. Beneath the table three children, one but an infant, played with a dog.

Michael had been down these halls of horror far too many times to react to the cloying hands of the beggars that groped at them as they moved on. The ladies, however, made the mistake of digging into their handbags so often he was sure they would go home without a coin.

From every shadowed corner came the sounds of weeping or groaning, whether from sickness or desolation no one could say. By now most of the women had gone pale and begun to look somewhat ill, making Michael feel a bit ashamed of his earlier crankiness. They had, more than likely, never experienced anything near the squalor of Five Points before today.

He did not doubt their sincerity. The simple act of submitting to a tour through such a vile place indicated they at least had the sensitivity to think of others less fortunate than themselves. There was little enough human decency and Christian charity in this city; certainly he had no right to be faulting the few who displayed a measure of it.

Michael stepped out of the way, allowing the ladies to sidestep a drunk sprawled face down in the hall. Waiting for the women to pass, his attention was caught by one in particular, who appeared to be lagging a bit behind the others. A slender, straight-backed young woman, her rich chestnut hair was caught in a thick chignon that seemed to defy the frivolous bonnet perched on top of her head. She walked with a slight limp, scarcely noticeable, and her expression was not so much one of revulsion as compassion. Her attention seemed to have been caught by something just ahead, and he turned to look in the direction of her gaze.

Her eyes were fastened on a little girl who was huddled just outside a closed door. The young woman stopped when she reached the child, separating herself from the rest of the group who walked on, accompanied by Officer Price. Michael was about to urge the straggler on, but he hesitated when she stooped down to gaze into the child's face.

When she spoke, her voice was low, and, as he would have expected, unmistakably refined. But it was also a voice touched with genuine warmth and concern.

The woman had soft hazel eyes and a small oval face with a nearly pointed chin. So fine-boned was her frame that she seemed to bend beneath the heavy weight of her hair. But a note of firmness in her voice and the strong line of her jaw belied any hint of frailty.

Smiling, she reached out a hand to the

child, who regarded her with a mixture of distrust and awe. "Hello," said the young woman, withdrawing her hand when the little girl ignored it. "Is this where you live?"

Suspicious eyes burned out of a dirty, bruised face. The little girl, about five years old, was clad only in a filthy sack of a dress. Her body was covered with grime and sores, and Michael knew a moment of rage at the thought of parents who would allow a child to go around in such a state.

"My name is Sara," said the soft-voiced young woman. "Won't you tell me yours?"

The child studied her for another moment, then answered in a whisper, "Maggie."

"Maggie," the woman repeated. "Why, that's a *lovely* name! And is this where you live, Maggie?"

The little girl nodded, staring at the woman across from her. The distrust in her eyes had given way to puzzlement, and as she gaped, she sucked the thumb of a grimy hand.

To Michael's amazement, the young woman dropped down to her knees in front of the child, seemingly mindless of the fact that her fine wool suit would be instantly ruined by the grime covering the floor. "Do you have any sisters or brothers, Maggie?" she asked, touching the child lightly on the forearm.

The little girl jumped back, as if unaccustomed to being touched, at least in so gentle a manner. The young woman immediately dropped her hand away.

"Brothers," the child finally answered in the same hushed tone. "Me has two brothers."

Michael noted the thick brogue as southern Ireland, most likely County Kerry. Appraising the child more carefully, he decided she'd be a fair little thing were that wee pinched face scrubbed clean and her long black curls combed free of their tangles.

"Aren't you frightened out here in the dark, Maggie?" the woman asked. "Shouldn't you go inside, with your mother?"

The child hunched her shoulders. "Uh-uh," she murmured, shaking her head. "Not allowed."

The young woman — Sara — looked confused for a moment. "You're not allowed to go inside your rooms, Maggie? Why is that?"

"Mum is visiting."

"I see. Well, couldn't you visit, too?"

Again the child shook her head. "Not allowed. Mr. Tully wouldn't like it."

Sara's eyes narrowed. "Mr. Tully? That's your mother's guest?"

The little girl stared as if she didn't understand.

"Mr. Tully only visits with your mother?" Sara asked tersely.

When the child bobbed her head stiffly up and down, Michael expected the refined young woman to either blanch or blush. She did neither. Remaining as she was, on her knees, she put a hand to the riot of black hair falling over the little girl's face, smoothing it back from her temple. "Well, Maggie, I can see that you're a very good girl, obeying your mother as you do. I wonder if she would allow you to have a sweet?"

The child's face brightened, though her eyes still held a glint of uncertainty. "A sweet?"

"A peppermint," Sara said, fumbling inside the pocket of her skirt. "Would you like one?"

The little girl's eyes went from the young woman's face to the piece of candy she held out to her. Finally, she nodded, extending a dirty hand. Sara smiled, pressed the candy into the outstretched hand, then got to her feet.

"I must go now, Maggie," she said, "but if I may, I'd like to come back soon and visit with you."

The child stuffed the peppermint into her mouth like a greedy baby bird, then looked up. "Will you bring more sweets, then?"

"I certainly will. Now, you must stay right here, Maggie, close to your own door, until your mother is . . . is finished with her visit. It's not a good idea for you to go wandering about the building. Will you do that, Maggie?"

The little girl nodded distractedly, her attention wholly absorbed in the peppermint. Michael moved to escort the young woman on down the hall.

"I suppose there are hundreds of others just like her trapped in this dreadful place," the woman said after a bit.

"Aye, and she's in better shape than most," Michael bit out. "See here, Mrs. —"

"It's *Miss,* Sergeant Burke. Miss Sara Farmington."

"Yes, well, Miss Farmington, you told the child you'd be back —"

"And so I shall."

"I don't mean to offend you, Miss Farmington," Michael said with an edge in his voice, "but a lady would not dare to enter Five Points without a police escort. And, begging your pardon, these little . . . junkets into the district take a great deal more of our time than we can actually spare on such —"

"Foolishness?" she finished for him, then stopped, and turned to look into his face.

Michael was somewhat taken aback by her direct scrutiny. Behind that gentle, unassuming gaze he caught a glimpse of a formidable, iron-clad will. He was also struck by the fact that Miss Sara Farmington reminded him a little of Nora — at least Nora as he remembered her.

"Do you know, Sergeant Burke," she said thoughtfully, "you're quite right. I don't believe any of us ever stopped to consider the ramifications of taking you away from your duties."

Her frown of concern left no doubt as to her sincerity, and Michael suddenly felt awkward. She seemed a true lady, after all; he hadn't meant to insult her. "Don't take offense, Miss Far—"

"Oh, I'm not," she hastened to reassure him. "Not at all. It's just that you're absolutely right. We simply didn't think. Crime is running rampant in our city, and here we are, expecting the police to play bodyguard so we can go exploring. It's really quite unforgivable. And totally unnecessary."

"Well, now, you can't be coming into this terrible place by yourself, Miss Farmington. You can see that it's no place for a woman at all, much less a woman alone."

"Oh, you needn't worry about that!" she said, laughing. "None of us is brave enough to come down here *alone!* But in the future we shall enlist the help of some of the gentlemen from our congregation. They should be more than capable of providing us an escort."

"Miss Farmington, even the *police* dread coming in here! And we *never* come in unarmed!" Michael was horrified at the thought of some silk-vested deacon attempting to see to the safety of this fine young woman and her friends. "If you *must* come, then it should be only with a police escort. But I cannot help wondering — why are you so determined to come at *all?*"

She seemed to enjoy his discomfiture, her eyes twinkling with amusement. But as he watched, her expression abruptly sobered. "Sergeant Burke, we want to help these people — and we believe we can. I know this probably sounds like nothing more than womanly idealism to you, working as you must amid truly deplorable conditions. But we happen to think that, with enough planning and financial backing, we can make a real difference in Five Points. We're prepared to plan for years, if necessary, and to spend a considerable sum of money in order to turn this into a decent place to live."

Michael shook his head. "It's been talked about before, Miss Farmington, many a time, with no results, none at all. You've seen the poor souls for yourself — their wretchedness. What could you possibly hope to accomplish that would make any difference for them?"

She straightened her shoulders and looked him square in the eye. "What we will do, Sergeant Burke, is to pray, praise, and proceed."

Michael stared at her. "Begging your pardon, I — ?"

She smiled. "That is the scriptural order of things for God's people when they prepare to conquer a heathen nation. Read your Bible, Officer Burke — oh, I'm sorry, your faith doesn't really encourage that, does it?"

Michael could not contain a slight smile at her flustered expression. "Well, as a matter of fact, Miss Farmington, I am that rare creature, an Irish Protestant who can actually read — and *does* read, especially the Scriptures. I might point out that some of my Catholic friends can also read. And do."

One eyebrow went up in challenge. "But not the Bible."

He shrugged. "Some do, some don't. That would not seem to be any of my business." He gave her a look to remind her it was also none of hers.

"Your rebuke is noted, Sergeant," she retorted with a dryness that made a grin break across his face.

They walked the rest of the way in silence, Michael pacing his stride to her slight limp. When they reached the downstairs landing, the others were waiting to continue the tour, giving Michael no opportunity to apologize to the young woman for his rudeness.

By early afternoon they concluded their tour and led the ladies out of Five Points to their waiting carriages. Turning onto Broadway, Michael pulled in a deep, cleansing breath of fresh air, his first since entering the slum that morning.

He felt a faint edge of disappointment that he'd been unable to talk more with the plucky Sara Farmington. Just as quickly, he was struck by a feeling akin to shame. How could he be seeking the company of another woman when he had only recently committed himself to marriage with Nora? But he immediately justified his attraction to Sara Farmington by deciding it was her vague resemblance to Nora that had piqued his interest in her in the first place.

He spent the rest of the way back to headquarters in prayerful thanks that Morgan had written when he did, asking for help for his family and Nora's. If the lot of them had taken it upon themselves to make the crossing with nobody waiting on this side, they might well have ended up in Five Points, with all the rest of its hopeless victims.

Through Morgan's intervention, Nora and her family would be spared that particular hell. With that thought — and the thought that in only a few weeks he might be a husband again — Michael quickened his step and lifted his face to catch the sun. Giving his nightstick a bit of a twist, he then continued up Broadway with the jaunty, purposeful step of a man whose life has taken on new purpose and challenge.

30

Nora's Turning

I know where I'm going,
I know who's going with me,
I know who I love,
But the dear knows who I'll marry. . . .

OLD IRISH BALLAD (ANONYMOUS)

The Green Flag

They had been at sea almost three full days before Nora finally read Michael's letter.

The first day out she had been too devastated, too dazed to think, much less read. The second, she had suffered the assault of a peculiar sort of illness — not seasickness, exactly, at least not like that of the other passengers close by. She had not endured the same painful retching, had not even lost the contents of her stomach. All the same, she'd been ill enough that she could do nothing more than lie weakly on her berth, staring up at the ribs of the moldy ceiling as the bile from her stomach rose and ebbed, filling her mouth with a bitter, nauseating acid.

Today her stomach had stopped its pitching, but she still felt lifeless, enervated, and lay in the same benumbed stupor. Only in the vaguest sense was she aware of her surroundings: her bunk mate, the young woman who had glared at her so fiercely their first day at sea, now lay flat on her back, moaning and weeping in despair between bouts of retching. Katie Frances was curled in a tight ball at the bottom of the bunk, wheezing with every breath she took, while the silent Johanna looked nearly as dazed as Nora felt.

All around them rose the mingled sounds of suffering. Those with the strength to cry out filled the air with a mixed chorus of prayers and curses, pleas for mercy and screams of agony. Babes wailed, grown men raged, and women keened.

Throughout the day, Daniel John had appeared often, at times coaxing her to eat or take water. When she refused, he would go away, only to return later — mostly, she supposed, to satisfy himself that she still lived. Evan Whittaker had come around once or twice, staying only long enough to ask if there was anything he could do for her, shuffling back to his bunk when she quietly assured him she needed nothing.

By evening of the third day, she still had not made the slightest effort to move further from the bunk than the privy, had not bathed or combed her hair or taken food. Part of her nagged that she had no right to continue in this fashion, that it was thoughtless and selfish to ignore her own family and the orphaned Fitzgerald children; another part dully responded that it no longer mattered.

A terrible, vile stench surrounded her, and she made the effort to pull herself up on the bunk to look around, throwing a hand to her head when it began to spin. Knowing she was weak to the point of collapse, she caught two or three deep breaths, then waited until the danger of fainting had passed.

Finally she was able to haul herself the rest of the way up. Dragging her legs over the side of the berth, she glanced around at her surroundings, appalled at what she saw and smelled.

Alice, her bunk mate, and the two little girls at the foot of the berth were asleep, all three lying in their own messes from being ill. Nora's stomach pitched, and she fought against being sick. She put a hand to her sticky, brittle hair, then to her face, grimacing when she saw the dirt and oil that smudged her palm.

Her throat was sore and painfully dry. Mostly, she felt disheveled and disoriented — and disgusted with herself and the putrid conditions around them. Instinctively, she attempted to smooth her bodice, staying her hand when she touched the envelope close to her heart.

Retrieving Michael's letter from inside her dress, she glanced around, hesitating. She supposed she should make an effort to clean up their berth, but she wasn't at all sure she had the strength. Besides, she had put off reading the letter long enough; the berth could wait.

Her head ached with a dull, nagging throb, and her hands trembled as she opened the envelope, pulled the letter free and began to read:

> Dear Nora Ellen . . . I hope you will remember your long-ago friend, who still remembers you with much affection. . . .

Evan Whittaker had been brooding for most of the evening. He knew what he wanted to say to Nora Kavanagh, had prayed over it as much as he was able, given his light-headed state. As yet, however, he had been unable to muster the courage to approach her with his suggestion.

There was always the chance she would take him the wrong way, become offended or even angry. His intention — his *only* intention — was to help, if he could. He could not deny his growing admiration and somewhat unsettling concern for the grieving young widow. She *was* lovely, after all — even in her frailty and her unhappiness, she was like a rare, delicate wildflower, exquisite and fragile and elusive.

Obviously, she should not be alone. She needed someone to look after her. He had promised Morgan Fitzgerald to care for her and the others as if they were his own. And he would keep that promise if at all possible. Admittedly, it would be no sacrifice on his part to look after Nora Kavanagh; she was the kind of woman who somehow called forth one's manly, protective instincts. In her own unique way, she was really quite wonderful.

In thirty-six years, Evan had never loved a woman, had never had a romance. Always too shy to initiate a relationship — and too set in his ways to respond in the unlikely event that a woman should take the initiative with *him* — he had resigned himself to living his life alone. It was not such a bad life, really: he had his work, his church, his books. He managed. Now that he would be starting a new life in a new country, however, he thought it might be wise to give some consideration to starting over in other ways as well. Where was it written, after all, that he need remain a bachelor for the rest of his years?

Suddenly realizing the direction his thoughts had taken, he blinked, then pressed a hand to his mouth in dismay. It might not be *written,* but he had always assumed as much, and now was certainly no time to be thinking about changing his spots. What he must do, above all else, was to make every effort to fulfill his vow to Fitzgerald. He would do his best to look after Nora Kavanagh, ease the journey, help with the children. To anticipate anything more was absurd.

Still, if she came to depend on him, trust him . . . who could say? Perhaps later . . .

Nora still sat on the side of the berth, her feet planted heavily on the floor. Stunned, frozen in place by what she had just read, she stared into the shadows.

Her mind could not take it in. Added to everything else, this was simply too much. An offer of marriage from a man she had not seen for more than seventeen years? How else could she respond but with shock and bitterness — a bitterness directed not at Michael Burke, but at Morgan Fitzgerald.

Morgan. She had seen his clever, conniving hand in it at once. It was all too clear what he had done. Hadn't he admitted, just before leaving Thomas's cabin, that he, too, had received a letter from Michael? He had played the innocent, like the consummate rogue he was, telling her as little as possible, all the while knowing exactly what he'd been up to. Obviously, he had taken it upon himself, in his proprietary, arrogant way, to try to order her life for her. Why would he do such a thing? Sure, and he must have realized it would humiliate her.

Anger and the pain of betrayal nearly doubled Nora over. She hugged her arms to her breast as if to hold herself together. Choking on unshed tears of fury and humiliation, she drew deep, shuddering breaths to control her trembling.

She had believed he truly cared for her. At the last, she had cherished his outburst of emotion, had clung to it. Had it all been a lie, then, just another attempt to pacify poor little Nora, to keep her from going to pieces on him and making things more difficult?

No. No, she did not, *could* not, believe that. His heart had been in his eyes, his true heart revealed at last. What she had seen in his face had been real, at least at that moment.

It was obvious what had driven him to do such a daft thing. As always, he simply believed her to be too weak, too helpless to manage on her own. The man had ever believed she needed a keeper; since childhood, he had treated her like a wee, frail thing to be pampered and patronized.

For an instant — only an instant — the thought skirted her mind that perhaps, out of the depths of his caring, he had simply taken it upon himself to ensure her safety and well-being, that he had not meant to be so heavy-handed. But just as quickly came a fresh wave of shame at the position in which he had placed her, *whatever* his motives might have been.

Merciful Lord, what had he told Michael?

That they were destitute, starving, in dire need of charity?

Just as we are . . .

She squeezed her eyes shut against the painful truth, willing herself not to weep. She *hated* being dependent on others, had always despised the shame of it, yet had been forced to endure all too much of it in her life, from her childhood on.

Nora opened her eyes. What if she were wrong? What if Michael meant all he said, that his son was in sore need of mothering, that he himself was in need of a partner to share his life? What if he *did* remember her with affection, after all, and did truly want her as his wife?

Don't be a fool! Nora's mind argued. *Morgan's stamp is all over this thing! Why would any decent man with a brain in his head go offering to wed a used-up woman he hasn't seen or heard from in years?*

Besides, whatever was behind it, did they really think she would consent to marry a man she no longer knew, a man she didn't love? She had rejected Michael once; had he and Morgan forgotten that? If she had not loved him enough to marry him then, when they were close and knew each other well, what in heaven's name led them to believe she would marry him *now,* and the two of them strangers?

She sat up a little straighter, trying to ignore the throbbing at the base of her skull. Glancing down at the pages of the letter strewn across her side of the berth, she grabbed them up in one angry sweep, intending to shred them to pieces.

Startled, Nora jumped as Evan Whittaker moved out of the shadows. Still clutching the letter in one hand, she nodded to him.

"I hope I didn't startle you, Mrs. K-Kavanagh," he said uncertainly, stopping a few feet away from the berth. "It's . . . good to see you sitting up at last. I hope you're feeling b-better?"

"Aye, a bit, thank you. But how are *you,* Mr. Whittaker? Is your arm giving you much pain?"

"Some. But nothing I c-can't tolerate." With his good hand, Whittaker moved a small stool closer to the bunk. "May I?" he said, waiting for her nod of assent before he sat down.

To Nora, the Englishman looked ghastly: pale, ill and more than a little shaky. Pain had lined his smooth forehead and carved deep brackets on either side of his mouth, adding years to his once almost boyish countenance.

"Am I disturbing you?" he asked abruptly, half rising from the stool as his gaze went to the letter in her hand.

"No — no, not a bit," she assured him.

"Yes, well . . ." He relaxed only a little. Then, clearing his throat, he leaned forward.

"I, ah, was wondering if we might . . . talk? There's something . . . I'd like to, ah, d-discuss with you. If it's no b-bother, that is."

Nora shook her head, sensing the man's difficulty. Obviously, he was struggling to find words for whatever he intended to say. "It's no bother at all, Mr. Whittaker."

"Yes, well . . . you see, k-keeping in mind that you've been through a great deal . . . you've had a terrible time of things, after all . . . and it does seem to me that it must be rather frightening for a woman, crossing the ocean more or less alone. Oh, you have your son, of course, I don't m-mean to denigrate Daniel. He's such a fine boy, so collected and mature for his age. Still, it has to be most difficult . . ."

He stopped, his expression frozen in dismay. "Oh, dear, I'm saying this b-badly . . . I knew I would . . ."

Having no idea how to help him, Nora offered a weak smile.

Whittaker rose suddenly, reaching out to a nearby beam to steady himself. "I would like," he said, his voice gaining a bit of strength, "to offer my p-protection to you, Mrs. K-Kavanagh. For the duration of our journey . . . and for as long as you might desire, afterward."

Nora's mouth went slack as she stared at the man. "I'm sorry?"

"Please, Mrs. K-Kavanagh understand that in no way do I mean to be forward!" he blurted out. "I wouldn't want you to think —"

Whittaker stopped and swallowed with difficulty. Even in the dull glow from the lantern, Nora could see him flush and was torn between conflicting emotions of sympathy and annoyance. *Even to a mild-mannered man such as this, she appeared helpless and weak, in need of an overseer!*

As he stood there, looking none too steady on his feet, he clenched and unclenched the fingers of one hand. "I only meant to say, Mrs. K-Kavanagh, that it would be my pleasure to act as your . . . ah . . . protector . . . for the duration of our voyage . . . and for as long as necessary after we reach New York. After that . . . well, ah, I'd b-be most flattered if you would consider me as a . . . a friend, at least."

The poor man looked about to faint. Nora was at a loss. Half fearful that he might topple over at any moment, half angry that yet another man perceived her as helpless, she forced a note of steady calm into her voice. "I — truly, I don't know what to say, Mr. Whittaker. I'm very grateful to you, of course . . . but you've already done so much for me and my family —"

"Oh, please," Whittaker interrupted, pulling a handkerchief from his vest pocket and wiping it over his brow with a trembling hand, "you need say n-nothing! Nothing at all. I only wanted to m-make you aware of the fact that . . . that I respect you greatly, and care deeply about your welfare. And that of your son, of course," he added quickly. "D-Daniel and I have been getting to know each other quite well, and he's a wonderful b-boy. Wonderful . . ."

His words trailed off, unfinished. Nora felt an unjustified stirring of anger. She was being entirely unfair. This good, shy man was willingly making himself miserable on her account, pledging his protection to a virtual stranger, to a woman who must look no better than a deranged harridan at the moment. And, clearly, the very act of making himself understood was a torment, timid soul that he seemed to be.

Indeed, she *liked* Evan Whittaker and owed him much; that his intentions were the best, she had no doubt. But he, too, had seen something in her, some flaw in her character, that marked her as inadequate. God in heaven, what was there in her demeanor that made her appear simpleminded and incompetent to these men?

She sat up a bit straighter, having to grope at the limp mattress when she was hit by a new surge of dizziness. Seeing her sway, Whittaker put a hand to her shoulder. "I've upset you! I'm so sorry —"

"No, no, it's not that!" Nora protested, forcing herself to sit upright, unassisted. "I'm still . . . a bit weak, is all. No, I'm — my goodness, Mr. Whittaker, I'm not perturbed with you at all, simply overwhelmed — by your kindness."

He stooped slightly to peer into her face. "Please d-don't feel you need to say anything more, Mrs. K-Kavanagh. You're really quite weak, and I didn't intend to cause you additional d-distress. I — just b-bear in mind that I will count it a privilege to d-do whatever I can to make this journey easier for you. Now then," he said with more firmness, "I'm going to leave you alone so you can rest."

He turned to go, then stopped. "You will let me know if there's anything I can d-do?"

Nora nodded and managed another faint smile. "Of course. And — I do thank you, Mr. Whittaker."

Still somewhat dazed, she watched him stumble off to the men's quarters. Truly, she did not know what to make of the man.

At the moment, she wasn't sure she cared. She had had her fill, and then some, of coming across as incompetent to the men with whom she came in contact. From now on, she would do whatever she must to avoid even a hint of weakness, any sign of dependency. She was a woman grown, after all, with a son and three orphaned children who had nobody else in the world.

Deliberately, and with a strange new sense of purpose, she took the pages of Michael

Burke's letter and, one by one, tore them into pieces. As she watched them flutter to the floor, she knew an instant of panic.

Perhaps she should have at least saved his address . . . what if —

Shaking off the thought, she closed her eyes. *Dear Lord, I am sick to death of being a weak, clinging woman. I ask you now to do whatever you must to make me strong . . . strong in your power, strong enough, Lord, so that others will no longer feel such a need to take care of me, indeed strong enough that I might begin to look after others for a change. Oh, I'm that frightened, Lord. Sure, and you know I am terrified of what may lie ahead for all of us. But in the future, Blessed Savior, couldn't we just let my terrors be our secret — yours and mine? Please, Lord?*

Nora opened her eyes and, for the first time in her life, stretched her hands up, toward heaven. Crying out in a harsh, desperate whisper of a plea, she begged, "*God, change me! Oh, my Lord — change me!*"

31

The Most Fearful Dread of All

The fell Spectre advanc'd – who the horrors shall tell
Of his galloping stride, as he sounded the knell.

AUTHOR UNKNOWN (1858)

They had been at sea nearly a week when Evan took a turn for the worse. His fever soared, and his wound began to fester and burn as if somebody held a fiery brand to his skin. Still, there were others in sadder condition, and it was their need, not his own, that sent him stumbling to the surgeon's quarters late at night.

He found Dr. Leary sprawled in his bunk, his eyes glazed. He looked about to pass out.

"I'm sorry," Evan said stiffly, not meaning it. "I know it's late, but you're d-desperately needed in steerage. We have people down there in their extremities."

The surgeon lolled where he was, peering at Evan with eyes that would not quite focus.

Dr. Leary's quarters were cramped and

reeked of whiskey and mold. Evan was struck by a bout of weakness and, head pounding, his wound on fire, he groped for the open door to keep from falling.

"There's something terribly wrong b-below," he said thickly. "Not seasickness. M-much worse. Please — you *must* come! People are dying!" The surgeon had not been seen in steerage since the day after they sailed, and Evan found it almost impossible to keep from screaming at the drunken man to do his job.

"The Irish are always dying," muttered Leary drunkenly. "Why should I be the one to circumvent their destiny?"

A terrible fury rose in Evan as he stood studying the dissipated wreck of a man across the room. Was this all the help they could expect, this drunken failure who could scarcely speak? God help them all, they *would* perish!

"You are Irish yourself, man!"

The surgeon grunted. "Don't be reminding me."

"Dr. Leary," Evan tried again, the words sticking to his palate, "we have two c-corpses in steerage, and from the looks of things this night, we will have m-many more before sunrise. If you do not c-come with me and come now, I promise you I will return with a number of the largest, b-brawniest men on board and we will *drag* you below! Good heavens, man, you're a *physician!*"

Leary glared at Evan for another full minute. At last, he hauled himself up from the berth, teetering wildly as he stood. He grabbed at the corner of the desk to break his fall. After another moment, he yanked his bag off the desk and pitched toward Evan. "Let's go, then."

Fighting back his revulsion, Evan put a hand to the man's arm to help steady him, but the surgeon shook him off with a grunt of protest.

"C'mon, Englishman, show me your corpses. And don't be getting so rattled about it." He stopped long enough to wag a finger in Evan's face. "You'll be seeing plenty more of them before this crossing is done."

The surgeon laughed, then lurched through the open doorway. "That's the truth, you know. There'll be plenty of corpses for the greedy old Atlantic on this voyage. She'll claim those she wants — she always does!"

The doctor looked back over his shoulder, squinting at Evan with a peculiar grimace of a smile. "And who can say but what they all would not be better off in the bosom of the sea than where they're going, eh?"

Less than an hour later, Leary, white-faced and suddenly sober, faced the captain in his quarters.

"I tell you it's the *Black Fever!*" the surgeon exploded, ducking his head beneath the low rough-beamed ceiling. A big man, he felt more confined in Schell's cabin than in his own, though the captain's room was far more spacious. Schell's Spartan quarters were oddly inhibiting, like a foreign laboratory. Sterile, cold, and restricted.

"Typhus?" Schell sat calmly, his smooth hands folded on his desk. As always, the desk top was uncluttered and bare, except for the ship's log and a sextant.

"Call it what you will," Leary spat out, "it's certain doom! This is disaster aboard a ship, and well you know it!"

Frigid blue eyes fixed the physician in place like a bug on a pin. Even in the somber lantern glow, the red scar on Schell's face blazed its anger. "How many?"

"Dead, do you mean? Two so far: at least half a dozen down with it, though. It can take the lot of them before it's done — but, then, I don't have to tell *you* that, now do I? You've seen it all before."

The captain's thin mouth pulled down only enough to cause a faint break in the marble mask of his face. "Tell no one but the bosun and First Mate Clewes. They will confine steerage below decks."

"*All* of them?"

Schell lifted his eyes to regard Leary with a cold, exaggerated patience. "Of course, *all* of them," he said, still not raising his voice. "It would hardly make sense to isolate only a few, now would it?"

"They'll have no chance, none at all, locked in there together like rats in a barrel!"

Schell remained silent, watchful. Leary could hear the man's shallow breathing, saw the cold eyes freeze over, but just enough of the whiskey remained to dull his normal sense of caution. "I should think you'd want to deliver most of your cargo alive, Captain, if you're to earn your fee."

"*Our* cargo," Schell said smoothly, his accent thickening somewhat, "has already been paid for, the fee collected — from *your* countrymen. The only thing left for us to do is to put them ashore in New York. After that, it's entirely the problem of the . . . what do you call them? The *runners*."

Leary glared at the man across from him. Schell was an unfeeling, cold-blooded monster. The man had no soul. No soul at all.

"Send Clewes and the bosun to me," said the captain, turning his back. "And stay sober."

Leary stared at the back of Schell's head, debating whether his surgeon's knife would penetrate that granite-hewn skull. At last he turned and lunged out of the room, in a mad race for his bottle.

Fiabhras dubh . . .

The Black Fever. Typhus. The fearful malediction began to circulate steerage within hours, bouncing from berth to berth, striking raw terror into the hearts of all who heard it whispered or moaned.

No disease was more dreaded, none more horrifying than the prolonged, agonizing terrors of typhus. No swift, merciful death, this, but days of suffering and slow destruction, a lingering agony that transcended every other known form of human misery. Even to speak its name aloud was to unleash the full blast of hell's wrath.

Black Fever aboard ship meant unavoidable epidemic and unimaginable suffering. Tonight, aboard the *Green Flag*, it meant sorrow upon sorrow.

In the Castlebar gaol, Morgan Fitzgerald thought about Nora aboard the ship to America and Daniel John at her side. He thought about his fine horse, Pilgrim, wondering what had become of him. He even thought about Whittaker, the Englishman. Then, despite his intentions to avoid the subject, he turned his thoughts to his approaching death.

There had been no trial — not that he had expected one. He knew well enough how things would be. One night soon, his cell would open. Hooded men would lead him out and put him onto a horse. He would be taken outside the town, to a deserted stand of trees — convenient for a hanging — and that, as they say, would be that. The end of him.

It had happened before, and it would happen again, *was* going to happen, to *him* this time. He had no hopes of a surprise or a last-minute miracle. He doubted that God was of a mind to perform miracles for an outlaw. And that was what he was, all right — an outlaw.

To the magistrates, he was the worst kind of outlaw — an Irish rebel who happened to have a passing good education, who could write a fair essay that might stir Gaelic blood and heat nationalist passions. He had robbed and raided, he had insulted the authorities and embarrassed their superiors. Of course, he might have survived all that if he had been ignorant — ignorant and entirely lacking in political interests.

Oh, he was a dead man, and that was the truth.

He should pray for his soul, Joseph Mahon had said, and Morgan knew the priest had it right. The thing was, he didn't know how — where to begin, what to say. He had gone too far. Over the years the stains of his sins had run together, eventually draining into the sea of a past from which he could no longer draw the slightest hope of a future.

Besides, only a penitent should pray for his own soul, one who sorrowed for his sin and wished it gone. Morgan supposed he was sorry for whatever wrongs he had committed in his lifetime, was *deeply* sorry for any that might have brought hurt or harm to his fellowman. But, in truth, the greatest sorrows in his soul were mostly self-centered: He grieved the loss of his loved ones, and he grieved the desolation of his country.

Had he known a way to create remorse within himself, he would have done so. But there was a terrible deadness in his spirit that seemed beyond reach. And so he waited, strangely impassive, knowing he would swing. Other than wondering when it would come, he was not as overwhelmed by the thought as he probably should have been.

Joseph Mahon, the priest, felt swept under by a great wave of defeat as he prepared to pray for the neck — and the soul — of Morgan Fitzgerald.

Joseph Mahon, the man, felt despair and anger as he knelt beside the bed in his room behind the chapel and considered the kind of death the brash young poet would endure.

Joseph had seen men hang, had rubbed his own neck at the snap of the noose, beheld the final agony of their last moments. He could not bear the thought of Morgan Fitzgerald facing such an end. The man was an outlaw, a renegade, a rogue. But, oh, what God could do with such a man, with such a valiant heart and mighty spirit!

Yet only a fool could not anticipate Fitzgerald's end. There would be no trial; the rumor was all over the village and the county, and Joseph had not been at all surprised to hear of it.

He had tried to stop this mad rush to the gallows, had spent days pounding on the door of every magistrate in the area who might have helped to stay the hangman's rope. But everywhere he went, he heard the same sound: the toll of doom for Morgan Fitzgerald.

And yet he knew that somehow it must be stopped. The man waiting in the Castlebar gaol, waiting to die, must be saved, spared from the noose at all costs. The country was in dire need of this man, would be in even greater need of him in the days to come.

The priest had a single hope — only one — to save Morgan from the gallows. Aidan Fitzgerald, Morgan's father, had given him that hope with his final confession, before he died of the drink.

But how could he salvage that hope, how could he use it in Morgan's behalf, without violating both Aidan's confession and his wishes for his son?

How, Lord?

There was a man. One man, in Dublin, who could turn the tide. If he would.

Joseph prayed. Prayed for light, for a word of wisdom, for a work of power that would save a man's life — and his soul as well.

32

Secrets Aboard the *Green Flag*

Abandoned, forsaken,
To grief and to care,
Will the sea ever waken
Relief from Despair?

(ANONYMOUS — NINETEENTH CENTURY)

Daniel and his mother fought their way up the ladder to the hatch, gripping the splintery rungs with fierce determination. Behind them, hands grasped and shoved in an effort to push upward and free themselves from the stench of illness and death that now permeated steerage.

At the first clang of the morning bell just after daybreak, the ladder became a prize sought by every able-bodied person in steerage. Reaching the foredeck first didn't necessarily guarantee an early place at the stove; that boon was reserved for those holding bargaining power with the deck cook, such as bribe money or flattery from a pretty lass. Still, there was a mad rush every morning to reach the caboose, the fireplace that served as a cooking stove for steerage passengers.

The race for the hatch was even more frantic than usual this morning. All were in a fever to flee the misery of their quarters — not so much to gain the advantage at the caboose, but to escape the common dread of being confined with dead bodies.

Two had died late in the night, an elderly grandmother and a wee lass. Not long after, wild rumors had begun to sweep the entire deck. There was even talk of the Black Fever, though nobody seemed willing to say for certain as yet.

The victims had been left to lie in their bunks after the surgeon's cursory examinations. Dr. Leary had been in a fierce hurry to leave, ignoring the questions and pleas of the frightened passengers trying to crowd him.

With the surgeon himself in such a bother, Daniel thought bitterly, *is there any wonder the passengers are eager to flee?*

Despite the pall of death and the ominous rumors, his own heart felt lighter this morning than it had in days. For the first time since boarding the *Green Flag*, his mother seemed to be her old self again. Oh, her sadness was still painfully apparent, but at least she had eaten her meals two days in a row.

Today she had come for him before the morning bell, not long after he awakened.

He'd seen at once that she had combed her hair and scrubbed her face.

Smiling at him, she handed him one of the two cooking pots she was carrying. "You must have a warm breakfast this day, Daniel John," she said, much as she might have had they still been at home in the village. "It's important to eat and build our strength, so we can ward off the fever."

"Then you believe that's what it is, the Black Fever?"

Averting her eyes, she nodded, then answered in a strained voice. "I have seen it before, several years ago in the village. From what they're saying about the bodies, I've no doubt it's the typhus."

Instead of the fear Daniel would have expected, she seemed surprisingly steady and matter-of-fact.

Now, as they clung to the ladder, waiting for the hatch to open, she still appeared resolute and in control. Glancing back over her shoulder, she said, "We'll bring breakfast back for Katie and Johanna. They're minding Little Tom so I can go above decks. And we'll fix enough for Mr. Whittaker as well, though if he's as ill as you say, I doubt he'll be able to eat."

The Englishman had grown worse all through the night, flush-faced and hollow-eyed with the fever, going on like a crazy man in his sleep. "I'll have a look at him as soon as we come back," his mother went on. "Oh — and Daniel John, I'll need the medicine box. Katie is some fevered, too."

"It's under my bunk," Daniel John said, his spirits plummeting with her comment about Katie. Uneasily, he remembered how pale his friend had looked the day before, how listless and weak she appeared every time they were together. "Mother, you don't think Katie —"

He broke off when the hatch suddenly opened, letting in a thin veil of light from early dawn. Behind him, the big-bellied, peevish man from a neighboring bunk prodded his back, and Daniel instinctively kicked out a leg to keep from being knocked off the ladder.

Only five or six people were in front of him and his mother, so he had no trouble hearing the sailor who now stood in the hatchway, staring down at them with hard black eyes. "Go back to your quarters, all of you! No one is allowed above decks this day! You're under quarantine until further notice from the captain!"

"*Quarantine?* For *what?*" A redheaded man at the very top of the ladder blasted out the question.

"There's two of you dead of the Black Fever, that's for what!" the sailor retorted, his mouth screwing up with contempt.

"By whose say-so are we quarantined?" called out another man, this one halfway down the ladder.

"The surgeon's! Now get below, the lot of you!"

"But how long will you be keeping us down here?" cried out the man at the top.

"I wasn't told." The crewman started to close the hatch, then stopped when a thin, gray-faced woman standing near the bottom of the ladder cried out. "You can't just be keeping us locked up down here, in this — pit! Why, we won't be able to cook our food! We can't even get to the privies!"

Her outrage caught fire and set off a round of furious protests. People began to fight their way higher up the ladder, toward the hatch. Those still on the floor now started to move, until soon a swarm of hands was clawing at the ladder, threatening to topple everybody on it.

"You'll stay below deck until you're told otherwise!" shouted the sailor, shaking his fist through the opening of the hatch. "Now get down to your hole where you belong!"

With two meaty hands, he gave the red-headed man at the top of the ladder a hard shove, enough to cause him to reel backward. The man shouted as he swayed, then toppled helplessly from the ladder, causing the woman and little girl at his back to lose their balance. The ladder itself creaked and shook.

Daniel grabbed his mother around the waist with one hand, bracing the two of them against the hull with his other arm as their cooking pots went clanging to the floor. The burly man at his back let go an oath. Daniel shot him a look over his shoulder, shouting, "Get *down!* Get off the ladder!"

The man cursed him again, but turned and yelled the same warning to those behind him. Finally, one by one, they lowered themselves to the floor. After a moment, Daniel and his mother followed.

While some went to help those who had fallen, others clustered at the foot of the ladder, murmuring and looking about in fear and anger.

An elderly hawk-nosed man on a cane yelled up at the sailor, who still stood in the hatchway, scowling down at them. "God have mercy, man, you must at least help us to get the corpses out of here! We can't be leaving dead bodies lying about!"

The sailor glared at him, cursed, then heaved the door shut with a bang.

Within seconds, the angry murmurs of the crowd swelled to enraged threats and invective. Daniel could smell the fear in the air. Questions flew among the bunks, met by dread predictions and cries of alarm. Soon a general wailing went up. Women wept, children whined, and the men cursed and raged among themselves.

Suddenly, from across the room came a high-pitched shout of terror. "*Fiabhras dubh! Fiabhras dubh!* It *is* the Black Fever!"

Careful not to crack his head against the low ceiling — which was actually the underside of the main deck — Daniel stretched, craning his neck forward to see where the cry was coming from. At the opposite end of the men's quarters, a fair-haired boy who looked to be about his own age was hunched over a lower bunk, wide-eyed with fear. *"Their faces! Oh, God, have mercy, their faces — they're almost black!"*

Daniel lunged forward, but his mother grabbed his arm, holding him back. "*No!* Stay away!"

He froze, staring at her.

"Let only those who have had the fever and survived it go near the bodies," she said, clutching his arm. "It's not as dangerous for them. The rest of us must do whatever we can to slow its spread!" Her eyes bored into his. "We have too many people depending on us to come down with the fever, Daniel John. We must stay well!"

Daniel looked from his mother to the bunk across the room. A number of men had gathered near the frightened boy and now stood staring at the occupants of the berth. "But what can we do? How can we possibly *not* come down with it, locked up in this . . . *dungeon!*"

He broke off, dismayed at how easily he had surrendered to his fear. Even in his own ears, he sounded like a panicky child.

"We will do what we must," said his mother, her voice unexpectedly gentle. Still clasping his arm, she added, "And you can be sure there will be much to do. But, first, we must see to Mr. Whittaker. Now, hurry and get the medicine box for me."

Daniel looked at her, confused as much by this new, unsettling show of strength as by the chaos surrounding them.

"Daniel John, *please*. I'm frightened, too. But we must do what we can while we're still strong!"

He saw the look in her eyes, a plea for him to be a man, at least for the moment.

The panic rising in his throat threatened to reduce him to blubbering, but, catching a deep breath, he nodded and followed her down the aisle.

Evan strained to focus his eyes on the face lowered to his. The bunk, the stinking lantern hanging from the ceiling — even the woman's face — swayed drunkenly in front of him.

Now he stared into twin faces, two Nora Kavanaghs. He saw himself reflected in both pairs of eyes. The eyes were worried . . . or was it fear that stared back at him?

He tried to speak, but someone had sewn his mouth shut. There was a weight on his tongue, a hot coal . . .

In lieu of speech, he attempted to lift his

hand, to make a signal of sorts. But his arm had been tied to the bunk. Pain held it fast; his other hand was free, but stiff and numb, lifeless.

He struggled to sit up, but hands held him down, pressing him into the bunk.

"It's all right, Mr. Whittaker. We'll take care of you. Be easy now, just rest yourself and be easy . . . it's all right." Both faces spoke as one, smiling with kindness.

Hot . . . he was so hot . . . and a host of knives stabbed, slicing into his shoulder.

The twin Nora Kavanaghs were saying something, their voices echoing, drifting away. . . . Young Daniel hovered closer, frowning, his eyes burning, heating Evan's skin even more. Why did the boy look so frightened?

Again he tried to speak. Nothing came. Humiliated, he felt tears track his cheeks . . . hot tears . . . scalding hot, like his skin and the pain in his shoulder.

"Please don't struggle, Mr. Whittaker. We'll take care of you . . . try to rest." The boy's voice was thin, distant, fading . . .

Something cool touched his forehead . . . so good. He mustn't weep . . . what would she think? He didn't want her to think him weak. He was supposed to be taking care of *her* . . .

33

Where Is God?

If it be stormy,
Fear not the sea;
Jesus upon it
Is walking by thee.

JOSEPH SHERIDAN LEFANU (1814–1873)

Daniel straightened, his gaze going from Evan Whittaker, who lay writhing on his berth in obvious agony, to his mother, her eyes frantic, her face pale with alarm in the swaying light from the overhead lantern.

With trembling hands she gingerly parted the torn sleeve of the Englishman's shirt to examine his bandaged shoulder. The vile odor issuing from the blood-soaked wrappings forced Daniel to turn away momentarily, but his mother continued to hover over Whittaker, shaking her head worriedly while tending to him as best she could.

"Daniel John, we *must* have the surgeon, and soon!" she whispered hoarsely. "His wound is infected, I'm sure of it. He's failing badly!"

"I *tried,* Mother!" Both he and Hugh MacCabe, the farmer in the next bunk, had made three futile attempts that day to get a crewman's attention by banging on the closed door to the hatch. "They wouldn't answer us!"

His mother glanced toward the ladder, unused for over two days now, except for those times when someone would ascend it out of sheer desperation, to hammer on the door in appeal. They *were* desperate; a number among them were bordering on hysteria. They might just as well be in prison, so hopeless did their plight seem.

The stench in steerage, intolerable before, was now unbearable. The very act of breathing had become another kind of misery. Beneath most bunks lurked wet, soiled rags, rotting food scraps, even feces. Without ventilation, the overpowering odors of stale air, human waste, and rank filth filled the entire dungeon-like hold with fumes deadly enough to fell a sailor — had one taken it upon himself to venture down into this pit of horrors.

Barred from the latrines, without access to fresh air or cooked food, the doomed passengers were falling ill by the dozens from seasickness, diarrhea, and fevers. Three new cases of suspected Black Fever had developed. Even now, a new corpse lay in the men's section, an old man who had screamed the entire night before dying.

Nothing in Daniel's worst nightmares could have prepared him for the horror of this pit in which they were trapped. He felt himself to be existing in a dark abyss, as if the sea itself had swallowed the *Green Flag* and was now bearing it upon some dread course of doom.

Darkness engulfed them, a shroud of evil drawing them in, closer and closer each day. Last night he had fallen asleep to the cries of the suffering and dying, his last thought a silent cry of his own: *Where is God in the midst of all this madness, this misery? When evil is so powerful a presence . . . where is God?*

Just as quickly, another question seized his thoughts to torment him. *How could Morgan have done this to us?*

Hadn't he bothered to investigate the ship and its crew? Daniel couldn't believe he would have set them aboard had he held even the slightest suspicion about the ship. Yet how could he *not* have known? He had made the arrangements, after all.

But what did it matter now? There was no turning back, no escape.

And no Morgan to settle their grievances. It was up to *him* now to do whatever he could to protect his mother and the children.

And to help Evan Whittaker.

Daniel looked down at the Englishman. Drenched with perspiration from the fever, the man was out of his head with pain. His once-neat white shirt was ripped and blood-stained, his thin face smudged with grime. Daniel was struck by the thought that without the odd little spectacles Whittaker always wore, he looked surprisingly young and vulnerable. Strange, up until now he had not thought of Whittaker as young, and certainly not as a vulnerable human being like himself.

A fresh surge of emotion coursed through him as he realized anew the debt of gratitude they owed this man who had involved himself in their misery and now lay suffering in their midst — all because he had tried to help them.

Greater love hath no man than this, that he lay down his life for his friends . . .

But we *weren't* his friends, Daniel thought, a lump rising to his throat. We were virtual strangers, even enemies, when Evan Whittaker risked his life for us. We were nothing to him, nothing more than unfamiliar names and foreign faces.

From somewhere deep inside his spirit, something stirred. A slow, gentle kind of warmth began to rise from the very depths of his being.

And suddenly Daniel had the answer to his question. He knew where God was.

He was *here,* in the throes of their wretchedness. In the midst of their suffering. In the sacrificial love of the pain-racked Evan

Whittaker. In this humble heart from which the love of Christ had so freely flowed. God was *here*.

Still stronger and brighter than the evil that lurked all around them, seeking an opportunity to conquer, *God was here* —

"Daniel John?"

He blinked at the sound of his mother's voice, looked from her to Whittaker.

"You must try again. Perhaps someone will come this time."

"Yes, all right. I'll go right now, Mother. I'll go and pound on the door of the hatch until *somebody* comes. I'll *make* them open it, or drive them mad trying!"

Nora's eyes swept over her son with a questioning look. Then she nodded and turned back to Whittaker. Crooning to the delirious man as she might have a child who needed soothing, she continued to swab his flushed face with gentle strokes. "Aye, you try again, Daniel John. Mr. Whittaker cannot go on so. We must get help for him at once!"

Daniel scurried up the ladder, ignoring the splinters that pierced his hands. Reaching the top, he pounded as hard as he could on the door. When his efforts were met by silence, he shinnied back down to grab an iron pot lying discarded amid some rubbish in a corner.

This time when he reached the top of the ladder, he began to crash the pot against the door, over and over again, shouting like a wild thing as he pummeled the rotting wood. *"We've a dead body in here! Open the hatch and help us take him out!"*

At last, the door flew open, and the sailor in charge of passing down their daily ration of water appeared in the opening. His face was ugly with rage as he glared at Daniel. "Stop with that racket, you little Mick!"

Daniel reared. Flinging the cooking pot to the floor, he squeezed his left arm and leg through the opening, past the sailor's brawny frame. Then, grabbing hold of the coaming, he managed to push by the crewman, throwing him off as he hit the deck at a run.

He had no idea which direction to go, where he would find Dr. Leary, but he headed aft, toward the stern, hurtling down the deck like a fired arrow in search of a target.

It came as no surprise to William Leary, the surgeon, that Abidas Schell had a stone for a heart. He had known the man too long to believe otherwise. Thus far this voyage had only served to confirm what he already knew.

Schell stood now, stiff and straight on the quarterdeck, entirely indifferent to Leary's protests on behalf of the poor wretches in steerage.

Leary was sober for a change, a condition in which his temper flared far more quickly than when numbed with whiskey. Schell's arrogant coldness had already torched the surgeon's anger, and with every minute's passing the flame blazed that much higher.

To make matters worse, Leary was as edgy as a wounded polecat about the storm blowing up. Already the Atlantic breezes had increased to strong winds. The tightly tuned rigging hummed and keened as the waves lifted the ship's stern, sweeping the deck with spray.

Leary wiped the salt foam from his face and raked a hand over the muscles at the back of his neck, strung tight with tension. The thought of a storm at sea never failed to make his blood run cold, but battling a storm with a daredevil captain like Schell at the helm made it freeze in his veins.

The grim-visaged captain was using the pretext of preparing for the approaching storm to ignore Leary's presence, but the surgeon wasn't fooled. This man was entirely capable of barking out a set of clipped, precise orders while absorbing half a dozen other conversations at the same time.

Schell simply had no interest in, no compassion for, the poor devils below.

Leary almost wished he were as heartless.

He felt a sudden, vicious stab of spite at the expression on the captain's face as he watched the crew work feverishly to bring in some of the standing sails and double-reef the topsails.

He knew it set Schell's teeth on edge, having to haul in canvas. The man would fly every possible square foot of sail he dared, running the ship to the limit of her potential. The few knowledgeable seamen on board — and they *were* few — grumbled nervously from time to time that they would all eventually suffer for their captain's irresponsibility. One or two had even dared to challenge Schell's orders, but he had ordered them flogged senseless, thereby putting an end to any further questioning of his judgment.

Making another attempt to get Schell's attention, Leary now moved to stand directly in front of the man. "At least let them take turns coming up, just long enough to suck in some fresh air," he said. "A few at a time will do no harm, and the healthier we can keep them, the better off we will all be."

"The entire steerage is under quarantine and will be until I'm assured of no further outbreak of typhus." Schell's reply was distracted, his gaze set above, to where a nimble-footed youngster was climbing a towering mast.

Finally, he lowered his eyes to look at Leary. "As the surgeon, I should think your concern would be for the welfare of the entire ship, not just the few Irish paupers in steerage."

"Few?" Leary shot an incredulous look at Schell. "There are over two hundred of them down there!"

The captain shrugged.

"And what about those poor Chinese girls you've got locked up in the cabins with the opium? They're children, God help us! Just children! Is there *nothing* that means as much to you as gold?"

He paused, enraged at the other man's lack of response. "Well, answer me this, man, what happens if you deliver your Irish unfortunates and your little-girl whores dead instead of alive? Where will that leave your *business* then, eh?"

Schell's icy blue gaze never wavered, but the threat in his voice was unmistakable. "I believe our arrangement had your blessing, *Doctor*. It was you, after all, who handled the negotiations."

Leary swallowed. "You gave me no choice, and you know it," he muttered, forcing himself not to shrink beneath Schell's frigid stare of contempt.

"Doctor! Dr. Leary — please, sir, you must come!"

Leary whirled around, and Schell blinked in surprise as a wild-eyed boy came upon them at a run.

It was the young colt of a lad who was traveling with the injured Englishman. Gasping for breath, he looked faint, perhaps even ill.

"What are you doing here?" Schell's voice cracked like a gunshot. "How did you get abovedecks?"

Panting, the boy looked from Leary to the captain. "Please, sir, I'm sorry, but we need the surgeon badly! My friend, Mr. Whittaker, may be dying!"

Schell glared at the boy as if he were a worm. "Denker, here!" he called out to a nearby crewman. "Put this beggar back down in steerage where he belongs."

"*No!* Not unless the surgeon comes with me!"

Schell made no move for an instant. Then, without warning, his hand shot out to slap the boy across the cheek with enough force to make him reel.

Instinctively Leary put up a hand, as much to ward off the enraged captain as to steady the boy. But Schell had already dropped his arm, the implacable mask once more in place.

The sailor he had summoned now moved behind the boy, yanking both his arms hard behind him. The lad struggled, crying out. His eyes flashed with fury as he stood, legs outspread, facing Schell.

"Our fares are paid," he said, his voice trembling with resentment. "We're entitled to a doctor, and that's all I'm asking!"

"You're entitled to be strung up on the ratlines," retorted Schell, pointing to the tarred ropes used as a ladder, "if you so much as open your mouth once more. As it is, you've earned yourself a night in the wheelhouse."

"Oh, give over!" Leary blurted out. "I was going below tonight anyway, to check the lot of them. I'll go with him now instead of waiting."

For an instant he thought Schell would refuse, would stick to his intention of locking the boy up. A muscle tightened at the corner of one eye, and the nasty scar seemed to pulse and blaze. But at last he gave a short nod of dismissal, telling the sailor, "Let him go. There's more important work to be done than wasting time with an Irish beggar boy."

"Come on, you little fool!" Leary snapped, now angry with himself for stepping in. His impulsive defense of the boy would serve neither of them well.

Taking the lad by the arm, he half-dragged him back up the deck, grumbling all the way. "Why would you be fretting yourself so over a stinking Englishman is what I'd like to know? What is he to you? Not worth incurring the wrath of a man like Schell, I can tell you."

"Mr. Whittaker saved our lives!" The boy twisted in an attempt to tug himself free from Leary's grasp. "We can do no less for him."

Leary looked at him. "What you'd best be doing is staying out of the captain's way from now on unless you've a mind to end up at the end of a lash! He makes no distinction for age."

"He has no right to flog a passenger! I know that much!"

"You know nothing at all!" Leary shouted, again grabbing him by the arm and bringing him to a stop. "*Nothing!* Schell is the law on this ship, and you are no more than a flyspeck to him. If you value your skin, you'll stay out of his sight!"

The boy was quiet for a moment, his piercing blue eyes making Leary increasingly uncomfortable.

"What kind of a ship *is* this?" he asked in a low voice. "Not what we were told, that much is certain."

Leary flared, tightening his grasp on the lad's arm. "I don't know what you were told, boy, but you'd best listen to what *I'm* telling you. You'll do neither yourself nor your family any good by making trouble. Stay quiet and stay out of the way if you hope to see America."

Leary studied the boy for a moment more, relaxing his grip slightly but still holding on to him with care.

"All right, come on now," he ordered, somewhat mollified as he again started to tug the lad along beside him. "If you want me to have a look at your Englishman, give me no more grief. And if you've more than a pea for a brain between your ears, you'll not show your face outside steerage again until you're told. This ship is a dangerous place for meddlesome children."

The boy's gaze stabbed at Leary's conscience. For an instant he felt as if his defenses were being cut away, layer by layer, and his soul laid bare. Something in those eyes belied the youthful countenance, something old and wise beyond the lad's years.

Chilled by the thought that he had been seen for what he was, Leary gave the boy's arm a vicious yank and quickened his pace still more.

Nora pressed her clasped hands against her lips, her gaze going back and forth between the scowling physician and the semiconscious Evan Whittaker.

In his delirium, the Englishman had struggled so fiercely against the surgeon that Daniel had to help hold him down.

"Please, Doctor, can you give him something for the pain?" Nora ventured uncertainly, somewhat intimidated by the doctor's rough impatience.

Ignoring her, he straightened, his shoulders bent slightly to keep his head from grazing the ceiling. For a moment he continued to stare down at Whittaker's shoulder, his lined face twisted into a taut, resentful grimace.

"There's nothing for it but to take the arm."

The words were spoken with such a resentment it almost sounded as if he were indicting Whittaker for his failure to heal.

The room swayed. Nora stared at the surgeon, then Whittaker. "*No . . . oh, no!* Please, there must be another way . . . some medicine —"

"I said I'll have to amputate!" snapped the surgeon, still not looking at anyone but Whittaker. "It's his arm or his life."

"But he's not aware enough to even have a say in it —"

The physician turned to look at her. "He *has* no say in it, woman, if he wants to live!"

Dear Lord, all this is happening to him because of us! It's so unfair; he saved our lives, and now . . . this?

"If you . . . if you amputate, will he live?" Daniel John's voice sounded thin, tremulous. Nora saw the dismay in her heart mirrored in her son's eyes.

The surgeon's lower lip rolled down even farther. "I can't promise that. He might live if I take the arm. But he'll die for certain if I *don't!*"

Doesn't he care? Whittaker might be a stranger to him, but he is a doctor, after all.

Nora stepped closer to Whittaker, looking down on him. His face was tracked with perspiration and grime, etched with pain.

She felt ill. Ill and sad. And guilty.

He did it for us. It's because of us this is happening to him.

"I'll have to go and get my instruments," Dr. Leary said. "We'd best get to it right away. He's in bad shape."

"Just be sure that's *all* you get. You'll be sober when you operate on him."

Nora's head shot up at Daniel John's sharp words. The surgeon whipped around to face him, eyes flashing.

"I saw the shape you were in when you treated his wound." The lad's voice was as hard as any man's. "You were *drunk!* I wouldn't be surprised if it wasn't your fault the wound went bad."

"Why, you —"

"You know I'm right!" Daniel John stood, stepping out from Whittaker's bunk to face the surgeon. "I'm only asking for your word that you'll come back sober. He's important to us."

"He's English," the surgeon sneered.

"He's our *friend,*" countered the boy. "He saved our lives. Now you will save his."

Nora stared in wonder as the surgeon's angry glare slowly wilted, then dropped away entirely.

His shoulders sagged, his face went slack, and then he gave a short nod. "See to him until I get back," he muttered gruffly. "I won't be long."

As soon as the doctor walked away, Nora let go the tears she'd been choking back. Daniel John came to her, pulling her gently into his arms.

She could feel her son's trembling as she

wept against his shoulder, but his arms were strong and his voice still steady. “At least this way, he has a better chance to live, Mother. That’s the important thing — that he live.”

Wetting his shoulder with her tears, Nora desperately hoped that Evan Whittaker would feel the same when he awakened.

34

The Keen Comes Wailing on the Wind

I hear all night as through a storm
Hoarse voices calling, calling
My name upon the wind.

JAMES CLARENCE MANGAN (1803–1849)

Morgan Fitzgerald stood in the middle of his cell, wondering why the gaol was so uncommonly quiet tonight.

For more than an hour he had heard none of Cummins the gaoler's vigorous cursing, no prisoner complaints, no rattling of chains or slamming of doors.

It was as dark as it was quiet. Even the candle that usually lighted the corridor seemed to have been forgotten.

Outside, the wind set up a mournful wail, and Morgan shivered. A breath of dread whispered at the back of his neck — from the keening of the wind or the cold of the cell, he couldn't say.

Not for the first time since being locked up,

he thought of the flask he had once carried. He'd given up the drink years before, while still a young man, once he saw himself headed down the same road as his father. Tonight, though, he thought he would not mind a taste or two.

He smiled grimly in the darkness. Had he known back then that his choices ran to dying with a noose around his neck or a tumbler in his hand, he just might not have been so quick to smash the flask.

He was exceedingly bored. The candle he'd managed to badger from Cummins had burned itself up last evening, so he couldn't see to read or write. This would have been bad enough in itself, but it was more vexing than it might have been, thanks to that sly priest, Joseph Mahon.

The man had slipped a worn copy of the Scriptures inside his belongings. On the cover was fastened a note.

Now Joseph knew him well enough to know he could never resist a good tale. His vague message had been meant to pique Morgan's curiosity, and so it had.

Morgan, the note had read, *there's a tale inside about a foolish fellow who thought he could escape God by running in the opposite direction. More than a little like you, I should imagine. I thought perhaps you might want to see for yourself the lengths to which our Lord will go to get our attention and change our course. His name was*

Jonah, by the way, if you care to look him up . . .

Morgan knew the story of Jonah, of course, but, partly to appease Joseph and partly out of idle interest, he had read it again.

And again.

Even now he found himself wanting to read it once more, at length. Something about Jonah and his great fish captured Morgan's attention in an odd sort of way.

At times, like now, he even found himself musing that this cell was not unlike the fish's belly — cold and wet and dark.

At any rate, he was eager for Cummins to bring his evening meal so he could nag him for another candle.

In the meantime, he wondered where the irascible rat who had become his nighttime companion was hiding himself.

Oliver, Morgan had named him, in memory of Cromwell, of course. And wasn't the dull-witted rodent nearly as predictable as old Oliver himself had reportedly been?

Each evening just after Cummins left Morgan's plate, the rat would slink out of its hole and actually try to beat him to his supper.

For the first two or three days, Morgan had let the creature have the offensive mess in its entirety, for he could not stomach it. At that rate, however, he would have ended up too weak to attend his own hanging, and so he determined to teach the greedy Oliver some manners, making him wait until he himself arrived at the last few bites and set the plate to the floor.

Either the rat had tired of his paltry leavings, or else the gruel had finally killed him off. Morgan suspected the gruel.

The cursed tooth had begun to ache again this afternoon. Morgan wished he had the stomach to yank it out, but the thing was a piece of himself, and these days he was not eager to part with even a rotting tooth. If nothing else, the pain was a reminder that he was still alive.

He heard the jingle of keys and turned. The door opened to frame both Cummins, the gaoler, and Joseph Mahon, the priest, in the flickering glow from the candle Cummins held.

In the dim, weaving light the men's faces took on an eerie pall, giving them an almost spectral appearance. The gaoler's heavy-jowled face was set in a fierce, relentless expression, while the priest stared at Morgan with a peculiar, speculative look in his eye.

Morgan met his stare with a questioning look of his own, then turned to Cummins.

His shoulders tightened instinctively as the cold finger of doom began a slow descent down his backbone.

The question no longer seemed to be whether Whittaker would survive the amputation of his arm, but whether he would live long enough for the amputation to take place.

Daniel watched the Englishman with anxious eyes, his own face flushed with dread of what was to come. Whittaker had not spoken for over an hour, other than to moan or mumble something entirely incoherent.

Much to Daniel's relief, the doctor had returned in a short time, sober. With him he brought a number of ominous-looking medical instruments, the sight of which had made Daniel's mother quickly turn her head away.

Whittaker lay on a rough wooden table at the end of the steerage compartment. The surgeon, an apron bound around him, had just returned from scrubbing his hands in a bowl of hot water, water he had taken time to heat before returning. He snapped at a number of inquisitive onlookers, chasing them off to their own quarters with a string of curses and threats.

Now he stood, studying Whittaker. After a moment he raised his eyes to look first at Daniel, then at his mother.

"One of you will have to stay and help," he said shortly.

Daniel's heart slammed hard against his ribcage. He looked at his mother's ashen face, swallowed, and said, "I'll stay."

He didn't miss the pool of relief that instantly welled up in his mother's eyes. But, pressing her lips into a tight line, she shook her head. "No, Daniel John, I will stay. You —"

"Mother," he interrupted, "I'm going to be a surgeon, remember? This is something I will have to do myself one day. I will stay with Whittaker."

Their eyes held briefly; then she gave a slight nod and backed away, retreating to a nearby place against the hull.

"If he starts to wake up, give him as many drops of this as he can manage."

Dr. Leary's graveled voice jerked Daniel's attention back to the table and Whittaker. Taking the small bottle the surgeon handed him, he asked, "What is it?"

"Laudanum. Opium. It'll ease the pain some."

"Some? Don't you have anything stronger?"

The surgeon glanced up from assembling his instruments on a tray beside the table. "Even if I did, I wouldn't chance giving it to him, the shape he's in. His heart is battling for every beat. Pain never killed a man," he finished curtly. "Too much opiate has killed more than one."

Daniel swallowed down his growing panic. "I'd like to pray, please."

The surgeon turned. "As you like."

"I'd . . . I'd feel better about things if you would pray as well."

"I'm not a praying man," replied the doctor, turning away.

"And what kind of man are you, then, Doctor?"

Daniel's quiet question seemed to fluster the surgeon. Pretending to search the inside of his medical case, he delayed his answer. "A man who has seen far too much to believe in a God who hears prayer," he finally muttered, turning back to Whittaker.

Daniel scrutinized the stooped, weathered-looking surgeon. Something in this man belied the gruffness he seemed so determined to project, and he found himself wondering if the doctor's hard exterior was as impenetrable as he had first believed.

Daniel hesitated another instant, then bowed his head and closed his eyes. In a soft, not altogether steady voice, he prayed for the skill of Dr. Leary, for the success of the operation, and for angels to stand guard and minister to the unsuspecting Evan Whittaker.

"And I pray that when he awakens, Lord, he will forgive us for the tragedy we have brought upon him."

Daniel opened his eyes, blinking at the sight of the knife the surgeon now held in his hand.

"Come around to this side," the doctor ordered. "You scrubbed your hands as I said?"

Daniel nodded and crossed to the other side of the table, where the doctor had laid out the instruments.

He tried to swallow, but found his throat swollen shut.

"This is the saw I will need when I'm finished with the knife," the surgeon said, pointing out each instrument as he reeled off their names.

"This other is the Hey's saw," he went on. "Silk for sutures, here. Now, then, you stay close, hand me each as I ask for it." He glanced at Daniel. "You all right, boy?"

Daniel moistened his lips, nodded.

The surgeon studied him. "You must not get sick on me, mind. You're sure you are up to this?"

Daniel dragged his eyes away from the instruments, looked at the doctor, and nodded stiffly.

The physician bent over Whittaker and set to work. "So you've a mind to be a surgeon yourself, then?"

"Aye," Daniel replied in a shaky voice, his eyes widening as the doctor ripped off what remained of Whittaker's torn shirt, then flushed away the blood from the wound with a bucket of cold water.

"Tonight may just change your mind."

Daniel's eyes went to the knife in the surgeon's hand, followed the movement of the blade as it targeted Whittaker's upper arm.

The room swayed. The table rocked back and forth.

Daniel panicked, sure he was about to be ill — or, even worse, that he might faint.

Then he saw the knife suspended in the air and the surgeon lift his head, frowning as he let go an oath. "It's the storm," he growled, holding the scalpel poised until the rocking ebbed. "This ship is damned, that's certain! I told Schell, I told him he would pay . . ."

Daniel could make no sense of the man's wild muttering. But he knew well enough the importance of a steady hand on the knife.

Grinding his teeth, he hugged both arms to his body, holding his breath as the surgeon began to cut.

Whittaker's eyes were still shut, but he screamed — a terrible, piercing scream.

Tightening his own arms around himself, Daniel screamed, too, a silent, suffocating scream that tore at the walls of his heart and made his chest swell until he thought it would explode.

Dimly he became aware of the doctor's rough demand. "The *saw,* boy! *Hand me the saw!*"

Whittaker screamed once more when the saw met bone. Then his head lolled to the side as if he were dead.

The ship rocked, creaking and groaning, swaying like a drunken whale. The table danced on the floor.

The surgeon stopped, waited, then returned to his task. His face was flushed, slick with sweat, his eyes boring through the bone along with the saw.

The ship rolled, and Daniel pitched forward. He reached to steady himself and the table, to hold fast.

His stomach recoiled at the motion of the ship, the sight of the surgeon's blood-soaked apron, the sound of the saw severing Whittaker's arm.

Oh, dear Lord, I am sick . . . so sick . . . I mustn't retch . . . I mustn't faint . . .

Seawater streamed through the overhead vents, spraying the table, Whittaker, the surgeon.

Passengers shrieked. Prayers and curses were lifted, fighting to be heard against the squeal and crack of the ship's timbers, the crash of the waves.

The wind itself seemed to be screaming with pain as the surgeon finally separated Whittaker's arm from his body.

Daniel squeezed his eyes shut against Evan Whittaker's tragedy and cupped both hands to his ears to shut out the hellish sound of torment shaking the very hull of the ship.

The demented face of a woman rode the storm aboard the *Green Flag*.

Sheathed in a gossamer gown, hair flowing, her twisted features were set straight ahead. One arm was raised, the hand balled to a fist. The fist gripped a piece of green silk, flapping madly in the wind.

The wild eyes of the *Green Flag*'s masthead seemed to follow the frenzied movement of the crewmen as they fought the gale-driven waves splashing over the deck.

The force of the waves knocked sailors off their feet, hurtling them forward, sweeping some the entire length of the deck. Timbers cracked, blocks fell, spars broke loose and went down in a tangle of rigging.

On into the howling night the woman leaped across the waves, pointing the way with the flag in her upraised arm, daring the gale to slow her speed.

Engulfed by the blackness of the sea and the night, the woman appeared to be fleeing a different Darkness.

35

To Set the Captive Free

And thus we rust
Life's iron chain
Degraded and alone:
And some men curse, and some men weep,
And some men make no moan:
But God's eternal Laws are kind
And break the heart of stone.

OSCAR WILDE (1854–1900)

It was taking Cummins and the priest a powerful long time to get around to telling him he was about to swing.

After fifteen minutes or more of idle blather, Morgan had enough. They might just as well get to it, since all three knew exactly why they had come.

Joseph Mahon obviously still hoped to shrive him, and Cummins no doubt wanted to be the lad to lead him to the noose.

Joseph had already sat down twice, only to haul himself up again and go pacing around the cell as if *he* were the one confined. Morgan thought it a bit peculiar that a priest like Mahon, who by now had to be an old hand at hearing the confessions of the condemned, should have such a difficult time of things with yet another sinner.

Cummins, too, seemed in an odd mood. Rather than the glee Morgan would have expected from him, the man's face was so sour it could have curdled a pail of new milk.

"So, then, Joseph, where have you been hiding yourself these days? You haven't been ill, I hope?"

Even as Morgan said the words, it struck him that indeed the priest *did* look ill, so lean you could blow him off your hand. Joseph Mahon was killing himself over his parish. Morgan would have wagered that both he and Oliver the rat had been eating better than the priest.

Mahon stopped his pacing and came to stand directly in front of Morgan, in the middle of the cell. In his right hand he held an envelope and a paper rolled into a tube — the legal go-ahead for his hanging, Morgan assumed. The hand holding the papers trembled so fiercely Morgan's instinct was to reach out and steady it with his own.

Instead, he shot the priest a grim smile in an attempt to make things easier for him. Splaying his hands on his hips, he stood, legs wide, studying Mahon with a rueful expression.

"It's all right, Joseph. Haven't we both known it was coming, and soon at that?"

The priest contemplated Morgan for what seemed a very long time, looking away only once to glance at Cummins.

"Morgan," Joseph Mahon finally said, his quivering hand tightening on the papers, "it is not what you think, lad."

Morgan frowned, waiting.

"Morgan," Joseph Mahon said again, lifting the paper in his hand and holding it up like a signpost, "you have been granted a pardon. A *conditional* pardon, mind you. But you are saved, Morgan. You are saved from the rope."

Morgan stared at him. He dropped his hands down to his sides, looked about him. The room seemed to swim. Even the ceiling tilted a bit, and the floor on which he was standing rose as if to hurl him backward.

"What are you saying to me, Joseph?" he grated out.

The priest reached out to put a hand to Morgan's forearm. "It's true, lad. You will not hang."

His heart pounding, Morgan looked to Cummins. The gaoler sat, hunched over like a lump on the sagging mattress. He wore the dark, angry face of one who has had the rug yanked out from under him.

"A pardon, is it?" Morgan parroted, turning back to Joseph Mahon.

"Aye, lad," said the priest, quickly adding, "a *conditional* pardon."

"I don't believe it," said Morgan, then repeated the words softly. "I don't believe it. How could this be, Joseph?"

"It is true, Morgan," the priest assured him. "You are saved. By God's grace, you will live."

For one appalling instant, Morgan felt he would disgrace himself by bursting into tears of stunned relief. Recovering, he looked at the papers in Joseph's hand.

"Is that —"

The priest nodded. "This is your pardon, Morgan. And a letter."

"A letter? A letter from whom?"

Morgan reached for the papers, but Joseph put up a restraining hand. "Wait, lad. Sit down, now, for we must talk."

Morgan managed a jerky nod. "How, Joseph? How could such a thing happen?"

The priest gave him a long look, then took his arm and motioned him toward the bed. Cummins immediately jumped to his feet and went to stand on the opposite side of the cell, as if Morgan's nearness might contaminate him.

"It came about," said the priest, waiting for Morgan to sit down, "through your grandfather."

While Morgan sat staring at him with burning eyes, struggling to shake off the buzzing in his head, Joseph Mahon turned to

Cummins. "I will talk with him alone now."

The sullen line of the gaoler's mouth pulled down even more. "I'm to see the pardon delivered," he said, crossing his arms over his chest, "and its terms accepted before the prisoner is released."

Mahon narrowed his eyes. "The pardon will be *delivered,* and *I* will tell you when the prisoner can be released! Will you insult your own priest by doubting his honor, Francis Cummins?"

The gaoler grumbled but finally turned and let himself out the door.

The priest sat down beside Morgan. "I know you are surprised, Morgan. I will explain what I can."

Morgan's own hand was shaking as he rubbed one side of his beard. He looked at the priest.

"Surprised?" Morgan repeated blankly. "Oh, I am not *surprised,* Joseph. I am dumbfounded!"

Avoiding Morgan's eyes, Joseph sat staring down at the floor.

Morgan noted that the priest's hands were still trembling. *Weakness,* he realized. *It isn't dread over approaching doom after all, but illness and exhaustion that has made him quake so.*

"Much of what you will want to know, Morgan, is in this letter," said Mahon, handing both the envelope and the scrolled sheet of paper to Morgan without looking at him. "There are some things I cannot tell you, not without violating your father's last confession."

Morgan looked down at the papers in Mahon's hand, then took them. "My father's —" Morgan stopped, groping to make some sense of the priest's words. "What is all this you are telling me, Joseph? About my father — and a grandfather? I have no grandfather, at least none I ever knew."

He paused, and Joseph Mahon turned and met his eyes, nodding. "Aye, lad, I know that. You thought you had no real family, other than your father and Thomas."

"That's the truth. But how is it that *you* know?"

"I have just returned from Dublin, Morgan. That's why I have not come to the gaol for some days now."

"Dublin? What is in Dublin?"

"Your grandfather. Your mother's father."

"My — Joseph, what is this about?" Morgan put a heavy hand to Joseph's arm, but, feeling the thin, fragile bones beneath the sleeve of the priest's cassock, he immediately gentled his touch.

Mahon looked away. "Do you remember your mother at all, Morgan?"

"No. I never knew her."

Still staring at the floor, Mahon asked quietly, "Did you know that she was half English?"

"Aye, I knew that, well enough," Morgan muttered.

The priest turned to look at him, his eyes widening with surprise. "Aidan told you, then — about your mother?"

Morgan shook his head. "Thomas. Thomas told me. Our da spilled it to him one night when he was on the bottle," he said tightly, remembering how his young heart had sickened at the thought of British blood in his veins.

"How much did Thomas know?"

"How much?" Morgan looked at him, then shrugged. "That was most of it. Our mother was the daughter of an English politician and a Dublin woman who left the church to marry."

"That was all? Did you never wonder what happened to your mother?"

"She died," Morgan said quietly, avoiding the priest's probing gaze. "When I was still a babe. I never knew her at all. She died, and his grief for her set our father on the road. He never got over her death, you know. Her dying killed him as well."

"It was hard for you lads, you and Thomas," said Joseph softly, as if remembering. "Aidan was a . . . a difficult man. A broken man. You must have wondered about your mother, what she was like?"

"Aye, we did," Morgan admitted. "Da would not speak of her, told us nothing of their life together, and so I made up a picture of her in my mind when I was small. The picture became so real that she almost seemed to live, at least at night, in my dreams. Even now," he said with a faint smile, "I can see the face I gave to her. It was a lovely face —"

Catching the maudlin note in his voice, he broke off and got to his feet. "Ah, well, what boy does not want a lovely mother? Joseph, I will ask you again: How is it that you know these things, and what is all this leading up to?"

"Aidan told both you and Thomas that your mother's people were dead as well as herself, did he not?"

Morgan nodded. "He did."

The priest sighed, his eyes roaming over the dark, barren cell. "I suppose he felt it best, safer for you boys." He regarded Morgan with a thoughtful gaze for a moment. "But it was a lie. Your grandfather still lives, Morgan. And it is to him you owe your freedom."

For a fleeting instant, Joseph caught a rare glimpse of vulnerability in Morgan, and it pierced his heart all through.

He had known this immense, strapping young man since he was a lad — long enough to know he was not the callous outlaw his reputation suggested. The Morgan Fitzgerald Joseph knew might very well possess the ferocity of a lion and the cunning of the wolf after which he was called. But he was also a man with an infinitely tender heart that belied his strength, a heart easily pierced and supremely capable of deep, intense pain.

Joseph remembered the boy Morgan had been, with his wild copper curls and his too-long legs and his habit of hurling endless unanswerable questions during the catechism classes. Brilliant and eclectic, he had been a rebel even then, a rebel with a hunger for knowledge and a fierce intolerance of easy answers. The lad had often reminded Joseph of a young animal, stalking the most elusive prey known to man — Truth.

"Sit down, Morgan," he said. "Sit down here beside me."

Morgan did as he was told, but the look he gave Joseph was guarded and not altogether friendly.

"The letter you hold is from your maternal grandfather. He has written to you with an explanation of the terms of your pardon, which he secured on your behalf. I will tell you the little I can without violating the confessional, but the rest you must learn for yourself, inside that letter."

Morgan studied the envelope in his hand for an instant. "How did you know where to find him?"

"Oh, *finding* him was no problem," Joseph said. "He is a well-known, powerful man — a member of the aristocracy. He sat in

Parliament for years, owns vast estates both in England and in Ireland, and has great influence. No, it wasn't difficult at all to find him," he repeated. "He's an old man now, of course, retired because of age and poor health. But your friend, Smith O'Brien, helped me gain an audience with him. He knew a man who knew another man, don't you see, and the next thing that happened, I found myself in your grandfather's library."

Joseph leaned toward Morgan. "And what a library it *is*, Morgan! You would lie down and die of ecstasy just to see it, and that's the truth!"

"Joseph, I care nothing about my — about this man's library! Just tell me whatever it is you think I should know and be done with it. If it's true that I am about to be freed from this place, the sooner the better for me!"

Joseph nodded. He thought he understood Morgan's confusion. To spend years with no family at all and then one day to learn of a grandfather who is no more than a stranger — an English stranger — would be a hard thing. A hard thing, indeed.

"Your father's family was ancient Gaelic — among the very oldest of Irish stock. Not wealthy at all, but learned people, most of them teachers and priests. Aidan was educated, first in France and later in Dublin at great financial sacrifice. To his family, knowledge was all, nearly as important as life itself."

"Aye, the old man often rambled on about the sanctity of education when he was drunk," Morgan commented brusquely.

Nodding, Joseph went on. "Your mother's family — at least on her father's side — was English, only a step or two removed from nobility. Wealthy, influential —"

"— and thoroughly Protestant," Morgan finished dryly.

"That's the truth. Your grandmother left the church in a great rush to marry her English lover, and it was immediately hushed up that their spotless Saxon bloodline had been some tainted with a touch of the Roman Irish.

"Your father was a poor student when he met and fell in love with your mother. By that time her family was so entrenched in their wealthy English Protestantism that the news of their only daughter's love for a starving Roman Catholic brought as much horror as if she had asked their leave to wed a leper.

"Your father's family was no more pleased. They cherished their Irishness and their Catholicism every bit as much as the girl's family did their Anglican ways. Both families threatened the young lovers with expulsion if they did not part.

"Well, the long and short of it," Joseph continued, feeling a renewed wave of sadness for the young couple who wanted only to be left alone with their love for each other, "was that your mother and father *would* be married, and so they defied their families — and their religions — and ran off to some godforsaken village in County Kerry to be married by a civil official.

"Over the years their poverty forced them to move from town to town. Aidan kept a school wherever he was needed, or else worked at odd jobs to keep food in their mouths.

"When Thomas was born, Aidan's father — his mother had died — relented and asked them to come home with their babe. Things were better for them for a time, but when the old man died, nothing was left to them except a house on which they could not pay the rent.

"Your mother was carrying you by then, and after you were born, she sickened for some weeks, then died. Aidan tried to keep you boys with him, but he had no money and was drinking something fierce all the time. So he went to your mother's family and offered the two of you — you and Thomas — to them."

As Joseph watched, a stricken look came over Morgan's face. "He gave us *away?* Is that the truth?"

"It wasn't like that! He was wild with grief, desperate to save you and your brother from starving. The family agreed to take you both, and gave Aidan some money to go away. He had to sign papers giving up all claim to you, had to promise he would never attempt to see you again. At the last minute, he couldn't do it. The papers were signed, the money in his pocket, but he reneged on the agreement and ran away, taking both you and Thomas with him.

"Apparently they tried for months to locate the three of you — even offered a reward. But Aidan went on the road like a common outlaw, hiding in the woods, stopping off in remote villages, until the family finally lost his scent. After that . . . well, as you know, he did the best he could. But by then he was a beaten man.

"The rest of it . . . no longer matters. There are private, personal things a father would not want his sons to know, only his priest."

Morgan was silent for a long time. He sat slumped over on the bed, his broad shoulders sagging, his rugged face pensive. Joseph reached once to touch him, thought better of it, and dropped his hand away.

"So that is where the money for my education came from," Morgan said softly. "He stole it from *them*." He was silent for a moment, thinking. "How did my grandfather manage a pardon for me? And *why?*" He turned to look at Joseph. "And these *conditions* you mentioned — what are they?"

"Your grandfather has the power to obtain most anything he pleases," Joseph replied. "As to *why,* you are his blood — his only grandson, Morgan — and he is sorry for what he did to your parents. Truly sorry."

"Of course, he is," Morgan sneered. "You still haven't told me what the conditions are."

"Morgan, he is an old, sick man. Probably he has little time left on this earth. It is altogether likely his remorse is genuine. I believe it is," Joseph said firmly. "As for the conditions, they are more than fair. He asks only that you refrain from further 'illegal activities.' And he wants to see you. He wants you to come to Dublin once you're released."

"He wants to *see* me?" Morgan uttered a short, ugly laugh. *"When hell is an iceberg!"*

Again Joseph reached to clasp Fitzgerald's shoulder. "Morgan —"

Morgan shook him off with a violent shrug. He shot to his feet and went to stand in the center of the shadowed cell. "If seeing him is a part of the pardon, tell him I'll whistle as I swing!"

He tossed the envelope and the pardon to the floor.

"Don't be a *fool!*" Ignoring the pain in his back, Joseph got to his feet and hurried to rescue the papers.

Facing Morgan, he pressed the envelope and the pardon into his hand. "I understand your bitterness, lad, and I don't blame you. But it will gain you nothing to go on nursing your poison. That paper is your freedom! Do not let your anger get in the way of your good sense!"

His face livid, Morgan waved the papers in the air. "Why, after all these years, Joseph? Answer me that! Why should I go toadying to a man who as good as murdered my parents? His own *daughter*, for the love of heaven! Why should I do anything for a man like that?"

Joseph looked at him, choosing his words carefully. "Because he is soon to die and wants to see his only grandson while there is still time."

At Morgan's grunt of disgust, Joseph shook his head and put up a hand to quiet him. "And because *you* will die if you do not go, if you refuse to let him help you. You should do this thing out of mercy for him, and for the sake of your own life most of all. I cannot think you would need more reason than that."

The younger man's back stiffened. He squared his shoulders, lifted his chin. Standing there, so straight and towering, he looked for all the world like one of the ancient warlords.

Oh, God, soften his pride, the priest prayed silently. *Quench his anger! Do not let him be such a fool as to deny the freedom he holds within his hand even now . . .*

When Morgan turned back to him, Joseph was amazed to see the lad's eyes glazed with unshed tears. So, then, a struggle *was* going on.

Indeed, Joseph wondered, had there ever

been a time when a battle was *not* going on inside that searching, tormented spirit?

Savior . . . tender Shepherd of our souls, reach out to your prodigal son and draw him back into your loving arms. Give him, at last, the peace that has eluded him all his life . . .

Moments passed, and the silence in the room hung heavy and thick with dread.

Finally Morgan turned, his face set in an unreadable mask. "I suppose," he said in a strangled voice, "I do not want to hang, after all. I will accept the pardon. I will go to Dublin."

Their eyes locked and held. "God be praised," murmured Joseph. "God be praised."

An hour later, Morgan walked out the back door of the Castlebar gaol into a clear, star-studded night.

He stopped just outside the door. There, a few feet away, stood Pilgrim, tethered to a fence rail.

As soon as Pilgrim saw Morgan, he went berserk, pawing the ground and squealing with excitement.

Stunned, Morgan bolted toward the horse. He crooned to the big stallion in the Irish, stroking his sides, patting his noble head.

At last he swung around to Joseph, just coming out the door. "How did you manage this?" he asked, a smile breaking across his face. "Where was he?"

With one arm tucked behind his back, the priest started toward him. "Cassidy hid him in the woods, took care of him. I only found out where he was last night."

Then, fixing a stern frown on Morgan, he withdrew what he had been holding behind his back.

Morgan's harp. His *broken* harp.

"What is the meaning of *this?*" The priest's voice was sharp.

Morgan shrugged.

"Can it be fixed?" Joseph asked, handing it to Morgan.

Hesitating, Morgan glanced at the strings hanging limply from the broken block of willow. Finally, he reached for it, nodding. "Aye, it just needs to be glued and restrung."

The priest studied him for a long moment. "The same is true of yourself, I'm thinking."

Morgan looked at him.

"God is calling you back, Morgan Fitzgerald," Joseph said, his tone softening. "How long will you turn deaf ears to His voice?"

Morgan stared at the diminutive, frail priest with real affection. "I have much to thank you for, Joseph Mahon. My freedom, my life — even my horse, it seems. How do I tell you what is in my heart?"

"You have *God* to thank," the priest replied. "I was only His hands and feet. It's

Him you should be telling what is in your heart."

Morgan inclined his head, smiling ruefully at the priest. "As you say, Joseph. Still, I owe you much."

"Then repay me by grieving for your sins and turning back to your Savior. I could hope for no greater payment."

Morgan studied him, wondering at the kind of great soul it took to make such a man. "You mean that."

"Of course, I *mean* it! I have stormed the doors of heaven for you, Morgan Fitzgerald! Can you not at least go knocking on your own behalf?"

Morgan managed a lame smile. "I suppose I can try, Joseph. But do not be surprised if the doors are permanently locked against me."

"Even if they are, lad, you hold the one key that will open them."

"The key, Joseph? What key would that be?"

"Christ in your heart, Morgan."

"Ah, I doubt He would live in a heart like mine, Joseph. Not now, not after all I've done."

From a great distance away, as if floating down from the ancient mountains of Mayo, came the memory of the Englishman Evan Whittaker's voice: *"He means to have your attention . . . and your heart . . . and one way or another, He will. Be warned, Morgan Fitzgerald, for the Ancient of Days and the Shepherd of your soul is in pursuit of you . . . and there is no hiding from Him."*

Morgan suddenly thought of Jonah . . . the cold, dark belly of the fish . . . his gaol cell. Had the Castlebar gaol been his fish?

God, what was happening? He was sniveling, sniveling like a boy . . .

"Will you pray with me, Morgan?"

"*Now,* Joseph?"

"*Now,* Morgan."

And so they knelt there, on the cold, wet earth in back of the Castlebar gaol.

With the weary priest at his side, the warm, familiar breath of his horse at his back, the prodigal prayed. And listened.

Above them in the night sky, the stars of heaven blinked in wonder.

"Do you still believe in the Man named *Jesus,* Morgan . . . the Man who was nailed to a cross on Calvary?"

"I do, yes," Morgan said softly, silently voicing the precious name in his heart for the first time in what seemed an age.

Jesus . . .

"And do you still believe," the priest went on, "it was the very Son of God whose hands and feet were nailed to that tree, Morgan?"

"Aye, I do." His voice grew softer still, choking on a wave of long-suppressed tears.

"And do you know that He died for you . . .

indeed, would have died upon His cross even if there had been no sinner in the world that day *apart* from you?"

God, oh, God, that's the truth, isn't it? You died for me, would have died for me alone . . .

Morgan Fitzgerald was weeping, his heart breaking.

"Lord, oh, Lord Jesus, forgive this sinner . . ."

Morgan, my son, I love you. You are mine.

"Even now, Lord? Even now?"

I have always loved you, Morgan. Even now . . . now and forever.

The priest and the prodigal wept, and heaven sang.

36

Whisper of Darkness

Be Thou my wisdom, Thou my true word;
I ever with Thee, Thou with me, Lord.
Be Thou my battle-shield, sword for the fight,
Be Thou my dignity, Thou my delight.
Thou my soul's shelter, Thou my high tower;
Raise Thou me heavenward, power of my power.

ANONYMOUS (EIGHTH CENTURY)

For three days Evan Whittaker lay suspended between life and death. Unconscious, seemingly unaware of everything but pain, he seldom moved except to thrash back and forth in the throes of his suffering. He made no sound except to add his intermittent groans and cries to the cacophony of despair that rang throughout the steerage quarters day and night.

Throughout the entire time, Nora felt that Whittaker had somehow escaped the *Green Flag*, had managed to slip away to a secret place, where he now awaited the Lord's decision as to his fate.

When, on the evening of the third day, he began to rouse, she nearly panicked. From the hour of the surgery, she had prayed for his recovery, yet dreaded his awakening. What would she say to him when and if he finally came to and found himself missing an arm?

Even as his eyes fluttered open to fix a glazed, uncomprehending stare on her, Nora looked frantically around the men's quarters for Daniel John. He was nowhere in sight. Only moments before, he had taken Little Tom to the back of the compartment to relieve himself, and they had not yet returned. MacCabe, the Galway farmer who was Whittaker's bunk mate, was gone as well.

A garbled word from Whittaker made Nora turn back to him.

"Hurts . . ."

Leaning close, Nora put a cloth to his head. "Shhh, now, Mr. Whittaker, I know it must hurt something fierce, but you are going to be all right, truly you are. You will be just fine."

His eyes closed for an instant, then opened again. Nora thought she saw a faint glimmer of recognition.

"Mrs. . . . Kavanagh . . ."

He *was* coming around! He would need the surgeon . . . somebody.

"Daniel John! Oh, thank the Lord!"

The sight of her son coming up the aisle, tugging wee Tom by the hand, made relief spill over Nora.

"Take Little Tom to the girls, and come back. *Hurry!*"

Glancing from her to Whittaker with surprise, Daniel turned before the words were out of her mouth. Pulling the little boy up into his arms, he hurried him off to Katie and Johanna.

He was back in a moment, his eyes anxious as he came to stand next to his mother.

As if sensing the movement, Whittaker's eyes flickered open. His lips were cracked and bleeding, his face still bruised and scraped from the fall he'd taken at the time of his shooting.

"What . . . happened?" he finally managed.

Nora's throat ached with despair as she reached out to smooth a strand of limp blond hair away from his forehead, gently, as she might have touched an ailing child.

Merciful Lord, what do I say? There are no words that can make this any easier for him.

"You . . . you have had surgery, Mr. Whittaker," she choked out. "Three days past now."

"Surgery?" His head lolled to one side, and his eyes closed again, only for an instant. "What sort of . . . surgery?" When he opened his eyes again, his gaze was more focused.

Oh, God, how do I tell him the terrible truth? I want to comfort him, but there is no comfort for such a thing as this.

"Your arm, Mr. Whittaker . . . the wound

was badly infected, you see. The surgeon . . . Dr. Leary . . . he —" She glanced at Daniel John for support, but the boy's attention was fixed on Whittaker, his eyes glistening with pain and sympathy.

Nora's mouth went dry as she turned back to Whittaker. "The doctor said there was . . . no other way if you were to live. He said . . . it was the only thing to do." The words stuck in her throat.

Whittaker's eyes met hers, and Nora suddenly felt the man absorb her horror. Slowly, he reached his right hand across his chest to touch the empty space at his left side.

Nora could feel his shock — the sudden, awful emptiness — as if it were her own. She swallowed, held her breath, nodding at the anguished question in his eyes.

"He *had* to do it, Mr. Whittaker," she managed to say, strangling on the words. "You would have died if he had not . . . operated."

Whittaker's hand continued to move, fumbling, passing over the blanket once, then again. All the while he continued to stare at Nora, as if expecting her at any instant to tell him he was dreaming, that his arm was right there, just as it had always been.

"I'm so sorry, Mr. Whittaker," Nora choked out. "It was the only way."

His eyes froze on her face, bleak and mute. Nora swallowed down the knot of despair in her throat, unable to speak. At last Whittaker squeezed his eyes tightly shut and turned his head away.

Nora cast a pleading glance at Daniel John, and he put an arm around her waist to steady her. "We'll take care of you, Mr. Whittaker," he said, his voice trembling as he repeated the assurance. "We'll take care of you. You'll be fine in no time at all."

Nora wasn't sure exactly what she had expected from the Englishman. She would not have been surprised if he had screamed or lashed out in a fit of hysterics.

What she had not anticipated was the stillness of the man, the lack of even the slightest display of horror or anger or outrage. He lay there on the bunk, eyes closed, quiet as a shadow. Once he opened his mouth in a soft, sobbing sound. Other than that, the only indication of his grief was a silent tear that crept from the corner of his eye, then made a slow descent down his scraped, lightly bearded cheek.

Instinctively, Nora reached to blot it gently with her fingers.

Its dampness mingled with her own tears as she lifted a hand to brush them away.

To Daniel's surprise, Dr. Leary came again that night to check on Whittaker.

He had appeared each day since the surgery, briefly, but showing what appeared to be genuine interest in his patient. During each visit, Daniel had thought him to be reasonably sober.

Until tonight. As had been the case when he'd first tended Whittaker's wound, the surgeon showed up reeking of whiskey, obviously unsteady on his feet.

Angry, Daniel was relieved that his mother had gone to lie down. He would not want her exposed to the surgeon's foul mood — or his foul mouth — when he was drunk.

Glaring at the man, he kept him under close scrutiny as Leary checked Whittaker's bandages with clumsy hands. Once, Whittaker gasped with pain at the doctor's careless touch, spurring Daniel to lunge forward and throw a restraining hand on Leary's arm.

The surgeon shot him a glazed look, then glanced angrily down at the hand clutching his arm.

Daniel didn't move. "Why did you come here like this?" he challenged.

"Like *what?*" the surgeon snarled. "Keep your hands to yourself!"

"You're drunk!"

"You're impertinent!" Leary shot back, shaking him off.

"What is it with you?" Daniel pressed in a low voice. "You seem a *good* surgeon when you're sober enough to mind what you're doing. Why do you do this to yourself, and to those who depend on you?"

The surgeon straightened, brushing the back of his hand across his brow as he fixed Daniel with a sullen glare. Beneath the swaying glow from the overhead lantern, Daniel saw a subtle change in Leary's expression. Resentment gave way to a look of weariness. The doctor's features, indeed his entire body, seemed to slump in defeat.

"That's the truth," he mumbled, averting his eyes. "I *was* a good surgeon once. More than good, some said."

"You still are," Daniel countered awkwardly. "Or you *could* be if you'd only leave the whiskey alone."

Replacing a roll of bandages in his case, the doctor slanted a disdainful glance at Daniel. "You know nothing, boy. Nothing at all. Let it be."

"I know your hands were deft and steady the other night when you performed Mr. Whittaker's surgery. Just watching you . . . it made me want to be the best physician I can be."

It was true, Daniel realized. In spite of the agony of watching Whittaker lose his arm, the terror of the entire procedure, he had been fascinated, even inspired, by the surgeon's obvious skill. He could not comprehend how a man of Leary's ability could descend to such an abysmal level.

Daniel stared at him for a moment. Then, sensing the futility of trying to reason with the man in his drunken state, he asked, "Did you bring more laudanum as you said you would? He's in fierce pain most of the time."

The surgeon gave him a blank look.

"You forgot!" Daniel accused him. "He needs *something* for the pain!"

Leary nodded distractedly, waving him off. "I'll bring it down later. Later tonight."

"No, you won't," Daniel grated, knowing full well the surgeon would be passed out on his bunk within the hour. "I'll go with you and get it myself. He needs it *now.*"

The doctor twisted his mouth into an obstinate pout. "You're not allowed above decks. You're in quarantine."

"You're the surgeon!" Daniel challenged. "Sure, and you have the authority to make an exception. Besides, it will save you a trip," he added spitefully. "You must have more important things to do."

Leary leveled an exasperated look on Daniel. "Oh, all right, then!" he said, snapping his medical case closed. "Come along!"

Daniel took time to ask that Hugh MacCabe keep a close watch on Whittaker until he returned, then leaned over to reassure Whittaker himself. "I'm going with the surgeon to get something for your pain. You'll be all right until I get back?"

Whittaker's attempt at a smile failed, but he managed a light squeeze on Daniel's hand to indicate he had heard.

Looking at him, Daniel felt a great rush of affection course through him. Who would have thought this quiet, retiring man would own such an infinitely heroic heart, such a brave, steadfast spirit?

A renewed determination to help his English friend rose up in Daniel. Indeed, thanks to Evan Whittaker, his faith in the Spirit of God working in mankind had been restored.

In spite of men like Dr. Leary.

A fierce, overwhelming wave of homesickness slammed into Daniel as soon as he crawled out onto the open deck. He stood, breathing in the smell of the salt sea, letting the cold, clean air wash over him like a gift.

Unbidden came the thought of home, the dark waters of the bay, the sagging pier, the sea-stained cottages, Killala . . .

Home! So strong were the memories, so powerful the longing, he nearly went to his knees. Shaking off the yearning thoughts, he gave the surgeon a hand up. Leary swayed a bit, grabbing for the rail to steady himself.

In an attempt to throw off his melancholy, Daniel started up a running conversation with the physician — mostly one-sided — as they headed aft.

"How long have you been a ship's surgeon?" he asked, lifting his face to catch the spray off the water.

"Years" was the only reply from the doctor.

"Why did you do it?"

The surgeon darted a startled look at him, making Daniel wonder at the man's jumpiness.

"Why did I do *what?*"

"Take on a shipboard practice instead of one in the city? Do you love the sea so much?"

An indecipherable look crossed the doctor's face. "No," he bit out, "I've no love for the sea!"

"Then why?"

"Why are *you* so blasted curious?" Leary grumbled, making it clear further questions would not be tolerated.

Daniel shrugged, turning his attention to the night sky, the dark, vast Atlantic surrounding them. A dizzying sense of space and freedom . . . *precious freedom* . . . swirled around him as they walked. He could almost ignore the stiffness in his legs from inactivity, the weakness of his body from lack of proper nourishment.

All that mattered was being out in the open, the stench of dying and misery replaced, at least for the moment, by the clean, sharp scent of salt air, weathered canvas, and sea-aged wood. His heart swelled to hear, instead of the requiem of hopelessness that rose from steerage, the chorus of gusty ocean winds and flapping sails.

So keen was his temporary sense of

well-being he forgot the surgeon's impatience and blurted out another question, one that had nagged at him almost from the time they had come aboard. "Why is it I never see any of the cabin passengers?"

The doctor's shuffling gait faltered for an instant. "And how would you be seeing anything at all when you are confined to the kennel?"

Ignoring the man's jibe, Daniel tried another tack. "Are they afraid to come out because of the typhus?"

"You need not concern yourself with the cabins! We are carrying only a scant few passengers, as it happens. This is not an ordinary passenger ship, at least not this voyage."

"True enough," Daniel said softly. "I had already figured out this is no ordinary ship."

The surgeon was not so drunk as to miss Daniel's pointed remark. "And what is that supposed to mean?"

Daniel shrugged, deliberately not answering.

Without warning, the doctor seized his arm, stopping them both where they stood. Three sailors standing nearby, playing out a line, glanced over at Daniel and the surgeon with no real interest.

"Boy, you are entirely too fresh! You'd do well to forget what you may *think* you know and concentrate on minding your own business — which has nothing at all to do with this ship!"

In reply to the doctor's outburst, Daniel appraised him with a growing sense that the man harbored an entire horde of guilty secrets — secrets that somehow involved every passenger on board.

The nagging at the back of his mind had been there almost from the beginning. There was something very wrong about the *Green Flag*, and he was convinced Dr. Leary was a part of it.

On his way back from the surgeon's quarters, laudanum in hand, Daniel gave in to his curiosity. He would have a closer look at the cabin area.

The mention of the cabin passengers had seemed to set off an alarm in the furtive surgeon. Whatever secrets the *Green Flag* was hiding could be found, he was convinced, in the cabin area.

If he were discovered, he could truthfully claim permission from the surgeon to be out of steerage. If it came down to it, he would pretend he had lost his way going back to his quarters.

Nervously glancing behind him every few steps, he started up the deck, staying inboard and stopping to hide in the shadows when he spotted a member of the crew.

He was only a few feet from the cabins when the sound of angry voices stopped him. Ducking down behind a stack of wooden chests, Daniel peered around the corner, watching.

He saw a big hulk of a sailor framed in the doorway of one of the cabins. He appeared to be adjusting his clothing. Almost nose to nose with him stood Captain Schell!

They were having a terrible row about something. A few feet away another seaman stood and watched.

Shivering in the damp shadows, Daniel crouched down a little lower. He could still see what was taking place, could hear every word of their angry exchange.

"You were warned!"

The captain's steel-edged voice grated with fury. He held a lantern high, trapping the sailor in its light. "You were told not to go near the cabins! What do you think you are doing?"

The crewman attempted a wide-gapped smile. "I thought I heard something, is all, Captain! Thought I'd best have a look. The door was unlocked."

Schell froze the man in place with a threatening glare. "You thought you'd have a look, all right!" The captain's voice cracked like a pistol shot. "Thought you'd take your pleasure like the rutting pig you are, that's what you were doing!"

"Aw, Captain, what's the harm? I was just breaking one of them in, you know. What difference does it make? That's what they're for."

Schell's face went livid, engorged with contempt. "Yes, that's what they're for! But not for the likes of *you!*" He broke off, back-handing the sailor across the face.

The man's head reeled. Daniel caught his breath, and put a hand to his cheek at the memory of his own encounter with the captain's vicious temper.

"Garbage!" Schell hurled at the sailor. "*You are garbage!* That is *cargo* in there, do you understand? This entire ship is *cargo!* And you are to have nothing to do with the *cargo* beyond loading it and unloading it!"

The blood pounded in Daniel's head, making his ears ring. His stomach knotted even tighter as he went on watching.

The captain reached past the man to yank the cabin door closed, then turned to bark an order over his shoulder.

The crewman behind him stepped up. "I want to know who left that door unlocked!" Schell grated, pointing to the cabin. "And you pass the word that if I hear tell of another man interfering with the cargo of this ship, he will be flogged until the deck runs red with blood!"

Turning back to the offending sailor, he moved the lantern closer to his face. "Well, you stupid fool, let us hope she was worth a keelhauling." His voice was low but thick with menace. A brief slash of a smile appeared, then faded as he stood watching the crewman drag the protesting sailor down the deck.

Holding his breath, Daniel watched Schell turn the handle on the cabin door and push it open. He stood just inside the doorway, lifting the lantern to inspect whatever lay within.

Somebody inside the cabin was crying!

Daniel pulled in a ragged breath, biting down on his bottom lip hard enough to bring blood.

After a moment, the captain turned and closed the door, this time locking it with a key before walking away.

Daniel stayed where he was for a long time after Schell disappeared. His heart banged wildly against his ribcage as he huddled in the shadows, trying to understand what he had just witnessed.

At last he got up his nerve to creep over to the cabin door and put his ear to it. Hearing nothing, he lifted his hand and touched the door, hesitating a moment before rapping lightly. When there was no answering reply, he again tapped softly on the door.

After another long silence, he glanced around uncertainly. With the lantern gone, the darkness on the deck was thick and relentless. But it wasn't the darkness of the night that gripped Daniel, trapping him in a surging wave of panic. It was another kind of darkness, one so cold and reeking of corruption it could almost be touched.

It was the darkness that rode the waves with the *Green Flag*, a presence that permeated the entire ship. He could hear its whisper above the tormented cries in steerage, over the roar of the waves above docks, in the secret shadows of the passenger cabins, even in the wind that flew the sails.

He had sensed the darkness before, had heard its whisper, felt its touch, smelled its decay. Tonight he thought he at last understood what it was.

The darkness had taken on a soul of its own. The soul of the *Green Flag*.

Back in steerage, Daniel gave Whittaker a dose of the laudanum, then propped himself up in the bunk next to the Englishman, watching him.

What he would give to tell Whittaker about this night: what he had seen and heard, what he suspected. But Whittaker was in pain most of the time, and when he wasn't, he was sleeping. It wouldn't do to bother him with anything that might cause him upset.

He would have to wait until the Englishman was stronger, had at least begun to mend. Then he would tell him. Perhaps Whittaker would understand, would know what to do.

With a rush of dread, Daniel felt the presence of an Enemy aboard the ship. Unseen, unknown . . . but real. Terribly real.

He was suddenly frightened, as frightened as he had ever been. How could he hope to defend himself or his loved ones against what he could not see?

We are not contending against flesh and blood, but against the powers of an unseen world.

How did one fight against a whisper, an elusive presence, a shadow of evil?

Put on the entire armor of God . . . the belt of truth, the breastplate of righteousness, the shoes of peace, the shield of faith, the helmet of salvation, the sword of the Spirit — God's Word.

Pray . . . plead . . . watch.

Slipping down off the bunk, Daniel dropped to his knees and began to pray.

37

Afternoon Encounters

A little love, a little trust,
A soft impulse, a sudden dream,
And life as dry as desert dust
Is fresher than a mountain stream.
So simple is the heart of man,
So ready for new hope and joy;
Ten thousand years since it began
Have left it younger than a boy.

STOPFORD A. BROOKE (1822–1916)

New York City
Late April

It was an almost springlike afternoon in New York. The air was gentle, the sky was clear, and on this part of the street in front of the Tombs — the Hall of Justice — there was no ripe smell of manure droppings or piled up garbage.

The entrance door had been propped open, but Michael Burke had come all the way outside and stood leaning up against one of the huge Greek columns that guarded the front of the building. At his feet, a baby boy lay sleeping in a basket.

He had found the infant abandoned in the dark hallway of a Mulberry Street tenement, wrapped only in thin rags, hidden in the same basket in which he now slept. When a thorough questioning of the building's tenants and surrounding neighbors yielded no clue as to the baby's parents, Michael had brought him back to the station and filed a report. Now he waited for an agency volunteer to pick up the foundling and take it to one of the designated hospitals or protectories.

While he waited, he read over the ship arrival notices in *The New York Packet.* These days he faithfully checked every issue of the *Packet.* If the ship had left Killala near the end of March, it had been at sea for nigh on four weeks by now. That being the case, it could arrive in the harbor as early as next week.

Of course, he had no way of knowing exactly when it set sail. Nor had he any certainty that Nora and her family were aboard.

The past few weeks of waiting and wondering, hoping — and occasionally dreading — had been the most exasperating, nerve-wracking experience in Michael's memory. Not to know if Nora was coming, and if she was, how she would react to him after so long a time; whether she would be willing to marry him; how her boys and Tierney would get along if they *should* wed; where he was going to put so many people . . .

He could not remember a time when his mind had felt so cluttered, so heavy, so fragmented.

Added to this was his concern over the increasing amount of time Tierney was spending in the employ of Patrick Walsh.

The boy was working almost every Saturday, from daylight to dark, out at Walsh's posh palace on Staten Island — and that was in addition to his regular after-school job at the hotel.

Lately Michael sensed a gap widening between him and his son. It grated on him, but he had to concede a certain amount of jealousy about Tierney's adulation for his employer. Walsh had achieved an impressive record of successes for an Irish immigrant. But Michael wanted Tierney to value some things more than money and influence and achievement — things like integrity and Christian principles, for example.

Yet, every time he raised the subject with the boy, Tierney would fire back that *he* was the one always encouraging him to "better himself." Since Michael could not deny the truth in the challenge, their debates always ended in a deadlock.

It was no wonder he was sleeping poorly, when he slept at all, and even less wonder he could not seem to concentrate on anything more complicated than the ship arrival notices.

His attention was suddenly diverted by a hackney cab slowing in front of the building. As soon as the two gray horses clopped to a halt, the driver leaped down to assist his passenger.

Surprised, Michael watched as Sara Farmington stepped from the carriage, gave instructions to the driver, then started toward the front steps.

Again he noted a faint limp in her stride, though her posture was straight and confident. She was wearing a fine spring suit, soft blue with white piping, and a somewhat more sensible wee hat than he observed on most women.

She smiled as soon as she saw him. Michael straightened, stepped out from the column and greeted her.

"Miss Farmington? Don't tell me you're here for another jaunt into Five Points so soon."

Still smiling, she glanced from him to the sleeping infant in the basket behind him. "Not today, Sergeant Burke, although I *did* intend to request an escort for next week. This afternoon, however, I'm here to relieve you of your little burden."

She went to the foundling and, stooping down, lifted him carefully from the basket. The infant slept on as she cradled him gently against her shoulder.

"You've come for the child, then?"

"That's right," she said distractedly, studying the face of the sleeping infant. "I volunteer for the Infants Hospital on Wednesdays and Thursdays."

"You are a busy young woman, Miss Farmington," said Michael, gazing at her with interest.

She shrugged. "There's no need to be idle in New York City. Especially these days, with the population exploding as it is."

Her eyes went to *The New York Packet* Michael held. "Do you have family scheduled to arrive soon, Sergeant Burke?" she asked, rubbing the baby's back as she inclined her head toward the paper.

Michael glanced at the *Packet* in his hand. "No. That is, not family. But friends."

"I see. When do you expect them?"

"As early as next week, possibly. But I don't even know for certain they are coming," he added. "I've been watching the notices, just in case."

The infant stirred a bit, cooed, and Sara Farmington smiled down at him. "Well, I hope they arrive safely. What ship are they booked on?"

"The *Green Flag*. It's a small packet, I believe."

"I'm not familiar with the name. I'll have to ask my father. Perhaps he'd have some information for you."

"Your father?"

"Yes, he's very informed about the vessels coming into New York," she replied, shifting the infant to her other shoulder. "I'll see if he knows anything about your friends' ship."

"Is your father employed at the harbor?"

She looked at him, her eyes glinting with a faint light that appeared to be amusement. "Well, actually," she said, "Father's in the business of building ships. But he haunts the harbor all the same, so he might have some information for you."

A bell went off in Michael's mind.

Sara *Farmington.*

Lewis Farmington, the millionaire shipbuilder! Farmington was a contemporary and close friend of John Jacob Astor. Astor, himself an immigrant from Germany, had made his fortune by investing the profits from his fur trade in farmland on Manhattan Island. Farmington, like McKay of Boston, had amassed a sizable fortune of his own by building some of the finest — and fastest — sailing ships in the world.

"You're not Lewis Farmington's daughter?" Michael blurted out, immediately dismayed by his lack of tact.

To her credit, Sara Farmington grinned at him. Her response was genuinely unaffected. "I'm afraid I am."

"Oh, I'm sorry!" Michael stammered, suddenly feeling awkward and crude and — very *Irish.* "I didn't mean to be rude; I simply hadn't connected the names."

"It's all right," she quickly assured him. "You weren't rude at all."

Michael still felt the fool, but wasn't she being grand about it?

Sara Farmington changed the subject with ease. "I think I'd like to walk for a bit, with the baby, before taking him back to the hospital — it's so beautiful today. Would you like to keep me company, Sergeant Burke? Do you have time?"

"Yes, of course," Michael said, pleased that she asked. "But let me carry the little fellow. He's underfed, but still a bit of a chunk."

"Why do you suppose he was abandoned?"

Michael frowned, reaching for the baby. "We find dozens just like him every month, many already dead. I suppose it's often a case where the mother is unmarried or unable to care for them. At any rate, the number is increasing as the city grows."

"It's difficult for me to understand how a mother could actually abandon her own baby," she said quietly, her gaze lingering on the fair-haired infant's face.

"No offense, Miss Farmington," Michael said grimly, "but if you've never been hungry and frightened — perhaps even desperate — it's not a thing you *would* understand."

His remark brought her up short, and he felt impatient with his own gruffness. But it was the truth, after all. How could those who had never known want even hope to understand those who had never known anything else?

Miss Farmington seemed a fine lady — a compassionate one, that much was certain — but to his way of thinking she could spend the rest of her life doing her bit of work in the slums and still never fathom the hopelessness of the poor wretches she was so determined to help.

There was, after all, no changing the fact that she was a Farmington, not a Flanagan.

His blunt statement made Sara stop and think.

"Yes," she said quietly, "I'm sure you're right." Watching the brawny sergeant heft the infant against his chest with one large hand, she couldn't help but wonder if the man spoke from experience. Had *he* ever been hungry or desperate? He *was* an Irish immigrant, so it was more than possible he knew whereof he spoke.

Holding the infant with one hand, the sergeant offered a supporting arm to Sara until they reached the bottom of the steps. Watching him as he instructed the hackney driver to wait, she noted how very small the baby looked in his arms.

He seemed a man of many facets, this Sergeant Burke. One might think him a hard man were it not for his eyes. His handsome face — and indeed it *was* handsome — at first glance appeared somewhat stern, perhaps because of the deep lines that bracketed his mouth and webbed out from his eyes.

But the eyes spoke a different tale. They reflected the varying colors of the man. They were wounded eyes. Sara sensed that the strapping Irishman had endured deep, personal pain. Not to mention the fact that he must daily encounter things no decent man could ever hope to forget. But they were also eyes that loved life, good-natured eyes that looked out upon the world with humor and tolerance and great kindness, as if they liked most of what they saw.

While he wore the marks of an old pain, the scars appeared to be fading. Sergeant Burke was a strong, determined man, unless Sara was very much mistaken. A survivor.

And most likely married.

The unbidden thought made Sara blink.

Well, what if he were? It was certainly of no concern to her, she reminded herself as they walked. "How long have you been in New York, Sergeant?" she asked, feeling a need to lighten her own tension.

"Almost seventeen years now."

Sara would have guessed a shorter time. The Irish lilt in his speech was still evident.

"I see. And do you have . . . family?" she asked as they started up Franklin Street.

He nodded, glancing over at her with a faint smile. "A son. Tierney. He'll soon be fifteen, though I'm finding it hard to believe."

"Tierney? That's an Irish name, I imagine."

"Aye, my wife chose it."

So there was a wife. "I see. Then your wife is also Irish?"

"She was, yes." He hesitated only an instant, then volunteered, "My wife died when the lad was small."

"Oh, I'm sorry," Sara said softly. *An old pain . . .*

"I'll be marrying again, perhaps," he said abruptly, darting a glance at her that made Sara wonder if he had spoken without thinking. "If my friends do come over, that is," he added quickly. "And if my proposal is accepted."

"That's . . . wonderful for you," Sara said lamely, unsettled and somewhat confused by the faint edge of disappointment she felt at his blunt announcement.

"It's nothing definite, mind," he put in. "I've written to ask, that's all. Nora may have a different notion entirely."

"Nora," Sara repeated softly. "Such a lovely name."

"We were children together," he offered in his brusque way. "Grew up in the same village. Her husband died last year, as did her little girl. Things have been hard for her, with the famine and all . . ." He let his words die away, unfinished.

"I see," Sara said awkwardly, "Well, I hope things work out for both of you."

He gave a small nod, but said nothing more. They walked on in silence for a time before Sara stopped. "I should get back with the baby, I suppose."

"Aye, he seems to be waking up," said the sergeant, glancing down at the squirming infant against his chest.

For a moment he stood regarding Sara with a questioning gaze. A smile flickered in his eyes, then reached his mouth. "I'm curious, Miss Sara Farmington," he said. "Why is it you do what you do?"

She frowned. "I beg your pardon?"

He continued to study her. The intensity of his gaze would have seemed bold from any other man, but Sara felt not the least bit offended.

"You're the daughter of a very important man. Why, then, do you spend most of your days in the slums?"

The question was a familiar one. When she was younger and still not altogether certain as to exactly what was expected of a Farmington, Sara had occasionally been very wicked, affecting the frivolous, somewhat addlepated behavior people seemed to expect from the idle rich. She had given that up as soon as she'd realized that her feigned foolishness was exactly what they approved of.

These days, she no longer played such games. She was not at all impressed about her station in life, but on the other hand she didn't take it for granted. Most of the time, she was glad to be the daughter of the wealthy, influential Lewis Farmington. It gave her the means to do many of the things she believed needed doing.

Besides, she liked her family. Father was a wonderful man, if a bit eccentric — eccentric by society's standards, that is. He loved to work with his hands, and he didn't care nearly so much for the money he made as he did for the fine ships that made the money. He was always generous in helping to fund Sara's "projects," and wasn't above harassing his friends and associates to do likewise.

Her brother, Gordie, was also a dear, though his wife Doris was a terrible bore. Doris *was* impressed with their station in life, and determined that everybody else should be as well. Poor Gordie had to sneak *his* contributions to Sara's "projects" out from under his wife's avaricious eye.

"Miss Farmington? I'm sorry, I had no right to ask you such a question."

Apparently she'd been silent so long he was worried he might have insulted her. Sara shook her head, smiling to reassure him. "It's a perfectly natural question, Sergeant," she said honestly. They turned now and headed back toward the hackney. "I just don't happen to have a very good answer for it. I suppose I do what I do because I think it's what Jesus would have done if *He* had been born wealthy instead of poor."

Sergeant Burke slowed his pace and shot her a surprised look.

"I promised Him when I was still a little girl that I would be as much like Him as I possibly could be," Sara tried to explain. "I didn't realize until I began to grow up how difficult it was going to be to keep that promise, mostly because of my father's money."

By now they had reached the cab, and the driver was eyeing them curiously. Still holding the baby, the sergeant continued to watch Sara with a half smile. His close scrutiny made her feel awkward, but the obvious approval in his gaze also made her feel . . . good.

"If I may venture my opinion, Miss Farmington," he finally said, his voice quiet but warm, "I think you have kept your promise in a grand way." He paused. This time when he smiled it was broad and friendly. "Now then, I believe you mentioned something about needing an escort for another excursion into Five Points next week?"

Sara stared at him, then grinned. "I did indeed, Sergeant."

He helped her into the cab before handing over the infant, now wide awake and beginning to make more insistent threats. "Would next Monday suit you, then, Miss Farmington?" the sergeant asked, leaning close as she adjusted the baby on her shoulder. "About two o'clock, say?"

Bouncing the infant gently up and down to soothe him, Sara returned his smile. "It would suit me just fine, Sergeant Burke."

As the cab pulled away, Sara looked down at the baby in her arms and sighed deeply. She was almost twenty-six years old and had already faced the likelihood that she would remain a spinster. She wouldn't have trusted a single one of the eligible suitors in her own crowd. In the first place, most of them were terrible bores who couldn't carry on a conversation about anything but making more money and gambling it away. In the second place, she was quite sure they were more attracted to her father's fortune than to her.

Then, too, there was the matter of her being lame. It didn't bother *her* all that much, except for those times when the aching in her leg kept her awake most of the night, but she supposed many men were put off by it.

It seemed the few really interesting men she met — and they *were* few — were already married, or at least about to be.

Like Sergeant Burke.

Again she sighed. After a moment, however, her mouth twitched. She put a hand to her lips to catch the giggle rising in her throat.

How *would* the cream of New York's society react to the idea of Lewis Farmington's only daughter being smitten with an Irish "copper"?

Sara glanced down at the baby. He had stopped his complaining and now lay quiet, staring up at her with a miniature frown and wide eyes.

Impulsively, Sara drew him as close as she dared, taking care not to squeeze him too tightly. During the remainder of the ride to the hospital, she cuddled the warm little bundle to her heart, pretending he was her own.

Half an hour later, Michael was walking south on Elm, his step somewhat lighter than it had been earlier in the day. Miss Sara Farmington seemed to have a cheering effect on a person, she did.

Again today he had noted that something about the young woman reminded him of Nora. That, of course, was why his heartbeat increased a bit when she was close by.

Still, she was a wonder on her own. Certainly she set aside the idea that all wealthy young women were vapid and foolish. She was as sharp-witted as any man Michael had ever met, and seemed to have the purpose of her life well in focus.

Glancing around his surroundings, he frowned in exasperation. The street was ankle-deep in mud and refuse, its stench sickening in the warm temperatures. The rotting smell of garbage, the clamor of children playing in the street, and the barking dogs darting wildly in and out between heaps of rubbish intruded into Michael's thoughts of Sara Farmington. It seemed wrong, even disrespectful, to be thinking of her in the midst of these surroundings. Perhaps he was being foolish, but he deliberately put the thought of her out of his mind.

He had reached the corner of Elm and Duane when he heard the barking of a horde of wild dogs, then gunshots.

His stomach knotted. Whipping around the corner onto Duane, he spotted a middle-aged Negro, pistol in hand, shooting randomly into the midst of a pack of dogs.

One after another fell into a bloody heap in the mud, while those still alive darted back and forth, yelping and barking as if caught in a net. Others, wounded but not quite dead, lay whimpering helplessly in their pain.

In an instant Michael grasped the fact that this was apparently one of the Negroes paid two dollars a day by the city to rid the streets of wild dogs. He froze, his hand going to his gun even as he took in the grisly scene.

Across the street, he spied three little boys, the smallest scarcely out of didies, all huddled together, watching wide-eyed as the Negro took aim at a bedraggled black-and-white pup. The little mutt was racing around in circles as if it had gone berserk from all the commotion.

A cry went up from the frightened little boys across the street when they saw the Negro's intent.

What Michael saw was the likelihood of a bullet hitting one of the children.

With a cry, he lunged forward, raising his gun and taking aim at the Negro. *"Drop your gun! Throw it down!"*

Slowing his stride as he approached the man, he again warned the man off the dogs. "I said, get rid of the gun!"

The man was either deaf or an idiot. Waving the gun at the pup, he ignored Michael entirely.

At the same time a big, mean-looking black dog bared his fangs and planted his feet in the mud in direct challenge to the Negro.

Heart pounding, Michael yelled once more. This time the man turned, bringing the gun around with him.

Michael's eyes swept the scene, taking in the black dog, the Negro's gun now trained on *him,* and the panicked little boys. He turned his own gun on the black dog.

Suddenly the dog leaped from the ground, hitting the Negro full force.

The man screamed as the dog slammed into him with a roar. The Negro's eyes were stunned and panic-stricken. His arm went up, and the gun went off.

Michael's chest exploded into a fireball, and the afternoon sun fell to earth.

38

A Clashing of Swords

In that spectralest hour, in that Valley of Gloom,
Fell a Voice on mine ear, like a wail from the tomb . . .
For here were my cords of Sleep suddenly broken,
The bell booming Three;
But there seemed in mine ears, as I started up, woken,
A noise like fierce cheers, blent with clashings of swords,
And the roar of the sea!

JAMES CLARENCE MANGAN (1803–1849)

The rumor circulating steerage claimed they would see America within days, perhaps as early as next week. Each time she heard the word being passed among the aisles, Nora was struck by a new wave of anxiety.

Folding the blankets from the girls' bunk, she stood holding them in her arms, staring across the room at the children. Except for Katie, who was too weak and wrung out to be petulant, they were bored, and growing more and more restless in their confinement. They had all lost weight and looked unhealthy. The sparse remainder of the few provisions they had carried on board was now entirely ruined, invaded by weevils and rats. They were subsisting on their ship allowance, which was scarcely enough to keep them from starving.

They were all weak, Nora included, all ill to some extent. Even those who thus far had managed to escape the typhus still suffered the effects of stale air, insufficient food and fresh water, not to mention the deadly fumes of sickness they were forced to endure day and night.

Still, the children had their rare moments of cheerfulness, and Daniel John was one of the reasons. Tonight he had a group of a dozen or more in the corner, entertaining them with his harp, he and an elderly man with a squeeze box.

Nora tried not to think about the squalid floor where the children had flopped to listen. Katie, wee Tom, and at least a dozen others had made a ring around the musicians and sat, nodding their heads and patting their knees in time to the music. Even the deaf Johanna, taking her cue from the others, rocked to and fro in her silent world to a rhythm only she could hear.

Thank the Lord for the children, Nora thought, watching them. At times they almost managed to make life's madness and troubles bearable.

But what would become of the children once they reached America?

Apprehension twisted like a rope around her heart. Starting over in a new land all alone would be frightening enough in itself, but starting over with a son and three young children in tow was enough to make her quake with terror. She had absolutely nobody to depend on except herself — and they had nobody to depend on except *her*.

Why . . . oh, why had she thrown Michael's letter away? He was their only link to this new land. He would have helped them — indeed, had wanted to help them!

Foolish! So foolish! In her mindless pride, she had thrown away their best hope. Why hadn't she thought of the young ones instead of herself? Now they would be completely alone, with nobody who would care — who would even *know* — they had arrived! In her selfish disregard for the consequences, she had tossed away the address of the one person who might have made a difference for them!

What in the name of heaven would she do with these children? She could not fail them; she must not. She and Catherine had promised each other years ago to look after each other's children should it ever become necessary.

In addition, there was Evan Whittaker to think about. Obviously, they could not abandon him, not after all he had done for them.

What worried her most was the question of where they would live, once they arrived. The money from Morgan would not last long, not with so many to house and feed. She would have to arrange affordable lodging until she could find a job.

A job. *God have mercy, what kind of job could a widow with a houseful of children hope to find?*

Angry with herself, she turned and began making up the bunk. She *must* not do this, she *would* not give in to her old fears! Worry over the terrors of the lurking unknown would defeat her before she ever stepped off the ship. She must think things through, stay calm, try to plan.

It helped to remember that she had a son who was no longer a child. Daniel John was smart and strong and always eager to do what was asked of him, and then some. He must go to school, of course, but that didn't mean he couldn't work part time.

They would manage. They *had* to manage.

But on the heels of her resolve came a fresh stab of regret at her thoughtless haste in destroying Michael's letter. If Morgan knew what she had done, he would be livid with her!

On the other hand, if Morgan knew what *he*

had done to *them*, he would be devastated.

Morgan. She must not think of Morgan. It only made things harder than they already were.

Evan was trying to wake up. He thought he heard music . . . a harp . . . the bright sound of children. He wanted to listen, but the sounds swelled and died away into silence.

He fought to open his eyes, but they were too heavy, and he was too weak. It didn't matter. Whether he was awake or asleep, the days and nights remained the same.

He passed the time in a twilight world induced by the laudanum, drifting through the slow-rolling hours in a haze of pain and macabre dreams. He never quite slept, but simply hung suspended in a drug-induced web, where his nightmares were the only reality.

Tonight was no different. He was awake, yet not awake, aware but without any real sensations — except for the pain. Even that was easier now, almost bearable. He was healing, that much was certain. Even the sullen Dr. Leary had made a grudging snarl of approval the last time he'd examined his . . .

Stump. Say the word. Say it!

He tried to force the word from leaden lips, but it remained only a hateful thought.

You no longer have an arm. You have a stump . . .

For days now, he had struggled to face the reality of his circumstances. Between the ebb and flow of an opium stupor, he tried out a number of words and descriptions, searching for one that did not sound quite so grisly.

He was a man with one arm. A one-armed man. He'd had an arm surgically removed. Amputated.

He was a cripple . . . he had a stump. He would never be whole again . . .

There. That was further than he had gone before. And as far as he would ever need to go. There was nothing else to be said.

Lord . . . oh, Lord, why did you allow this to happen to me? Didn't I do what you asked? Didn't I go where you sent me? I was obedient, I even managed to put aside my cowardice, to trust your guidance, your power . . . Why, Lord?

The pain that seized him now was far worse than all the physical agony he had endured so far, a pain that went beyond bodily suffering. Indeed, the distress of body was nothing compared to the anguish of soul that now closed over him, weighing him down like a sodden grave blanket.

From somewhere . . . a dark, shadowy place he had not known existed within him . . . came a whispering, an ugly hiss of accusation:

God betrayed you, didn't He? He let you down completely, after everything you went through to obey Him! He let you down . . . He failed you . . . failed you . . .

Evan shuddered, stiffened in horrified denial. Again the dark pit in his spirit gaped open, and the whisper grew more insistent:

You trusted Him . . . you've always trusted Him. Well, just see how He's rewarded your trust. Look at yourself . . . look at your ugly self . . .

His Bible . . . where had he put his Bible? Desperate, he pushed himself up on his right arm, looked around, but all was a blur. Where were his eyeglasses? His heart thudding madly with the effort, he patted the bunk around him, stretching to peer down at the floor. There was no sign of the eyeglasses or the Bible.

He tried to squirm to the edge of the bunk to feel beneath it, but was overwhelmed by a dizzying surge of nausea.

Sinking back onto the bunk, he threw his arm over his eyes and waited for his head to stop spinning.

Why did God allow this to happen? You were only doing what was expected of you, just as you always have. You've always done your best, you've been a good man, a decent man, lived an honorable life. But does God care about any of that? Does He care about what you're going through right now, at this moment . . . does He even know?

Something cold and depraved was breathing on Evan's soul, struggling to suffocate his faith.

"Jesus . . . Savior . . . Jesus . . ."

Over and over he mumbled his Shepherd's name, clinging to it like a shield.

Finally, out of his memory, the words came, light exploding in the darkness:

"The Lord gave, and the Lord has taken away; blessed be the name of the Lord."

He has failed you . . .

"Shall we receive good from the hand of God and not trouble?"

He allowed it to happen . . .

"He wounds, but He binds up . . . He smites, but He also heals."

If he's really as powerful as you seem to believe, why didn't He keep you from this dread thing? Why didn't He save your arm? Where was His power when you needed it? Where was He then?

"In his hand is the life of every living thing and the breath of all mankind."

He took your arm . . . He made you ugly and repulsive . . . He made you a joke, a caricature of a man . . .

"But the Lord sees not as man sees . . . He looks on the heart."

He has deserted you, you fool! Why shouldn't you deny Him and start anew?

"I know that my Redeemer lives . . . though He slay me, yet will I trust in Him . . ."

"Mr. Whittaker? *Mr. Whittaker!* Are you all right? Is there something you need?"

Evan opened his eyes. It was the boy,

Daniel, peering down at him with worried eyes. "What is it, Mr. Whittaker? Can I get you anything?"

"Oh . . . no . . . I . . . I'm all right." As if coming out of a fog, Evan's mind began to clear slowly.

"Do you need the laudanum, Mr. Whittaker?"

"*No!* No," he said again, this time more quietly. "No more laudanum. I'm . . . I b-believe I'm feeling somewhat better . . . I don't want any more laudanum. But perhaps . . . one thing . . ."

"Aye, sir, what is it?"

"My B-Bible . . . do you think you could find it for me? I, ah, I like to k-keep it handy. And my eyeglasses . . . I can't seem to find them either . . ."

"They're under here." The boy reached into a small box at the foot of the berth and handed Evan his eyeglasses, then his Bible. "I put them away until you were ready to read again."

Fumbling, Evan set his eyeglasses in place, noting grimly that even such a simple task was awkward for a man with only one hand. Then he held the Bible to his chest for a moment.

Frowning with concern, Daniel bent over him. "Are you quite sure you're feeling better, Mr. Whittaker?"

Nodding, Evan lay the Bible beside him. "I

am now, yes," he said, managing a weak smile. "There *is* something else you could do for m-me, though, Daniel — if you don't m-mind."

"Of course. Anything at all, sir."

"I want you to g-get rid of the laudanum. Right away. All of it."

The boy's gaze was skeptical. "*All* of it, Mr. Whittaker? Are you sure?"

Evan reached to grip the boy's forearm. "Yes, I'm *very* sure! I . . . I don't b-believe I'll have any further use for it, and it . . . it makes me sleep too much." He paused, then added, "Tomorrow, once my head clears a b-bit more, perhaps you would help me get up, walk around a little. I must start b-building up my strength."

Daniel nodded, his eyes still uncertain. "I'll be glad to do that. If you're sure you feel strong enough."

Evan put a hand to his cheek, grimacing at the feel of a full growth of beard at his fingertips. "Oh, my. Do you suppose you could help m-me get rid of this as well? I must look dreadful."

The boy studied him soberly. "I'll help you shave, of course, if that's what you want, Mr. Whittaker. But I believe Mother's right — you look right snappy with the beard."

Evan blinked. "Snappy? Your mother said that?"

Daniel nodded, smiling. "We were going to

try to convince you to leave it, once you felt more yourself."

"Oh." Evan blinked again. "Well, I — *snappy*, you say? Perhaps I'll wait a bit . . . just for a while, before I d-decide."

"I'm truly glad you're feeling better," Daniel said quietly. "I've missed our talks."

Evan studied the boy's thin, strongly molded face, the fine, noble head, the genuine goodness in the deep blue eyes. "As have I, Daniel. I'll tell you what," he said briskly, patting the opposite side of the bunk, "why don't you sit down right n-now and k-keep me company?"

The boy looked at him, then sank down onto the bunk beside him. After a second or two, he wet his lips and said, his tone hesitant, "Mr. Whittaker, are you truly feeling stronger now? Strong enough that I could confide in you about something — something that's been a fierce worry to me? There's been no one else I could tell, and I need to know what you think about it."

"Why, of course, Daniel." Immediately curious and concerned, Evan twisted to prop himself up, finally waiting to allow Daniel to help by plumping a coat beneath his head like a pillow.

"All right, now," he said, feeling more comfortable than he had since the surgery. "What seems to be bothering you? Tell me everything."

* * *

As Daniel talked, he felt a wonderful sense of relief settle over him. He hadn't realized just how much he had come to depend on Whittaker's precise, matter-of-fact way of putting things in order. Being able to confide his suspicions and fears about Captain Schell and the ship went a long way in relieving the anxiety he'd been carrying around for days.

His relief was short-lived, however. Reaching the end of his tale, he caught his breath and sat, waiting. When Whittaker remained silent, Daniel could stand it no longer. "So, then, Mr. Whittaker, what can we do? How can we find out what's going on?"

Whittaker regarded him with a solemn, worried expression, still delaying his reply. After another long silence, he drew a deep sigh and began to rub his right temple as if his head ached. "Well . . . I d-don't know that there's anything we *can* do, Daniel, at least until we're off the ship."

"But we *must!* If we wait until we leave the ship, it may be too late for — for whoever is in the cabins! Besides, what difference will it make, our leaving the ship? We'll be total strangers in New York — we won't know how to help ourselves, much less anyone else!"

Still massaging his head, Whittaker closed his eyes. Only when Daniel saw how weary and pale he looked did he realize he'd been talking far too long.

"I'm sorry, I've tired you out," he murmured, sliding down from the bunk. "I'll go so you can rest."

"Wait." Whittaker opened his eyes, put his hand to Daniel's arm. "Before you go, there's something I think we should pray about. Here," he said, indicating that Daniel should kneel beside his bunk. "I want us to pray that God will p-put some p-people in the city for us."

Daniel looked at him. "I don't understand."

Propping himself up a bit more, Whittaker explained. "When the Apostle Paul was in Corinth, the Lord appeared to him in a vision one night and told him to g-go right on doing what he'd been sent to do — proclaiming the Gospel — and not to be afraid, because God had many people in the city."

Whittaker paused, sinking back onto the berth. "God does that for us, I believe. When we're in His will and facing the unknown, He puts some of His people in 'our city.' In other words, He sends His own to help protect His own. Let us pray that He'll put some of His people in New York City for us, Daniel."

Daniel sank down to his knees. Whittaker did the praying for both of them, but when he was done, Daniel added his own silent petition: *Lord, there are many of us, so if you have plenty to spare, would you please put a great number of people in the city, enough to go around?*

* * *

It had already occurred to Evan that it might not be only the mysterious occupants of the cabins who were in jeopardy. The more he mulled things over — Schell's vicious explosion of temper the night Daniel had gone above in search of the doctor, the boy's suspicion that Leary was hiding something, either about the captain or the ship itself, and the recent confrontation between Schell and the sailor — the more apprehensive he became about the captain's character. Who could tell what kind of perfidy the man might be involved in, might have involved the entire ship in?

As to the unseen passengers in the cabins — he had read enough about white slavery during recent years to suspect the *Green Flag* was involved in something of that nature — perhaps in other illegal cargo as well. Where prostitution flourished, opium could often be found in partnership. Indeed, the drug was becoming as much a plague in American and European cities as it had been in the Orient for centuries. Thanks to the fast-sailing packet ships and the burgeoning populations in cities like New York and London, running opium and foreign prostitutes from one country to another had become a highly profitable activity.

Eyes closed, a hand to his head, Evan fretted over the fact that Daniel was disappointed in him. The boy was obviously hoping for some sort of plan as to how they might help whoever was hidden in the passenger cabins.

But as far as Evan could see, the best plan at the moment — the *safest* plan — was to pretend they knew nothing, had noticed nothing at all out of the ordinary, at least until he could attempt to find out more about the dark-natured Captain Schell and his drunken surgeon.

When the surgeon came to examine him and others in steerage later that night, Evan was ready for him.

He was somewhat relieved to see that the man was, as usual, in his cups. A drunken tongue wagged far more freely than a sober one.

Leary was putting the finishing touches on a fresh bandage. "You're looking feistier than I've seen you for a time," he said thickly. "Must be feeling more yourself."

"Yes, I b-believe I am. I'm actually beginning to get used to the idea of having . . . only one arm."

"Might as well," slurred the surgeon. "You'll not be changing things."

Compassionate soul . . .

"That's true," Evan agreed through clenched teeth.

"There are artificial limbs, you know," Leary said, straightening. "You might want to see about one later, after you're entirely healed."

Evan swallowed, thinking of all the hook-handed pirates in his adventure novels. "Perhaps," he managed to say. "I've heard rumors that we'll see N-New York soon. How much longer, do you think?"

Leary scratched his grizzled cheek, obviously groping for a lucid thought in the blur of his brain.

"A week, ten days, says the captain. If the weather holds."

"That soon?" A mixture of relief and apprehension washed over Evan.

Leary fumbled with rewrapping a roll of bandages. Without looking up, he simply grunted a neutral reply.

"I say," Evan ventured, watching the man closely, "what sort of cargo does this ship carry? I don't believe I remember hearing anything about cargo."

The doctor paused in his fumbling to look at him. "I'm the surgeon, not a sailor. I wouldn't know about cargo."

"I see." *What accounted for the guilt plastered over the man's face?*

"Well, perhaps you'd be willing to advise me of the procedures once we arrive in New York," Evan continued, trying another tack. "What can we expect, once we're ready to leave the ship?"

The surgeon's eyes seemed glued on the

roll of bandages. "There'll be people there to help you. The captain has seen to all the arrangements, I'm sure."

Evan sensed the man was sidestepping. "Yes. Well, ah . . . what k-kind of . . . arrangements, exactly?"

The surgeon seemed to resent every syllable he uttered. "You'll need to pass through quarantine, have a medical examination." He paused, then uttered a nasty laugh. "Which will be anything but thorough, you need not worry."

"My . . . surgery? It won't prevent m-me from leaving the ship, will it?" Evan asked, his concern genuine.

Again the doctor laughed. "Nothing much prevents you from passing quarantine unless you are black with the typhus or already dead."

Evan stared at the man. "Yes. And . . . where do we actually g-go, once we're permitted to leave the harbor?"

Averting his gaze, the surgeon closed his medical case. "I told you," he said, half under his breath, "the captain has arranged for people to be there. Guides for the lot of you. You needn't worry."

Something in the man's furtive demeanor — in spite of his drunken vagueness — sent a warning directly to Evan's brain.

He suddenly knew that they *did* have something to worry about, perhaps more than he'd first feared.

39

A Tale of Deception

And the world went on
between folly and reason
With gladness and sorrow by turns in season.

JOHN DE JEAN FRAZER (1809–1852)

In Bellevue Hospital late the following Tuesday afternoon, Sara Farmington sat by the bedside of the sleeping Sergeant Burke, thinking about how different the day was to have been.

Instead of venturing into Five Points with the Irish policeman as her escort, she had ended up in this dreary hospital ward, feeling unsettled and vaguely ill at ease.

A curtain had been drawn around the cubicle for privacy. The sergeant had been sleeping ever since she arrived — almost two hours ago, she realized with surprise. It was an oddly disturbing sensation, seeing such a big, vigorous man lying vulnerable and silent in a hospital bed. Shirtless, his entire chest was swathed in thick bandages, stained in two or three places with dried blood.

To Sara's eyes he looked gray and drawn and ill. As she watched, he stirred slightly, muttering something in his sleep Sara couldn't catch. Instantly, she tensed, perching forward on her chair. But after another second or two, he groaned, threw a hand up over his eyes, and quieted.

She sighed, leaning back as her mind reviewed the last few hours that had led her to Bellevue. She had arrived early at the Hall of Justice, expecting him to meet her there, only to be told by the desk officer that the sergeant had been shot just last week — the very day they had last been together! — and was now recuperating in the hospital from a serious chest wound.

Thank heaven she had asked Uriah to drive her carriage today, rather than depending on a hackney! The elderly Negro driver had frightened half a dozen other teams off the streets as he followed her bidding to take her to Bellevue at once.

Framing her face between her hands for a moment, she deliberately avoided thinking of the weakness that had seized her upon learning Sergeant Burke had been shot. Nor did she dwell on the overwhelming tide of relief that had swept through her the moment she heard he would be all right. For now, it was enough to sit here beside him, pretending that when he woke up he would be glad to see her.

Immediately, another discomforting thought thrust itself into her mind, forcing out her feelings of relief. Did she dare tell him of her father's response to her queries about the *Green Flag*?

She glanced over at him, wondering just how much he really cared for his . . . Nora.

Stop it, you ninny! she silently reprimanded herself. *The man is as good as engaged, with a sweetheart sailing the Atlantic to be with him. All you can hope for is to be his friend, to be of help to him if there's any way you can. Now, for heaven's sake, stop behaving like a giddy schoolgirl!*

"They did not tell me I was dying, those rascally surgeons. But what else could it mean, finding an angel at my side?"

Sara shot bolt upright on the chair, her eyes snapping open. "Sergeant Burke! Oh — I must have dozed —"

He was lying with his head turned toward her, watching her with a mischievous, if feeble, grin.

Flustered, Sara stammered out an apology, feeling decidedly foolish to think he'd been lying there staring at her, even as she sat thinking of *him!* "Gracious, here I am, waiting for *you* to wake up, and *I'm* the one who falls asleep!"

"Well, I must say, Miss Farmington, it's grand to wake up to the sight of you instead of that prune-faced old Harrison."

"Harrison?"

" 'Harrison the Harridan,' I affectionately call her," he explained sourly. "She fancies herself a nurse, but between you and me I'm convinced she's actually a British spy they've turned loose in the States to get rid of all the Irish coppers."

"I'm relieved to see that you're feeling better," Sara remarked dryly. "I heard you very nearly died, but you seem to be making a remarkable recovery." That was an exaggeration, of course, but the glint of amusement in his eyes *was* reassuring.

His smile turned to a scowl. "No, and I did not 'very nearly die!' " he groused, waving one hand in exasperation. "I could have left this chamber of horrors long before now if I could only find somebody to give me my trousers!"

Immediately his face flamed. "Sorry, Miss Farmington. It's little time that I spend with proper young ladies — I'm afraid I tend to forget my manners." Glancing down at himself, he gave the blanket a tug to cover his torso.

Suppressing a smile, Sara looked down at the floor, but not before noting that his hand trembled slightly on the bedding. Obviously, he was weaker than he wanted anyone to know.

"I *am* glad you're doing so well, Sergeant Burke. Your surgeon and the nurses seem delighted with your progress."

"That's because they can't wait to be rid of me," he muttered. "Harrison claims I am the most provoking patient she's ever encountered."

"Somehow I'm inclined to believe her," Sara said. "I can't imagine how this could have happened and I didn't hear of it. I'm certain there was nothing in the papers."

One dark brow lifted cynically. "They'd not be advertising the fact that a policeman got shot by another city employee."

"A city employee? But I thought the desk officer said it was a Negro shooting dogs in the street!"

"It was. Those boyos are paid by the city to do just that — rid the streets of wild dogs. This fellow, however, had fortified himself with a bit of the rye before he went on duty. Both his aim and his brain may have been somewhat unsteady," he concluded with a grim smile.

Sara shuddered. "That's horrible."

"My getting shot or the dogs?"

Her mouth twitched. "Both."

His expression sobered. "Well, it's done, and I'm alive, for which I'm thankful. I mean to be gone from this place by the end of the week, though. I *must* — the ship may be in the harbor by then, and I intend to be there when she docks."

Sara frowned as she considered him. "You can't be serious, Sergeant! You'll be in no condition to leave the hospital by then. Besides," she added, "you don't actually have a specific arrival date for the ship, do you?"

He shook his head. "Not yet," he admitted. "I don't suppose you remembered to ask your father if he knew anything of the *Green Flag*?"

Sara swallowed, wishing she could avoid answering his question. "As a matter of fact, I did."

The sergeant's eyes widened with interest. "Did you now? *And?*"

Taking a deep breath, Sara turned on the chair to face him more fully. "Well, at first he wasn't able to tell me very much at all. The name of the ship wasn't familiar to him."

Disappointment clouded his expression, and Sara quickly added, "He did get the name of the captain, however."

"The captain?"

"Yes. Father had one of the men at the yards do some checking on the ships scheduled to arrive during the coming weeks. Apparently the *Green Flag* isn't listed, but it's commanded by a Captain *Schell. Abidas Schell.*"

"Peculiar name," he commented. When Sara said nothing more, he rubbed a hand down the side of his face, frowning, and went on. "Will knowing the captain's name make it possible to find out when the ship is due to arrive?"

"Well . . . possibly," Sara replied, wringing her hands in her lap. "Sergeant Burke, as it happens, this Captain Schell . . . is a familiar name to my father." She hesitated, and caught a deep breath before going on. "Apparently, he's not a — a reputable person."

The sergeant's eyes darkened. "What does that mean, exactly? What makes a ship captain disreputable?"

She sighed. "I suppose I might just as well tell you exactly what Father told me," she said reluctantly. "It would seem that this . . . Abidas Schell . . . is nothing more than a common criminal. Most likely he's only managed to avoid prison by never staying in any one port long enough to be caught. He's a known smuggler — opium, munitions, and other . . . other illegal cargoes. Father said he's been involved in slaving and almost every other criminal act covered by maritime law."

Michael pushed himself up on one arm, staring at her. Sara flinched when she saw the sharp flash of pain that crossed his face with the effort.

"That's not . . . quite all," she said tersely.

His eyes narrowed.

"It seems that on a number of occasions Schell has also been known to sell his entire list of steerage passengers to some of the larger, more sophisticated runners."

Sara shrank at the thunderous look that

now settled over his face. Of course, a police sergeant would know only too well what that meant.

Until recently, it had been common practice for a certain despicable kind of thief to board a ship as soon as it appeared in the harbor with the sole purpose of bilking the bewildered, frightened immigrants out of their money and belongings, all to the profit of the runner's employer, usually a tavern owner or a company.

Preying on their fear and confusion, the runner could easily wheedle his way into their trust because he was of their own kind — Irish runners plundered the Irish, Italians the Italians, and so on. The poor aliens were completely ignorant of the practice. Within moments, the unscrupulous parasite would be on his way out of the harbor with an entire family, or families, in tow, leading them to a "respectable boardinghouse they could afford, where they would enjoy the companionship of other souls from the auld sod while planning for their future."

The swindler would take the unsuspecting family to his employer's boardinghouse — most often a squalid tavern or tenement. There they would be charged an exorbitant rent for holing up with several other families in the same filthy, often unfurnished room. During their stay, their funds would swiftly disappear, along with most of their possessions.

These days, a new, more vicious practice was springing up, according to Lewis Farmington. Now unprincipled captains were selling their entire steerage lists to the runners of highly organized brokers. With this prepaid arrangement, all the steerage immigrants were turned over to one runner, who met the ship when it arrived and then proceeded to make a killing with a minimum of effort.

Apparently, the captain of the *Green Flag* was one of the innovators of this merciless brand of thievery.

"I must get out of here!" Pushing himself up as far as he could, the sergeant turned white with the effort and immediately collapsed onto his pillows.

With a cry, Sara shot up off the chair. "Don't be foolish! You see how weak you still are — why, you'd fall on your face before you made it past the door! The surgeon said you'll have to stay here for at least another week, perhaps longer."

"I will *not!*" he bit out, his voice shaking with rage and weakness. "I *can't!* I can't just lie here, knowing Nora and the others are at the mercy of that — *pirate!*" Even as he spoke, he balled one large hand into a fist, grinding his jaw against an obvious onslaught of pain.

"Sergeant, there is absolutely nothing you can do until the ship actually arrives!"

"But there's no knowing when that will

be!" His face was pinched, his eyes burning with frustration at his own helplessness.

"I'll find out," Sara assured him. "I promise you, I'll find out."

"How?"

"Father will know a way, I'm sure. I'll talk with him the moment I get home. But *you* must promise *me* in the meantime you'll not try anything foolish! You're not nearly strong enough to be up, and you'll be of little help to — to your friend, Nora, if you injure yourself and have to lie abed for *weeks!*"

He was furious. Furious and grieved. Sara knew instinctively that this man had never in his life had to depend upon anyone other than himself. And here he was, flat on his back, almost wholly dependent on a crotchety nurse and a lame society spinster.

Watching him, Sara breathed a prayer that God would enable her to help Sergeant Burke. Otherwise, she had no doubt at all that he would ultimately risk his life to save the woman Sara was trying her utmost not to envy.

"I do not understand how Morgan could do such a thing," he muttered, staring at the ceiling with hard eyes.

Sara strained to hear. "Morgan?"

"My best friend in Ireland," he said. "He arranged the passages for Nora and the others, or at least *had* things arranged." Shaking his head in disbelief, he said, "He could not have known. He would never have put Nora aboard if he had any knowledge of Schell's reputation. He was deceived; he *must* have been!" Breaking off, he looked at Sara again. "God help the man who betrayed him. He will rue the day, and that's certain."

Sara stepped closer to the bed. "Sergeant, I must leave, but I'm asking you to promise me that you will do exactly as your surgeon and your nurses say."

When he remained stubbornly silent, she pressed. *"Sergeant?"*

He glared at her, his wide upper lip curled down in a terrible scowl.

Sara drew herself up. "Sergeant Burke, I will agree to gather your information for you only if *you* agree to take proper care of yourself! It's entirely your choice."

The glare heated to a boil, and Sara recalled rumors she had heard about the Irish temper. Still, she held his gaze with a frigid stare of her own.

"All right, all right, then!" he snarled, again trying to haul himself up on one arm, this time succeeding. "But you'll let me know right away once you learn the arrival date, mind! I intend to be there when that ship enters the harbor, and neither you nor anybody else will be stopping me!"

Sara rolled her eyes, entirely unintimidated by his masculine bluster.

A thought struck her, and she felt she

should ask. "Your son — is there anything you'd like me to do for — *Tierney,* is it — while you're in the hospital?"

A look of surprise crossed his face. "That's kind of you," he said somewhat grudgingly, "but I'm sure he's fine. He comes every day that he can, and he seems to be getting on well enough. Tierney's almost a man — he can manage."

"Yes, of course," Sara said dryly. "Men always . . . manage."

She turned and did her best to flounce out of the room. Flouncing was difficult, of course, when one was lame, but Sara thought she managed it rather well, under the circumstances — until she heard his deep voice, laced with amusement, at her back.

"Did you know, Miss Farmington, that you are really quite lovely when you're fussed?"

Sara managed not to stumble as she flounced through the door.

40

How Far the Shore

Our feet on the torrent's brink,
Our eyes on the cloud afar,
We fear the things we think,
Instead of the things that are.

WILLIAM B. McBURNEY (c. 1855–1892)

It took three days for Lewis Farmington to ferret out the information Sara had requested regarding the arrival of the *Green Flag*. Throughout the entire period, Sara routinely cajoled and nagged him to do all he could on behalf of Sergeant Burke.

They had dinner alone Friday evening, just the two of them, in the long, narrow dining room of their home on Fifth Avenue. As was his custom, whether entertaining guests or simply enjoying his daughter's company, Lewis Farmington was attired in his black dress coat and silk neck cloth.

Bending to kiss him on top of the head before seating herself, Sara noted his appearance with approval. "You're looking very elegant tonight, Father."

She wasn't flattering him. In her estimation, Lewis Farmington *was* a fine-looking gentleman. His hair had gone entirely to silver, but had thinned very little. His almost black eyes usually danced with fun; his figure was trim, his skin ruddy from all the hours spent outside in the yards rather than inside his office.

Glancing up from his newspaper, he watched Sara closely as she sat down and rang for Ginger to begin serving.

"And you look harried," he said, regarding her with a speculative expression. "Just as you have all week."

Sara smiled sweetly at him. "Please ask the blessing, Father."

After he prayed, her father transferred his critical eye to Ginger as she set a silver soup tureen in front of him.

"How many years," he said with deliberate emphasis, "is it going to take before you stop trying to foist that seasoned dishwater off on me, woman? Must I tell you again? *Take away the soup! I do not like soup.*"

The striking, middle-aged black woman slanted an unconcerned look at him. "Soup is a part of your meal," she replied, making no move to take away the tureen. "Polite gentlemen eat their soup."

"Polite gentlemen have polite housekeepers."

Ginger smiled, all pearly teeth and flashing

dark eyes beneath her white turban.

Sara grinned into her own soup as she lifted her spoon. Her father and Ginger had been engaged in an ongoing argument for almost as long as she could remember. When it wasn't soup, it was something else. They loved to argue, and both were extremely creative in their efforts. How many times had she enjoyed the stunned reactions of dinner guests who happened to witness a session of informal banter between Lewis Farmington and his British West Indies housekeeper? Close family friends knew, of course, that Ginger would lay down her life for Lewis Farmington or any member of his family, just as they were aware that Father held *her* in high respect, with an almost brotherly affection.

Sara waited until Ginger brought her father's serving of pot roast and set it down in front of him with a pointed thud — alongside the soup tureen — before asking her daily question.

"*Well,* Father?"

He forked a generous bite of meat into his mouth. "Well, what?" he finally said.

"Father —"

"I want you to answer a question for *me,* my dear. I would like to know," he said solemnly, pausing to take a sip of water, "the exact nature of your interest in this . . . Irish policeman."

"Sergeant Burke."

"What?"

"He's a police sergeant, and his name is Burke," Sara said matter-of-factly.

"Yes. Well, is this . . . *Sergeant Burke* simply another one of your projects, or is there more to this than you're telling me?"

"No, Sergeant Burke is *not* another one of my projects, and, no, there is no more to this than I've told you," Sara said patiently. "As for the nature of my interest, I've already explained that to you: The man was shot in the line of duty and is presently incapacitated. I'm trying to do him a simple favor, that's all."

"Why?"

Sara looked at him blankly. "Why?"

Swallowing a bite of potato, he glanced over at her. "Why would you want to do a favor for a man you scarcely know?"

"Because he needs help," Sara answered easily, meeting his gaze. "And because I like him."

He appraised her for another moment, then resumed eating. "Very odd behavior, a girl of your background becoming friends with an Irish copper."

"My behavior has always been odd for a girl of my background, just as yours is frequently considered odd for a man of your position. Indeed, we are probably the only two people among our circle of acquaintances who aren't shocked by our odd behavior. That doesn't bother me in the least. Does it bother you, Father?"

"Not at all!" he said with a grin, lifting his fork in an unmannerly fashion. "I rather enjoy myself, don't you?" Without waiting for an answer, he went on cheerfully, "All right, then, since you assure me there's nothing improper about this, ah, concern for the sergeant, I will tell you what I've learned."

Sara replaced her spoon, beaming at him excitedly. "Then you *do* have news! Tell me!"

"It's nothing definite, you understand," he cautioned as he went on devouring his meal, "but I should think it's fairly reliable. Poston at the yards did some investigating for me, and in the process he talked with the captain of the *Yorkshire*, one of the Black Ball packets. They just came in today, and he thinks they may have overtaken this *Green Flag* two days ago. The *Yorkshire* is supposed to be the fastest ship built, you know," he explained rather petulantly, "although I think we have one nearly ready to launch that is far superior. At any rate, if he's right — if it *was* the *Green Flag* they passed — she should be coming into the harbor as early as tomorrow or Sunday, I'd say."

Tomorrow or Sunday! Sara's mind raced. There was so much to do and scarcely any time in which to do it! If this awful Captain Schell was the scoundrel his reputation touted him to be, the people on that ship could be in dreadful danger.

Of course, she reminded herself, Sergeant Burke didn't even know for certain his friends were actually *aboard* the *Green Flag*. Was she being altogether foolish, intending to rush to the rescue of a ship filled with immigrants who might be strangers to both her *and* Sergeant Burke?

But they were human beings, whether they were known to her or Sergeant Burke or not! That in itself was reason enough to try to help them.

Turning to her father, she studied him for a moment.

When he raised an inquiring eyebrow, Sara ran a finger around the rim of her porcelain teacup, thinking.

"Father, I wonder if I might enlist your help?"

He pursed his lips. "I suppose you're referring to this ship thing."

Sara nodded. "Knowing what we know, I really think we at least have to make an effort to help those people."

"Would it do any good to remind you that we don't know for certain those people *need* our help?"

"I'm afraid not."

Lewis Farmington sighed and pushed his plate away. "I thought not," he said mildly. "Very well, then. What, exactly, are you going to drag me into *this* time?"

On Friday evening, the steerage passengers were given extra water rations. Nora used hers to launder a change of clothing for all of them, including Whittaker.

She used one of their precious last scraps of soap, scrubbing as many items as she could until the water was no longer clean enough to make a difference. With the help of Katie and Johanna, Daniel John strung a line from the iron plate on the hull where his bunk was secured to the next bunk across the aisle. Nothing would really dry, of course. Steerage was too damp and very cold, plus the fact that the damage incurred during the storm allowed continuous leakage of the sea. But Nora felt better — less like a squatter — just to have made the effort.

While the children hung up the laundry, she applied salve to the sores on Little Tom's knees, rubbed raw from playing on the rough floor of the deck. She was as gentle as she could possibly be with the tyke, but he whimpered, trying to push her hand away. "Hurts!" he chanted accusingly.

Poor wee wane. Just that morning he had asked for his "mum" again. Most of the time he seemed to have accepted Catherine's death, but on occasion, when he was sleepy or fretful, he still called for her. It nearly broke Nora's heart.

"You're very close to the F-Fitzgerald children, aren't you?" Evan Whittaker stood beside her, dangling a piece of rope in an effort to distract the little boy so Nora could tend to him.

"Aye, I am. We were more family than friends, always popping in and out of one another's houses and the like." Memories flooded her mind, making it impossible for her to go on.

"Have you thought about what you'll d-do once we reach America? With the children, I mean?"

Nora squeezed her eyes shut for a moment. When she opened them, she set wee Tom to the floor, and he went at a run toward his sisters and Daniel John.

"I think about it all the time," she answered truthfully. "But there are only questions, never answers."

"Mrs. K-Kavanagh, I will help you — and the children — however I can."

Nora turned, lifting her face to look at the Englishman. He had been staying up, walking around the deck, for longer periods of time each day. But one glance revealed the frailty and weakness of the man. He had a long way to go before he would be able to help himself again, much less anyone else.

"You are kind, Mr. Whittaker. I do not know how I will ever repay you for your kindness to us."

Pulling up a stool across from her, he braced himself on the rim of the bunk until he'd managed to sit down. Nora instinctively reached to help the man, then withdrew her hand, sensing her gesture would not be welcome.

"Friends d-don't concern themselves with repayment, Mrs. Kavanagh," Whittaker said, his face pale from even this small exertion. "And I *would* like to think that, after all we have g-gone through together by now, we are friends."

Nora regarded him with genuine liking. "Mr. Whittaker, no soul ever had a better friend than yourself."

He flushed a bit, but looked extremely pleased. "In that case, d-do you suppose you could stop c-calling me 'Mr. Whittaker'? Just plain 'Whittaker' or 'Evan' will do between friends, don't you think?"

"I do, yes." She paused, then added, "And I think you should call me 'Nora,' if you please."

"Thank you . . . *Nora.*"

Nora liked the way he said her name, so soft and carefully that he made it sound like music.

"Are you excited, now that we're nearing New York?" Whittaker asked.

Nora turned to replace the tube of salve in the box beside her. "Excited?" She shook her head. "Frightened is what I am."

"Yes. I confess that I share your f-fear. Still, I'm sure the Lord understands and considers our anxiety. I'm d-doing my best to trust Him in this."

She looked at him. Of course he would be frightened. What would become of an ill, one-armed man in a foreign country?

What would become of them all?

She wished she could share his belief that God was aware of and concerned about their circumstances. But these past weeks of hell aboard the *Green Flag* had convinced her of what she'd only suspected back in Killala: God had withdrawn His blessing from them all. Apparently, He had judged them and found them guilty and was now meting out His punishment on a rebellious people, herself included. Not a soul on this evil ship had managed to escape His wrath.

After a long silence, Evan cleared his throat and looked away from her. "Are you still missing your son . . . Tahg . . . very much, Nora? I know losing him . . . in addition to your other losses . . . m-must have made all this even harder for you."

She looked at Whittaker, saw his gentle frown of concern as he asked the question.

"Aye, I will always miss him," she answered quietly. The image of Tahg's white face, his pain-filled eyes flashed before her. Instinctively, she put a hand to her throat, touching the wooden cross that lay next to her skin, the cross carved by Owen and worn by Tahg up until his death.

"It isn't likely I will ever stop missing him," she said softly, "Tahg and the others. So many gone, so much lost —"

Her voice broke, and she stopped for a moment until she could regain her composure. "But I would not wish them back. Not now, not knowing the torment they would have had to endure if they had lived. My sorrow for them all will go on, but I am grateful they were spared . . . all this."

Their eyes met, and Whittaker gave a slow nod of understanding.

Later that night, Abidas Schell sat at his desk, writing in his journal, making what would be one of the final entries for this voyage:

Light winds, N.E. by E. Weather pleasant, but some fog. Saw two land birds, much weed. Should spot a pilot boat by morning.

Should enter the Narrows late tomorrow night or early Sunday. . . .

In his cabin, William Leary, the ship's surgeon, sat hunched over his desk, half drunk, but still sober enough to handle a pen.

Smoothing the paper with a trembling hand, he held the pen suspended as his thoughts wandered.

He was writing the letter now, rather than

later. Later tonight he would be too drunk, and tomorrow he would be too busy with preparations for arrival. After tomorrow . . .

He would not think beyond tomorrow.

With any luck, he would sleep tonight, once the letter was completed. By tomorrow night, they should be sighting New York. Finally, this latest nightmare would end.

For him, the nightmares were about to end altogether. He would make no more voyages with Abidas Schell.

The pistol was safe in his medical case, hidden beneath the bandages. He had not yet decided whether to use it on himself alone or on the both of them. Either way, he would be free of his demon.

At least in this life.

Shaking off any thought of the future, he began to write, penning the only address he could think of:

The New York Police Department. . . .

"We'll need to go to Sergeant Burke first thing in the morning," Sara said to her father, "and at least get a description of his . . . intended. I don't imagine he can help us much beyond that, unless he happens to know exactly how many are traveling in her party."

"How long has it been since he's seen this woman?" asked her father, finishing his custard.

"Almost seventeen years or thereabouts, I

believe. Let's hope she still looks somewhat like he remembers her. We need at least one person we can identify rather quickly."

Lewis Farmington met his daughter's eyes over his teacup. "He's going to marry a woman he hasn't seen in seventeen years?"

Sara shrugged, toying idly with her custard. "He's a very unusual man, Father."

"Mmm. Either that or a perfect fool."

"He's no fool," Sara said quietly, but with marked emphasis.

He darted a sharp look at her. "Sara, are you quite sure you're not taken with this man yourself?"

Jabbing the custard with her spoon, Sara answered bluntly, "I could be, I imagine, if he weren't committed to somebody else." She looked up at him, saw the mixture of doubt and worry in his eyes, and added, "But *I* am no fool either, Father. You needn't concern yourself."

She glanced up to find him still searching her face. "Very well," he said, blotting his lips with his dinner napkin. "We will have Uriah drive us to Bellevue in the morning."

41

A Meeting in Dublin

And sweet our life's decline for it hath left us
A nearer Good to cure an older Ill:
And sweet are all things, when we learn to prize them
Not for their sake, but His who grants them or denies them.

AUBREY DE VERE (1814–1902)

Nelson Hall was a great rambling structure, a vast entanglement of Georgian dignities, sprawling palisades, and endless wings that seemed to have sprung up at will, with no real pattern or purpose in mind.

Not quite a castle but more than a mansion, it reigned to the north of Dublin, near the coast and almost directly below Drogheda. Its uniformly gray landscape was relieved in the distance by deep emerald hills, soaring gulls, and pearl-white clouds swirling in from the coast.

Morgan thought it the most hideous affront to architecture he had ever seen.

He had noticed it before, of course, during

his roamings — indeed, had stopped to study it from a distance any number of times.

Until today, however, he had never viewed it as the palatial home of his own grandfather.

Richard Avery Nelson. Retired member of Parliament, philanthropist, art collector, descendant of a Cromwellian toady whose reward was this valley of fertile land and rolling hillside.

Early on Saturday morning, Morgan hitched Pilgrim to a fence post, then went strolling up to the immense front door. He had deliberately decked himself out in his tattered blanket-cloak, muddy boots, and worn frieze trousers.

An aristocratic looking footman, clothed entirely in black except for his frosty linen, appeared in the doorway before Morgan could lift a hand to the brass knocker. The man took him in from head to toe in one scathing glance, but to his credit he did not so much as blink an eye at the sight of this rabble who had the audacity to appear at the front door, rather than the back.

As the elderly servant chose not to dignify the shabby caller with even a glint of acknowledgment, Morgan bluntly announced his business.

"I am here to see Richard Nelson."

The man's face was a stone as their eyes met and held. "For what purpose?"

"Ah, that would be personal, I'm afraid."

The footman lifted his eyes upward a fraction, an indictment of this ragman's impertinence. "Sir Richard does not receive. He is indisposed."

Morgan regarded him with lively amusement. "The thing is, you see, I am invited."

"Invited?" A blinking of eyes, a lifting of brows, a clearing of throat. "By whom?"

"By himself."

Silence. Finally, "And you are . . . ?"

"His grandson," Morgan said with a nasty grin. "Would you be announcing me now?"

Nelson's library was everything Joseph Mahon had proclaimed it to be. Thousands of books, hundreds of them rare and carefully preserved, filled a cavernous room that smelled of aged leather, rich wood, and years of lemon oil.

Morgan's first surprise came when the old man behind the desk stood for the first time. This, then, was the source of his ungainly height and wide shoulders. Odd; he'd always assumed his and Thomas's long legs had been passed down to them from the Fitzgerald clan.

Richard Avery Nelson looked to be well into his eighties. His hair was white, his face a map of years. But his back was still straight, his shoulders broad, and his eyes clear and discerning.

Bracing both hands palms down on top of

the desk, he surveyed his grandson with a keen, discerning gaze. In his prime, Morgan thought, the man across from him must have presented an imposing sight.

Nelson stood waiting, almost as if he half expected Morgan to approach him with an outstretched hand.

Morgan stopped several feet short of the desk, meeting the old man's appraisal with one of his own.

"You are Morgan Fitzgerald."

"I am."

"My grandson."

"So you say." Morgan's eyes went to the old man's hands splayed widely on the polished desktop. They were trembling.

"The fact that you are a free man confirms it."

Morgan stood, legs apart, hands behind his back. If this was about obligation, he would not be staying long.

The old man beckoned to a comfortable-looking leather chair near the desk. "Please, sit down."

"I believe I will stand, thank you."

"As you wish." With stiff movements, Nelson sank down onto his own chair. "I assume you have read my letter by now."

Morgan nodded. "It was very informative." Hesitating, he added, "I suppose I should be thanking you for my pardon, though I wonder why you bothered."

"You're of my blood."

"No doubt I am as grieved over that fact as yourself."

The old man nodded, as if he had expected this. "You are very bitter. I rather imagined you would be."

Morgan uttered a short laugh. "Now, why would I be bitter? You disowned my mother, ruined my father, and chose to ignore every drop of the harm done until you heard I was about to wear a noose. Sure, and there is nothing in that to make a man bitter."

In spite of his diatribe, Morgan was beginning to feel a bit uncomfortable under the old gentleman's calm, almost sorrowful scrutiny. He wasn't sure what he had expected to find here — self-righteousness, perhaps, certainly arrogance and condescension — but not the serenity emanating from this mild-mannered old patriarch.

"You may say whatever you wish to me, young man. I probably deserve the worst of it. But we can save each other a great deal of time if you'll simply listen to me first, and listen with an open mind."

Morgan stared silently at him.

"I wanted to see you," Nelson said, ignoring Morgan's sullenness, "to tell you I am sorry for whatever pain I caused your father, as well as you and your brother."

Morgan found himself wondering if the old man was dying and this was his idea of a deathbed confession. But he did not look to be dying, and he did not seem the type to make superficial confessions even if he were. He remained silent, waiting.

"As I explained in my letter, I was a pompous fool when I was a younger man, but to be fair you must realize I was a victim of my own upbringing and environment. I thought my daughter's love for your father was irresponsible and foolish. I handled it miserably and then was too proud to do anything about it. One thing you must believe," he said, looking up from his hands, "your grandmother and I would have been good to you and your brother had Aidan not run off with you. Our willingness to raise you both was quite genuine."

Morgan spoke for the first time since the old man had begun. "A magnanimous gesture, I am sure. You hoped to save us from our Irishness, from Rome — and at the same time, from the devil," he bit out resentfully. "All by separating us from our father."

To his surprise, the old man did not argue. "That was a part of it, I imagine. And, of course, I simply lost my head altogether when Aidan ran off with the two of you and the money we'd given him —"

"Aye," Morgan broke in roughly, "thanks to you, we all went on the road like animals."

"Yes. And that was shameful." Nelson stopped and looked away for a moment before turning back to face Morgan. "I will tell you once more, just as I told you in my letter — I am deeply sorry. I was a fool, and I realize I caused a great deal of pain for you, for *all* of you. I shall go to my grave regretting any hurt I brought upon you and your brother."

"My brother is dead," Morgan said flatly. "As is my father."

The old man's expression grew even more pained. "I know."

"You wrote all this in your letter," Morgan said impatiently. "Why, then, did you demand I come here?"

Nelson folded his hands, his eyes going over Morgan's face as if to measure what he saw there. "I know before I answer that you will not believe me. But I swear to you that I am telling you the truth, and I mean every word of it with all my heart. Promise me you will listen and say nothing until I am done."

Shifting from one foot to the other, Morgan gave a grudging nod of assent.

For a moment the old man's eyes took on a distant, haunted expression, as if his thoughts had temporarily wandered past this room to a faraway place. "I have spent most of my life in this country. Indeed, it has become *my* country, in a way I cannot explain. It means far more to me than England ever did. I have grown to love the land, and, believe it or not, the people."

He leaned forward, regarding Morgan with

frank directness. "At the same time," he went on, "I have come to know great sorrow over what the country of my birth — England — has done to this land. Out of old prejudices and ignorance and indifference, England has run roughshod over this small and ancient island, trampling an entire noble race into the dirt."

The old gentleman now had Morgan's undivided attention, if not his trust.

"I am nearing the end of my years, and over the last half dozen of them I've become much better acquainted with the God to whom I once gave only lip service. Much to my surprise, I've found great joy in becoming His friend, as well as trying to be an obedient son. Perhaps that's why He's gradually, over the past few months, chosen to show me at least a small part of His concern and love for this island."

Morgan drew his hands into white-knuckled fists at his sides.

Nelson nodded, as if sensing the younger man's cynicism. "I know," he said, smiling sadly. "It's difficult for you to believe that God would reveal His love for Ireland to an Englishman. Still, it's true. He has shown me, during my times alone with Him, that the tragedy of Ireland grieves His heart. I long to do whatever I can to make a difference on this island, but I'm afraid there's very little I *can* do, with my health failing as it is. Therefore, I need to look to someone else, someone with the youth and energy to accomplish what I cannot."

He paused, then with a sweep of one hand, said, "Morgan, please — won't you at least sit down? I won't keep you much longer if you choose to go."

Morgan hesitated, but finally dropped down onto the chair the old man indicated.

"I want you to know that I've made you my heir. My only heir."

Morgan gripped both arms of the chair, half rising. "You — *no!* I don't want a shilling from you!"

Again came a wan smile. "I understand. But it's not entirely for you. That's why I asked you to come, so I can explain."

Morgan frowned skeptically, but relaxed into the seat again.

"I have been reading your writings," said the old man with a look that conveyed genuine admiration and interest. "In fact, once I learned who you were, I made it my business to read everything you've written — your poems, your essays, your songs — everything I could put my hands to. Actually, that was what motivated me to demand that you refrain from your . . . illegal activities. I could not bear the thought that such a valiant heart and a mighty pen would be silenced on the gallows."

Still, Morgan waited, trying to steel himself

against the power of the old man's words.

"Morgan, we both know there is a planned rising, a rebellion that many of your friends are trying to foist upon the people. And we both know just as certainly that, if it comes, it will fail — and very possibly destroy any future Ireland might have as a free country."

Morgan softened enough to nod his agreement.

Encouraged, the old man continued. "I am making you my heir because I believe with all my heart that you possess the wisdom, the genius — and the *love* for this suffering island — to make a difference. Men like you can speak to the hatred that has been the root of Ireland's struggles for centuries."

When Morgan would have interrupted, Nelson put up a restraining hand. "It has been given many names, many guises, but at the heart of all the conflict and the anguish is *hatred.* It has *always* been hatred!" The old man leaned forward, his eyes burning. "Hatred between the English and the Irish. Between Protestant and Catholic. Between tenant and landlord. Hatred that repeats itself and feeds on itself from one generation after another."

Knotting his hands together, Morgan bent his head to them for a moment, as if deeply grieved. He was unable to deny the man's sincerity any longer. Nelson's love and sorrow for the land laced his every word.

"Great evil has been done to this ancient, beautiful island," the old man continued. "And great evil has been done *by* her. But in the end, no matter how righteous, how just, each side believes its cause to be, *hatred* is still the wall that holds any hope of compromise, any chance of resolution, beyond reach."

He appeared to be tiring suddenly, and Morgan felt an unexpected sting of concern for the old man as he went on speaking in a weary, somewhat tremulous voice.

"I happen to believe that men like you, Morgan — men who have a gift for seeking and finding God's truth and then communicating it with vigor and power — may well be the only hope of saving Ireland from total destruction. All I can do is provide you with the security, the funds, to make it possible for you to devote yourself to your writing on behalf of your country.

"I foresee a day, unless these foolish prejudices and ungodly hatreds can finally be destroyed, when this island will run red with the blood of brother against brother, father against son, even mother against daughter."

Suddenly he leaned back in his chair, his shoulders sagging as if he had exhausted himself. "I am asking you to stay with me a while, Morgan, to get to know me — and allow me to get to know you. I yearn to know your heart, your whole heart, and to share mine with you."

Straightening slightly in his chair, he turned a look of appeal on Morgan. "You are my *grandson!* My blood runs through your veins! I am asking for only a few days, a few weeks, if you would. In the meantime, whether you agree or refuse, I want you to know that I've already drawn up the papers, amended my will. My estate will make it possible for you to dedicate the rest of your life — if you are willing — to saving this land you love so much.

"Morgan . . . Morgan," he said softly, his eyes beseeching, "your words stir a man's heart as no drumbeat ever will. They pierce the human spirit as no sword ever could! You speak with the voice of Ireland's heart, the voice of truth and hope and the promise of freedom. *Morgan . . . son of my son . . . please, forgive this old fool! Allow me to at least be your friend, if not your family.*"

Morgan's hands tightened still more on the chair arms. His gaze locked with the old man's, and what he saw there shook him to his very soul.

He might have been gazing into his own face, fifty years from now, with all the grief and shattered dreams of one who has never known the enduring love of a family. In Richard Nelson's stricken eyes, he saw his own lonely heart.

On the heels of that revelation came the thought, not without its own touch of irony, that twice now his neck had been saved — and both times by an Englishman!

And last came the reminder that he himself had been forgiven, and his offenses had no doubt grieved the Lord more than those of the old man seated across from him.

Who, then, was he to withhold forgiveness from Richard Nelson?

"Many in the movement are counting on me to speak out on behalf of the rising," he said hesitantly.

The old man nodded. "Smith O'Brien being one of them."

"He is a good friend. I respect him."

"But he has been drawn into something he can no longer control." When Morgan remained silent, Nelson pressed, "Do you deny it?"

Reluctantly, Morgan shook his head. "But that doesn't change the fact that he is counting on my help."

The old man studied him for a long moment. "Do you believe in this rising? Do you believe it's best for your people?"

Morgan met his eyes. "No," he said, again shaking his head. "I believe it could finish them."

"Then why not do what you can for *all* Ireland, rather than for only a few? That is the opportunity I am trying to afford you, son."

Morgan looked down at his hands, then at the old man's face. And he knew what he must do. What *God* would have him do.

"Aye . . . Grandfather," he said quietly, testing the name on his lips and finding it far easier to say than he would have guessed. "Aye, I will stay with you a while, and we will talk of Ireland."

42

Survivors in a Strange Land

Wail no more, lonely one, mother of exiles,
wail no More, Banshee of the world!
— no more!
Thy sorrows are the world's, thou art no more alone;
Thy wrongs, the world's.

JOHN TODHUNTER (1839–1916)

Hundreds of emigrant vessels put into New York City every year, sometimes as many as thirty or forty a day, bringing hundreds of thousands of steerage passengers from their respective countries — the majority of them from Ireland and Germany. Thousands died before they reached New York, but new babies were born every day aboard ship.

Some of the vessels brought opium into the city, along with whiskey and prostitutes. Others carried typhus, smallpox, and cholera. Hundreds of cases of disease managed to slip by the cursory quarantine examinations, escaping into the city to contaminate entire neighborhoods.

New York had become a refuge for the homeless, the destitute, the suffering. In return for her open door, she inherited disease, labor dilemmas, and some of the worst slums in the world. Within the city, among her tenements and revival brownstones, inside the mansions along Fifth Avenue and the shanties on Vinegar Hill, resentment and rebellion had begun to breed.

But to the immigrant in search of hope and a new life, the city still loomed as the Promised Land, the Golden Shore, the American Dream.

Aboard the *Green Flag* this Saturday morning, hearts had begun to stir and hopes had begun to rise.

They would soon be in New York City.

The directive came down from the mate on the foredeck to begin the final scrubdown. With it came the shocking order that all mattresses, pillows, and bed covers were to be tossed overboard with the refuse and leftover food.

Finally, they were given the heartening news that their captain had arranged for them to be met by reputable guides who would lead them to clean, respectable, and affordable lodgings. They were sternly warned to take no heed of other individuals who might try to lure them away from the ship, for these despicable characters preyed on helpless foreigners, robbing them of their valuables and taking advantage of their women.

This information brought exclamations of "Thanks be to God!" and whispers of horror at what might have become of them had it not been for the captain's foresight. The voyage had been a dreadful experience, but perhaps they had judged Captain Schell a bit too harshly. He had been looking out for their welfare, after all.

The order to throw their mattresses and bed covers overboard, however, was met with a great general outcry. To many of the destitute in steerage, their bedding represented the sum total of their personal belongings, virtually all they had to bring with them into the new world other than the rags on their back. But when the mate warned that to disobey could mean weeks spent in quarantine, they rushed to do as they were told.

Soon, the sea around them was mucked with mattress ticking, blankets, and baskets of rotten food. At the last, and against the heart-rending pleas of their loved ones, the bodies of three recent typhus victims were thrown callously into the sea, along with the other cast-offs.

Nora and the children worked in a frenzy alongside the others, scrubbing the walls and floor with sand, then sluicing them down, even drying the timbers with hot coals that the crew provided from the galley. Within a few hours, the former hellhole had taken on a tidy, almost comfortable appearance. Certainly any inspector appraising the *Green Flag*'s steerage would now have only marks of approval for what he saw.

Once they were done with the cleaning, Nora scrutinized first the children, then herself, with a choked exclamation of despair. They looked like filthy squatters!

Appalled at her own condition — her dress was in tatters, her hands grimy, and she smelled of seawater and sweat — she was equally dismayed at the appearance of the children.

"We cannot go ashore looking like tinkers!" she declared. "We will use a bit of the water to wash ourselves before changing into fresh clothes."

"Don't fret so, Mother," Daniel John told her, already stripping Little Tom out of his raggedy shirt. "Your friend, Sergeant Burke, will understand. He made the voyage himself, remember?"

Physical pain shot through Nora at his words, immediately followed by an even stronger surge of guilt. From the beginning, she had told no one, not even her son, of Michael Burke's questionable proposal of marriage. As far as the others knew, he was simply an old friend standing by in New York to help them get settled.

Nor did they know she had selfishly torn up his letter and address. All of them — Daniel John, the children, even Whittaker — had hopes that there would be at least one friendly face waiting for them in this city of strangers. Why, only the day before, Daniel John had repeated to her a conversation he'd had with Whittaker about this very thing, explaining how they had prayed that God would put some "people in the city" for them!

What if Michael Burke's proposal had been God's way of doing just that — and she had gone and ruined things for them all?

Now they were entirely on their own. Ashamed and dismayed, she realized she would have to tell them the truth, and soon.

But not now. There was no time. For now, the truth would have to wait.

The most recent announcement from the mate on the foredeck brought shouts of joy and relieved weeping below.

"Steerage passengers are now allowed above decks!" he proclaimed through a megaphone. *"The captain hopes you will enjoy your first sight of America! You should be able to see Staten Island within an hour or so, perhaps sooner."*

The ladder almost collapsed with the rolling weight of groping hands and shoving bodies as those who had survived the nightmare of steerage clambered up to the hatch in pursuit of freedom.

★ ★ ★

William Leary had carried the letter in his shirt pocket ever since he'd written it, along with the key to the cabins, waiting for the right time and a trustworthy messenger. In the pocket of his seaman's jacket he fingered the pistol.

When he saw the Kavanagh boy help the Englishman through the hatch, he cornered them, hauling them both to one side.

The boy, in a fever to get to the rail, shot Leary an impatient glare.

"Here, now, listen to me!" the surgeon muttered, glancing furtively around to see that no one nearby was paying any heed to them. "I have only a moment, and there's something I need to ask of you!"

Pretending to make a cursory examination of the Englishman's surgery, he spoke in a harsh, frenzied whisper. "Take this letter to a policeman as soon as you get off the ship!" he urged. "It is vital! Promise me you will give it to nobody else — only a policeman!"

The Englishman and the boy looked at each other, obviously bewildered.

"Promise me!"

"Yes . . . all right!" the Englishman agreed, regarding Leary with a measuring stare as the surgeon pressed the letter into his hand. "B-But what —"

"No time for questions! Just guard the letter!" Leary paused, adding, "All you need know is that it will help to put Abidas Schell where he belongs — and perhaps save a number of future victims at the same time!"

Turning abruptly to the boy, he snapped, "Are you a lad to be trusted?"

The youth shot him an indignant look, followed by a grudging nod.

"Take these keys, then," Leary told him, pressing them into the boy's hand. "They open the first two cabins. A pilot will be coming aboard to guide the ship into South Street, to tie up. You must unlock the doors and take the children who are inside the cabins to the pilot. Only to the *pilot,* mind — *not* the medical officer! Do you understand me, lad?"

The boy stared at the keys in his hand as if they would set his palm ablaze. "Children? What children?"

"Little girls!" The words ripped from Leary like a wailing on the wind. "Little girls who have been sold for evil use! You must get them out of those cabins while the pilot is still on board! Can you do this, lad?"

The boy's head came up slowly, and Leary saw understanding begin to dawn in his eyes. "Aye," he said, his voice hard. "I will do it, you can be sure."

"One thing more," Leary said, his words spilling out in a ragged stream. "Whatever you do, be sure you do not go with the captain's 'representative'! Plead illness —" He returned his gaze to the Englishman. "Say you think you have the typhus, say whatever you must. Just don't let yourselves be taken!"

Leaning toward them, he hurried on. "Even quarantine is to be preferred over the place where he would take you. You think you have known hell aboard this ship, but you have known no hell at all until you've seen Five Points!"

Several members of the crew were beginning to close in around them now, herding the immigrants already on deck out of the way to make room for others pouring through the hatch.

The blood pounding wildly in his ears, Leary locked gazes with the Englishman. "Once you are free of this ship, tell others the truth about what you have been through. It is happening on other vessels as well, a growing number of them. People should know."

Feeling the man's hand on his arm, Leary glanced down.

"How did this happen?" Whittaker rasped. "Morgan Fitzgerald would never have booked passage for his family on a coffin ship like this had he known!"

"I have no knowledge of any Fitzgerald!" Leary said, his eyes sweeping the crowd pressing in on them. "It's all done through brokers. Sometimes I act as a go-between for Schell, when the brokers are booking for Irish immigrants."

The contempt blazing out from the Englishman's eyes seared Leary's skin. "In other words, you sell your own countrymen to the devil! *Why?* What could possibly make it worth your while to betray your own people — and with most of them already half dead at that?"

Leary averted his gaze from the disgust that filled Whittaker's countenance. "There is no more time," he said gruffly. "Just guard the letter and the keys if you want to save some lives."

Before the Englishman could hurl any further questions at him, the surgeon turned and began to push his way through the mass of confused immigrants that now filled the main deck. Consumed by his need for the bottle as much as his resolve to be done with his final voyage aboard the *Green Flag*, he pushed a number of bewildered passengers aside and stumbled almost blindly toward his cabin.

In New York that Saturday morning, Michael Burke was lying in his hospital bed, talking somewhat glumly with his son, Tierney, when Sara Farmington and her father walked in.

Stunned but pleased, he managed a stammering introduction to Tierney, who immediately gave up his chair to Miss Farmington. Stuck for words, Michael could only stare at his unexpected visitors with amazement, especially when they explained the reason for their visit and what they planned to do after they left.

"If it *was* the *Green Flag* that the *Yorkshire* passed just two days ago, Sergeant Burke," Sara Farmington was saying, "the ship should be coming into the harbor at any hour now. It would be a great help if we at least knew what your friend Nora looks like. We need you to describe her for us as best as you can remember."

Michael was surprised at how vivid his memories had remained. Describing Nora to the Farmingtons was no trouble at all — he could see her in his mind almost as clearly as he had the day he had kissed her goodbye and sailed for America.

"She's just a wee thing, a slip of a lass," he told them. "Back then she had hair the color of a raven's wings and the loveliest gray eyes — huge eyes, like a little girl's — but sad. Nora always had such sorrowful eyes . . ." He spoke softly, his words drifting off to join his memories.

Preoccupied with her own troubled thoughts, Sara said little to her father as they drove away from the hospital.

Sergeant Burke had appeared so weak this morning; he almost seemed to be losing ground instead of getting better. Stopping in the hallway on the way out of his room, Sara had voiced her concern to the ward nurse — Harrison — but received nothing more than an impatient mumble about a "punctured lung taking time to heal."

Sara wasn't so sure the sergeant's condition was entirely due to his injury. She thought she'd sensed an uncommon moroseness about the policeman, a dulling of the spirit that wasn't at all like him.

Ninny! Listen to yourself; you'd think you knew the man well! He's little more than a stranger to you!

Still, his frustration at being incapacitated might be slowing down his recovery. More than likely, the sergeant was used to being in control and was finding it difficult to deal with his present helplessness.

She could not shake the memory of the look that had settled over his face as he described his Nora.

How she wished for the day when a man would speak of her in the same lovely way! And with such a look in his eyes!

She sighed deeply. That man would *not* be Sergeant Burke. He was still in love with his Nora, no matter how many years lay between them.

Abruptly, she turned to look at her father, only to find him studying her with a troubled gaze. "Did you see his face when he spoke of her, Father? We must help him! We must help Sergeant Burke find his Nora with the raven hair and sorrowful eyes."

Taking her hand, her father squeezed it gently. "And we shall, dear," he said, still searching her face. "We shall. We'll stop at the Hall of Justice on the way and enlist the help of some of Sergeant Burke's fellow officers." He paused. "Sara — are you all right, my dear?"

Sara met his gaze with a level one of her own. "Yes, Father, I'm quite all right. I'm simply feeling anxious about a friend. You understand that, don't you?"

Her father put an arm around her shoulders. "Yes, my dear. I understand very well. And I'm extremely proud of you."

A thought kept nagging at Michael, worrying him, refusing to let go.

"Tierney?" He turned to look at his son, again seated on the chair next to his bed.

"Aye, Da?" The boy leaned forward.

Studying Tierney's lean, intent face, Michael silently questioned his judgment, yet felt the urgency inside him peak. "You used to haunt the docks regularly. You know them well, do you not?"

Frowning, Tierney nodded. "Sure, I do."

His decision made, Michael pushed himself up a bit. "I want you to go after the Farmingtons, go with them to the harbor. I don't know why exactly, but I'd feel better if you went along."

His son stared at him for a moment, then leaped off the chair and bolted from the room.

Long after Tierney had gone, Michael lay staring at the bleak ceiling of the ward. *He* should have been the one to go to the harbor, not his son. It seemed that everybody else was looking after *his* responsibilities these days.

As much as the thought rankled, and as worried as he was about Nora and the others, the knowledge that Tierney was standing in for him at the harbor gave Michael a certain amount of reassurance.

Why it should be so, he hadn't the faintest idea.

43

People in the City

I turned my back
On the dream I had shaped,
And to this road before me
My face I turned.

PADRAIC PEARSE (1879–1916)

The uniformed officer designated to pilot the *Green Flag* into port stood facing the wide-eyed immigrants, giving them their first glimpse of a real American.

Smart and wiry in his white uniform and peaked hat, he dazzled them with his smile and air of authority. Then, with the crew's assistance and Captain Schell's dark, hovering presence, he proceeded to pilot the ship expertly through the Narrows, the channel between Staten Island and Brooklyn.

This was his favorite part of the job.

Trying to look everywhere at once, Daniel craned his neck to take in the placid bay, the green hills, the fine houses in the distance. All around them in the water were other boats and ships: medical boats darting from one ship to another, longboats, anchored clippers. Hundreds of people thronged the dock, some dressed in odd, foreign-looking clothing, others decked out in fine apparel.

It nearly took his breath away! He was determined to commit to memory every splendid detail, for he intended to remember this day when he was a very old man!

He turned to his mother, who stood with Little Tom in her arms, tears coursing down her face. "We will be fine, Mother," he said, raising his voice above the noise on deck. "God will put some people in the city for us, just as Mr. Whittaker and I asked. You will see."

His mother dragged her eyes away from the harbor scene to study his face. "Do you truly believe that, Daniel John?" she asked in a choked voice. "That we will be all right, at last?"

"Aye, I do, Mother." Even as he said the words, Daniel realized he *did* believe so. He had no idea what lay ahead, but somehow over the past hours an unshakable conviction had seized his heart, an assurance that the Kavanaghs and the Fitzgeralds — yes, and Evan Whittaker, too — had a future here in New York City.

"A future and a hope," he said firmly to his mother. "That's what God is giving us. I believe that with all my heart, Mother, and you must believe it, too."

Still she wept, and Daniel promised himself at that moment that he would do whatever he could in the days and weeks ahead to wipe away her tears, to make her smile again.

"Don't be afraid, Mother."

She shook her head. " 'Tis not fear. I was thinking of Tahg. And Thomas. Wishing they had made it this far, that they could have seen —" Her voice broke, and she made no attempt to finish her thought.

Daniel nodded to let her know he understood, but beyond that, he had no means of comforting her. Her loss was his as well, her sorrow his to share. What was to be said, after all? No words could make a difference. There was no changing the reality that Tahg was gone; Thomas, too. And the both of them would be sorely missed.

But those who remained must somehow go on, and going on, do more than simply survive. They must *live.*

Over his mother's head, he met Evan Whittaker's eyes. Standing between Katie and Johanna, the Englishman looked frail and weak, his expression a blend of both hope and sadness.

"Well, then, Mr. Whittaker — we made it. We survived to see America!"

Whittaker managed a smile. "We did indeed, Daniel. We survived."

"Thanks be to God . . ."

Surprised, Daniel realized the soft words of praise had come from his mother.

Again his gaze locked with Whittaker's, and the Englishman nodded slightly, still smiling as he turned to Daniel's mother and echoed her words.

"Yes, thanks be to be God."

The harbor rang with the sounds from the ship — familiar sounds heard every day, yet somehow unique to each vessel. Dozens of immigrants fell to the deck and prayed. Others wept for the land and the loved ones left behind. Children shouted and laughed with excitement.

They *had* survived. They were here at last, in America. It was time to commit the past to yesterday, with all its suffering and sorrow and shattered dreams. It was time to go in search of new dreams, new hopes, new beginnings. Time to look forward, to start over.

In the confusion and noise blowing over the deck, nobody heard the gunshot that came from the direction of the surgeon's cabin.

Engulfed by excitement and his own turbulent emotions, Daniel very nearly forgot the keys he had tucked down inside his jacket pocket. Turning to shoot a meaningful look at Evan Whittaker, then assuring his mother and the Fitzgerald girls he would return straightaway, he quickly slipped backward into the crowd.

The deck was all chaos and clamor as he melted into the throng of immigrants lining the deck. His heart was pounding, his hands clammy, but nobody seemed to take notice of him.

He half expected a flock of children to come pouring out onto the deck the instant he turned the key in the first lock. When no one appeared after a moment, he stuck his head cautiously inside the door. With sick amazement, he saw half a dozen young Chinese girls huddled together in the corner, staring at him with terrified eyes.

Daniel motioned that they should follow him, but they didn't move. Frowning, he made his voice as urgent as he could, again gesturing frantically that they should leave the cabin. At last, one of the bigger girls got to her feet, taking a tentative step forward.

Daniel smiled at her, nodding encouragement.

Immediately, she stopped dead-still, her dark almond eyes measuring him with fear and distrust. Daniel made no move, no gesture whatsoever. Finally, the girl once more began to creep toward him, her eyes never leaving his face. At last the others got to their feet and followed behind her.

Gulping in a huge breath of relief, Daniel waited until they passed by him, then went to unlock the other cabin. He went through the same gesturing and posturing as before until another group of frightened young girls slipped silently past him, out the door.

After a number of awkward attempts to reassure them that he meant only to help, he started down the deck in search of the pilot, twelve girls trailing behind him.

By the time they came in sight of the white-uniformed American, it was too late for the dumbfounded Captain Schell at his side to do anything more than stare at Daniel with murder in his eyes.

Tierney had caught up with the Farmingtons not long after they drove away from the hospital. He rode in their stylish carriage only as far as the Hall of Justice. From there, he continued on to the harbor in a Black Maria, one of the horse-drawn patrol wagons used for transporting prisoners. Five policemen recruited by Lewis Farmington accompanied them.

Near the dock, a cluster of dandified runners quickly parted and scattered as the Black Maria pulled into their midst. Tierney and the five policemen jumped from the patrol wagon before it stopped, falling in behind Mr. Farmington and his daughter as they headed toward the gangplank.

Lewis Farmington was probably one of only half a dozen men in New York City who wielded enough power to board an immigrant vessel over the objections of two medical officers and an entire crew of sailors.

Board it he did, and, although he attempted to dissuade Sara, she was at his side. Behind them came Tierney Burke with an entourage of New York's finest.

The men headed directly for the quarterdeck. Sara fell back, immediately beginning to search the crowd for a small woman with black hair and enormous gray eyes.

As they converged on the pilot, Lewis Farmington's gaze went to the hard-looking, scar-faced man standing stiffly beside the white-uniformed navigator. A fury bordering on madness burned in the man's gaze. That and his cap identified him as the degenerate captain of the *Green Flag*, Abidas Schell.

As the policemen descended on the captain in a wave, Lewis Farmington and the Burke boy stopped just inside the ring of curious onlookers. Close to the American pilot, an immigrant boy stood like a sentry in front of a group of terrified Oriental girls. The lad was almost shouting, trying to make himself heard over all the commotion.

Two of the policemen moved to take charge of the frightened girls, at the same time ordering the immigrant boy to identify himself.

Both Lewis Farmington and the Burke lad

started when the youth gave his name.

Sergeant Burke's son hesitated only an instant before lunging forward, thrusting himself into the melee, shouting the boy's name.

"Daniel! Daniel Kavanagh!"

The tall, curly-headed Irish boy whirled around, searching the sea of faces, his eyes quickly coming to rest on Tierney Burke, who had stopped only a few feet away.

The two youths stood staring at each other for a moment, then Tierney moved forward. The grin he shot at the Kavanagh lad brought a smile to Lewis Farmington's face as well, especially when he heard the boy's greeting.

"Pleased to meet you, Daniel Kavanagh! I'm your new bunk mate, Tierney Burke! Welcome to America!"

He paused for a moment, cocking his head. "Say, it's a relief to see all those girls aren't your sisters!"

Lewis Farmington wished he could have captured the gaping look of astonishment, then relief, that washed over Daniel Kavanagh's face. "You're . . . Michael Burke's son? You came . . . to *meet* us?"

Tierney Burke nodded, and the Kavanagh lad looked for all the world as if he'd just been presented with the gift of a new brother!

Sara was beginning to panic. Her lame leg hindered her progress through the throng of pressing bodies, and only now was she beginning to realize the utter futility of trying to find one vague face among hundreds.

She decided she'd best thread her way out of the crowd and go in search of her father. She was really quite vexed with both him and the Burke boy — it would have been nice if at least *one* of them had stayed with *her!*

Edging sideways, inward of the ship, her eyes skimmed over a heavy-jowled man wearing a crumpled cap who stood shouting angrily at an entire horde of confused-looking immigrants. At the front of the crowd stood a woman, holding a small boy in her arms, with two obviously frightened little girls just behind her. At her side stood a thin, somewhat ill-looking man with glasses, a beard . . . and an empty sleeve.

The woman appeared to be arguing violently with the nasty-looking man, with considerable input from the one-armed fellow at her side. Sara glanced away for a moment, peering closely into the ranks of the mob of immigrants milling around the deck.

Suddenly, a man whose badge identified him as a medical inspector parted the crowd. He wore an angry, authoritative expression, and Sara began to push forward to hear what he was saying. Seeing one of the city policemen now heading directly toward the inspector, Sara looked back to the woman with the child in her arms.

Her heart stopped, then skipped and raced.

A slip of a lass . . . hair the color of raven's wings . . . and huge sad eyes . . . This woman looked faded and worn, not at all like the girl Michael Burke had described. Her dark hair, graying at the temples, was pulled back, and her cheekbones protruded from a drawn and sunken face. Yet, she *was* the right size, and her eyes . . .

"*Nora!* Nora Kavanagh?"

The woman's head snapped around, and enormous gray eyes anxiously searched the crowd. The one-armed man at her side pointed toward Sara.

Sara again called out to her, pushing strangers out of her way. Shoving forward, she ignored the pain in her leg as she attempted to close the distance between them.

Finally, she reached the dark-haired woman, who stood staring at her with a thoroughly stunned expression.

"You *are* Nora Kavanagh, aren't you?" Sara asked breathlessly.

The huge eyes studied Sara.

"Aye . . . aye, I am Nora Kavanagh," she said in a soft, wondering voice. "But how is it you know —"

Hesitating only an instant, Sara put a hand to the woman's arm, wincing at the fragile bones beneath her fingers. She had no idea who the haggard-looking man with the empty sleeve might be, but he was obviously with Nora Kavanagh. Nodding briefly to him,

Sara then turned back to the woman.

"Sergeant Burke gave me a wonderful description of you! My name is Sara Farmington, and I'm . . . a friend of the sergeant's. I've come to take you to him."

Nearly an hour later, with the entire Kavanagh family and the Fitzgerald children finally gathered together on the dock, along with the weary-looking Englishman called Whittaker, the Farmingtons stood watching the bizarre procession coming down the gangplank.

Three grim-faced policemen led Abidas Schell and the medical inspector onto the dock, while two others took charge of the little Chinese girls.

Last came two crew members with a stretcher, bearing the body of the surgeon, found dead by his own hand in his cabin.

Nobody spoke until the entire procession had disappeared into the crowd on the dock.

The Englishman finally broke the silence. "Miss Farmington?"

When Sara turned to him, she felt an instant's surprise at the kindness and the warmth she encountered in the man's eyes. She found herself wondering what the story was with this Evan Whittaker. Nora's introduction had been most peculiar, identifying him only as "our good friend, to whom we owe our lives."

He was fumbling to pull something from his pocket as he spoke. "I've already showed this letter to one of the policemen who came with you. He said Sergeant Burke would want to read it also. If you and Nora would see that he gets it . . ."

Sara reached for the letter, then stopped. "You take it, Nora."

Nora looked at her, hesitated, then took the letter from Evan Whittaker, who turned and began talking with the boy, Daniel, and Tierney Burke.

When Sara felt Nora's hand on her arm, she turned, smiling at her.

"You *did* say that Michael will be all right?" Nora asked softly, her eyes still worried and fearful. "You are sure?"

"He's going to be just fine!" Sara assured her. Impulsively, she took the woman's thin hand and squeezed it gently. "Especially now that he has someone to help look after him. He's a stubborn man, your Sergeant Burke!"

Nora studied her with a searching gaze. "Yes," she said uncertainly. "Yes, Michael was always . . . stubborn." Hesitating, she ventured, "You — you are a good friend of Michael's, then?"

Their eyes met and held. "Yes, I am," Sara answered quietly. "And I'd like very much to be your friend as well, Nora."

44

A Reunion

But one man loved the pilgrim soul in you,
And loved the sorrows of your changing face.

WILLIAM B. YEATS (1865–1939)

Tierney Burke was determined to beat the others to the hospital.

The voyagers were on their way to the Farmington mansion to "freshen up" before going on to Bellevue, but Tierney had declined the invitation to accompany them. Instead, he set off at a dead run from the harbor. Leaping fences, ignoring the mud, he didn't slow down until he reached the hospital grounds.

Nora was pretty! She actually was! He couldn't wait to see Da's face when he got a look at her. Of course, she *did* look a bit older than he had pictured her — but little wonder, what with the famine and the long voyage.

And, of course, she would still be grieving for her eldest son, who had died before they ever set sail. Of all Nora's children, it seemed only Daniel was left.

At least *he* appeared to be fine. And he was sharp as a tack, that was certain! They were going to get along swell! Daniel Kavanagh must have dozens of tales to tell of Ireland and their trip across the Atlantic — and Tierney planned to hear them all!

Approaching the hospital entrance now, he slowed down to a trot. As soon as he cleared the door, though, he took off at a run down the hall, ignoring the angry squawk of a long-faced nurse who had to duck out of his way.

He started talking even before he was all the way into the room.

Nora glanced down over the clean gingham dress Sara Farmington was hastily adapting to the newcomer's thin frame.

She was still dazed from the incredible kindness of the Farmingtons. After rescuing Nora and the others at the dock, both Mr. Farmington and this fine-looking daughter had insisted on taking them all home for a bit before going to the hospital.

Home? The place was a *castle!* Nora had never even seen the *outside* of such a house, could not possibly have imagined the luxury she encountered within! And now she stood in the middle of this sumptuous bedroom, staring at herself in a full-length looking glass while Sara Farmington pinned and tucked her own gingham dress to fit Nora. She had even helped Nora wrap her hair in a neat twist at the back of her neck.

While Nora was being readied for her meeting with Michael, the children were downstairs in the kitchen, being fed.

"They can stay here while you're at the hospital," said Sara, standing at Nora's shoulder as she appraised the Irish lass in the mirror. "Father thinks your British friend, Mr. Whittaker, needs medical attention right away. He's sent for our physician."

Nora turned, studying the young woman next to her. "How can we ever be thanking you for —"

"You can't," Sara interrupted firmly, taking Nora by the arm and leading her from the bedroom. "Come along now. You look wonderful. We mustn't keep Sergeant Burke waiting any longer."

Sara took her at once to the library, where they were met by another surprise. Sara's father had offered Whittaker a job!

Lewis Farmington stood in front of the elegantly carved mantel, his hands tucked inside his waistcoat pockets. "You'll never imagine, Sara!" he announced cheerfully as soon as they entered. "It seems I've found myself a personal secretary at last! Mr. Whittaker here has had years of experience in just that capacity. With an English lord, no less!"

"Why, that's wonderful, Father. But does Mr. Whittaker know how terribly disorganized you are?"

Farmington beamed. "He says he likes a challenge."

Nora looked at Evan Whittaker, whose pale countenance was flushed with obvious pleasure. He met her gaze with a nod and a smile, and Nora could almost read his thoughts: God had, indeed, placed some of His people in this city.

Lewis Farmington had not quite finished taking charge. "As for you, Mrs. Kavanagh —"

"Nora — please call me Nora."

"Nora," he continued, "Sara and I would like it very much if you and the children would consent to stay with us for now. We've more than enough room, and our housekeeper desperately needs someone to share the responsibility of running this household." He paused, smiling at his daughter, who was still holding on to Nora's arm. "Sara, you see, is entirely too busy with her projects to be of any use to Ginger. We need a dependable, capable woman like you around the place."

Dumbfounded, Nora could only gape at the man as he went on. "Ginger — that's our housekeeper — will continue her duties, of course. What we'd like you to do, Nora, is to oversee some of the things she doesn't have time for. You might even want to help Sara with some of her projects, if you've a mind to interfere with other people's business."

Unexpectedly, Nora felt her eyes fill with

tears. "You're so kind . . . I . . . I don't know what to say . . ."

"Well, you can say *yes,* of course!" boomed Mr. Farmington.

"Father," Sara said, turning to Nora, "it's a wonderful idea —"

"I thought so —"

"— but Nora and Sergeant Burke . . . well, I believe that he's hoping . . ."

Nora stared at the young woman beside her. Had Michael *confided* in her, then, about his . . . proposal?

Again, Lewis Farmington took the situation in hand. "If Nora decides to make other plans later, we'll understand, of course. But that will take time; meanwhile, she and the children can visit with us. What do you think, Nora?"

The man's dark eyes were warm with a kind of . . . *knowing,* almost as if he understood Nora's confusion and inward conflict. Lewis Farmington was offering her shelter, Nora suddenly realized. A safe place . . . a resting place . . . until she could get on with her life.

Ignoring the tears that now spilled over from her eyes, Nora moistened her lips and said, "I . . . am most grateful, Mr. Farmington. The children and I would be happy to stay here. And I would like very much, I'm sure, to work for you."

"Nora?"

Sara's soft voice helped Nora check her tears.

"I'll take you to Sergeant Burke now. I'm sure he's getting very anxious."

Nora nodded, swallowing hard against a new surge of panic.

The Lord had been good . . . so good. He had affirmed His love in immeasurable ways this day, meeting their every question, their every fear, their every need, with infinite caring. Indeed, He had not abandoned them, after all, as Nora had feared. Today He had proven to her the reality of His presence in ways she could never have imagined.

But now . . . now, Michael was waiting. And Nora was suddenly frightened again.

Nora's legs quaked beneath her as she approached Michael's hospital room. She was certain she would fall on her face before she got through the door!

Glancing down over the dress Sara had loaned her, she knew an instant of dismay. She was nothing but bones! He would think her ugly . . .

"You look *lovely*, Nora."

She turned wild eyes on Sara, who was very nearly holding her up.

"Everything's going to be all right," Sara said quietly, smiling. "You'll see. Go on now. He's waiting."

Just outside the door, she hesitated again,

swallowing down the taste of her terror, fighting for a deep breath. Her stomach was knotted, her heart hammering like a wild thing. For a moment she did believe she was going to be ill!

Thank the dear Lord the others had not come with them. At least if she disgraced herself, there would be no one to see.

No one except Sara Farmington. And Michael.

Nora had never felt so foolish, so . . . vulnerable as she did at that moment. She had survived the Hunger and a nightmare ocean voyage, but she was suddenly quite certain she would not survive this meeting.

Sara Farmington pushed her through the doorway, then disappeared.

Michael sat on the edge of the bed, his hands braced at his sides. He appeared to be having a serious discussion with his son in the chair across from him.

The boy shot to his feet at the sight of Nora.

She stood waiting, just inside the room, staring at the two of them with anxious eyes.

In his American clothes, a blue woolen shirt and dark blue trousers, this man seemed a stranger.

Then he looked up, and Nora's heart leaped to her throat.

He was older, but still Michael. The dark eyes had lost a bit of their mischief, perhaps, but they were just as kind. His thick hair was still the color of chestnuts, with touches of silver here and there. The chin was still arrogant, as if he would take on the world. And win.

Leaning on the arm of his son, he got to his feet. The broad shoulders were stooped as he stood there, watching her, and for an instant pain crossed his features.

The boy stayed in the room only long enough to look from one to the other, then again. Then, shooting Nora an encouraging grin, he slipped past her, through the door.

Nora dragged her eyes back to Michael. Seventeen years hung suspended between them. It seemed a lifetime.

Finally Michael reached out a hand to her. "So, Nora Ellen," he said in a strangled voice, "you are here at last."

Nora bit her lip, searched his eyes.

This was no stranger . . .

"Aye, Michael," she said, taking a step toward him. "I am here at last."

Later, they sat on the side of his bed — he was unable to stand yet for any length of time — and talked.

She told him about Tahg and wee Ellie and Owen, then about Thomas Fitzgerald and Morgan.

He told her about his wife and Tierney and his job.

She told him about Evan Whittaker, how he had saved them and looked after them so faithfully. She told him about the voyage, the evil captain, the poor little Chinese girls, and about the tragic surgeon who had shot himself.

She gave him the surgeon's letter, and he read it aloud, pausing in places when Nora would make a strangled cry of dismay.

"He murdered his own *wife?*" she cried, once Michael finished reading.

He nodded. "She was dying in agony. He couldn't bear to see her suffer, so he got drunk and gave her an injection to end the pain — to end her *life* — not knowing her brother saw the whole thing."

"And the captain . . . Schell. He was her brother?"

Again Michael nodded, folding the letter and laying it on the table beside the bed. "Schell was already involved in white slaving and opium running. He started blackmailing the doctor then and there, and it never stopped! Threatened to tell the medical authorities, the surgeon's son —"

"And after all those years the son died, too!" Nora cried. "Oh, that poor, doomed man!"

"Don't feel too sorry for him," Michael said grimly. "He was the one who acted as go-between for Schell and a number of brokers, selling out entire steerage lists. Apparently that's what happened when Morgan's men arranged your passage. They thought they were dealing through a reliable Irish surgeon!"

They both remained silent for a long time. At last, clearing his throat, Michael took her hand.

Nora looked down, then glanced back at his face.

"Can we talk about a more cheerful letter now?" he said with just the ghost of a smile.

"Michael — you needn't say anything more," Nora put in quickly. "I know this was Morgan's idea, that he arranged everything —"

Frowning, he lifted a hand to quiet her. "I don't know what you *think* you know, Nora Ellen, but I can tell you I only wrote the truth in my letter. I want to marry you, lass. I want that very much."

Averting her eyes, Nora shook her head. "Michael, you don't want to marry me! We haven't seen each other in all these years, why — you can't possibly take on such a responsibility!"

He stared at her for a moment, then reached for her other hand, holding both firmly in his. "Listen to me, Nora! Listen to the truth. I *do* want to marry you! It's all I've thought about for weeks now!"

He paused, still gripping her hands. "Nora, I am a lonely man. I want you in my life. I want to make a home with you. I know we have much to learn about each other, that it will take time. If you're not ready to be a wife to me in the . . . intimate . . . sense, I will wait. Even if you never want anything more than friendship and companionship from our marriage, I will accept that. But you must know the truth, lass, and the truth is that I want your presence in my life.

"We were good friends once — we still are, I hope." He paused. "Can you think of a better foundation for a good marriage?"

"Michael —"

"Say yes, Nora. This is what is best for both of us, for our children."

"How can you be sure of that, Michael? After all these years —"

"Nora," he interrupted, "you once told me, when you were still a wee, scrawny thing, that I had a way of always making things come out right. Do you remember?"

She did.

"Nora . . . don't you see, lass? Some things simply don't change."

She stared at him, watching the old confident grin spread across his good-natured face.

"Now, Nora, before you say anthing more, I have a favor to ask," he said, still smiling.

"What sort of a favor would that be, Michael?"

"Seventeen years ago I asked you to marry

me and come to America. You turned me down, and I kissed you goodbye with a great sorrow."

She nodded, acknowledging the memory.

His eyes went soft as he moved to pull her into his arms. "Now, lass, seventeen years later, you are in America, and I am again asking you to marry me. I would also like to kiss you hello."

Nora made no protest when he leaned toward her. His lips touched hers, gently . . . so gently. A brief, unsettling memory flashed across Nora's mind — a memory of Morgan Fitzgerald, his fierce embrace, his urgent last kiss, his eyes filled with love . . .

"Nora?" Michael's voice called her back, and she shuddered.

His eyes probed hers, questioning. "Is something wrong?"

"No — no, Michael, of course not," she stammered. And then another memory invaded her mind: Evan Whittaker, hovering over her in the midst of his own terrible pain, offering to be her protector during the horrifying voyage to America.

And suddenly, in the deepest part of Nora's spirit, a light began to dawn. Hadn't she prayed, while still aboard the *Green Flag*, that God would give her the strength to be dependent only on *Him*. Hadn't she pleaded with Him to change her, to make her adequate for whatever might lie ahead?

She turned her eyes on Michael's face. There was a nobility there, a goodness and strength of character. This man would never renege on his promises, never leave her, as Morgan had. This man would remain true to his word. She could *trust* him, and he was waiting.

But there was another who would always be true to His Word. He would never leave her either. She could trust Him. And He was waiting . . .

At that moment, a strange, unfamiliar warmth rose up inside Nora, and she knew the Lord's presence as she had never known it before. He was waiting . . . waiting to answer her prayer . . . but waiting for her to take one step of faith before He answered . . .

And suddenly Nora knew what that step had to be. Before she could ever place her trust in, or offer her heart to, another man, she must first learn to lean on her Savior . . . she must learn to trust His love, His will for her life.

Perhaps she *would* marry Michael . . . someday. But not now, not so soon . . . not yet.

"Michael," she said softly, her eyes brimming with unshed tears, "I cannot marry you."

"Now, Nora, just —"

She hushed his protests by touching a

finger to his lips. "Listen to me, Michael," she urged him. "I want you to understand. I *need* you to understand."

And so he listened as Nora revealed her heart. She confessed her shame and her terror, her doubt and her despair. She admitted her need for healing, explained her need to learn to trust, to try on this new strength she believed the Lord wanted to give to her.

Little by little, as she spoke, Michael's expression began to change. Confusion gave place to understanding, frustration to acceptance. Friendship deepened, made room for respect.

"Michael," she finished, "I *do* love you. I have always loved you . . . in a very special way . . . and I do not doubt that I always will. But before I can love you — or any other man — with the fullness of a woman's heart, I have another journey to make."

He frowned, and she hurried to reassure him. "Oh, this is a different kind of journey, Michael! It's a journey . . . of faith. And today . . . right now, at this moment . . . I'm taking the first step."

Before Nora left the hospital, Michael asked another favor . . . and a promise.

"If he's willing . . . let your son come and stay with Tierney and me for a while," he urged her. "Just for a time. Until you're settled. I'd like the boys to become friends, and Tierney was so looking forward to having another lad about the house. I'll make sure he gets good schooling . . . and you'll see him often, whenever you want. Would you think about it, at least, Nora? For me, and for my son?

The promise was more a puzzle, and yet Nora was inclined to grant it. "I want your word," Michael said, gripping both her hands in his and searching her gaze, "that you will obey your heart. When the time comes that your heart sings love for a man, Nora, promise me you'll not let it be silenced by uncertainty or foolish pride. Promise me, lass, that, whether the song is for me . . . or for another . . . that you will give love's song a voice."

After a long silence, Nora leaned to kiss him gently on the cheek. "Aye, Michael . . . dear friend . . . I do promise."

Epilogue

Dublin
Late June

Morgan Fitzgerald had located this fine shop during his first month's stay at his grandfather's estate. The blind shopkeeper was a reputed master at fixing broken instruments, especially fiddles and harps.

While he waited for Mr. Higgins, the shopkeeper, to go in the back and have the wife tally his bill, Morgan pulled out one of the letters he'd been carrying in his shirt pocket more than a week now.

Unfolding it, it occurred to him that he was even able to smile a bit when he read the words these days. There was still some pain behind the smile, but it was not nearly so sharp as it had once been.

Daniel John had penned a message of his own, tucking it in with a more detailed letter from Michael. They had posted the letters to Joseph Mahon, in hopes the priest would see that they reached Morgan, if indeed he still lived.

He read them both regularly, but it was the lad's to which he most often returned.

Leaning up against a broad, double-door cabinet, his eyes again scanned the last page, which was mostly about Whittaker.

The enterprising Englishman seemed to have landed himself a job with Lewis Farmington, the wealthy shipbuilder who had not only helped to rescue them all, but had even taken Nora and the children into his home for the time being.

> . . . Whittaker says his new position is a great improvement over his old job, because Mr. Farmington is such a fine man. He also says he is thankful that he is right-handed.
>
> I like Tierney a lot, and although I miss being with Mother and the Fitzgeralds every day, I have to admit it was a better idea, my staying with Uncle Mike and Tierney for now. There is no room here for all of us, and the Fitzgerald children need Mother with them.
>
> Johanna is like a shadow to Tierney when we're all together; can you imagine that? It's odd, how he seems to understand exactly what she means, though she can't speak a word. He's more than kind to her, and very patient.
>
> Sure, and you were right about Uncle Mike, Morgan — he is a grand fellow! He is very kind to all of us and treats Mother with great gentleness and consideration . . .

Morgan glanced up, rubbing a hand over his eyes. How long would it be before the thought of Nora would no longer wring his heart dry?

"Well, then, sir, here is your instrument."

The shopkeeper's voice brought Morgan back to his surroundings. "I hope you will be pleased with it."

Returning the letter to his shirt pocket, Morgan turned and smiled at the man before remembering Higgins' blindness. "I've no doubt but what I will."

"That is a fine harp, sir," said the shopkeeper, "a very fine harp, indeed. I was pleased to repair one of such antiquity. You play it often, do you?"

Morgan laid the requested sum and an extra sovereign on top of the counter. "Aye, she has been a grand friend to me," he replied, examining the harp before tucking it under his arm.

With a word of thanks to the shopkeeper, he turned to go.

"Is it a minstrel boy you are then, sir?"

Morgan stopped, glancing back over his shoulder as he considered the question.

At last he nodded and smiled. "Aye, Mr. Higgins. That is exactly what I am. A minstrel boy."

Caressing the harp with a reassuring touch, he flung open the door and walked outside.

It was a fine afternoon in Dublin, and the

Irish sunshine set the big man's copper hair ablaze as he slung his harp over his back and stepped into the street.

The minstrel boy to the war is gone,
In the ranks of death you'll find him,
His father's sword he has girded on,
And his wild harp slung behind him.
"Land of song!" said the warrior bard,
"Though all the world betrays thee,
One sword, at least, thy rights shall guard,
One faithful harp shall praise thee!"

A Note From the Author

When I first began to research the idea for *Song of the Silent Harp*, I discovered a strong religious thread throughout the history of Ireland. I hope I have communicated to my readers a clearer understanding of how Christianity influenced the lives of some of America's Irish ancestors.

During those years of study and writing, I became aware that it is virtually impossible to separate the past from the present. The struggles and successes, the trials and triumphs of our forebears, make up not only a rich heritage but also contribute in immeasurable ways to what we — and our world — are today. Like young Daniel Kavanagh, I believe that, from God's perspective, yesterday, today and tomorrow are one vast *panorama*, a continuing epic which our Creator views in its entirety, from the dawn of time through the present to eternity.

Further, history *does*, indeed, repeat itself. Most experiences of the past continue to happen. The horrors of famine and hopelessness that surround many characters in *Song of the Silent Harp* still exist. Month after month, year after year, the innocent victims of war, disaster, political indifference and oppression go on suffering and dying, just as they did in Ireland during the Great Famine.

Government programs and private charities cannot begin to meet the escalating demand for worldwide assistance. I believe the Christian church should be at the very front of international rescue operations, for it is the *church* that bears the responsibility — and the privilege — of giving love to a world that needs it.

I invite you to join me in finding practical ways to help. I have selected World Relief Corporation, but there are many organizations that provide an opportunity to put faith and love into action. One person *does* make a difference.

B. J. Hoff

At the author's request, a percentage of her royalties for *Song of the Silent Harp* are paid directly to World Relief Corporation, the international assistance arm of the National Association of Evangelicals (NAE). Founded in 1944, World Relief attempts to meet the physical and spiritual needs of people on every continent.

World Relief is a church-centered ministry of compassion, offering help and hope to victims of war and disaster, famine and poverty. In addition to their international projects, they assist with the resettlement needs of refugees in the United States. Information on World Relief can be obtained by writing to:

World Relief Corporation,
P.O. Box WRC,
Wheaton, IL 60189